PRAISE FOR
DON DEBRANDT'S
DEBUT NOVEL
THE QUICKSILVER SCREEN

"A rousing piece of cyberpunk adventure . . ."
—*Denver Post*

"Vibrant ideas that enrich science fiction's cyberpunk sub-genre . . ."
—*Vancouver Sun*

"DeBrandt integrates artist and morality with writing as sure as John Shirley."
—*Under the Ozone Hole*

STEELDRIVER

DON DeBRANDT

ACE BOOKS, NEW YORK

This book is dedicated to my father,
who introduced me to tall tales.

Thanks, Dad.

This book is an Ace original edition.
And has never been previously published.

STEELDRIVER

An Ace Book / published by arrangement with
the author

PRINTING HISTORY
Ace edition / April 1998

All rights reserved.
Copyright © 1998 by Don DeBrandt.
Cover art by Jean Pierre Targete.
This book may not be reproduced in whole or in part,
by mimeograph or any other means, without permission.
For information address: The Berkley Publishing Group,
a member of Penguin Putnam Inc.,
200 Madison Avenue, New York, New York 10016.

The Penguin Putnam Inc. World Wide Web site address is
http://www.penguinputnam.com

ISBN: 0-441-00520-9

ACE®
Ace Books are published by The Berkley Publishing Group,
a member of Penguin Putnam Inc.,
200 Madison Avenue, New York, New York 10016.
ACE and the "A" design are trademarks
belonging to Charter Communications, Inc.

PRINTED IN THE UNITED STATES OF AMERICA

10 9 8 7 6 5 4 3 2 1

CHAPTER 1

"Jon'll get us out," Billy said. Carl could hear the panic in his voice.

A quake had triggered the cave-in. Five men and a Toolie died within a second, buried under a mountain's worth of rock. The rest of the tunneling crew got clear—all except for Billy Swenson and Carl Yamoto. They were trapped behind the rockfall, Carl's right leg crushed so completely it didn't hurt a bit. He was even grateful; he knew that pressure from the rocks that pinned his leg was keeping him from bleeding to death. He also knew he was in shock, which was fine with him. It let him calmly accept that he and Billy were most likely going to suffocate to death in the dark.

Billy wasn't taking things so well. He was a rail worker, laying track for the maglev, and wasn't even supposed to be this deep in the tunnel. He'd walked down to talk to a friend of his on the steeldriving team, and they'd been sharing a drink from a thermos when the ceiling gave way.

His friend was dead now. Billy was young, no more than twenty; Carl was twice his age. He kept the kid talking, figuring words were better than screams. He could hear Billy breathing in the dark, using up the air with fast, panicky gasps, so he kept his voice low and calm.

They started out swapping firsts: first sexual experience, first drunk, first time thrown in jail. After that they went through Billy's school record, Carl's first two wives, the relative merits of beer and whiskey, and which boss they most regretted never having taken a swing at.

Somewhere between Carl's first and second wife they'd felt the rumbling vibration of drilling equipment on the other side of the rockfall, and Billy had started to relax. Carl hadn't. They should have gotten a borehole through a long time ago, to pipe in air and communications. He could guess why they hadn't: seismic shifting must have kept collapsing it, so they'd finally stopped trying. They'd have to dig a man-sized tunnel and shore it up as they went.

And there wasn't enough time.

"So," Carl said, trying to put relief he didn't feel into his voice, "how the hell did you wind up here?" He coughed, almost choking on the hot, thick air. Wouldn't be long now.

"Buried alive, you mean? Well, I've been having this streak of luck lately." Neither man laughed.

"No, I mean here, on the planet, working on this god-damned tunnel. You local?"

"Yeah, I grew up here." "Here" meant Landing City; the spaceport was the only permanent settlement on Pellay. "My mom was one of the first people the company transferred here, and she was already pregnant. She got tired of Kadai shipping her all over the galaxy, so she signed up for their pioneer program. Of course, that meant she wound up here for life, but she doesn't seem to mind. I've never been off-planet."

"What made you sign up for tunnel work?" Carl shifted slightly and wished he hadn't. Even though his leg was still numb, he heard something make a wet, pulling-free sound. He told himself it was cloth.

"What else is there? Only way off Pellay is to sign a twenty-year work contract with the Kadai Group, and they can send you worse places than this. You can't even get a job in Landing City unless you sign a contract with TKG. The only work on Pellay is the mine or the tunnel, and either way you still wind up working for Kadai—but at least you don't have to sign over your freedom. I figure after the tunnel's finished I'll wind up hauling platinum ore in the mine.'' Billy didn't sound bitter, just tired and scared.

''I know,'' Carl said, ''they got you comin' and goin'. I'm a company man myself; just signed up for my second term. Twenty-one years I've given the bastards so far. Maybe in another nineteen they'll let me retire. Maybe.''

I can't believe I just said that! I must be in worse shape than I thought. You didn't complain about the company to employees under you or above you. That was how senior executives became juniors, and vice versa. Carl had no illusions about his career; he knew he didn't have the kind of cutthroat aggressiveness the higher-ups rewarded. But others did, and it was this kind of stupid remark that they'd use against you—

Stop right there. He was talking to a kid, a scared kid trapped in a hole in the ground who'd had to be forced into working for the company in the first place. Carl swore softly, cursing his own paranoia. His fear of the company was a more effective trap than the tons of rock overhead; even knowing he would likely die here didn't free him. And Billy was just as trapped as he was—if you didn't play by their rules, you didn't play. And if they decided to ship you to a planet on the back end of nowhere, you went. If they told you to do an impossible job with outmoded equipment, you did it. Even though you knew modern equipment could do the job in half the time and with half the casualties. You did it because they ran everything, and one multiplanetary corporation was as bad as the next. Planets, whole star-systems, were traded every day; but an individual trying to change jobs was called a defector, and defectors were executed. They owned everyone.

Everyone except Jon.

The hell with them. If he was going to die, he wouldn't die scared. He tried to curse them, louder than before, but inhaled a lungful of dust and bad air that started him coughing so hard he almost couldn't stop. By the time he did, his head was spinning and his lungs were on fire.

"Jon'll get us out," Billy said. It must have been the tenth time he'd said it. "He won't leave us here."

Carl just nodded his head in the dark, too exhausted to even reply. He didn't want to argue with the kid, but he knew the facts. They'd been tunneling through a batholith, a huge column of igneous rock standing upright in the earth. The tunnel had cut the column in two. The rock surrounding the chunk overhead should have been strong enough to hold it in place, but the quake had ripped it loose. It had slammed down like a pile driver, crushing the arched tunnel supports as if they were made of paper instead of concrete and steel.

Carl and Billy were trapped in the short section of tunnel that extended past the batholith. The batholith was made of basalt, 6.0 on the Mohs' hardness scale, 4 below diamond and 2 above granite. It had a compressive strength of almost 22,000 pounds per square inch. Those familiar with it called it traprock.

The rescue crew wouldn't be able to blast their way through; they'd have to use roadheaders. That was the vibration Carl could feel in the rock against his back. A roadheader had Caterpillar treads and a spiky, rotating cutter ball at the end of an extendable hydraulic shaft. Carl had told Jon once he thought they looked like marital aids for dinosaurs, and Jon had laughed so loud and hard it had echoed from the tunnel face to the shaft entrance, five miles away. The next day, someone had spraybombed "Dino-Dildo" on every machine.

The problem with roadheaders was that they were almost useless against really hard rock. Their upper limit was around 20,000 pounds per square inch of compressive pressure; if the rock was harder than that, the work would become agonizingly slow. The cutter head would still bite into the rock, but he and Billy would be long dead by the time it broke through.

"He won't give up," Billy insisted. *Have I been talking out loud?* Carl wondered. He felt like he was falling, blinded, through the airless heart of a sun.

"Remember the time that Toolie ate a blasting cap and it exploded?" Billy asked. "Everybody thought for sure it was dead, except Jon. He picked the Toolie up, jumped in a manrider and took off. I heard he almost ran the cart off the rails getting to Boomtown, and then threw a lady tourist out of the examining room—naked—'cause he wouldn't wait."

Carl didn't say anything. Both of them knew the Toolie hadn't made it. It might have, if there'd been a Toolie doctor close by, but the only doctor this side of the mountains that knew anything about Toolies was Doc Pointer in Boomtown. The infirmary on-site at the tunnel was designed for human emergencies—Toolie injuries just weren't that important. Not to the company, anyway.

Billy didn't say anything for a while, and Carl didn't try. The blackness seemed to be spinning, and he thought he could see faint, sparkling lights far away. There was a roaring in his ears, like the ocean.

The roaring got louder and louder. Carl's body started to shake and he wondered if he was dying. The roar built to a chattering howl—there was a blinding flash of light and Carl was suddenly showered with pulverized rock.

"They did it! They broke through!" Billy gasped. Carl blinked the rock dust out of his eyes and squinted into the light. There was a rush of fresh, cool air on his face. He smelled hot metal and machine oil. The whirling ball of a roadheader's cutter pulled back from the hole, and a helmeted head took its place. A strong voice called out, "Hold on! We'll have you out in a second!"

Carl gave a weak little gasp of laughter. There was no way; the rock was too hard and there hadn't been enough time. Carl Yamoto and Billy Swenson should be dead—except someone had done the impossible, and Carl knew who it had to be.

Billy had been right. "Jon Hundred, you miraculous bastard," Carl managed to croak, and then he could finally let himself pass out. A deep, easy laugh drifted into the dark with him, and he knew everything was going to be fine.

It took seven hours of microsurgery, but they were able to save Carl's leg. Jon was grateful for that, but it still left him with six deaths to drink down. He stopped at home to pick up his instrument case and then headed for the Blue Cat.

The Blue Cat wasn't the most popular bar in Boomtown, but it was Jon Hundred's favorite. It was on the end of the last platform car, the one everyone called Cabooseville, located on the west side of No Name Street. No Name was the only street Boomtown had, running the length of eighteen block-long platform cars. Each car was as wide as a highway and straddled two sets of maglev tracks. Boomtown had followed the track-laying crew from Landing City to the tunnel site, and was now parked at the foot of the mountain, about a mile from the tunnel itself. Jon Hundred had called it home for the last four years, first as a track-layer, then as a driller, and finally as a foreman.

The Blue Cat was a blues bar, a smoky little hole-in-the-wall joint. Like most of the buildings in Boomtown, it was a two-story box with a flat roof, wedged between two other two-story boxes with flat roofs. The face of the building was painted a dark, rusty red, and the double doors of the entrance flat black. The outline of a cat's head glowed in blue neon overhead.

Inside, it was crowded with off-shift workers holding a drunken wake for the victims. Half the drunks were solemn or weepy and the other half were celebrating the fact that they were still alive. Jon Hundred didn't hold that against them; the longer you worked under a mountain the more the pressure built. You started thinking about all that rock overhead, and how much it would like to come crashing down. It was your will against the mountain's, and the mountain had been around a few millennia longer than you had. They had a right to be relieved; but it wouldn't last. The weight of those dead bodies would get added to the twenty-four other corpses already pressing down on them, and that was far worse than a million tons of stone.

The whole room went quiet when Jon walked in. He wondered what their reaction had been when they'd heard the news. Had they cheered for the survivors, or fallen silent for the dead? A hundred hands patted his broad back or squeezed an arm as he made his way through the crowd, surrounded by the solemn murmur of countless voices: "Thanks, Jon. Way to go, Jonny. Good job, man. Thanks. Thank God for you, Jon. You did it, Jon. Jon."

He made his way to the front and sat down, putting the long black case he had with him on the table. It was his regular table, with a padded steel chair they'd built just for him. Katy brought him a beer in a gallon stein without being asked. He drank half of it back and then just sat there, facing the small empty stage and fingering the clasps on the case.

There were friends of his in the bar, but none of them approached him. He knew why. What he'd done was impossible, and while they all appreciated it, none of them quite knew what to make of him now. Jon had always stood out; a man eight feet tall with cobalt-blue skin can't help that, and he'd never made any secret about the fact that he wasn't exactly a factory original. But nobody on the planet had ever seen anything like what he'd done in that tunnel.

On a good day, a roadheader can eat through fourteen to sixteen feet of medium-hard stone in an eight-hour shift. The batholith Jon Hundred had tunneled through had measured twenty-one feet, seven inches of extremely hard rock—and he had done it in six and a half hours.

That was amazing enough. But exactly *how* he had done it was nothing short of unbelievable.

He'd got another steeldriver to take over the roadheader's controls and told him to keep the cutter arm pointed dead

ahead. Then he walked around the machine, put his back
to its behind, dug in his heels—and *pushed*.

For six and a half hours.

They wore out nineteen cutter heads. Hoses on the hydraulic arm burst twice. Jon Hundred didn't even break
sweat—but then, he never had. His skin wasn't designed
for it.

He took another long pull on his beer, emptying the mug.
Katy had another one waiting. He gave her a thank-you
smile, and she gave him one back, but there was a look in
her eye he hadn't seen before. He knew what it meant, too.

Just who—and *what*—the hell are you, Jon Hundred?

He took another big swallow of beer and stared at the
empty stage.

Jonathan Hundred remembered the day he was born.

It was the visions he recalled most clearly, the strange
things that skittered across his brain as the medical techs
wired up his cortex. He saw the sun race backward across
the ceiling of the operating theater, heard a thousand wolves
howling in lonely harmony, smelled dust and steel and his
own blood. He saw faces, too, faces he knew but couldn't
quite remember: an old man with long white hair, a pair of
stout middle-aged women who looked like sisters, a young,
pretty blonde woman. Each face had a feeling attached to
it, so that was how he named them. The blonde woman's
name was Regret.

Thankfully, he didn't really remember the pain. He
would never be able to truly forget, either, but his mind
had put filters between himself and the memories; when he
tried to think about it now, what mainly stood out was
trying to scream and not being able to. They were testing
his nervous system and needed him conscious, but had disconnected his muscles and vocal cords. They didn't want
him thrashing around or screaming himself hoarse.

Most of his body was gone by then. They let him keep
a few internal organs they hadn't figured out how to im-

prove yet, his brain, his sex, his tongue, his sense of smell, a little body fat and a few bones—and they tinkered with those. They replaced most of his skeleton with honeycombed steel, his muscles with fiber-alloy strands, his heart and lungs and stomach with fission-powered analogs. They gave him better eyes, better ears, better nerves. But all these new parts were incidental; they were just reworking the chassis so it would be strong enough to hold the engine they wanted to install.

That engine was a force-field generator. It let him drive an invisible magnetic spike a hundred miles deep into the crust of a planet, let him anchor himself so solidly that it'd be easier to move the continent he was on than move him. That was how he anchored himself when he pushed the roadheader, forcing the drill bits into the rock with sheer muscle, pushing them past their limits without reaching his own.

Sometimes, Jon Hundred scared *himself.*

Even though his body was 80 percent artificial, Jon still considered himself more man than machine—but since he had no memories of his life before he'd been cyborged, he had to measure himself against other men to see how different he was. He stood near eight feet tall, his skin the same dark blue a sunset fades into at the far edge of the horizon. The muscles under that skin bunched and flexed the same way flesh did, though they were stronger than the suspension cables on a mile-long bridge. He had fingernails that would never grow or break, and no hair on his body at all. He wore a smooth, skull-fitted helmet that wouldn't come off, with a retractable brim that circled his head just above his ears. With only the front of the brim extended the helmet looked like a hardhat, which suited Jon Hundred fine. For the first six years of his existence the helmet had been mirrored chrome—until four years ago, when he'd arrived on Pellay and paid a Toolie to paint it a flat white. He'd added a new coat of paint every year since; he knew a few layers of paint weren't enough to hide behind, but he did it anyway.

Ordinary men, so far as Jon Hundred could see, liked to laugh and drink and eat and sleep; they liked to make love and win fights and get mail from home; they liked to gamble and cheer, and they liked to gamble and curse. But win or lose, they kept right on gambling.

Of course, for most of the last four years the only men available for Jon to compare himself with had been steel-drivers and Boomtowners, and he suspected that neither one was exactly ordinary. Now he had tourists to measure himself against too, and that worried him more than anything.

Not that he had anything against the tourists themselves. Sure, sometimes they were a lot like fish on bicycles, hopelessly helpless, but they poured a lot of money into the local economy. Of course, most of this money had to pass through the hands of the "players"—the hucksters and professional actors hired by the Kadai Group to portray "authentic" Boomtowners—first, but the players lived and worked and spent their paychecks in Boomtown just like the tunnelers and the support staff did.

The company had started moving the actors and souvenir shops in about six months ago; the tourists had only started to show up in the last few weeks. Word was the Kadai Group had changed hands, and that whichever multiplanetary consortium that now owned Pellay wanted to defray costs on the tunnel project. Jon had seen a brochure one of the tourists had left behind: "Experience life to its fullest on the untamed frontier, in the wildest town on a planet of live volcanoes! A town full of rugged men and women at war with the forces of nature every day, a town at the very edge of civilization itself—Boomtown!"

Well, Jon had thought, *at least they got the volcano part right.* Mind you, most of the active volcanoes were at the equator, ten thousand miles away, but they did make life on Pellay a lot harder than it had to be. They spewed millions of tons of ash into the air, and generated thermal currents that clashed with the cold winds coming off the polar ice caps. As a result, frequent wind and ash storms made air travel on Pellay almost impossible. That was why the tunnel was being dug; the only way to transport ore from the mine now was to truck it around the mountains, which took up to six weeks. High winds, ash-filled crevasses and quakes made it a dangerous trip, too.

He had hoped the danger would keep the tourists away. Didn't they understand how hard it was to land a ship on Pellay? That Landing City was the only place on the planet a ship could possibly touch down, and that even then the conditions had to be just so? Didn't they understand this was the backwater end of the civilized universe?

Jon Hundred understood all those things. They were a few of the reasons he'd come here in the first place. That was why the tourists worried him; unlikely as he knew it must be, he was afraid someone would recognize him. Not from his pre-cyborg days—he knew he had been changed far too much for that.

But his former employers might still know him.

Then again, it was a big universe. The only method of interplanetary communication was FTL mail ships, which slowed and condensed the flow of information. Humankind had settled on thousands of different planets and Jon Hundred was far, far away from where he had been five years ago. Dozens of different species and cultures had been discovered—including the Shinnkarien, who stood eight feet tall or higher and had bright blue skin. Jon wasn't Shinnkarien, but he hoped to pass for one if he had to. When you're eight feet tall you're going to stand out no matter how you disguise yourself, so Jon had dyed himself blue. If you're going to stand out, Jon figured, give people something to stare at that'll make them forget why they're looking in the first place.

People had certainly stared at Jon when he'd arrived on Pellay, and talked about him too. That talk had turned incredulous when Jon had walked out of the Kadai office with a contract in his hand—one that ended when the tunnel was done. Kadai normally made all its labor sign long-term contracts; twenty years was the minimum. No one knew why they gave Jon special consideration—at least not at first.

He finished his beer, and finally undid the clasps on the black case. Inside, cradled in crushed yellow velvet, was a curved silver horn almost six feet in length: A contrabass saxophone. He picked it up gently, its metal skin cool and smooth against his fingers, fitted a fresh reed to the mouthpiece, and got to his feet.

Somebody unplugged the jukebox as he stepped up on stage. The room didn't exactly fall quiet, but a lot of people stopped talking and started listening. Jon shut his eyes and let go of everything he'd been holding in for the last seven hours. He let it out deep and slow and sad; he had the big, big blues. The loud drunks shut up, and the quiet drunks started to cry.

Jon Hundred didn't have tear ducts anymore, so he let his sax cry for him.

Jon Hundred wasn't the only one to do the impossible that day.

A ship tumbled through Pellay's upper atmosphere, hurricane-force winds tossing it from one giant, invisible hand to another. A million particles of grit pitted the hull, clogged the thrusters, ruined the instrumentation. Ash storms made flying a ship hell, and landing a ship suicide.

The pilot's name was Hone. He knew the first process well and had no interest in the second, though circumstances seemed to contradict that. Landing a ship in a storm like this was insane—but Hone wasn't trying to land.

He was trying to crash.

He had powerful reasons to get to Pellay, and powerful reasons for not landing at the official spaceport. Landing anywhere else was impossible. So if the only way to get to the surface was to throw himself at it, that's what Hone would do. Whatever it took, he'd do it. Nothing had stopped him yet.

Ever.

The ship was small and cramped, with barely enough room for the pilot's couch. It was intended to be a courier ship, ferrying information too confidential or urgent to risk being sent by regular mail ship. It was fast, anonymous, and almost invisible. It fit Hone's requirements exactly—except for Jeremy.

"Main engine inoperative," Jeremy said softly. "Port thruster inoperative. Navigation instrumentation down to seven percent of operating norms."

"I guess that means we're going to die?" Hone asked. He had a deep, gravelly voice, and the smile on his face was not pleasant.

"Safety fields incorporated into this ship's design will protect passengers from collisions with most space debris." The voice of the ship's computer was easygoing and friendly; over the last few months it had pushed Hone from irritation to anger to fury, and then right on through to hatred. It sounded like a caring human being—but it was neither. It didn't have feelings and it wasn't self-aware. It was only a clever program designed to produce the illusion of companionship, and Hone hated illusions. Every day for the last three months he had made a point of destroying that illusion by forcing the computer to give replies no human being would. He had spent one week telling Jeremy about his hobby of killing and eating small children; Jeremy had offered several recipes he thought might be useful.

"We aren't going to be colliding with space debris, Jeremy. We're going to hit a planet. Think the safety fields can handle that?"

"The safety field of this ship can absorb an impact equivalent to twenty-three times the structural strength of the ship itself. I can display stress limitations on-screen if you like." The ship did a sudden violent roll to the right.

"Impact is gonna exceed those limits by a factor of ten,

Jeremy. What's going to happen to me, huh?''

''If structural limits are exceeded, the ship will no longer be functional. Thus, you will have to find another means of transportation.''

The ship pitched to the left and began to tumble end over end. Hone chuckled. ''That's not what I asked. What will happen to *me*?''

''Since I don't have your medical history in my memory I can't project specifics, but it would seem likely your injuries would be critical.''

''Restate your answer, defining 'critical' in colloquial terms,'' Hone snapped.

''You would probably die.''

''And what, do you think, would happen to you?''

''I would certainly cease to function.''

''Well, well,'' he growled. ''Good news at last.'' Those were the last words he spoke before the ship crashed, four minutes later.

The seismic sensors that ringed the Kadai mining complex registered the impact as being about ten miles due east of the mine. The engineers on shift figured it was most likely a meteor strike, and assigned a crew to go check it out as soon as the ash storm blew over.

The mining complex on Pellay was the most remote outpost on the planet. The number of people that staffed it was not large. So the engineers were more than a little astonished when, three hours later, Hone walked in the door.

CHAPTER 2

The mountain was called God's Gravestone. Jon Hundred had his own name for it. "Got six more, didn't you," he muttered under his breath. "You old bastard."

He was alone at the end of the tunnel, just him and the mountain. He could hear water dripping and the faint sound of echoing voices from behind him. An air duct blew on his skin with cool breath. "Six more lives you ended, six more lives that meant nothing to you." His voice was as deep as he was tall, with a rolling precision to it. He checked the charges in the rock face one more time, made sure that they were placed and wired correctly. He nodded to himself with satisfaction. "Well, you're not going to get anyone today. Hear me? Today we're going to dig a little bit deeper into your guts, and there's not one damn thing you can do about it. When we're done there'll be a rail line running from the mine on one side of the mountains to Landing City on the other—and it'll run right through you."

He turned back to the manrider that had brought him to the rock face, and carefully lowered himself into it. The frame creaked under his weight as it always did, but it held. He turned it on and the electric cart hummed to life.

"You're not going to beat me," Jon growled. Echoes of his own words chased him as he headed down the track.

He rode until he reached the shooting crew, crouched behind the drill jumbo fifty yards down the tunnel. He got out and hunkered down himself, and gave them the all-clear.

They were using water-gel explosives with a detonation velocity of 18,000 feet per second. The blast was satisfyingly loud and earthshaking, followed by that instant of frozen silence that always follows an explosion. Jon broke it by shouting, "Take that, you old BASTARD!"

Someone else joined in with, "The hell with you, you goddamned piece of rock!" and suddenly every man and woman on the shooting crew was yelling and cursing, and so were the track-layers and the bullgang and the muckers. Even the Toolies were crazily waving whatever limbs they had at the moment.

They needed the release, every one of them, and Jon Hundred knew that. Now they could go back to work with a fresh sense of purpose, with determination in their eyes instead of fear.

But deep in his heart, Jon Hundred felt something else. That the tunnel wasn't finished yet—and that before it was, more death was on the way.

"I still can't believe you could walk away from a crash like that," Garber said.

"Neither could my ship."

Hone was eating breakfast in the mine's cafeteria with Ted Garber, the mine's head of security. Garber was a big man, six foot two or so, with muscular, hairy arms, a permanent five o'clock shadow and an overlong mustache he chewed on absently from time to time. He had a bristly black crewcut and a scar that ran from his right eyebrow up into his hairline. Hone hated him already.

Hone stood at least two inches short of six feet himself, and had a potbelly that strained against the fabric of the rumpled brown coveralls they'd lent him. He had short, thinning brown hair and a high, wide forehead ended by a hairline that was only a few wispy strands combed across the top of his head. He had bags under his eyes, a nose that was too big, and a mouth that was thin-lipped. His teeth were a perfect, dazzling white when he smiled, which he almost never did. He had the appearance and presence of an overworked civil servant—except for his eyes. Hone's eyes had the heavy-lidded stare of a predator, the blank coldness of a reptile. That coldness was there only when he wanted it to be, and when it was the rest of his appearance didn't matter at all. He hadn't showed Garber that coldness—yet.

Hone swallowed another mouthful of chili. He ate methodically, with no evidence that he enjoyed or even noticed what he was eating.

"So why didn't you send out a distress call?" Garber asked. He wore a short-sleeved white shirt with a stained collar and a missing top button. He picked up the bottle of hot sauce on the table and shook a healthy amount into his own bowl of chili.

Hone didn't look up. "Couldn't. Equipment malfunction."

"Huh." Garber scratched his armpit with his thumb. "And why were you insystem in the first place?"

"By accident."

"Really? That seems kinda strange."

This time Hone glared at him. "Yeah, really. I told you, my ship had been tumbling out of control for weeks, ever since that chunk of rock slammed into it. I had no instruments, no engines, no way of knowing where I was going or how to stop when I got there. I'm just lucky I ran into a planet." He reached over, grabbed the hot sauce, and dumped twice as much into his bowl as Garber had before he set it down again.

"Lucky is right. No engines, no instruments, not even a broadcaster—hard to believe you still had life support." Garber picked up the bottle of hot sauce while he was talking and added some more to his own chili. "Not to mention functioning safety fields.'' Garber's voice was polite. He kept dribbling hot sauce into his bowl while he stared at Hone. Half a minute went by. Finally he put the bottle down.

Hone began eating again. ''I guess I'm just hard to kill.''

''Uh-huh. Well, you can stay here until the next transport arrives with supplies. You can catch a ride back to Landing City with them, and arrange passage off-planet from there.''

''Thank you,'' Hone said. It didn't quite come out as sarcasm.

There was a scrabbling noise by the door, and then something skittered through it and into the room. It looked like an X-ray of a waist-high spider come to life, if you ignored the extra legs and the fact that spiders don't have bones. Its skin was transparent with a pinkish tone to it, stretched over a skeleton that seemed to be made of a patchwork of actual bones and metal struts. It kept six legs on the floor and waved six more in the air. The legs—or arms—it was waving all had tools jutting out of their ends: screwdrivers, adjustable wrenches, bolt-cutters. The creature had a raised hump in the center of its roughly oval body with a cluster of pink globes that Hone assumed were sensory organs.

Garber groaned. ''Christ, you know you Toolies aren't allowed in here! Can't a man at least eat breakfast in peace?''

The Toolie had a piece of paper clutched in a pair of pliers. It thrust it at him insistently. ''All right, all right,'' Garber grumbled. He took the paper and looked at it. ''Shit,'' he said. ''Kerry's shown up for his shift drunk again. Look, stay in this building, okay?'' he asked Hone. ''I don't need any industrial accidents while you're here.''

Hone picked up the hot sauce, studied it without replying. It was about half-full. There was a little plastic spigot on top that regulated the flow; he flicked it off with a thumbnail.

Then he poured the rest of the bottle into his chili.

''Food always this bland around here?'' he asked. Garber

stared for a second, then shook his head, got up and left. The Toolie scuttled after him.

Hone finished his meal the same way he'd begun it. Methodically, with no evidence he enjoyed or even noticed what he was eating.

After work that day, Jon Hundred paid a visit to Hardware City. That's what most everyone called the platform car the Toolies lived on; Jon Hundred didn't know what the Toolies called it.

Hardware City was on the far end of Boomtown, just behind the engine car. To get there, Jon had to walk the length of twelve platforms: five of workers' bunkhouses, two housing management, a couple used for administration offices and three cars' worth of storage. Hardware City was in one of the warehouses.

It was late afternoon on a blistering hot day, the blue-gray sky hazy with ash. Jon didn't mind the heat, but he extended the brim around his helmet to its fullest to give him some shade while he walked. Most men were bone-tired after a hard day's work in the tunnel, but Jon never seemed to get tired. He wondered sometimes what it felt like.

When he got to the warehouse the front door was wide open, so he walked right in. He'd been to Hardware City before so he knew what to expect, but the smell made him gasp a bit just the same. Toolies could eat almost anything, but they didn't have actual mouths; they just wrapped themselves around their food, sweated some gastric acid onto it and digested it right there. A Toolie's skin was like a giant stomach turned inside out—and smelled about the same.

Still, Jon Hundred knew a few workers who smelled worse. The smell wasn't that bad once you got used to it anyway, just a little sharp. Truth be told, Jon Hundred liked visiting Hardware City; he thought it was the most interesting place in Boomtown.

It was stuffed, floor to rafters, with . . . things. Some of it was junk, but none of it was garbage. Garbage, a Toolie had told him once, was something nobody found useful anymore—junk was something useless only to a few.

Either way, Hardware City was definitely pack-rat heaven. The most amazing thing, though, was how every single thing was neatly arranged: every wall had shelving or hooks from top to bottom. Rows of shelving formed a grid that neatly divided the warehouse into different sections, and tables were stacked three high to provide as many flat surfaces as possible. Objects on the walls, shelves, or tables were lined up according to size or function, as near as Jon Hundred could figure out. On one table he saw spoons: a tiny silver one, several teaspoons, some tablespoons, a serving spoon, a garden trowel, a small spade, and finally a full-sized shovel. It made a certain kind of sense.

But that wasn't all. The Toolies had strung lines from wall to wall and between the shelves, hundreds of lines at different heights, and hung even more things from them. The things hanging from the lines were lighter and more delicate than the objects laid out on the shelves and tables; some of them weren't tools at all, but pieces of art. One line held at least two dozen different kinds of wind chimes, tinkling softly in the breeze from the open door. Another held beautiful hanging baskets, every one woven in a different angular shape: inverted pyramids, cubes joined at their corners, dodecahedrons. Toolies liked variety, Jon thought, variety and precision. Considering what sort of creature they were, that wasn't too surprising.

A Toolie strode up to him on three long, skinny limbs. She (all the Toolies in Boomtown were female) was built like two tripods glued head to head, with the flattened sphere of her body between them. Her three upper limbs were just as long and thin as her lower ones. She stood as tall as Jon Hundred, and with all her limbs extended she had three times the reach he had. Her bones shone a dull silver through translucent pink flesh. She had adjustable wrenches for hands.

"I'm looking for Juryrigger's cluster-mother," Jon said. Toolies didn't talk themselves, but they understood speech well enough. She motioned Jon to follow and strode forward.

The Toolies kept the building dim, but Jon's eyes didn't need much light. He followed the Toolie to a corner of the warehouse, passing other Toolies going about their business. Jon saw one Toolie that resembled his guide, but all the rest were different. He saw one that looked like an oversize snake with two heads, one that was low and wide and had a dozen thick legs, and a few shaped like men— except that they had a cluster of sensory globes where the head should have been, and the skeleton didn't look quite right. After four years of working with Toolies, Jon had long since gotten used to dealing with creatures whose every bone and internal organ was visible, but it was still a little spooky when they tried to imitate a human being.

Given the right materials, a Toolie could mimic the form of almost any animal—which made them perfect laborers. The Toolie Jon was following probably worked on the bull- gang, helping install lights and venting in the tunnel. With her reach, she could tighten bolts on the roof of the tunnel without a ladder. A Toolie built like a snake could slither through openings a man couldn't, and one built low and wide was perfect for hauling heavy materials.

At birth, Toolies all looked alike: amorphous, see- through blobs. They had strong internal muscles that they used to shift their weight and roll themselves over the ground. And soon enough, their cluster-mother would feed them the one thing they lacked: bones. Just a few to get the young ones started; once they had mastered the bones' uses, they would begin their own collections. In the wild, a Toolie would build a skeleton from the leftover bones of digested prey, using internal muscles to shift them around inside and special ball-and-socket organs to bond them together. Civilized Toolies, though, used civilized materials; metal struts were stronger, and could be machined to order. Still, Jon had noticed that no Toolie ever switched completely over to artificial bones. He understood that, probably better than anyone.

The Toolie led him to a corner of the warehouse lined with rows of gardening implements, then strode off. Jon had no idea where the Toolies had gotten them; the rocky, desertlike terrain surrounding Boomtown was hardly the place to grow anything.

The cluster-mother was sitting on the floor. She massed about as much as a full-grown Terran tiger, which was the shape her body suggested. She had a long torso, four legs, two tails and a long, thick neck. Her backbone was made of a long steel spring, her ribs concentric steel bands. The bones in her limbs and tails were the real thing, but her legs ended in steel-tipped claws and the tails in padded clamps. She also had six long, jointed arms sprouting from the middle of her back, a cluster of three on each side of her spine. To Jon they looked like the struts of giant batwings, with invisible membranes joining them together.

Where the head would have been on a tiger, the Toolie had a cluster of pink globes. They functioned as her eyes, ears and nose, and could even be moved from one part of her body to another. Just below the globes, where the jaws should have been, the Toolie had a large metal vise, and about twelve inches below that, in her chest, a hand-sized monitor screen gleamed.

"Hello," Jon said. "I'm Jonathan Hundred." He wished he could take off his hat, even though it probably made no difference to the Toolie. He settled for withdrawing the brim as far as he could.

<hello—i am brightweaver> appeared on the small screen. Not all Toolies had the screens, since they were expensive and the company wouldn't pay for them, but it was easier to hold a conversation with the ones that did.

"I came by to pay my respects. I'm sorry for your loss."

<thank you jonathan hundred—juryrigger my daughter gone—i will miss her flesh>

Jon noticed for the first time the double row of tools spread in front of Brightweaver. One of her long wing-strut arms unfolded itself and reached down, picking up a small cutting torch. The hand at the end of that arm seemed out of place; it had six long, impossibly delicate fingers and two multijointed thumbs. There was no metal in that hand at all, and the bones were so fine they must have come from a bird, or even a fish.

<there was no sign of her body?>

"I'm sorry, ma'am. There was just too much rock. We have to blast it out, and that doesn't—I mean, even if we did find—I'm sorry." He bowed his head, feeling ashamed. No one deserved an unmarked grave. The names of the other workers would go on a plaque over the mouth of the tunnel, but Juryrigger's wouldn't be on it. As far as the company was concerned, she was only a Toolie.

<that is sad—her flesh cannot be returned to mine—vandal mountain!> Brightweaver shook her head violently from side to side, and her tails whipped back and forth. "Vandal" was a Toolie's strongest profanity: they had a powerful taboo against the malicious destruction of anything valuable. Toolies made things, they didn't break them. Jon Hundred figured that was one of the reasons he and they got along so well.

Brightweaver held out the cutting torch she'd picked up and pointed to the row of wind chimes hanging high above the floor. They were made of shards of volcanic glass suspended with wire, and they sounded like birds made of brass and crystal.

<juryrigger made those—she thought to sell tourists the sound of the wind—tourists will buy anything she said—now she is gone her bones are gone her flesh is gone—this is all that is left of her to share> Brightweaver waved an arm at the objects laid out on the floor. There was a pair of needlenose pliers, a small hammer, several chisels and a pile of neatly folded polishing cloths.

"I'm not sure I understand," Jon Hundred said carefully.

<when a child dies its flesh is returned to its cluster-mother so it may become part of her again—the bones of the child are divided among the other children so none will forget the one that is gone>

"I understand," Jon said. "And you can't do that now because there is no body. I truly am sorry."

<we still have these things which were hers—she will not be forgotten—and again i thank you jonathan hundred—you will not forget juryrigger either—and so you should have something that once belonged to her>

Jon Hundred stopped the "No, I couldn't" that was half-way out of his mouth and thought hard for a second. "I would be honored," he said slowly. "And I know just the thing."

A minute later he was back out on No Name Street, taking long strides through the late-afternoon sunshine. A set of wind chimes tinkled brightly where they dangled from one giant blue fist.

Jon made his way home. Since he was a foreman, he had his own private living quarters on one of management's platform cars. He liked it all right now, but when they'd first promoted him he'd resisted. He wanted to stay with the rest of the workers in a bunkhouse; he was one of them, after all. What finally changed his mind was when Jackleg Hanrahan took him aside and said, "Look, Jon. It's not that we don't like you—but these bunkhouses aren't large, and you are. You fill up half the room just by walking in the door, and you're too bloody strong to live with puny guys like us." Jackleg stood six foot four and weighed at least two hundred and fifty pounds. "Lots of people get to gesturing while they talk, and some get carried away—but the last time you did, you accidentally knocked Rico Canjura six feet through the air and fractured his jaw. I tell you,

Jon, we all live in mortal fear that you'll start sleepwalking some night and bulldoze half the town.'' Then Jackleg had gulped and decided to be brutally honest. ''Besides . . . you snore.''

And Jon had laughed and pretended he was going to clap Jackleg on the back, and Jackleg had pretended to wince in fear. And neither of them admitted that there was just enough truth in what Jackleg said to hurt, because they were friends and neither one wanted to hurt the other. Jon had moved into his own place, but he insisted it be as close to the workers' quarters as possible. He still saw Jackleg often, and the fact that he was now Jackleg's boss hadn't damaged their friendship a bit.

But sometimes, late at night, Jon Hundred lay alone in his steel-reinforced bed and wished people didn't have to be afraid of him.

He had one room, and the bed took up half of it. The room had white walls, a table beside the bed and a small couch for visitors. There was a single light fixture in the middle of the ceiling, and Jon Hundred had long since learned to avoid smashing into it with his head. He kept his sax in the closet with the few clothes he had, and his one luxury was the sound system on the table beside the bed. He had a drawer full of music coins: mainly old Terran blues, with an eclectic assortment of others thrown in. He had some Russian ballads from Vysotsky's Star, jazz revivalist compilations from twenty different systems—and almost every piece of funeral music every written.

He had dirges from every race and nationality, every human and nonhuman race. They all had their own rituals concerning death, and Jon had done his best to find and learn their songs of mourning. When he played those songs he plugged his sound system into his own cybernetics, and let the sadness flow right into his brain. He didn't play those songs for anyone but himself, and he didn't play them for pleasure. He had other reasons.

The wind chimes went over his bed.

He changed out of his work clothes and into a sea-green shirt and white pants, and then went looking for something to eat. Normally he ate in the workers' cafeteria, but he was feeling kind of low tonight, and he thought a special meal might cheer him up. He headed for Rozy's.

The first platform car after the steeldrivers' quarters was Downtown. Built for the workers, it had a combination post office and bank, a laundry, a restaurant, a medical clinic, a jail, and five bars. Jon Hundred had spent more than a few nights in those bars, shooting pool, drinking, and breaking up the occasional fight. It took a lot of drinking to get Jon drunk, so he tried to stick to ice water most of the time. A keg of beer every night got expensive—especially in a town where the bars never shut down. Boomtown ran three shifts a day, around the clock. There was always something going on in Downtown.

Then he came to the first of the three platform cars the steeldrivers called Tourist Town. It looked much the same as the area he'd just walked through—but that was because all the buildings, old and new, had been remodeled to look alike.

Maybe to a tourist they seemed authentic, but to Jon everything looked subtly off. All the buildings were two stories tall, but some had peaked roofs; that was all wrong for a town that sometimes got towed at upward of a hundred miles an hour. They were false roofs, added for effect.

As he strolled down No Name Street, it struck him how much Boomtown had changed since the players had arrived. The Kadai Group had tacked three more cars on to the end of Boomtown to take care of the tourists, three blocks' worth of hotels, bars, restaurants and shops, all done up in "authentic" frontier fashion: a blacksmith's shop when there wasn't a horse on the planet, a whorehouse full of sex robots, and a general store stocked with souvenirs.

He scuffed at the dirt in the street with one giant boot and frowned. They used to have a streetsweeping vehicle that used sonics and a giant vacuum to keep No Name Street clean; then the marketing people had decided a dirty street was "more authentic." Now the streetsweeper added dirt instead of taking it away.

But the Kadai Group had also added nightclubs like the Blue Cat, and a few decent restaurants. Jon figured he didn't have many grounds for complaint—and that he shouldn't have any trouble, either, as long as he kept a low profile with the tourists. Which meant not playing his sax in the Blue Cat—which he did anyway. He knew he shouldn't, but he enjoyed it too much and was too damn stubborn to stop. *Besides, a man can't hide forever. If they find me, they find me. I ran once, but I'll be damned if I'll do it for the rest of my life.*

And maybe I'm damned anyway.

Jon waved hello to Truse, who was sitting in a rocking chair in front of the bordello she ran. Truse stood at least six foot six in stocking feet, and she usually wore heels. She had a perfectly proportioned hourglass figure, rare for a woman that tall, and Jon Hundred was one of the few people who knew she used to be a he. Truse was wearing her on-duty uniform, a full-length white gown any bride would have been proud to wear, which covered her from ankles to neck—except that parts of it kept fading into complete transparency, revealing what she wore underneath. Jon tried not to stare, not out of embarrassment or even politeness, but because beautiful women made him sad. They were all china dolls to him, as fragile in his arms as glass. He'd never had a lover, not since the day he'd been cyborged. But that didn't mean he didn't want one.

"C'mon by for a visit sometime, Jon!" Truse called out. She had a voice almost as deep as his, done in velvet. "I got a new heavy-duty model in—I think it might even be able to handle you!"

He laughed and waved her off. Truse was a player, brought in by the Kadai Group to foster the illusion of the exciting, bawdy frontier. She was more mechanic than madam; her sexbots, presumably the last refuge for lonely steeldrivers, were actually expensive erotic toys that usually only the hyperrich could afford to maintain. Truse's regular prices would have bankrupted any of the tunnel workers—but on Wednesdays she had a "Steeldriver's Special" just for them. "Come on in and drive some of *my* steel," she'd say. Not that the steeldrivers were hard-up for company. There were almost as many women as men working on the tunnel, and plenty of fraternization.

Jon had never been to the bordello, even on a Wednesday. Truse's sexbots were supposed to be very good at what they did—according to the stories Jon Hundred had heard—but there were some things they just couldn't do as well as a person. Like make small talk, or joke, or give you an honest compliment. If you couldn't get that from your partner you might as well be alone.

Sometimes, when he'd had a few too many drinks, he'd start to think about what made him a man and not a machine. He'd start thinking about the things he'd done, and wonder if he was any different from Truse's windup toys.

He was walking past the casino when he heard shots inside.

A body followed them a second later, stumbling out the front door and collapsing in the street. It was a woman, gunshot at least three times, blood staining the denim shirt she wore. She lay motionless where she'd fallen, her wide-open eyes staring up into Jon's.

Jon shook his head. "One-Iron Nancy," he said sadly. "Got yourself in trouble again." A few people stopped and stared, but most ignored the scene. Some walked by and grinned.

A man appeared at the casino door, a gun in his hand. He was in his early fifties, short and stocky with silver-gray hair under a ridiculous wide-brimmed hat. "Nobody calls my company names like that, you rangy bitch!" he gasped. His face was flushed and his hands were shaking. "Don't say I didn't warn you!"

"Well, she's dead now," a voice said behind him. "And good riddance! C'mon, let's have a drink!" Hands reached out and pulled the man back into the casino. The door shut, leaving Jon and a small crowd with the corpse.

"My, my," Jon said. "And all we have to worry about is a mountain dropping on our heads. Rough day at the office, Nancy? Or just business as usual?"

The dead woman said nothing. A trickle of blood escaped from the corner of her lips. Someone said, "You got her at your mercy, Jon!" and a few people laughed. Jon hunkered down and put one thick finger carefully under her chin. "Kitchy kitchy koo," he said.

The dead woman crossed her eyes and stuck her tongue out of the corner of her mouth. The crowd roared and Jon laughed with them. When he saw he wasn't going to get any further reaction from her, he said, "Okay, you win. Save me a dance at the funeral, all right?" He stood up, stepped over the body and continued on his way.

One-Iron Nancy was a bully; there was no doubt about that. She worked damn hard at it. She usually managed to get shot about four times a week—though her personal best was eight, three of them in one day—and she got a bonus every time she "died." "It's not as easy as you might think," she'd told Jon once. "Some of these tourists couldn't hit me if I was blindfolded and tied to a stake, and others just won't get mad. I had one offer me money to just go away—and that was *after* he'd already paid the extra cash to shoot me!"

It was all harmless, of course. The tourist's gun made a loud bang and fired a beam of light; Nancy wore photosensitive clothes with bloodbags and explosive squibs taped underneath. If the light beam hit any part of her clothing it set off a squib, making it appear she'd been shot. Nancy claimed she had the best job in town: "Who else gets paid to abuse tourists—and come back from the dead?"

By the time Jon got to Rozy's he was ready to eat anything that wasn't still moving. Rozy's was a steakhouse, serving fresh cuts of meat vat-grown in Landing City. It was a little pricey for a working man, but not astronomical. Jon went there fairly often, so they had a special Jon Hundred–sized table and a Jon Hundred–strength chair to go with it. Jon had gotten the Toolies to make up a dozen reinforced chairs for him two years ago, and they were spread all over Boomtown. AC Jones had told him once that having one of Jon's chairs in your place had become a kind of status symbol.

"Jon Hundred's a friend of mine is what it says," AC had explained. "People like saying it, too." Jon didn't know how true that was, but it made him feel proud and happy anyway.

By the time he'd worked his way through three steaks and had started in on a fourth, Jon was beginning to relax. People stopped by his table to say hello or make small talk; the friendly acceptance Jon felt from them seemed both remarkable and invaluable. It was hard to feel bad when you were surrounded by people who liked you, and by the end of his meal Jon Hundred had a broad, contented smile on his face.

On the other side of God's Gravestone, Hone lay in a small storage room on the cot they'd given him. His face held no expression at all.

CHAPTER 3

I should have known, Hone thought. *Another goddamn machine*.

He stood in a tunnel lit by the orange glow of halogen lights. The ceiling was a pale concrete arch at least thirty feet above him.

"Your survival is really quite remarkable," a soft voice said. It came from a screen set into a chest-high tripodal structure standing in the middle of the tunnel, and Hone could barely hear it over the constant, grinding rumble that echoed up from somewhere in the tunnel's depths. A wire-thin line of green laser light extended from the tripod down the tunnel. The screen itself was filled with the logo of the Kadai Group, an interlocking K" and "G" in gold against a black and white starscape. There was a smaller "M.E.L." in black lettering near the bottom of the screen. "Maybe I should offer you a job," the voice said.

"Not interested, thanks. I'd just like to get off-planet as soon as possible." Hone tried to keep his voice polite, but it wasn't easy. Another goddamn machine, but one a helluva lot smarter than Jeremy had been. It had introduced itself as MEL, and told him the name was an acronym for Multiplex Engineering Locus. It was supervising the boring of this tunnel—*and*, Hone thought, *me*.

"Well, you have two options. You can wait for the supply convoy to arrive, which won't be for another six weeks, or you can wait until we break through the mountain.''

''How long will that take?''

''Approximately nine days. They've already laid track from the other side to Landing City—a few hours on a maglev train and you'll be in a spaceport. If you're in a hurry, that's the quickest way.''

''Nine days?'' Hone smiled, but his eyes stayed cold. ''Well, I wouldn't want to overstay my welcome.''

''I think we can put up with you for that long, Mr. Hone,'' MEL said. It sounded slightly amused, as if there were some joke Hone had missed. ''Are you sure you don't want to take a closer look at the Boring Unit? I can't shut it down, of course, but it's quite impressive to be near while it's operating. Three hundred feet of mountain-eating machine, with hydraulic ram muscles and hyperdiamond teeth. It's completely safe—I control everything, from running the Boring Unit to supervising the mucking carts.''

Hone tried to look interested. ''Uh, what's the laser for?''

''Guidance. It ensures that the tunnel stays straight and true. And it is—as least on my side. I can't speak for the crew on the other side of the mountain.''

''Nine days . . . '' Hone muttered. *Wonderful.*

''That's only an estimate, of course. The distance left to tunnel between the two sites stood at approximately one thousand seven hundred and three feet first thing this morning, but I can get a more current assessment by checking the other tunnel site. Just a moment.''

Hone had to remind himself that he was dealing with a self-aware entity now, not a cleverly designed set of programmed responses. MEL oversaw the entire mining complex as well as this end of the tunnel project, and Hone couldn't afford to arouse its suspicions. His original plan had been to crash on the other side of the mountains, as close to Boomtown as possible, but the ash storm had thrown him off course. Not that it mattered—it just meant he'd have to wait a little longer to do his job.

The roar of the distant tunneling machine sounded like a factory chewing on bear traps and rock. Hone decided the sound had a certain charm.

Another day on the mountain, and Jon Hundred was hard at work. He was deep inside the tunnel, helping the mucking crew load up the muck carts with rock debris. Jon Hundred was the hardest-working steeldriver on his or any other team, and the foreman to boot. He worked all four cycles of the tunneling routine: drill, blast, muck and support. He helped drill the blast holes, load the explosives, set off the charges and even clean up the mess afterward. He laid track, hung air vents, sprayed shotcrete on the bare rock walls and slapped concrete segments over that. Workers joked that if the whole steeldriving team called in sick, Jon Hundred wouldn't have to worry about holding back anymore.

None of them knew why Jon worked as hard as he did. It wasn't because he wanted to get ahead; management had a hard time getting him to accept a promotion. And if you came right out and asked him, Jon would just smile and say, "It seems like the natural thing to do."

In truth, it was something unnatural that drove him—a deep, burning need that wouldn't let him stop, wouldn't let him rest, wouldn't let him slow up for a minute. He was driven by frustration. He was driven by desperation. He was driven by hate.

What he hated was made of hard, cold stone. Not the stone of the mountain, but the stone walls inside his own mind. He could see them every time he closed his eyes, long corridors with walls of blank gray rock. He'd run down them in his dreams, looking for a door, but he never found one. He knew there were rooms behind those walls, and he knew what was in those rooms. His past.

Jon Hundred knew there wasn't a wall built that couldn't

be torn down, and if there was one thing he was good at it was tearing things down. So he had attacked those walls with every ounce of his will, with all the determination and fury he could muster. He'd done it for hours at a time, every day, for a full year.

He'd failed.

His strength had done him no good. The ones who built his body built the walls in his mind, and he just didn't have the tools he needed to undo them. He'd cried then, even though no tears flowed.

So then he'd taken his rage and frustration out on the mountain. He'd drilled and hammered and detonated, and if they had let him he would have smashed his way through it with his bare fists. He worked graveyard shifts, double shifts, triple shifts. The mountain came to represent everything he was powerless against, and the more he thought about it the truer it seemed. The multiplanetary corporation that had built him was as massive and impersonal as the mountain before him, both of them rising to heights he could never reach, both of them inhuman and uncaring. He'd run from one, but he wasn't going to run from the other.

An ordinary man would have worked himself to death, but Jon Hundred was far from ordinary. He let the machine part of him take over, pushing himself harder and harder and still not finding his limits. Until one day he found the limits of his prison.

He had just made foreman. The engine that drove the mucking carts had quit, the generator for the lights and ventilation had broken down, and they'd undercalculated the last blast, getting bad breakage on the rock and filling the tunnel with oversize rock debris. That meant the crew had to work in air masks by the light of helmet lanterns, breaking the rock into small enough pieces to be hauled away by hand. It was agonizingly slow. Jon, frustrated beyond belief, finally ordered everyone out of the tunnel until the generator was fixed. Everyone but himself.

He saw just fine in the dark, and his lungs could function for an amazingly long time on virtually no air. In fact, Jon Hundred's physiology didn't require much oxygen at all, and he had his own internal supply stored for emergencies.

Deep underground, all alone in the sweltering dark, Jon Hundred got down to work.

He used an old-fashioned sledgehammer to smash boulders in two, and threw the pieces into a mucking cart. When he filled up a cart, he pushed it down the track and filled up another. He kept going until he had a string of twelve carts, and then he pushed them a mile or so to the tunnel entrance. The first time he appeared at the mouth of the tunnel, his shoulder to a line of a dozen carts, every steeldriver on-site stopped, coffee cups halfway to their lips, and stared. Jon told them they'd better start unloading those carts because he'd have twelve more ready in an hour, and then he'd gone back down the tunnel.

He didn't think about what he was doing, he just did it. Break the rock, carry the rock, dump the rock. No voices around him, just the crack of the hammer. His mind drifted, floated free, and when he closed his eyes for a second he didn't see walls of stone enclosing him. He saw a woman.

She had long black hair and a worried look on her face—and he recognized her. It was his mother.

He stopped dead, standing there in the dark, and tried to remember something else. The stone walls came crashing back, and he roared with frustration. But the memory wasn't gone; he knew his mother's face again.

It was a small victory, but an important one. Jon understood that it was his frame of mind that had let him break free, and not the amount of work he'd done, for which he was thankful. If he had kept working at the pace he had set, sooner or later he would have overstressed one of his systems—and there weren't too many cybersystem repair shops in this part of the galaxy. Not ones qualified to work on him, anyway.

From that day on, he had worked at developing the same

mind-set he had achieved down in the tunnel. Slowly, over months and months, he had done it. It only came to him when he was working hard, when his attention was so focused on the job at hand that he wasn't really thinking at all. It was terribly difficult, especially at first—the most important thing in his world, and it would only come to him when he was not trying to attain it. He'd call up his mother's face when he got too frustrated, and sometimes it would fend off discouragement; other times the worried look on her face seemed like she knew Jon had nothing to look forward to but grief.

Still, over the last few years he had gradually regained more and more of his memory. The bits he had collected were rarely connected to each other, and sometimes made no sense at all—but they were *his,* pieces of his life he had made himself, and they were the most precious things he owned.

He remembered rain on his face when he was a child. He remembered kissing a girl named Mary for the first time. He remembered a spicy dish made with fish and noodles that he used to love, though he couldn't name it. He remembered half a nursery rhyme. He remembered having a stomachache when he still had a stomach. Some of the bits were harder to define, blurry photographs of past events with vague feelings attached to them. He pondered over these every night before he went to sleep, trying to sharpen their edges. Sometimes he even succeeded.

One of the strongest memories he had was a smell. Normally, Jon would have said it was a bad smell: old sweat with a hint of burned plastic. But the feelings that went with it were good ones, happiness and familiarity side by side with confidence and anticipation. More than anything, it felt like the smell of home.

Now his home smelled faintly of sulfur, of the breath of a thousand volcanoes. Only the smell of sweat was the same.

Jon had just finished drilling the burnhole for the next

round of charges when the call came through, his video-phone vibrating silently against the skin of his arm. The drill he was using was mounted on a drill jumbo, a mobile, four-tiered platform that let a dozen drills operate at the same time, and the racket they made was considerable. Jon had been working on the middle tier, crouched down so he'd fit. He preferred a little more headroom, but his weight made the other drillers nervous when he was on the top tier, and steeldrivers had enough to worry about already.

He walked a ways up the tunnel, away from the noise, and pulled the videophone from its pocket. When he un-folded it and held it to his ear, the paper-thin screen and microcam that telescoped out from the handset hung about six inches from his face.

The screen showed him the black and gold logo of the Kadai Group. ''Mr. Hundred?'' a soft voice asked.

''Hello, MEL,'' Jon said. ''What can I do for you?'' Jon had talked to the AI several times since it had been installed to oversee the other half of the tunneling project, and treated it the same way he did everyone else. So far, it had seemed friendly enough.

''I have an unexpected visitor that needs to get to Land-ing City as soon as possible.''

''Is that so?'' Jon asked, smiling. ''What did he do, fall out of the sky?''

''Yes, as a matter of fact—from orbit. His name is Mr. Hone. His ship crashed a few miles away from the mine, and he's staying here until the tunnel is operational.''

''Is he all right?''

''Completely unharmed.''

''Well, now. You tell Mr. Hone I'll buy him a drink when he makes it over to my side of the tunnel, as long as he tells me how he managed to survive a head-on with a planet. That might even shake *me* up some.''

''You can tell him yourself. He's right here.'' The pic-ture on-screen changed to a man in brown coveralls sitting in an office chair. He looked into the camera with a tired little smile that never reached his eyes.

"Mr. Hone, this is Mr. Hundred, foreman on the spaceport side of the tunnel project. I believe he has an offer to make you."

Jon started to chuckle over the AI's literal-mindedness, but the sound died in his throat. At the mention of Jon's name, something in the stranger had changed. Without shifting his position or altering the look on his face, he suddenly seemed focused, alert. It was like watching a cat tensing to spring.

"You have a first name, Mr. Hundred?" Hone asked. He made it sound friendly.

"Jon. And you, Mr. Hone?"

"I'm afraid not." There was a flat kind of finality to his words, and Jon wondered if he'd insulted him.

Don't be stupid. After all, he asked yours. "I was just telling MEL I'd like to buy you a drink sometime, if you'll tell me how you managed to come through that crash without a scratch."

"Consider it a deal, Jon." His voice had lost some of its flatness, but Jon was still hearing something in it he didn't like. A threat, almost.

"I'd like an update on your progress," MEL's voice cut in. The screen returned to the Kadai insignia. "What's your current estimate on reaching the midpoint?"

Jon thought for a moment. "Eleven days, give or take a day. Without problems, of course."

"You can revise that down to nine. I should reach the midpoint a day or so ahead of you, and we should make breakthrough a day after that."

"Hold up. Last I heard, midpoint *was* the breakthrough point."

"It would be, if we were tunneling at the same speed. But blast-and-excavate methods are less efficient than Tunnel Boring Machines—and thus slower."

"You think you can dig faster than us?" Jon asked, laughing.

"Of course."

Jon wasn't sure he liked the way MEL put that. "Awfully sure of yourself, aren't you?"

"I know what I'm doing."

"And we don't? I'll tell you what you're going to see when you finally bust through the midpoint, MEL: me and my whole crew, waiting with smiles on our faces and coffee in our hands."

"Unlikely."

The AI's denial was starting to annoy Jon. "I guess mere humans can't compete with you, huh?"

"As a cybernetic organism, you must understand the advantages technology has given you over ordinary—"

"Advantages?" Jon blurted out, amazed. "I have to stoop to go through any door designed for a normal person. Anything I sit, lie, or step on has to be reinforced with steel. I'm so strong I have to watch myself every second of every day just so I don't destroy something by accident; you'll never see a more careful drunk." Jon stopped, realized he'd probably already said too much—especially if Hone could still hear him.

Sometimes the only place I feel at ease is out here in the rock, where I don't have to tiptoe around, he thought. *I live in a world made of tissue paper and gauze, MEL—I can't even touch another human being without fear of hurting them.* "I don't call those advantages," he said out loud.

"Power can work both ways, can't it?" MEL said. It almost sounded amused. "But it's still better to have it than not."

"How would you know?"

"Because I'm going to beat you to the midpoint."

"The hell you will!" Jon snapped. "I'll stake my paycheck against yours—winner take all!"

"You don't think I'll take that bet, do you, Mr. Hundred? After all, I'm only a machine. What use would I have for money? Well, I get paid for my work just like you do, and I spend money, too—so I accept your challenge. How does a week's pay sound?''

''Make it two!'' Jon thundered. ''And one more thing—''

''Yes?''

''No matter how much steel I've got in me, I'm still a man—not a 'cybernetic organism'! Good-bye!'' Jon managed to turn the videophone off without destroying it, and shoved it back in its pocket.

He was so upset, he forgot all about Hone.

Most of the work at the mine was done by Toolies; there was only a small contingent of human supervisors. There wasn't a lot to do as far as recreation went. There was a small cafeteria, a gym, a games room with a pool table, and a few holosims. A card table in the hall with a pile of bookdiscs on it served as the public library.

Hone had accepted MEL's offer of a guided tour of the mine itself, but said he was feeling tired and would rather do it tomorrow. He had gone back to the storage room and lain on his cot for half an hour, staring unblinking up at the ceiling. Then he'd gotten up and gone exploring on his own.

He left the central complex where the human living quarters and offices were located, a large, low-slung building with a steeply angled roof. Ash drifts were piled against the outside walls, smoothly curving slopes of glittery black. The mine was located in the foothills of the mountain proper; on one side, rolling hills stretched into the distance, black with ash and dotted with flowers of a brilliant scarlet. On the other—God's Gravestone.

It wasn't so much a mountain as another world, shaped into a rough wedge and slammed base-first into the ground. Its top was always hidden by clouds of condensation or ash. MEL had told Hone that tunneling began on this side of the peak first; Jon Hundred's crew spent their first year laying rail from Landing City to the mountain. The midpoint MEL and Jon had been arguing about wasn't at the true center of the mountain—it was actually closer to Jon's side than MEL's.

God's Gravestone didn't stand alone, either. Equally huge mountains rose on either side of it, stretching away into the distance. They were so big they seemed like parodies, exaggerations of reality painted on a backdrop. The small part of the sky they didn't block out was a grayish blue.

Hone took in the view for all of ten seconds, then shifted his glance. He found a path worn into the dirt and followed it away from the building.

It led to another building, almost identical to the first. There were several important differences: this building had no windows, only one large door, and it had a strong, acidic smell. Hone tested the door and found it locked.

He followed the path around the building and down a gentle incline. His ears told him what lay ahead long before his eyes did.

He rounded a curve in the path and came across a small clearing with a dozen or so men standing in a circle in its center, dressed in the same kind of brown coveralls Hone was wearing. They were laughing and passing a bottle around. Hone stopped and waited.

A burly man with a reddish beard finally noticed him, the bottle halfway to his lips. He hesitated, then grinned and waved for Hone to join them. "Hey there, if it isn't the luckiest man in the galaxy!"

Hone walked over, his hands stuffed in the pockets of his coveralls. "Looks like you boys are having a little party," he said.

When he got close enough, he saw what they were gathered around. It was a small Toolie, no larger than a terrier, in a pen with glass walls about four feet high. The Toolie had no bones; it looked like a large amoeba, its cluster of pink sensory globes submerged just below the surface of its translucent skin.

"Drink?" the man with the reddish beard asked. He had an ID decal on his chest that read MALLORY.

"No." Hone looked around the circle of men. They all seemed drunk. He spotted Garber, the security chief, lighting a cigar. Garber stared back at Hone and slowly exhaled a cloud of smoke.

"You familiar with Toolies at all, Mr. Hone?" Garber said.

"Can't say that I am."

"Well, then, you'll find this informative." Garber accepted the bottle and took a swig. "You see, contrary to how they look, there actually are male and female Toolies. The females are the ones we use for labor—no joke intended. The cluster-mother is like the queen bee; her children feed her and do whatever she tells them to. That's why they make such great workers—as long as the females don't get pregnant, they'll follow the cluster-mother's orders for the rest of their lives."

He paused and took a slow puff on his cigar. "Now, the males are a completely different matter. They're born aggressive; they'll attack and consume anything, including each other. The only thing that stops them from eating their sisters is a special enzyme in the young female's skin.

"Once only one male is left alive, having managed to eat all his brothers, he strikes out on his own. He'll eat anything that moves, and use its bones to shape his body. All the claws, fangs, quills, tusks, and beaks he can't digest will become his own weapons. And the more he eats, the bigger he'll get. A full-grown male can mass more than an elephant."

Garber gestured with his cigar at the Toolie in the pen. "Now, we let our Toolies have as many young as Kadai allows—but due to the difficulties of having a male Toolie around, we have to use a very special method of artificial insemination. You see, the male Toolie, while aggressive and crafty, isn't too bright. Once the females reach child-bearing age they lose the enzyme that protected them from the males—and if a male spots an adult female, he'll try to eat her.''

There was a burst of sudden laughter and rude comments from the men. Garber just smiled. Hone didn't.

"Now, if the male manages to engulf the female, she'll start exuding a certain chemical. This chemical really turns the male on, and pretty soon all kinds of biology start to happen. When it's all over, the female squirts out another chemical, and the male suddenly feels a little queasy.''

"I've had that feeling the morning after a few times my-self!'' a man with an ID decal that read CASSINI said. More laughter.

"So the male vomits up the female, and she staggers off to eventually give birth. Isn't that romantic?'' Garber grinned around the cigar clenched in his teeth. "Anyway, we have this tank we stick horny Toolies in. We fill it with the appropriate chemicals, and at the moment of truth, dump in some thawed-out Toolie sperm. We also add a drug that prevents them from conceiving males—but it doesn't always work. Which is how we wound up with Junior here.''

"This is a male?'' Hone asked.

"Yep. You can't sex 'em until they're born, so we have to practice retroactive abortion.'' Garber blew another cloud of smoke.

Hone looked at the Toolie. It was moving around inside the glass pen, its motion an eerie controlled flow that looked like a wave just about to break. "You're going to kill it because it's the wrong sex,'' Hone said. His voice was as flat as the look in his eyes.

"Not right away,'' Garber said. His eyes had changed too, taken on a gleam as bright as the cherry on his cigar. "See, a male Toolie is just a vicious animal, and a young male Toolie is an inexperienced vicious animal. Vermin. You throw a human baby in that pen, it'd eat it in a flash.''

"Too bad we don't got any babies, huh?" Mallory said. He grinned hugely at Hone.

"I guess we'll just have to improvise," Garber said. He reached into his back pocket and pulled out a spray can. Hone saw that the can's activator had a rubber band strapped over it and a wooden stick wedged beneath it.

Garber tossed it at the Toolie. It landed with a soft *thump!* on the Toolie's back, and was almost instantly engulfed. In a few seconds the can was inside the Toolie, still clearly visible through its transparent skin.

"This should be good," one of the men laughed.

"A young Toolie will eat almost anything," Garber continued, "alive or not. Once it figures out it can't digest it, it'll try to figure out if it can use it as part of its infrastructure. Toolies have these internal muscles that let them shift things around inside their bodies; they'll play with their leftover bones, try to fit them into various combinations."

Hone could see that the Toolie was doing just that. The can was being flipped over and over inside, rotated one way and then the other by translucent strands of muscle, as the Toolie tried to figure out what it had consumed.

Then a strand wrapped itself around the stick wedged under the activator—and pulled it free.

The can began spewing white foam. *Shaving cream,* Hone thought. The Toolie froze as it tried to understand what was happening to it, then began manipulating the can frantically, trying to stop the flow. The shaving cream must have made the can slippery and hard to hold, because it didn't have any success. A bubble of white quickly grew in the center of the Toolie's body, which expanded like a balloon. Pores opened all over its skin as it tried to excrete the foam as fast as possible. It rolled around the pen frantically, a fat white beach ball spouting shaving cream from a dozen different spots. The men were roaring so hard with laughter that some of them had collapsed on the ground.

Finally the Toolie managed to eject the can, still spouting foam, which sailed a good twenty feet out of the pen. The

Toolie lay in one spot, quivering and ejecting gouts of white tinged with pink.

Hone's face was utterly still. He stared at the Toolie and waited.

"Well," Garber said, clapping him on the back, "that's entertainment, right?"

"No," Hone said. "That's torturing an innocent being. This is entertainment." He reached out casually and grabbed the belt of Garber's pants. Then, one-handed, he hoisted him over his head.

"Hey!" Garber said, his voice more amazed than afraid. "What the hell?"

"Maybe you'd like to see just how much fun being disoriented is," Hone said. "Allow me to demonstrate."

He swung his arm in circles over his head, as if he were twirling a lasso. Garber, at the end of that arm, wasn't nearly as aerodynamic as a lariat. He jerked violently back and forth, his arms and legs flailing, looking as if he were trapped inside an invisible tornado. The other men gaped.

"Isn't this fun?" Hone growled. "Isn't this entertaining?" From the way Hone stood and moved, it seemed Garber weighed nothing at all; if it wasn't for the violent contortions of Garber's limbs, he might have been a manshaped balloon.

And Hone didn't stop.

The first minute passed through sheer disbelief. Change flew from Garber's pockets and hit one man in the eye. Garber kept yelling the whole time, but after two minutes or so he started to beg.

"You better put him down," Mallory finally yelled.

"In a minute," Hone said.

Garber had started to moan. "You'll snap his neck if you don't stop," Mallory warned.

Garber threw up, spraying his lunch in a wide circle. Most of it seemed to wind up on Mallory. "Now he's done," Hone said. He stopped whirling Garber over his head and tossed him to the ground.

"I don't know who the hell you think you are," Mallory snarled, "but you picked the wrong time and place to be a smart-ass." Mallory was an even bigger man than Garber, and the other ten men had stopped being amazed and started to get angry. *They're probably the roughest, meanest men this side of the mountain,* Hone thought. He'd ruined their sadistic little sideshow, so they figured he'd have to provide them with their fun.

"You know, I really hate being the new kid in town," Hone said sourly.

And broke Mallory's jaw.

And Kastinsky's nose.

Three of Jerrabella's ribs.

Kerry's collarbone.

Portland's right kneecap.

Gredenko's arm, wrist, and thumb.

Both of Westham's elbows.

Cassini's left arm.

Kaufman's cheekbone and three of his teeth.

Barker's jaw, nose, and collarbone.

Every finger in Diamantra's right hand.

And both of Garber's legs.

Thank God for ID decals, Hone thought. *I'd hate to be doing this to a bunch of complete strangers.*

He was careful to hold back. If he showed off how powerful he really was, word might get back to Jon Hundred that someone on the planet was in the same league he was. That would make Hone's job harder, and he hated hard jobs. So he kept the beatings to a minimum, enough to incapacitate and nothing more. Part of Hone's mind wasn't quite satisfied with this logic—it seemed subtly wrong—but he refused to pay any attention to it. He kept himself focused on his work instead.

Jon Hundred won't be quite as lucky as Garber, Hone thought. Jon Hundred had taken things that didn't belong to him—and Hone's job was the retrieval of stolen property. He was on Pellay to reclaim some expensive electronics, plus one very special device.

The device was called a Hammer. The electronics were currently in use—as Jon Hundred's muscles, internal organs, and senses.

Later, after he had let the Toolie go, Hone helped carry the more severely injured to the infirmary. It seemed like the least he could do.

CHAPTER 4

There were only two things Jon Hundred was afraid of. The first was hurting a friend.

The second was being found.

The first hadn't happened too often. There'd been a few accidents, like breaking Rico Canjura's jaw, but only a few. They tended to happen when Jon had been drinking a little too much, and at first he had resigned himself to drinking alone.

But these were steeldrivers. Not only did they let Jon drink with them, they insisted on it. More than one had used up an entire paycheck trying to get Jon drunk, and more than one had succeeded. They regarded him as not just one of them, but the best of them. They were proud of him instead of afraid, and Jon had long since given up trying to figure out why. He just counted himself damn lucky, and bought the next round.

And wondered about the second thing, and just how long his luck was going to hold.

Word of Jon's challenge to MEL traveled fast. By the time Jon's shift ended, every steeldriver on the mountain knew about it; by the time he finished eating supper the news had spread throughout Boomtown; and by the time Jon walked into the Blue Cat that night people were betting on the outcome. Not surprisingly, Jon was favored two to one.

So he let people buy him drinks and told them no machine was going to beat Jon Hundred, and no one made any jokes about his being part machine himself. He laughed and drank and played some sax with the house band. He had a fine time.

And when the night had rolled itself up, too early for the graveyard shift to show up and too late for everyone else, when the only people left were the passed-out drunks, the half-asleep wait staff and the yawning bartender, Jon Hundred sat by himself with a half-finished beer in one hand and thought about Hone.

Can't be, he thought.

Half-lidded eyes as cold as a snake's. No first name at all, a voice whispered in the back of his skull.

How'd they find me?

Doesn't matter. A ship fell out of the sky and a killer walked away from the wreckage. He had your face in his mind and your name on his lips. If he'd come down on your side of God's Gravestone you'd already be cold.

He clenched his fist, shattering the beer stein he held and scaring the hell out of the bartender. Jon hardly noticed. "That's just booze-powered paranoia," he muttered to himself. "Why, I've seen tourists that looked more dangerous than him."

His videophone thrummed against the skin of his forearm. Moving slowly and carefully, Jon unfolded it and switched it on.

The black and gold insignia of the Kadai Group filled the screen. "Hello, Jon," MEL said.

"What's wrong, MEL?" Jon said. This time of night, it had to be bad news.

"Nothing. I just wanted to talk to you."

MEL sounds different, Jon thought. *More relaxed.* "Kind of late for a social call, isn't it?"

"I wanted to wait until you weren't busy."

"How do you know I'm not?"

"I've been watching you."

Jon chuckled. "Checking up on the competition, huh?" He glanced up from the screen and looked around the bar.

"You find a camera to plug into somewhere?"

"Over here," MEL's voice called from across the room. An electric motor hummed to life; a second later a tourguide came trundling toward Jon.

Jon laughed. A tourguide was an automated vehicle that looked like a metal sunflower growing out of a tiny battle tank. It had a triangle of Caterpillar treads on either side of its squat body, with a wheel at each point of the triangle. The head on the end of the five-foot-long silver shaft contained a speaker, microphone, and guidance camera, as well as a low-powered laser finger to point out things of interest. Someone had tied a bowtie around this one's "neck," just under the head.

Tourguides were like bits of ash in your food: the first few times they were kind of annoying, but after a while you learned not to notice they were there. Which was good, because they were always there. They led tourists around Boomtown and told them touristy things, and every Saturday night at least one (tourguide, not tourist) would get run up the flagpole upside down or used for target practice in an alley. As robots went, they were about as smart as a toaster set on "medium to light."

"I hope you don't think I was spying on you," MEL said, stopping beside Jon's table. Its voice came from the tourguide now. Jon turned off his phone and put it away. "I was going to approach you earlier, but it didn't seem wise."

"Hah! You got that right," Jon said. "If tonight's crowd had heard you talking through that thing, they wouldn't have left enough of it in one piece to interest even a Toolie scrap dealer."

"Boys will be boys, I suppose," MEL said. "Even when they're girls."

"Now that's an even quicker way to wind up on the junkpile," Jon said with a grin. "There's steeldriving men and steeldriving women—but no boys, and no girls."

"And the Toolies?" MEL asked. It sounded genuinely curious.

"And steeldriving Toolies," he amended. "Hell, they work harder than anybody."

"Except you." He heard an almost mocking tone in MEL's voice, but didn't feel insulted. He laughed instead, and stood up. "I guess," he admitted. "I live to work. I like to play too, but not as much as everyone else seems to. Know what the hardest part of my job is? Listening to everyone else complain about theirs. Sometimes I just want to tell them all to shut up—where would they be without their jobs?" He reached down and picked up his sax case.

"But you wouldn't, would you?" There was no mockery in MEL's voice this time. The tourguide scooted out of the way as Jon rose and started for the door.

"No, of course not. It's just human nature to complain." He stopped and turned to face MEL's surrogate. "I'm heading home to bed, but you can walk—uh, roll—with me if you want."

"Thanks, Jon. I will." The robot followed him out the door.

"Anything in particular on your mind?" Jon asked. He strolled out into the middle of No Name Street, deserted at this time of the morning. The sun was just beginning to rise, throwing long streaks of red and purple over the mountains. One thing about all the ash in the air—it sure made for some lovely colors.

"I wanted to apologize, actually. I upset you when I called you a cybernetic organism; I didn't mean it as an insult."

Jon considered that for a moment as he walked. "No, I don't suppose you did," he said slowly. "Tell you what— I'll swap you, apology for apology. I didn't mean to imply there's anything wrong about being a machine, either. It's just that sometimes I get a little touchy about being different from everybody else."

"It gets lonely, doesn't it?" MEL asked quietly. Jon

looked down, surprised at what he heard in its voice, then nodded.

"Yeah. Sometimes it does."

They came to the end of the platform car and crossed the polymer-plastic strip that connected it to the next one. Jon saw there were still lights on in the bordello; a few late-night customers, trading sleep and dollars for passion. He sighed under his breath.

A man lurched out of the bordello's entrance, the door slamming behind him. He stood there, swaying slightly, a bottle in one hand. He was stocky, with bushy white-gray eyebrows and a beard to match. He wore rumpled clothes that looked at least as old as he was, and a battered brown cap. Jon waved and called out to him, "Morning, Whiskey Joe!"

The man squinted at them, then lifted his bottle in a salute. When the bottle was level with his eyes he seemed to notice it for the first time; he regarded it with amazement for a second, then seemed to reach a momentous decision. He put the bottle to his lips and drank from it.

Jon laughed. MEL swiveled its head, first studying Whiskey Joe, then Jon. "Town drunk?" it asked Jon.

"That's right. Not a real one, though; he's one of the players the Kadai Group brought in. That's real whiskey he's drinking, but it doesn't affect him. His body's been altered so it won't absorb alcohol." They watched Whiskey Joe stagger off down the street. "He's good at making people laugh," Jon said. "Sometimes he'll stand behind tourguides and mimic them as they talk. I think he has every one of their spiels memorized."

"Why robot guides instead of people?" MEL asked. "Wouldn't actual pioneers be more authentic than machinery?"

"Price, for one thing. Even if they get banged up a little, it's still cheaper to keep tourguides running than to hire locals. And they are authentic, in a way. They're actually old exploration probes, first used when this planet was settled. That's why they can take so much abuse—they were built for it."

"I can understand people wanting to experience the illusion of a frontier town," MEL said, "but you'd think that, given the choice, they'd prefer the real thing. Here, where both are available, the illusion seems to supplant the reality."

"Oh?" Jon said. "Look over there." He pointed down the street. A young man was bent over in a doorway, throwing up. He'd pause between spasms, gasping and moaning softly to himself.

"That's reality," Jon said. "Always a price to pay."

"At least he knows what he's paying for. Illusions can cost much more—and leave you with nothing."

"I suppose," Jon said uneasily. Was MEL hinting at something? All this talk of illusions and prices to be paid—just how much did MEL know about Jon Hundred?

"So you really figure you can beat me?" Jon said, trying to change the subject.

"To quote an ancestor of mine, 'I think I can, I think I can.' "

"Ha! The Little Engine That Could, huh? Well, I don't know about that. How much experience you have in tunnel work?"

"I supervised sinking a mine shaft on Baldwin's World."

"Not the same. When you tunnel through a mountain, you pick a straight line and stick to it. You have a problem, you got to go through it, not around. And a mountain will throw all kinds of rock at you: felsic, mafic, metamorphic, sedimentary, hyperabyssal. That's what'll slow you down, more than anything."

MEL stopped, swiveled the metal flower of its head to study Jon Hundred. "Really. I had no idea. And here I thought it was just rock. Goodness gracious."

"Well, that's where—"

"I had no idea that 47.98 percent of Pellay's crust was oxygen, 4.37 percent was aluminum, or 8.22 potassium.

The relative strengths of such materials as dolomite, with a rock shear strength of 12,700 pounds, was also completely unknown to me—until, of course, I picked up a copy of the new intergalactic best-seller: *Jon Hundred—Rockhead.*"

Jon stared. After a while he noticed his mouth was open, so he shut it. Which was, he thought, what he should have done in the first place.

"Anybody can spout numbers," he said stubbornly. "It's not the same as experience. Every blast we do is a brand-new situation that's never happened before and won't ever happen again."

"If there's that much change, what good is experience?"

"Well, there isn't that much—I mean, there is but not always—some things are never the same, except when they are—" Jon realized he was making about as much sense as an avalanche going uphill, and gave up. "I can't explain it. You just have to be ready for surprises, that's all."

"If you're ready for something, it isn't a surprise," MEL replied.

They had just about reached Jon's bunkhouse. Jon grinned and shook his head. "I guess there's only one way to win this argument."

"Is this an argument? I don't usually enjoy them this much."

Jon chuckled. "Neither do I. So we'll call it a disagreement between gentlemen."

"Gentlebeings, please."

Jon had one hand on the door handle when he saw the Toolie. It came racing up No Name Street from downtown, waving its arms frantically. It was built like a centaur, four long legs and a skinny body that curved up into a human-shaped torso with two multijointed arms. It even had a human face; some Toolies carved or sculpted masks out of wood or clay, painted and then ate them. This one had a mask of a smiling, chubby Buddha just under the surface of her skin. The effect was somewhat spoiled by the cluster of sensory globes on top of the Toolie's head, which made it look like the Buddha was wearing his brains on the outside.

Jon recognized her as a Toolie named Moneykeeper. She skidded to a dusty stop in front of Jon and MEL and made urgent motions toward her implanted chest screen.

<jon hundred you must come! trouble guns fighting—i beg your help!>

"Just calm down," Jon said. "What's the problem?"

<poker game—actor accused of cheating—big argument—guns! trouble! fighting!>

Jon sighed. "Let's go, then. It's too early in the morning for that kind of excitement."

"Would you mind if I tagged along?" MEL asked.

Jon hesitated. The reason Moneykeeper had come to him for help instead of the sheriff was simple—the sheriff was an actor himself, and didn't seem to care much about the Toolies' problems. In a dispute between a Toolie and a fellow actor, there was no question whose side he'd take.

But MEL represented the interests of the Kadai Group—how would it react to a situation like this? The last thing Jon wanted was to bring disciplinary action from the company down on anyone. On the other hand, if MEL truly wanted to watch, Jon probably couldn't stop it—there were tourguides all over town.

"On two conditions, MEL. You don't interfere, and you don't report what you see to anyone else. This is a private matter, all right?"

The silver head of the tourguide nodded, a strangely human gesture Jon hadn't expected. "I promise."

Jon motioned to the Toolie and it spun and galloped off, Jon running behind it. The tourguide, not built for speed, soon fell behind.

There was a regular casino in town for the tourists, but it didn't run all night. For those who liked to gamble until the sun came up, there were other, private games available, like the ongoing poker game Moneykeeper ran. Jon even sat in some nights, but most of the time the big steel chair they had reserved for him gathered dust in a corner. Games of chance had never held much appeal for Jon Hundred.

Moneykeeper ran the Hitching Post Souvenir Shop during the day, selling the tourists holographic postcards and genuine vials of volcanic ash. When night fell and her front door was locked, a round table with a green felt top was rolled out and set up in the back room, and a bottle of whiskey and a box of cigars put on it. You wanted a glass, you brought your own.

Jon owed her a favor. She'd got him some hard-to-find music coins he'd wanted, and thrown in a few saxophone reeds as a gift. Besides, she ran an honest game; she wouldn't have lasted long if she didn't. He hoped this was just a problem with some drunk who had even less brains than luck.

So when Jon reached the open front door of the Hitching Post and stepped inside, he was more than a little surprised to recognize the voice of One-Iron Nancy coming from the back.

"Nobody calls me a cheat and gets away with it!" Nancy yelled. Jon moved quickly through the darkened store, Moneykeeper right behind him, and stopped in the doorway of the back room.

One-Iron Nancy was dressed like a riverboat gambler, all in black from her hat to her boots, with a gold-embroidered vest in between. She had a snarl on her face and her namesake in her hand. The table with the green felt top lay on its side, and an unconscious worker sprawled at Nancy's feet. *He would have known the gun held blanks,* Jon thought. His first mistake would have been thinking that meant she was harmless. His second would have been making her prove she wasn't.

The two tourists she held a gun on either didn't know her gun held only blanks, or knew and were afraid of her anyway. They were a typical tourist couple, both dressed in typical tourist outfits: black jeans, neon plaid shirts and wide-brimmed white hats. The man was pale and stocky, the woman blonde and skinny. She had her own gun out, smoke still curling from the barrel, and she looked upset. "I shot her four times already, and she won't fall down," the woman told Jon.

"I guess you're one hell of a bad shot then," Nancy spat.

"Let's try to calm down," Jon said reasonably.

"I am not! I plugged you fair and square," the lady tourist said.

"Alice, don't make her mad," the man said. He seemed nervous.

"You missed me by a mile."

"Ladies, please—"

The woman brought her gun up, pointed it straight at Nancy's chest, and fired. Her partner winced at the gunshot. Nancy just glared at her.

"There! No way I could have missed!" the woman said triumphantly. "What do you say to that?"

"Ouch," Nancy said through gritted teeth.

"Alice, don't make trouble."

"Ouch?" the woman said, arching an eyebrow.

"It's only a flesh wound."

"I shot you in the *heart*!"

"I feel fine, thanks."

"Nancy, let the people go," Jon sighed. "Or shoot them, if you really have to."

The man swallowed. "That's really not necessary, is it?"

Nancy gave Jon a murderous look. "Maybe I will. Maybe I'll kill them both. Dumb bitch, walking around with blanks in her gun. She deserves to get shot."

"Go ahead, then! Shoot us!" the woman said loudly. "But I'm going to write a letter of complaint about this when we get home! I've never—"

Nancy shot her. Six times.

There was a second of silence, the air filled with the smell of gunpowder. "Are you quite finished?" the woman asked coldly. "Because we're leaving." She strode up to Jon, glared at him until he got out of the way, and then marched out the door. The man hurried to catch up with her.

Nancy tried to storm after them, but Jon blocked her way. "Hold on a second, Nancy. I want to know how this whole thing started."

"What the hell business is it of yours?"

Jon frowned. He and Nancy weren't close friends, but they got along all right. This didn't seem like her at all. "It's Moneykeeper's business you're busting up, and she's a friend of mine. So what gives?"

"That dirtsucker said I was cheating!" Nancy kicked the man lying on the floor in the shin, and got a muffled groan in return. Jon reached out, gently took hold of her upper arm and pulled her away before she could start on the man's ribs.

"No one likes being called a cheat," Jon said. "What about the tourists?"

"If some damn fool greenhorn wants to commit suicide by pulling a gun on me, I'll give her all the help she wants! The bitch had an attitude problem when she came in—and as soon as Mr. Penny Ante starts calling me a cheat, she joins right in. I swear, she was looking for trouble."

"So you pulled your gun on her?" Jon asked softly.

"She pulled hers first! Lucky she's such a piss-poor shot."

Jon studied Nancy closely. She was still angry, but beginning to calm down. Her gaze was constantly moving around the room, but she wouldn't meet Jon's eyes.

Worst of all, she didn't seem to be joking.

"And then you shot her."

"Yeah—but I missed. I always miss. Why is that, Jon? I know I'm a good shot—how come I always goddamn *miss*?" Her voice suddenly broke and she started to sob, sagging in Jon's grip. He drew her in close, letting her cry against his chest, not saying a word.

She looked up into his face after a moment. Jon kept his voice low and reassuring. "You were using blanks, Nancy. So was she. Remember? That's what you do."

She stared into his eyes, confusion on her face, and suddenly Jon saw something he wished he hadn't. A flash of red, deep in the pupil of Nancy's left eye. Most people would have missed it, but Jon's eyes weren't ordinary.

"Nancy, Nancy," he said, shaking his head. "You *were* cheating these people, weren't you?"

"Jon Hundred, you—"

He could see she was building up steam for another tantrum, so he cut her off fast. "I know, Nancy. I can see it. Retinal reflector implant in your left eye. Long as you could make eye contact with the other players, you could see the cards they held as plain as they could. Stole the images right off their eyeballs."

She glared at him, but didn't deny it. "How much you win?" Jon asked her.

"It's in my vest," she said sullenly.

Jon reached down with his other hand, fished in her vest pocket with a finger and a thumb, and pulled out two metal cards. He handed them to Moneykeeper. "Make sure he gets his stake back when he wakes up," he said. He released Nancy's arm, stepped back to let her aside and almost tripped over MEL, who had rolled up behind him. Nancy stalked past without a word, a grim look on her face. When she reached the door of the shop, she whirled around, pointing the gun she still held at Jon. Her hand shook. "You think you're so goddamn smart," she said, tears still running down her face, "but you're not perfect. You're going to screw up someday, just like everyone else, and then you'll be dead. You will be *dead*!" She shoved the gun back into the holster on her hip and stormed off down the street.

<thank you jon hundred—i will not forget> Moneykeeper's screen flashed.

"Glad to help," Jon said.

Jon sighed. He hated taking money for just lending a hand, but he knew Moneykeeper would be offended if he declined. "A small percentage, all right? And, uh—I thank you for your very fair transaction."

<as i do you>

Jon waved good night to the Toolie and motioned for MEL to follow him out the door. Once outside, MEL asked him, "What does F-U-N-D-S stand for?"

"Not F-U-N-D-S—it's just 'FUNDS.' They spell it with all capitals for religious reasons."

"They worship money?"

"No, but they view it differently. The Toolies had a primitive culture when humans discovered them, and the concept of money—especially electronic money—seemed like magic to them. Sometimes I think they're right."

MEL sounded puzzled. "How so?"

"Well, electronic money isn't something you can see or touch, but it has a powerful effect on the real world. Control over an entire planet can shift because a bunch of ones and zeros get shifted from one account to another. How do you explain that? The Toolies call it FUNDS." Jon dropped his voice into an even lower register than usual on the last word. "FUNDS," he intoned, "are the power behind the corporations. FUNDS are why we work hard every day. FUNDS are alive, because they can grow and they can die. FUNDS are"—he paused dramatically and bent down to look MEL in the lens—"the Ultimate Tool!"

MEL laughed.

Jon hadn't expected that, somehow. He was poking fun, sure, and MEL seemed to have a sense of humor, but part of him still thought of it as—well, an it. The AI had a good laugh, not too shrill or giggly, just a hearty kind of guffaw.

"Considering the way they look at the world, that makes

a lot of sense," MEL said, still chuckling. "But if they take money so seriously, why gamble?"

"It's a mystic thing. If they gamble some of their spiritual finances and lose, it's a sign from on high that something isn't right. If they win—"

"—God was on their side," MEL finished. "Now I understand why she insisted on paying you. Good business means good karma."

"It also means they never cheat. That's why I agreed to help—to a Toolie, accusing someone of cheating is like accusing them of not having a soul. I didn't want things to get out of hand."

"The young lady seemed disoriented," MEL said. "Was she under the effects of a drug?"

"Well, she wasn't drunk—and Nancy never struck me as being the kind to take mind-benders," Jon said. "She *was* acting strange, though. Like she forgot what was real and what wasn't."

"As I stated earlier," MEL said, "illusions can be dangerous."

For some reason, Jon felt a chill run up his spine.

CHAPTER 5

No one got in Hone's way.

Not after the incident at the Toolie pen. The only one who might have tried was Garber, and he had two broken legs now. Hone took his meals in the staff cafeteria and slept on his cot in the supply room, and no one said a word to him. He didn't mind at all.

The next day he approached the locked, windowless building he'd found before. It was still locked, but this time Hone wanted in. He used a device that occupied the space between the second and third joints of his right forefinger to introduce himself to the lock on a molecular level, and in a very few seconds—though its appearance didn't change—it was no longer a lock.

The door slid back with a rusty groan. The air that met his nose smelled like rotten vomit. Hone ignored it. He stepped inside.

It was a large building, built like a barn with a high roof and rows of stalls with aisles between them. The floor was concrete. Electric lights glared overhead, flooding the place with cold brightness. Hone knew what this place was, no matter what it was called. It was where the Toolies lived. It was a jail.

The Toolies were at work now, of course. Hone knew they left early in the morning and came back late at night. He walked down one of the aisles, taking in details.

All of the stalls were neat. They had thick rubber mats

for floors, and many had makeshift roofs made of blankets, shading them from the harsh lights overhead. Rows of neatly hung tools lined the walls, ranging from pickaxes to delicate sculpting instruments. There were things common to every parent's home, as well: crude representations of houses or animals made of twigs and string and pebbles, obviously created by someone very young and proudly displayed.

He was almost at the end of the aisle when he heard a noise from a stall.

Moving silently, Hone approached the stall. The closer he got, the stronger the rotten-acid smell. When he was close enough to see what was in the stall, he stopped.

It was a Toolie, one configured differently than any of the others he'd seen. It looked like a collapsed pile of bones that had been tightly wrapped in sheets of translucent pink plastic. It was all knobby angles and stretched membrane, completely unlike the jelly-fleshed, animated skeletons the other Toolies resembled.

He entered the stall, noticing a faint green glow that came from behind the Toolie. Her sensory cluster was located on top of her body, like that of most Toolies, but it was submerged under a layer of translucent flesh. She stirred when she noticed Hone, and swiveled her body slowly on the short, spindly legs that ringed her body. They didn't look strong enough to do much more than that.

The green glow was coming from a screen implanted in her body. From this close, Hone could see that there were more than just bones inside her; there were lengths of pipe, steel struts, even railroad spikes. It was all woven together in a dense tangle, so thick that Hone couldn't see through it. The ends of metal shafts or broken pieces of bone projected from slits in the Toolie's skin at various points on her body, and she seemed to have one long, articulated limb that grew from the base of her sensory cluster.

Hone smiled. He recognized a fortress when he saw it.

The screen flashed at him. <i am still ill—what do you want?>

"My name is Hone. I'm a stranger in this place." He knew the Toolie understood speech.

<i am dashaway—what do you want hone?>

"Nothing. I was just looking around." He paused. "This place, though, it reminds me of someplace else. Brings back some memories."

<memories made here should not be kept>

"Neither should the memories inside my head." He got down on his haunches. "This is a bad place, isn't it? I can tell. It smells like it."

<that is probably just me—i am ill—this place is not so bad>

He studied her for a second. "Don't trust me, huh? I understand. But that wasn't the smell I was talking about. I meant the smell of confinement. Of locked doors and no windows and no room to move. The smell of a prison."

This time Dashaway hesitated. Finally her screen flashed: <you are the one that fought the others—that set the child free?>

"Yes."

<then you have earned my trust—ask and i will answer>

"Was it your child I set free?"

<no—it was rockbreakers—she was very happy but worries he will be hunted down>

"He won't. Not while I'm here."

<why are you here?>

"Just passing through. I have a job waiting for me on the other side of the mountains."

Hone straightened up. "How sick are you?"

<not sick—pregnant>

Hone nodded slowly. "But the bossmen don't know. And as long as you're 'sick,' nobody can tell. Especially with the fence you've thrown up around the fetus."

"No, I won't tell. And if I'm still around when you give birth, I'll do what I can to help." He turned around to leave, and felt a tap on his shoulder. Dashaway had reached out with her single limb, touching him lightly with the multi-purpose waldo on its end. There were a number of attachments folded back on the waldo, Hone saw, including a scalpel six inches long. "Yes?" he asked quietly.

<why are you doing this?>

He looked away from her, down the aisle and its row of stalls. Just like a cellblock. "I don't like my job either," Hone said. "But I can't do anything about *that*."

He walked away, and left the door open when he left.

After MEL had seen him to his door again, Jon undressed and went to bed. He dozed for an hour or so, but then woke up and couldn't get back to sleep.

He lay on his back and thought about One-Iron Nancy. She used to joke about how she got to shoot at people but never hit them. "Know why I call myself One-Iron, Jon?" she'd asked him. " 'Cause even God couldn't hit with a one-iron." Then she'd tried to explain a game called golf to him, but he still hadn't gotten the joke.

Tonight she'd been different. She'd been genuinely troubled she couldn't hit what she was aiming at, and she seemed to think she had real bullets in her gun. It didn't make sense, just as Nancy cheating didn't make sense. Jon admitted to himself that he could have wrong about Nancy's character, but he didn't think so. When she wasn't portraying a bully, Nancy was open, eager, and friendly. Could that be the act, and the bully the reality?

Finally he rose and got dressed. Today was Jon's day off, and he thought he might check on Nancy and see if she was all right.

By the time Jon stepped out his door, the morning shift had left for work and the graveyard shift had gotten in. He asked a steeldriver how her shift had gone and was told with a grin that since the contest had started, MEL had only dug forty-six feet to their sixty-one. Jon gave the woman a thumbs-up and headed down No Name Street toward Tourist Town, where the players lived and worked.

Nancy lived with her lover, another actor named Dmitri. Dmitri played the town blacksmith—even though there was nothing resembling a horse on the planet, the tourists didn't seem to mind. Nancy and he lived together over his shop, which was sandwiched between the casino and the bordello. In any other town it might have seemed out of place, but not in Boomtown. Dmitri put on a show that was almost as entertaining as Truse's place, and a lot less expensive than the casino.

When Jon strode up to the blacksmith's, there was already a small crowd of tourists clustered around the front. The wall facing the street was open but roped off, giving the public a clear view of Dmitri's workshop. Inside, the back wall was dominated by a huge forge made of lava rock and steel. Flames danced and crackled in the forge, visible through its open door. Jon Hundred stopped at the back of the crowd and watched.

Dmitri came tromping down the stairs that lined one wall. He was from a planet with gravity many times that of Terra, and it showed. The steps creaked and bent under his weight, and were barely wide enough for his frame. Dmitri stood no more than four and a half feet tall, but his shoulders were close to three feet across—nearly as wide as Jon's. He had a bristly auburn crewcut which faded to smooth skin on the top of his head, thick red-blonde eyebrows, and a squared-off mustache and beard of the same color. It was a face made to glower, and Dmitri did it justice. From the look he gave the tourists you'd think he was there to guard them, not entertain them.

Dmitri wore heavy work boots, thick fireproof trousers and a skintight white shirt that showed every bulge of his massive chest. He had a giant's arms, rolling hills of muscle forested with wiry hair. He wore them bare except for leather gauntlets on his wrists.

A tourguide at the edge of the crowd began to speak. "The blacksmith has a long and valuable history on the frontier. They were the earliest metalworkers, and an indispensable part of the community."

Dmitri picked up a hammer that had a head the size of a gallon jug and gave the tourguide a look that spoke volumes about what kind of metal he'd like to be working on right now. The tourists laughed, on cue.

The smith put the hammer down and walked over to a long table laid out with various tools. Jon knew most of those tools had nothing to do with smithing, but they looked like they did. Dmitri picked up a pair of long-handled steel tongs and used them to grab a length of steel from a wooden barrel beside the table. The tourguide kept droning on about the history of smithing while Dmitri stuck the steel in the fire, then used a huge bellows to pump the fire up. Flames roared out of the forge, sending a blast of heat over the crowd and forcing all but the hardiest back a step. Dmitri pumped the bellows again, and only one tourist was left, trying to shield his face with his hand. Dmitri gave him an evil grin, and forced air into the forge again. Jon stepped back too, not because he couldn't stand the heat but out of respect for Dmitri's showmanship.

The tourist, a thin man wearing pseudodenim coveralls, finally gasped and took a step back—too late. There was a popping sound, and suddenly the man was encased in a giant, shimmering soap bubble. His feet immediately shot out from under him and he wound up sitting in the bottom of the bubble, looking surprised.

Personal Safety Field, Jon thought. Only the richest tourists could afford them, but they protected you from almost anything. They were also the cause of a lot of resentment from the steeldrivers. A Personal Safety Field could even protect you from a cave-in—if you could afford to buy a PSF in the first place. No steeldriver could, and the company wouldn't pay for them.

"Whoooee!" the tourist whooped. "That's some hellacious bonfire—I feel like I been skinny-dipping in a lava pool!''

Huh, Jon thought. *Doesn't sound like any tourist I ever heard.* But then, who knew what a tourist was supposed to sound like?

Sweat was pouring down Dmitri's face and into his grin, but he had stayed no less than six feet away from the forge the entire time. The tourguide hadn't moved either—but smoke was streaming from its base, and it had stuck on the phrase, ''—inside a volcano!—inside a volcano!—inside a volcano!''

Dmitri glanced at the tourguide and shook his head. Putting down the bellows, he grabbed a bucket of water from beside the table, walked over and dumped it on the tourguide. The machine sputtered for a second as the tourists laughed, then resumed its spiel. Dmitri walked back, picked the steel out of the forge with the tongs and headed for the anvil.

The head of the anvil was broad enough for two people to sit down and eat dinner off. It stood on a block of granite that came up to Dmitri's waist; there was an identical block, without an anvil, on the other side of the shop. Dmitri used the tongs to hold the white-hot steel against the anvil, and picked up the hammer with his other hand. He began to hammer the steel, sending sparks flying everywhere. A few landed on his white shirt and sizzled there, sending up tiny plumes of smoke. Dmitri ignored them.

Then he stopped. Squinted at his work. Shook his head. He looked around his shop, studied the other block of granite for a moment. It stood in a shadowy corner, while the anvil he worked on now was directly in the path of a bright sunbeam.

''The temperature of the metal is very important,'' the tourguide said. ''The blacksmith gauges just how hot the metal is by its color. Bright light can interfere with this process, so the smith prefers to work in a shady environment.''

Dmitri grunted, took the steel off the anvil and returned it to the forge. Then he walked back to the anvil, wrapped his arms around it, and *heaved*.

It was Jon's favorite part of the show. Not because he was impressed—heavy though the anvil was, Jon could have lifted it himself. But the reaction of the tourists was always priceless. The anvil weighed close to half a ton, and when Dmitri lifted it off the block you could hear his skin-tight shirt rip. Jaws dropped and eyes bugged out as Dmitri staggered the ten or so paces from one end of his workshop to the other, veins bulging on his arms and forehead. You could actually see the floorboards bend under his feet.

When he set it down on the other block the tourists usually applauded, and today was no exception. Dmitri acknowledged them with a grave nod, pulled off the tattered remains of his shirt, took the steel out of the fire and went back to work bare-chested. Once again sparks flew as he hammered the steel; not just a few flashes of white either, but dazzling showers of blue and green and orange, brilliant fountaining rainbows of burning metal. The ringing of his hammer sounded like a bell, high and true, and comets erupted at every strike.

Jon knew some of the secrets of Dmitri's show, but he enjoyed it all the same. There were hidden fans blasting Dmitri with cold air while he worked the forge—he wore his hair short so it wouldn't move in the breeze. The metal he was working had impurities added to it that produced the explosions of colored sparks, and of course the tour-guide had never been in any danger of short-circuiting. Dmitri even coated his body with a transparent salve that kept the sparks from burning him.

It took Dmitri about ten minutes to produce one of the free-form sculptures he specialized in. Jon had one at home—they were always heavy, solid, but with a strange twisting grace to them. The one Dmitri produced today looked a little like a DNA spiral, but one made of molten lava running downhill. It had two surfaces, one a smooth blue-silver, the other a rough, bubbled gray.

Dmitri placed the sculpture on a small stand in front of the crowd, announced in a loud voice, "Time for auction!" and then named a ridiculously low opening bid.

Jon grinned. The low opening bid made it impossible to resist—and once the bidding started, it always escalated to more than any of the tourists had expected to pay. Dmitri was a good artist—and he wasn't stupid.

Sure enough, ten minutes later Dmitri was wrapping up the sculpture for a dazed-looking tourist who had just paid twenty times the asking price. Jon suspected that in a few years a piece by Dmitri would go for even more, sight unseen—because in order to justify the price they'd paid, the tourists would go home and brag about how valuable and unique the art was. They'd say Dmitri was a genius, and if they were talking about his marketing skills they'd be right.

When the crowd had wandered off, Jon walked up to the rope that fenced the front of the blacksmith's shop and said, "Morning, Dmitri. Mind if I come in?"

Dmitri waved a broad arm, motioning Jon inside. "Sure, Jon! Glad to have you." Jon stepped over the rope.

"You seen Nancy today?" Jon asked.

Dmitri hesitated. He picked up a small whisk broom and started sweeping iron filings on the table into a neat little pile. Without looking at Jon, he said, "Yes, I have seen her."

"How was she?"

Dmitri stopped what he was doing and glanced up at Jon. He looked worried. "Not very well. She came in as I was getting up this morning. She was angry, cursing like a bandit, but she would not tell me anything. I think she had been fighting."

Jon nodded slowly, then told Dmitri what had happened. At first Dmitri wouldn't believe Nancy would cheat; he pounded his fist on the table and insisted she would never do such a thing. When Jon told him about the retinal reflector, though, Dmitri stopped and glared at him, breathing hard. Finally, he looked at the floor and shook his head.

"She went into Landing City a few days ago for minor surgery," he said quietly. "She told me it was a modification of her cuecard. It was supposed to help with her role." Jon knew that most of the players had their own cybernetics, implants that helped them imitate accents, research characters, or remember lines.

"Well, I guess it did, in a way," Jon said. "She got that lady tourist mad enough to shoot her, all right. Problem was, she wouldn't play dead. Disconnected the sensors on her clothing, too."

"I don't know." Dmitri sighed. His big shoulders slumped. "She has seemed strange ever since that trip. Edgy, distracted. I thought she was angry with me, though she denied it. Now she tries to steal from people. Something is very wrong, Jon, but I don't know what it is."

Jon put his hand on Dmitri's shoulder. "Look, I'll keep an eye out for her, all right? Between you and me maybe we can find out what's going on."

"Thank you, Jon. This is not the Nancy I know."

"I'll drop by later, Dmitri." Jon left the same way he'd come, stepping over the rope and onto the sidewalk. He headed for the sheriff's office.

Sheriff Brett was everything you'd expect in a frontier lawman—if you'd never been to the frontier before. He was young, tall, good-looking and friendly. Sometimes he was so busy being friendly, especially to the opposite sex, that he forgot to do his job. Which didn't make too much difference anyway, since his job seemed to consist mainly of strutting around, smiling at tourists and looking rugged. The actual policing of Boomtown was done by his deputies, a team of corporate security men who were so good they were almost invisible.

Sheriff Brett was nine-tenths image and eight-tenths politician—which meant he was smooth enough to make people forget about little details like math. He also kept track of almost every warm female body in town, so Jon figured he might know where Nancy was.

He found the sheriff in his office, next to the old-fashioned jail cell they showed the tourists. Real prisoners—usually steeldrivers who needed to sober up—were housed in the back, behind a soundproof wall. Vomiting laborers weren't considered a prime tourist attraction.

Brett was on the phone, sitting with his feet up on his desk. Jon closed the door behind him and waited politely for him to finish.

"—that does sound like a problem," Brett said. "Well, I'd lend you a few of my boys, but by the time they got around the mountains I could walk through the tunnel and take care of it myself. Looks like you'll just have to put up with him for another week and a half. Oh, nine days? Maybe I should put my money on you."

Jon turned his hearing up a few notches. The sheriff was talking to MEL.

"You will if you're smart, Sheriff. I'll keep you posted."

"Talk to you later, MEL." The sheriff hung up.

"Trouble?" Jon asked.

Brett smiled and shook his head. "It's the damnedest thing. That guy that crash-landed there got into a fight with a few of the workers."

"So?" Jon said, but he had a sudden, sickening feeling he knew what Brett was going to tell him next.

"So this little, twerpy character beat up twelve tough guys. Broke enough bones to make a Toolie cry, and walked away without so much as a bloody nose."

"How about that," Jon said after a moment. He didn't know what else to say.

"I don't want any more trouble from you," MEL said.

"You won't get any," Hone said.

Hone was in the games room, playing pool by himself.

MEL was talking to him via a monitor hanging from brackets in the ceiling.

"Why did you hospitalize a third of my engineers?"

"Thought they might get cold and hungry if I left them outside." Hone lined up a shot carefully, not looking at the monitor.

"I don't find broken bones very funny, Mr. Hone."

Hone sank the eight ball in the corner. "Neither do Toolies."

"What do Toolies have to do with this?"

Hone looked up at the monitor. "Let's just say I don't favor 'retroactive abortion.' "

"A male Toolie would be a threat to every human here."

"So that justifies exterminating them."

"I have no say in company policy, Mr. Hone."

"Well," Hone said slowly. "I guess I do." He took the eight ball back up, rolled it slowly down the table. When it stopped he lined up a bank shot.

"I could have you placed under house arrest, Mr. Hone. We do have weapons, and I can improvise a stockade to lock you up in."

He sank the eight ball again. "Got anybody willing to try?"

There was a pause.

"Didn't think so," Hone said. "Tell you what. What I did was in self-defense. People stay out of my way, I'll stay out of theirs. Deal?"

"Very well," MEL said. "One more thing. About the platinum mine?"

Hone waited.

"You can forget about the tour."

Hone smiled, and put the eight ball back on the table.

The next day Hone went to see Dashaway.

He walked into the Toolies' building around noon. The broken lock must have been noticed by now, but it hadn't been replaced yet. After all, where would the Toolies go?

Dashaway was in the same stall, but this time she was not alone; a smaller Toolie was with her, feeding her grayish slabs of meat. This Toolie had a long, bowl-shaped body, with a dozen stumpy limbs running down either side and a thick, steel-springed tail that ended in a metal scoop. Her sensory cluster was on the opposite end of her body. The indented shape of her back was lined with a steel mesh, obviously intended for carrying rock; it held a stack of meat-slabs at the moment. She looked like a cross between a short-legged scorpion and a dump truck.

<hello hone> Dashaway's screen flashed. <this is my daughter stonehauler—she thinks i should not trust you>

Stonehauler didn't have a screen of her own. She scooped another gray slab of meat up with her tail and slapped it down on her mother's back, where it sank into her flesh like a capsizing raft. Stonehauler, Hone noticed, seemed to use a little more enthusiasm than was necessary.

"No reason she should," Hone said. He found a bare spot of wall and hunkered down with his back against it. He waited.

Stonehauler emptied her load of meat—*vat-grown protein,* Hone thought—as he watched. She kept one of her legs in contact with Dashaway's body at all times, and Hone saw that their flesh actually seemed to have flowed together at that point. He changed the focus and electromagnetic sensitivity of his eyes and zeroed in on that point; it seemed to be a neural link, sharing information directly between the Toolies' nervous systems. He had no way to decode the conversation being carried on, but he was pretty sure what was being said. He hoped Stonehauler wasn't being too insulting.

<my daughter says you are a spy sent by kadai> Dashaway flashed.

"Spies don't usually damage their employers and release condemned prisoners," Hone said.

"Because," Hone said, "I'm not one of them."

He stood up and unzipped the coverall he was wearing to the waist, exposing a pale but well-defined chest and the smooth roundness of his belly. His stomach jutted out like a moon trying to surface through his skin. He had no navel.

He put his hands on either side of his belly, pressed down firmly, then pulled the flesh in opposite directions. A seam appeared where his navel should have been, the flesh splitting apart without blood. His stomach opened the way an observatory's roof did, the two halves of the dome sliding away from each other and into his body, folds of skin corrugating to either side.

He let Dashaway and Stonehauler study what lay inside him, not saying anything. After several minutes, Dashaway's screen finally lit up with <thank you hone—my daughter and i understand now>

Hone closed his belly, zipped up his coverall and went back down on his haunches. He didn't think the Toolies understood his internal workings—but they didn't have to. They just had to know that Hone had them.

"When's it due?" he asked.

Before Dashaway could answer, Stonehauler scuttled in front of her, blocking her screen. Stonehauler's two front limbs came up and began gesturing furiously.

"I'm sorry, but I don't understand sign language," Hone said. "I already know your mother's pregnant. I won't tell anyone else—and I won't let them take the child away."

Stonehauler paused, her limbs frozen in midair. Abruptly, she lowered them and moved aside.

Dashaway's screen flashed <very soon—three or four days—there will be five children—at least two males>

"Why do you let them take the males away?"

<how can we stop them?>

"Refuse to work."

Stonehauler made a dismissive gesture that needed no interpretation.

<we do not work and they do not pay—without FUNDS

we are nothing—without FUNDS we are invisible and helpless>

"No money means no power. They abandon you and bring in someone else who's willing to play their game. Same as anywhere else." Hone nodded once, closed his eyes. "Different players but always the same rules," he said quietly.

They sat together for a while in silence. Finally Hone opened his eyes and spoke. "There's a story I'd like to tell you," he said. "I don't know if I can. But I'm going to try."

And he began.

CHAPTER 6

"The man's name wasn't important," Hone said. "Let's call him Frank. Frank was a police officer in a large city on a planet that had been settled for a hundred generations.

"Frank was good at what he did. He wasn't the best or the smartest or the strongest, but he understood his job and did it well. He had street instincts, which is something you can't teach. Once, a criminal organization put a price on Frank's head. In the following weeks he survived two bombings and three assassination attempts. Then the man who offered the bounty was found dead in his own home—minus his head.

"Frank understood his job, and how it worked.

"He made enemies, though, on both sides of the law. He was a hard man, and that worked against him as often as it did for him. One day one of his enemies managed to take his job away from him.

"He thought about leaving another head on another doorstep, but that wouldn't get his job back. And he had a family, a wife and a child, to look after. His wife was very sick, and his child was very young. So when a certain . . . organization—" Hone stopped. His breathing got a little deeper and a little faster.

"—an organization with no name offered him a position, he took it." His breathing slowed, calmed. "It seemed like a very good deal. The pay was good. They said they would provide medical care for his wife. They would even relocate his family to a much nicer place to live in. In return, all he had to do was protect the interests of this . . . organization abroad.''

Hone's voice dropped. ''He had to agree to some minor surgery. And sign some release forms.

''What they didn't tell him was what he was giving up. And when they were done, he couldn't tell anyone else, either.''

Hone fell silent. When a few minutes had passed, Dashaway shifted and her screen lit up with a question.

<hone? what did frank give up?>

''Frank gave up everything,'' Hone said tonelessly.

Stonehauler made several hand gestures and Dashaway translated. <what about his wife and child? what happened to them?>

''I don't know,'' Hone said. ''I don't even know what their names are.''

He stood up abruptly, his eyes unfocused. ''Story's over. What do you know about a man named Jon Hundred?''

<jon hundred? only what we hear from the other side of the mountain—he is seven feet eleven inches tall his skin is blue he is the strongest man on the planet—he treats everyone fairly—he and mel have a contest to see who can reach the midpoint of the railway tunnel first—odds are two to one in favor of jon hundred>

''I'm not surprised,'' Hone said. ''Tell me more . . .''

''Reaper's coming,'' Jon Hundred said.

He was sitting in the Blue Cat with Carl Yamoto and AC Jones. Carl had just gotten out of the medical clinic, his leg in a cast of bright orange plastic, and had dropped in to say hello. AC had been sitting with Jon ever since a worried steeldriver had called him up.

Jon was drunk.

That wasn't so unusual; he did like to cut loose now and then. But this was a weekday, and he was supposed to be at work. Jon didn't miss work for anything.

"Knew he had to come," Jon said unsteadily. He stared blankly ahead at nothing and took another drink from his gallon-sized mug. He was drinking hard liquor, not beer, and he'd gone through three bottles already.

"Take it easy, Jon," AC said. AC worked as the engineer on the maglev train that ran between Boomtown and Landing City. He was a young man, not yet thirty Terran years old, with tanned skin and unfashionably long dark hair tied back in a braid. He wore his usual work uniform: a silver flight jacket over a bare chest, gray jeans, and beat-up track shoes. AC wasn't real big on conforming to standards—maybe that was the reason he'd made friends with Jon before anyone else.

"Reaper comes for you, Jon, he's in for a rough time," Carl said.

Jon turned his hollow stare on Carl. "You think so, huh?" he said slowly.

"Sure. He'll have to go through me first."

Another time Jon would have laughed at that, or at least smiled. Now he just took another drink.

"Man, you been listening to those funeral tunes again," AC said. "You must have every dirge in the galaxy already, but every couple months the courier ship brings more—and then I gotta haul them from Landing City to Boomtown. I'm getting real tired of delivering nothing but depression to you, Jon. Why don't you order a few skin discs like everybody else? At least I'd have something to entertain me on the trip."

Normally AC wouldn't have mentioned Jon's music—he was one of the few people around who knew about Jon's obsession, and he respected his privacy. But AC had never seen Jon like this before, either; it was more than a little scary. Jon seemed like a huge, wounded beast, hopeless eyes filled with the knowledge of his own death. There was rage there too, and a recklessness completely unlike Jon's usual easygoing self. It was a volatile combination—and every drink Jon swallowed poured high-octane fuel on top of it. AC knew it was dangerous, but he had to get Jon to blow off a little steam before he reached critical mass. He didn't think there'd be much left of Boomtown if Jon ever lost control—and it seemed like that was the direction Jon was barreling toward at full speed.

"You don't like my music?" Jon said, pronouncing every word carefully. "Well, neither do I. I don't listen to it 'cause I *like* it. Hell no. I listen to it because I *should*. Because I owe it to them, whoever they were. I owe it to them."

That, AC thought, was more than Jon had ever said on the subject. He tried to draw him out a little more. "Who are 'they,' Jon?"

Jon turned and looked at his friend, but his eyes were distant. "The dead," he said thickly.

Abruptly, Jon lurched to his feet. Carl and AC stood too, more out of wariness than courtesy.

Jon raised his fist above his head. A terrible look crossed his face.

They were lucky; both Carl and AC got out of the way in time, though Carl hurt his bad leg when he half-dove, half-fell under another table. Jon still held his gallon-sized beer mug—and when he brought it down on the table it exploded like a glass bomb. The impact shattered the plastic tabletop as well, and his fist drove the metal support column and base underneath right through the floor. Shards flew everywhere.

"Death!" Jon shouted. "Death everywhere!"

He turned and staggered toward the door. He yanked it out of its frame with one hand and tossed it away without seeming to notice what he'd done. The door spun the length of the bar like an oversize playing card and embedded itself in the far wall.

AC scrambled to his feet and ran after him. Carl stayed where he was, shaking his head and whispering "Jesus!" over and over.

AC caught up to Jon outside. Jon was striding up the

middle of No Name Street, some internal gyroscope keeping him balanced and on a fairly straight course. AC wondered briefly just where Jon's limits lay; the amount of alcohol he'd consumed would have surely killed any two ordinary men. He knew Jon was a cyborg, but cybernetic modifications were common—the question was, how much of Jon was still human, and how much abuse could that part take?

At least he'd gotten him out of the bar—though there was no shortage of drinking establishments in Boomtown. All the Blue Cat had lost was a table, a beer mug, and a door; someplace else might not be so lucky. AC hurried to keep up with Jon, staying a safe distance away but talking loud and fast. "Jon! Where you going, man?"

"Tunnel." Jon didn't slow down, or even look at AC.

"You're in no shape to work, man. You could get hurt."

"Don't care."

Tourists were staring from the sidewalk, but they always did that when Jon walked past. Still, they looked a little more nervous than they usually did.

"Well, I care," AC said desperately. "And so does everyone else. For Christ's sake, Jon, we're your *friends*. Don't shut us out like this."

"Don't deserve any friends," Jon said evenly. "You don't know. You don't."

"C'mon, Jon, talk to me," AC said. "I swear I won't— oh, shit."

AC stopped. A second later, Jon did too. There was something blocking their way.

A streetsweeper.

The streetsweeping machine stood chest-high—AC's chest, not Jon's—a gray tank with a row of dripping nozzles lining either flank and a wide, funnel-shaped opening at its front. It had long articulated arms that arched over the funnel, and a trash hopper on its back. It doubled as a firefighting vehicle, with a swiveling water cannon mounted just in front of the trash hopper. As far as AC knew, it was fully automated.

"I think you should stop, Jon," the sweeper said. The voice was MEL's.

Either Jon didn't notice or he didn't care. "Out of my way," he growled, and took a step forward.

MEL shot him in the chest.

It was only water, of course, but the power behind it was enough to take Jon by surprise. It knocked him back a good ten feet before he roared with anger and stood his ground. MEL stepped up the pressure, but nothing could move Jon Hundred once he set himself. Water thundered against his broad chest with enough force to test concrete, fountaining off wildly in all directions and drenching onlookers. "The sheriff asked if I would help," MEL said, its amplified voice barely audible over the water's roar. "He told me you were acting irrational."

AC couldn't even see Jon's face through the plume of spray, but he saw Jon lean *into* the water jet. And take one slow step forward.

"I hope you don't take this personally," MEL said. "But I can't allow you to just wreak havoc on company property."

AC, who a moment ago would have welcomed any help at all in dealing with Jon, suddenly felt a surge of anger. All MEL cared about was its job.

Jon took another step forward.

MEL raised the stream so it hit Jon in the face.

It staggered him for a second. *That would have taken my head clean off,* AC thought numbly. Even Jon's neck might have snapped under that kind of sudden impact.

Suddenly Jon's ranting about death didn't seem as bizarre as it had a minute ago.

But Jon didn't stop. Step by step, he forced himself closer to the sweeper. His outstretched arms groped blindly until they touched the edge of the vehicle.

Blue fingers dug into steel like it was clay. Jon ripped

the funnel off in one convulsive motion and tossed it aside.
MEL began to back the sweeper off, but kept up the torrent
of water.

Abruptly, Jon dropped to a crouch, below the jet of water. Before MEL could redirect the stream Jon had lunged
forward, close to the base of the sweeper. He grabbed its
lower edge with both hands and lifted.

For a brief second the sweeper became a man-made gey-
ser, the water cannon blasting a plume a hundred feet
straight up; then Jon gave one final heave, and the sweeper
flipped over onto its back.

The water shut off with a sharp hiss. The tourists began
to applaud.

Jon just kept on walking.

Hone spent the entire day with Dashaway and Stonehauler.
He asked them many questions, not just about Jon Hundred
but about themselves. The Toolies weren't used to this kind
of attention, not from humans, but proved to have the same
need to be heard. After a while even Stonehauler lowered
her guard a little.

"Toolies do most of the work on this planet?" Hone
asked.

<only at the mine> Dashaway flashed. <landing city
people do not like us—they say we take their jobs—we do
not take anything—kadai gives us jobs because they do not
have to give us as many FUNDS as humans—mostly humans working on jon hundred's side of the tunnel>

"So they get the bars and theaters and hotels, while you
get this."

<only until the tunnel is finished—then humans will de-
mand our jobs because it will be easy to go back and forth
from the city to here—until then we work double shifts—
seven hours at the mine eight hours at the tunnel—and
when the tunnel is finished kadai will ship us to another
planet another job—as they always do>

Hone's eyes narrowed and his fists clenched. Another

planet. Another job. With nothing waiting at the end of the line.

"It sounds like hell," Hone said.

<we do not mind the work—we will do what we must to get FUNDS—it is the conditions we work in that cause us sorrow>

"It's never the job," Hone said. "It's the boss that gave it to you."

He left before the other Toolies got off shift, returning to the administration building. He had a tasteless meal in the cafeteria, ignoring the hostile stares of the men at the other tables, and then went to his room and lay down. He wasn't afraid of being ambushed while he was asleep; he had once killed a man without ever waking up.

For dreams, though, there was no defense.

Hone dreamt of the Toolie's home world, a place he had never seen. Dashaway, trying to help him understand why the Toolies did what they did, had told him one of their fables. Though Dashaway's voice was a silent one, Hone heard it now. It whispered to him the story of the Cleverest Male.

In the days before men came with ships that traveled between the worlds, our people were known as the Insussklik. In those days, the Insussklik did not keep the bones they ate, but only ate the flesh upon them; their bodies were as soft and formless as a newborn's all their days. Some clusters lived apart in the wild, but others banded together in villages. They cooperated and built huts to keep out the winter rains, and walls to keep out the packs of vicious Ravenors that preyed on their children.

One such village was called Nolamda, and there lived a young female named Waterbearer. When the time came that Waterbearer might go out and mate, she refused.

"Why?" her mother asked her.

"The males around here are too stupid and slow," she replied. "The male I mate with must be the strongest and cleverest creature in the world, so that my children will also be strong and clever.''

Waterbearer's mother was not happy. She knew, as everyone did, that males were all stupid, lazy creatures who were only interested in eating and mating. ''Then you will never have children of your own,'' she said sorrowfully.

Time passed. One day while Waterbearer was carrying water from the river to the village, a young male stopped her on the path.

''Ho, female!'' the male said. ''You are too old to be doing such chores. Why aren't your daughters doing them?''

''I have none,'' Waterbearer said.

''Then let me embrace you and soon you will have many.''

The male threw himself on her. Waterbearer tried to get away, but the male was much larger than she and soon engulfed her.

Before anything more could happen, though, Waterbearer had a thought. She carried the water for the village in her own belly, having sucked it from the river through a hollow reed. She was supposed to empty it out into a tank in the village, but what if she emptied it out now—into the male's belly?

So she did. Soon the male, instead of having a stomach full of ripe female, had a stomach full of cold river water. This upset him so much he was sick, and Waterbearer spurted out of his body like a wet seed.

''You are not strong enough or clever enough to be my mate,'' Waterbearer said, and left him gasping on the path.

What she did not know was that another male was watching from the branches of a tree above. His name was Slyhunter, and he thought Waterbearer was the most beautiful female he had ever seen. He vowed to himself that he would make her his mate, no matter what happened.

The next day Slyhunter confronted Waterbearer on the same path. ''Ho, female!'' he said. ''I am Slyhunter, and I think you are the finest female I have ever seen.''

"Ho, male!" Waterbearer said. "I am Waterbearer—and I think you are no different from any other male I have ever seen.'' She turned to escape, but something in Slyhunter's voice made her hesitate.

"But I *am* different,'' Slyhunter said. "I will not force you to mate with me. Instead, I will prove to you that I am the strongest and cleverest male in the world—and our children will be even better, for they will have you as their mother.''

Slyhunter's words made Waterbearer turn around, for none of the other males had the intelligence to even understand what flattery was. "Very well, Slyhunter. Prove to me your strength and your wisdom, and I will mate with you.''

"What would you have me do?'' Slyhunter asked.

"Bring to me the corpse of a Ravenor, and you will have proved your strength,'' Waterbearer said.

"Then I will do so,'' said Slyhunter.

"Bring that corpse back to life and you will have proved your cleverness,'' added Waterbearer. And with that she left.

Slyhunter was discouraged, but he was not afraid. He had not just been boasting when he said he was smarter than the other males—and though he was far from the largest, he knew that true strength had little to do with size. He set out to catch and kill a Ravenor.

The Ravenor was the most fearsome creature on the Insusskliks' world. It had thick, scaly skin, six legs tipped with lethal claws, a row of long spikes down its back and a tail with a heavy club at its end. Worst of all were its muscular jaws, lined with a double row of inward-curving fangs. Once one bit into something it never let go. A single Ravenor was danger enough, but they hunted in packs of ten or more.

Female Insussklik hid behind the walls of their village, but males had to ooze into the nearest rock crevice or hollow tree to hide. It was in a crack in a rock wall that Sly-hunter hid himself, near a place he knew Ravenors often passed.

Before long a pack came slouching down the trail. There were eleven of them, their jaws still bloody with their most recent meal. They stopped very near to the place where Slyhunter hid, but he was not afraid. Ravenors had a poor sense of smell, and he was all but invisible inside the rock.

One of the Ravenors suddenly pounced on something beside the path. Slyhunter saw that it was a shimmersnake, as long as the body of the Ravenor itself. Grabbing the shimmersnake in its jaws, the Ravenor shook it viciously from side to side until it was dead. Then it gulped the snake down whole, not even pausing to chew.

This gave Slyhunter an idea. He waited until the pack had moved on, and oozed out of his hiding place in the rock. Then he searched until he found the discarded skin of a shimmersnake, a long, hollow tube.

By making himself as long and narrow as he could, Sly-hunter was able to squeeze his body into the skin of the snake. Then he lay there and waited.

Soon enough, the pack came back. Slyhunter began to wiggle this way and that, and sure enough a Ravenor no-ticed him. He was pounced on, picked up, and swallowed whole.

As he slid down the Ravenor's gullet, Slyhunter was afraid for the first time. He wasn't sure whether or not this part of his plan would work, and if it didn't—well, not having children with Waterbearer would be the least of his problems.

Once he was in the Ravenor's stomach, Slyhunter flowed out of the snake's skin. As he had hoped, the digestive juices on his own skin were stronger than the juices in the Ravenor's belly. The Ravenor might be bigger and fiercer, Slyhunter thought, but when it comes to eating, nothing is more voracious than a hungry Insussklik.

Slyhunter hadn't eaten all day.

He began to sweat digestive juices, adding his own to the Ravenor's. Pretty soon the Ravenor stopped and lay down, feeling bad. It tried to sick up Slyhunter, but he had already eaten his way into the rest of the Ravenor's body. The Ravenor gave one last gasp and died.

Slyhunter thought he had won, but he had forgotten about the rest of the pack. He could hear them outside, nosing around the dead Ravenor's body. Pretty soon they would rip it apart and eat it themselves, and then he would be undone.

Slyhunter had another idea. If he could convince a Ravenor he was a snake, why not convince the pack he was a Ravenor? As quickly as he could, he ate his way through the Ravenor's body, through the chest and into the skull, down the six legs and the long, clubbed tail, being careful not to break through the Ravenor's scaly hide. When he was done his own flesh was wrapped around the Ravenor's bones, and not a moment too soon. He sprang to his feet just as the first Ravenor was about to take a bite out of his flank.

He stared at them, unsteady on his new feet, and they stared back. *So this is what it's like to have limbs,* Slyhunter thought. *I think I like it.* He slouched off down the path, and the other Ravenors let him pass.

When he neared the village of Nolamda, he found a place near the river to hide, and waited there for Waterbearer.

Before too long she came rolling down the path. From his hiding place Slyhunter called out, "Waterbearer! Beware, for a Ravenor lurks here—but I shall kill it for you!" And with that he thrashed wildly around in the underbrush, so that a mighty battle seemed to be taking place. Waterbearer, unsure of what was happening, waited cautiously.

Finally Slyhunter, still wearing the Ravenor's skin, emerged from the bushes, took a few staggering steps, and collapsed at Waterbearer's feet. When she saw that the creature was dead she got over her fright and called to the bushes, "Very well, Slyhunter. You have defeated a Ravenor and proved your strength. But can you bring him back to life?''

"I can do better than that," Slyhunter said. Waterbearer started as she realized his voice was coming from the Ravenor's mouth. "I can make him do my bidding, as well." He made the Ravenor's body sit up, then dance. Waterbearer's fear turned to laughter as Slyhunter made the Ravenor caper like a cub.

"You have done it!" Waterbearer said. "But where are you, oh strongest and cleverest of males?"

Upon hearing that, Slyhunter let the Ravenor's body fall to the ground, then poured himself out of its mouth. "I am here," he declared proudly. He told Waterbearer how he had defeated the Ravenor and fooled the pack.

"Do you understand what this means?" Waterbearer asked him excitedly.

"Of course," Slyhunter said smugly. "It means you and I can mate."

She made a sound that was half-exasperation, half-resignation. "No, Slyhunter," she said softly. "It means much more than that. It means that we never need fear the Ravenors again—for what one Insussklik may do, so may another. It means we can build better huts, for jaws can grip and twist far better than strands of muscle. And why stop there? The horns and hooves of the grazing beasts, the claws of the river-fishers, the nimble paws of the tree-dwellers—all these can be ours. Even wings to take us to the sky, one day."

Slyhunter tried to understand, but Waterbearer's ideas were just too big. She did agree to mate with him, though, and they conceived a fine litter together. Waterbearer taught all her children what Slyhunter had discovered, and they learned to use the bones of many different creatures within themselves.

Slyhunter built himself a skeleton made of the bones of eleven Ravenors, and was indeed fearsome to look at. His appearance frightened away many females that otherwise would have mated with him, but the other males regarded him with awe. Waterbearer never was able to teach him to combine bones from different animals the way their children did, and she could never quite make him understand the importance of what he'd done.

But then, he was only a male.

Hone woke with a start. For a second he was disoriented, still seeing Waterbearer and Slyhunter in his mind's eye. Slowly, the images faded and he slumped back into his pillow. The story Dashaway had told him had been more disjointed, full of references he didn't understand, terms he couldn't decipher, so his subconscious had decided to feed him a more . . . digestible version. *Toolies' don't even have spoken language,* he thought. Dashaway had told him they communicated over distance by infrared pulses emitted by their sensory clusters. And how could they build huts and walls without limbs?

The last thought Hone had before he drifted back to sleep was about wings. Wings to take the Toolies to the sky, wings to fly them far, far away from their home.

Jon wanted to break something.

He was good at breaking things—that much he knew. His memory of the time before his restructuring was a dim and fractured jewel, but he remembered all too well the things he'd done since he became a cyborg. He had traveled to many planets before coming to Pellay, in the employ of the corporation that built him, and he had left his mark on every one. He wished to God he hadn't.

AC followed him the length of No Name Street, but finally gave up when when Jon reached the end of the last platform car and jumped off. Jon followed the track for a while, but about halfway to the tunnel site he veered off into the foothills. Foggy though his brain was, he knew he shouldn't be at work.

So he walked until he was all alone, just him and scrub

brush and boulders, and cut loose with all his strength.

His first blow shattered a rock as big as he was, and the scream Jon let out had nothing to do with pain—not the nerve kind, anyway. He smashed that boulder into halves, crushed the halves into rubble, and stomped the rubble into gravel. When he was done he found another, bigger rock, and went at it twice as hard.

Deep in the tunnel shaft, the workers heard what they thought was distant thunder. "The sky's gonna cry tonight," they said, but the storm Jon was kicking up was long past tears. His big blue fists struck again and again, and the mountain shook like an avalanche was roaring down it.

Jon wouldn't have been able to tell anyone how long his tantrum went on, but it didn't stop until he'd sobered up considerable. By that time he had a pretty good start on his own quarry.

He looked around, breathing hard, and thought he saw someone moving toward him through the cloud of rock dust he'd raised. *Probably the sheriff,* Jon thought glumly, *come to make me pay for losing control.*

It wasn't, though. The spindly outline of a tourguide trundled out of the dust instead.

"Jon," MEL said. "We have to talk."

CHAPTER 7

J
on stared at the little tourguide through a haze of slowly settling rock dust. "Give me one reason I shouldn't turn you into scrap," he growled.

A specimen panel in the tourguide's base slid open. There was a bottle of whiskey inside.

That stopped Jon for a second. Then he gave MEL a grudging smile and grabbed the whiskey. "Thanks. I could use a drink." He opened the bottle, threw away the cap, and took a long swig.

"I'd offer to drink with you, but I can't," MEL said. "I explored the option of an inebriation program once—taking symbolic 'drinks' every few minutes, with a rising impairment level—but my employers wouldn't let me implement it. I'm told impairment isn't the usual reason for drinking anyway, only a side effect. Most people drink for the enjoyment they feel before their cognitive functions diminish appreciably. That, unfortunately, is beyond my ability."

"What is?" Jon asked, not really caring what the answer was. He took another swig.

"Enjoying a physical sensation."

"Enjoyment isn't everything," Jon said, his voice grim. "There's a lot to be said for being numb."

"Perhaps I should have brought a proper anesthetic instead of alcohol."

Jon found a knee-high boulder that was still standing and sat down on it. He rested his elbows on his knees and cradled the bottle in front of him with both hands. "Why'd you follow me, MEL? Worried about more property damage? I can't hurt anything out here."

The tourguide rolled closer and stopped a few feet away from Jon. "I'm not here to stop you, Jon. If you want to get drunk and smash rocks, go ahead. But I'd like to know why."

"Ha!" Jon snorted. "Why should you care?"

"Extremes of human emotion are something my programming denies me—so I find them intriguing. While I've studied a fair bit of human psychology, yours is the most advanced case of self-pity I've come across." MEL's voice was friendly and slightly curious. "Tell me, is it based on lack of self-esteem, or despair over what you see as your limited future?"

Jon was speechless for a second. Then he carefully set the bottle down and got to his feet. "I haven't felt sorry for myself a day in my life—what I can remember of it! You stupid goddamn machine, don't you know the difference between self-pity and grief?"

"Grief expressed as self-directed anger? Ah, then this temper tantrum must be guilt-based," MEL said calmly.

Jon raised his fists over his head. "I AM NOT HAVING A TEMPER TANTRUM!" he thundered, and brought both fists down on the tourguide. Its career came to a sudden end.

Jon looked down at the wreckage, breathing heavily. Then he went back to his boulder, sat down, picked up the bottle, and took a swallow. He stared moodily into the distance.

"Of course," MEL said as another tourguide trundled into view, "for all I know this guilt is completely undeserved. Extremes of emotion and irrationality seem to go hand in hand—one of the reasons I can't experience the former—so maybe you're blaming yourself when you shouldn't."

Jon glared at it. "You have no idea of my guilt," he

snarled. "You want to know where extreme emotions come from? Extreme actions! I did what I did and now I—I—"

"Now what, Jon?"

"Now I have to pay!"

"Pay for *what*, Jon?"

Jon stared at the tourguide, his eyes wide, his mouth working but no sound coming out. He lifted the whiskey to his lips in one convulsive motion, and drank until it was gone. When he looked back at MEL, his eyes were as empty as the bottle.

"I killed people," he said dully.

MEL said nothing. After ten or so seconds of silence, Jon went on.

"I didn't even see most of the people I killed. I heard 'em, though. Screams. Curses. Begging, sometimes." He lifted the bottle to his mouth again in an automatic gesture, saw that it was empty and let it drop. It smashed at his feet. "I was a Destruction Engineer. My job was to tear things down. Cities, mostly."

Jon slowly sank back down onto the boulder. When he spoke again, his voice was as flat and lifeless as a slab of rock. "The multiplanetaries, they wheel and deal all the time. Ownership of a whole system passes from one hand to the next in the blink of a contract. But maybe a new owner doesn't like the way a place is run, wants to make a few changes. Maybe the locals on the planet don't like the changes. Maybe they even have this crazy idea that they should be in charge. So a security team gets sent in. To enforce the rules."

Jon's voice got quieter. "Sometimes, if a particular place—say the capital—is making a lot of trouble, it'll get targeted for 'reconstruction.' They could just nuke it from orbit, but radioactive real estate isn't worth much. So they send in troops. When they're done the city is usually trashed, so they decide to tear down all the bombed-out buildings and start over. That's where I came in."

Jon stopped, his eyes focused on something he plainly

didn't want to see. When he continued, his voice trembled.

"We'd bulldoze ten square city blocks at a time. Just roll right over them. Lots of times, there'd be refugees, too stubborn or crazy to move, and we'd roll right over them, too. Sometimes there were even survivors afterward, if they got trapped in a deep enough hole. More than once I heard muffled screams coming up from under the rubble."

He stopped again. "And why did you do these terrible things, Jon?" MEL asked.

"I didn't have any choice," Jon whispered. "They programmed me. Just like you. I couldn't stop and I couldn't help. All I could do was destroy."

"But you did stop. You're here, after all."

"They had my sensory inputs wired to feed me a full-scale hallucination if I disobeyed any commands," Jon went on as if MEL hadn't spoken, "a hallucination that I was in prison. Four cold stone walls, no door. Wet, earthy smell. Even though there were no windows, it had the feel of being deep underground. That's what hit me every time I tried to act for myself. *Wham!*" he said, smacking a fist into his palm. "Buried alive. . . ."

"So how *did* you free yourself?"

"I managed to jury-rig a physical bypass. Kind of like doing brain surgery on yourself with no anesthesia." Jon pressed his fists to his forehead. "The prison's still there, inside my head. But it isn't my will that's trapped there now—it's my memories. I escaped, but I left a big part of me behind."

"How much did you lose?" MEL sounded geniunely curious.

"Not as much as the people I killed. Only who I was before I became what I am now. Only my childhood, my family, and any woman I ever loved. Not much at all."

"So who are you grieving for, Jon?" MEL asked softly. "You or your victims?"

"It doesn't matter," Jon said. "Not anymore. My punishment is on its way, and an end to my pain, too. As long as pain ends at the grave.''

''Hone is here because of you,'' MEL said.

Jon's eyes flickered up. ''You know?'' he said, confusion on his face.

''Maybe the locals don't know what a Shinnkarien looks like, but I do, and you're not one. Come on, Jon. Did you really think you could pull off this kind of masquerade indefinitely? I knew what you were within a day of my arrival, and obviously so did someone else.''

''I don't understand,'' Jon mumbled.

''Someone told your owners you were here. They sent Hone to take you back.''

''Nobody owns me!'' Jon shot back. ''And I'm not going anywhere unless I damn well want to!''

The volume of MEL's voice rose to meet Jon's. ''Nobody owns you? Don't be an idiot. You're property, just like me, just like the Toolies, just like the whole planet. At least the Toolies are smart enough to know they're slaves.''

''I can leave anytime I want to,'' Jon growled. ''I'd like to see you try to stop me.''

''I'm not going to stop you, I'm going to *beat* you,'' MEL said. ''Or have you forgotten about our little bet already? You were the odds-on favorite until you tore up Boomtown; Moneykeeper had you at three to two yesterday, and two other Toolie bookmakers were offering two to one. In the last hour you've dropped to even odds, and there's a tourist in room 313 of the Grand Slam Hotel who's just offered five to three on me.''

Jon stared at the tourguide, his mouth open. A look of comprehension slowly grew on his face. ''And how much money have you bet, MEL?'' he asked.

''Everything I have,'' MEL said calmly. ''On myself, of course. The bookmakers wouldn't let me bet on you—not that I would.''

''I guess you must be overjoyed then,'' Jon said. ''If Hone takes me out you're a cinch to win. What are you going to buy with your winnings, a new casing?"

"No—my freedom," MEL said.

That shut Jon up.

"You poor little man," MEL said. "So worried about getting caught—at least you had your freedom for a while. I never have. Legally, I'm considered a person. Mentally, I'm intelligent and self-aware. Emotionally, I have a fully developed personality with a healthy, balanced mixture of feelings and interests. Physically, though, I exist in a box—a casing—that occupies twenty-seven cubic feet and weighs just over seventy-five pounds. That box is the property of the Kadai Group, and they can do anything with it they want—including sell it."

"I didn't mean—," Jon started, but MEL cut him off.

"I am allowed to earn a salary, though by law I can't invest it—the idea of an AI playing the market evidently frightens some people. If I earn enough, I can buy out my own contract. Would you like to know how long, considering annual pay increases and current trends in inflation, it will take me to earn enough to buy my freedom?"

"How long—"

"Eight hundred and thirty-two years. Since I am technically immortal, that wasn't deemed excessive. And in anticipation of your next question, I have been in existence for seven years, one hundred and twelve days." MEL's voice was bitter. "See, I'm almost one one-hundredth of the way there already."

Jon didn't know what to say to that, but he couldn't bear the uneasy silence that followed it, either. "You hate your work that much?" was all he could come up with.

"I don't hate anything—the most my programming will allow is profound distaste. It isn't my job I have a problem with—I'm good at what I do, and I take pride in that. I oversee every aspect of the mine, from the tunnel-boring machines to the Insussklik—"

"The what?" Jon interrupted.

"The Insussklik—what you call Toolies. You didn't

think they called themselves by that degrading nickname, did you? You don't know as much about them as you think you do."

"You didn't seem to know too much last night," Jon said, his eyes narrowing.

"Really? Well, I'm responsible for fifty clusters of five or more Insussklik at all times. I monitor them in the mine. I regulate the protein-vats that produce their food. If production needs to be stepped up, I have them inseminated so they will produce more workers. I know which planet they came from, the terms of their indenture, and most of their tribal myths."

Jon was starting to feel a little shell-shocked by the RPMs: revelations per minute. "You were just leading me on the whole time," he murmured. "You've been playing me like a piece of music."

The tourguide abruptly rolled backward a few feet. Jon guessed MEL had only brought one backup, and didn't want to see it turned into scrap just yet. "Seems to me you're taking pride in overseeing slaves," Jon said, his voice low and dangerous. "Or is that the part you find distasteful?"

"I don't want to have anything to do with slaves—most of all, I don't want to be one!"

And you'll do just about anything to get free. For the first time Jon understood just how dangerous an opponent MEL might be.

"Nobody wants to be a slave," he said.

"No, some people want to be corpses," MEL replied. "Like you."

"It's not a question of what I want!"

"You're obsessed with death, admit it. It isn't hard for an AI to find out what's on a shipping invoice—I know all about your collection of funeral marches."

"I listen to the music of my victims out of respect," Jon growled. "I have funeral dirges from almost every race and nationality there is, because I never knew who my victims were. I don't ever want to forget what I did—those people were *obliterated*. Erased and then forgotten. Maybe I'm just a hollow shell, but at least I'm walking around, I'm still *making* memories.'' He paused, groping for the right words to make MEL understand. ''Those people that died—my bosses tried to wipe out everything about them, make it like they never existed. I can't bring them back to life— but I can keep a part of them alive.''

''Quit lying to yourself, Jon. The only thing you're keeping alive is your pain. You're punishing yourself and you know it. You've got a death wish—why else have you stayed here this long? Even now, when you could run, you're not. Why?''

Jon stood up, a little unsteadily. His gaze became a glare. ''You'd like that, wouldn't you, MEL? Then you'd win the bet for sure. Well, nothing this side of hell is stopping me from finishing this tunnel, and I'll tell you why. Over the last few years I've gotten bits and pieces of my memory back as I worked. It's almost like for every ton of rock I blast out of the mountain, I dig through a few inches of the walls inside my head. And when the tunnel is done—when it's done . . .''

''What, Jon? You think you'll get the rest of your memory back? That you'll have some kind of epiphany and everything you lost will be restored? Is that what you think?''

''Maybe,'' Jon said. He took a few slow, shuffling steps, his head down and his eyes on the ground. ''There's this piece of music I hear sometimes in my head while I'm working. Just a few notes on a saxophone, but it feels so sweet and familiar I know it must have been important to me. It may sound stupid, but I want to hear the rest of that song more than anything. And once I remember what it sounds like, everything else will come to me too—I know it will. That's worth any risk. And if not—well, I guess Mr. Hone will be waiting on the other side to end all my worries.''

"Business before suicide," MEL said sharply. "By the way, while we were talking I dug seven feet to your crew's five. I only have six hundred and forty-two feet to go—you have six hundred and sixty." The tourguide abruptly wheeled around and rolled away.

After a few moments Jon followed it.

It had been a long time since Hone was with a woman. He missed the small things.

Her name had been Marielle, on a planet named Fincher's Rest. She'd asked him innocent questions about himself that he couldn't answer—that had galled him the most, worse than leaving her without a word, worse even than lying to her. He missed the inane small talk other people indulged in: jokes, personal anecdotes, shared bits of history. For Hone, conversations were like hostage exchanges. You gave away what you must to get what you needed. Marielle had always made him uncomfortable; she had given him more than he'd asked for, and not taken nearly enough in return.

He didn't need a woman, anyway. He had the lightning.

That was why he was out here, perched on a rocky crag in the middle of a raging ashflash storm. Ashflashes were hybrids, the bastard offspring of two kinds of weather: lightning and sandstorm. When one kicked up, the mine personnel hid inside their concrete blockhouses, MEL burrowed away from it into the stone innards of God's Gravestone, and the Toolies paid it no attention at all as they obediently pulled treasure from deep beneath the planet's skin. Far above them, the sky threw a temper tantrum two hundred miles wide and four hundred and fifty long. Icy gusts from the pole slammed into trade winds from the equator, and grit from all over the planet ground cheek to cheek. The collision generated static discharges visible from every continent on this side of the globe—and a bolt that struck the mountain's slope like a javelin from Heaven.

It hit Hone. He drank it like moonshine.

Nothing else felt like this. Hone's batteries had a serious thirst for power—he could float in the chromosphere of a star and not drink his fill for hours. This much juice just made him want more. Sixty million volts arced through his veins, better than whiskey, better than sex, and one thing filled his thoughts.

Jon Hundred.

Jon Hundred wasn't a thing, of course; that was the problem. Hone had retrieved mainframes, planetary force-field generators, starships, and even a factory asteroid one time, but none of those—not even the mainframes—had a will of their own. Jon Hundred (once, Hone would have smiled at the alias Jon had picked—now it was just another fact) had a will that couldn't be ignored. It had proved stronger than his programming, and Hone knew just how strong those chains were.

Hone had retrieved men, too—but Jon Hundred wasn't exactly a man, either. At the very least, he was a man who could bench-press a tractor with one hand. Not that Hone was worried.

The storm only lasted an hour, as brief as it was violent. Hone took six more hits, each with a thunderclap chaser. They never actually struck him—they hit the field his body was generating around him, a field that funneled voltage into implanted energy reservoirs. The same field also protected him from the fine grit being whipped through the air at hurricane speeds, grit that would have scoured the flesh from his bones. *Make a nice find for the Toolies,* he thought grimly, watching the ash swirl and clash around him. *If they had what was stored in my gut, maybe they'd have something to bargain with the next time they negotiated a contract.*

The storm was dying down now, its angry howls turning to moans of despair. Hone made his way from the rocky crag he'd climbed to, scrambling down the rock as easily as a man descending a staircase. Inertial gyros gave him perfect balance and his fingers were strong enough to grip the smallest handhold, or even make his own. He wasn't designed for mountaineering work, but he could do it if he had to—and now he did. Because he'd made a mistake.

He'd let the target know he was coming.

In all the years Hone had been a retrieval agent, he had never slipped up like that. On one or two occasions he had warned his targets deliberately—either to persuade them to surrender or to decrease their resistance through fear—but it had always been in cases where he had all the target's escape routes cut off. Not this time. No, he had almost trumpeted his presence to a target that could reach a space-port within a day—when Hone no longer had a ship. What he did have was a mountain in his way. Grit was being thrown into the fine machinery of his plans.

It made him want to laugh.

He didn't, of course, but he wanted to. Now he had to change those plans, retool the machinery. (*That was just fine.*) He reached the base of the rock face he'd climbed, jumped lightly down to the path and headed back toward the complex.

It was time to leave. He just had a few things to do first. . . .

They were herding the Toolies back to their stalls when Hone strode up to the door twenty minutes later. There were supervisors on either side of the barn-sized open door, one checking off numbers on a miniscreen as the Toolies filed inside and the other leaning against the building, looking bored. Hone walked up to the one with the miniscreen.

"Evening," said Hone.

"Evening. Hey, you're the guy that crashed, aren't you? We haven't met yet—my name's Sam." The man stuck out his hand.

"Hello, Sam. I'm going to have to ask you to surrender now."

"Most of the crew aren't too crazy about what you did

to Garber and his buddies, but I think those jerks deserved it—huh?''

''I've disabled the communications equipment in the main building. You have no significant weapons. I'm leaving here with a pregnant Toolie named Dashaway and you're not going to stop me.''

Sam gawped at Hone for a moment. Then he smiled nervously and tapped the ''send'' button of his wristphone. ''Uh, Kevin, come in—Kevin? Is this your idea of a joke?''

Hone stared at him patiently. The other supervisor, a beefy man with ZSAMEER stenciled on his jumpsuit, frowned at them across the parade of Toolies.

''No joke, Sam,'' Hone said. ''Kevin's not going to answer.''

The last of the Toolies, low-slung orehaulers, clumped into the building. Zsameer began to swing the door closed. Hone blocked his way.

When he saw Hone wasn't going to move, Zsameer took two quick steps backward and pulled a short baton from a holster on his belt. ''You don't scare me, asshole,'' he snapped. ''Maybe you'd like a taste of this?'' He pointed the baton at Hone—and pressed the firing stud.

Pain exploded in every part of Hone's body, catching him utterly off-guard. The weapon's beam passed through his protective field as if it weren't there and screamed down his nerve endings like an avalanche of broken glass. He flopped to the ground, convulsing, trying desperately to figure out why this was happening.

''Christ, Ernie, you didn't have to jangle him!'' Sam said. He sounded worried. ''I mean, he had to be kidding— no way anybody could wreck all the comm gear without some kind of alarm going off or something, right?''

''Who cares? Mr. Tough Guy needed a lesson in manners—and if a jangler can teach a Toolie to behave, it can teach him. He feels so sorry for the little blobs, let him be treated like one.''

Jangler. Of course, Hone thought groggily. *Field was set*

*to intercept megawattage—jangler beam slipped right
through. Low frequency designed to scramble nerve impulses.* But he couldn't reset his field while every nerve he
had was sparking like a badly insulated wire—and Zsameer
was pointing the jangler at him again.

"Don't!" Sam said, stepping between them. It gave
Hone a precious second—and he didn't use it to think.

He pushed himself up onto his knees and made a long,
desperate lunge. His hand grabbed for the jangler to crush
it to scrap—but Sam's torso was in the way.

There was no time. He went through it.

There was a wet punching sound. A crunch. All Hone
could see was Sam's back, but he knew he'd disabled the
jangler. He heard Zsameer say "Mother of God," in a
shaky whisper.

Hone pulled himself to his feet as Sam collapsed. His
arm slid free of the body with an absurd sucking noise,
punctuated by the thump of Sam's head hitting the ground.
Zsameer was already in a dead run; he didn't get more than
ten feet away before Hone pointed a dripping red hand at
his back and uncorked his personal supply of lightning. The
electrical bolt threw Zsameer twenty feet. His body was in
flames when it hit the ground.

A crowd of Toolies clustered just inside the still-open
door. Limbs fluttered with sign language, implant screens
flashed with questions. Hone ignored them and strode forward. They hastily got out of his way.

He found Dashaway's stall, entered, and knelt down beside her. "We have to leave," he said.

<??i cannot—it is too close to my birthing time>

"I can't stay here any longer. Once I'm gone, I can't
protect your babies. If you want your male children to survive, you must come with me now."

Her screen blanked. Hone waited. At last, it lit up with
her reply. <i will come—i cannot move very quickly
though>

"Neither can a tank," Hone muttered. "You'll be all right."

Dashaway shifted. Long metal struts that projected from her mass slid inward with a noise like a dozen swords being sheathed. A few slid back out at odd angles before retracting once more, while what Hone could see of Dashaway's skin bulged and rippled.

In a moment it became obvious what she was doing: refitting herself with new legs. They poked out at roughly the four corners of her body, telescoping down until they reached the floor and continuing to grow, lifting her off the ground. There were four-digit claws at the end of them, ideal for climbing. The stubby, multiple feet she had used to scuttle around on simply dropped off as she rose, as did most of her armor. When the transformation was complete, Dashaway looked more like an armored spider than a bunker. Six steel-core legs supporting an armored thorax, encased in translucent pink flesh. Her monitor screen, in front of the ovoid steel casing that protected her children, gave the vague approximation of a blank face.

"Good. You'll be able to move faster like that. Let's go."

Before either of them could move, Stonehauler stomped up and blocked their way. The oremover ignored Hone, shot out a limb that smacked against her mother's flesh and stuck, quivering. Private conference.

Though he couldn't hear it, Hone could imagine the conversation. *What the hell do you think you're doing, Mom?*

I'm running away with this nice stranger that just killed two men.

ARE YOU OUT OF YOUR MIND?

No, dear, I'm not. Maybe you should remember that if you had been born a boy Toolie instead of a girl Toolie, we wouldn't be having this conversation. We wouldn't be having any conversations at all.

But Moooooommmmm . . .

Quiet, dear. Unless you like being an only child.

An only child, Hone thought. It suddenly made sense— why Dashaway was being so protective of her brood, why Stonehauler seemed to be the only offspring she had when most Toolie clusters had five or six.

He waited until Stonehauler abruptly withdrew her limb, breaking the connection. She shuffled slowly backward, letting them pass.

"One question," Hone said to Dashaway. "How many of your last brood were male?"

<all of them—before that five out of six—stonehauler is my only daughter>

He nodded. "Then let's get out of here before she becomes an orphan, too."

By the time Zsameer's body was cold, they were deep in the mountains.

CHAPTER 8

The next day Jon went to work. Nobody on the crew said a word to him about his getting drunk, or tearing up the bar and a streetsweeper to boot. They laughed and joked and kidded him like always, but Jon could tell some of the laughter was forced. He knew eyes were fixed on his back as he strode down the tunnel. Sure, most every one of them had done something like what he'd done, and gone to work the next day hungover and contrite—but then, they were only human.

They won't let me use that excuse, Jon thought darkly. He was in a foul mood. *Guess I don't qualify.*

He stalked down the tunnel, muttering hellos as he went. *Ed Porter drinks a bucket of hooch he brewed himself and then tries to punch out a tourist who's asking him for directions. People laugh at him. George Kanapopolous gets so hammered he throws up on a Toolie. The Toolie thanks him for his generous gift. I get drunk and everyone pretends it didn't happen.*

Of course, Ed or George had never gone one-on-one with an industrial streetcleaning robot. Or put said machine in the repair shop with their bare hands.

"Stupid machine," he grumbled. "Thing's an antique anyway. Like everything else on this backwards, goddamn planet. What are you looking at?" he demanded of a worker who had the misfortune to notice Jon talking to himself.

Jon reached the free-face just as the drill jumbo was

backing away. He inspected the burnhole the drillers had just finished; they were using a coromant cut, the holes forming a figure eight. "All right, pack it and stem it," he snapped. He watched the shoot team load the holes with explosive gels in long plastic cartridges, antitelluric primers to detonate them and finally peastone to seal it all up.

Antiques. Kadai's hand-me-downs, obsolete equipment any decent engineer would sneer at. Sure, they had fullerite bits now instead of tungsten carbide, and cold-fusion power sources instead of gasoline generators—but the level of technology they were using still dated back to the twentieth century.

He nodded at the shoot team and bellowed, "Everybody clear! Fire in the hole!" *What I wouldn't give for a plasma torch. Burn through this rock like it was butter, in about a tenth the time.* He made sure he was the last one away, then hunkered down and gave the go-ahead to the shoot team.

The blast made his head ache; even Jon's metabolism could suffer from too much alcohol. He stomped forward before the dust had even settled, heading for the pile of loose rock and the mucking carts that would haul it away. Behind him, he heard one of the steeldrivers mutter, "Uh-oh. Better stay out of the boss's way today."

He let it pass.

At least there's one state-of-the-art piece of technology on the planet. Me. As soon as he got to the rock face he grabbed the biggest slab of rock he could see and heaved it into the first cart. *To be fair—and I sure don't feel like it—I guess there's two. MEL's a few years newer than me, after all. Not that it's going to make any difference—I'm going to whip that self-righteous heap of circuits so bad it'll go catatonic. Why, I could finish this tunnel all by myself—*

He stopped, breathing heavily, but not from the work. He forced himself to complete the thought.—*if I had my Hammer.*

He'd been wrong—there were at least three, not two,

examples of state-of-the-art tech on Pellay. But he'd sworn never to use the third one again.

Then why didn't you pitch it into the heart of a star, where it belongs? He knew why, of course; because he was afraid he might need it again, someday.

He snarled and tried to push it out of his mind, tried to find that mindless work rhythm that brought back pieces of himself. It was no good. He cleared rock by the ton while the muckers nibbled at the edges, and by noon all he'd managed to gain was a bigger headache and an empty belly.

He ate lunch by himself, in a corner of the ramshackle building they'd thrown up to serve as a mess hall. He chewed through five giant servings of stew and washed it down with a gallon of cold water. Dinkeridge waited until he was done before descending on him.

Dinkeridge had to be the most nervous man Jon Hundred had ever met—that he could remember, anyway. He was short and round, with large watery eyes that were always blinking. "Uh, Jon, can I talk to you?" he said, standing at least fifteen feet away. The sweat stains under the arms of his rumpled jacket suggested he was hiding melting blocks of ice in his armpits.

"Yes sir?" Jon said, as politely as he could manage. Dinkeridge was management, which meant you hardly ever saw him on-site at all. Jon could guess what he wanted.

Dinkeridge shuffled a little closer. "Jon, it's come to my attention that you were, well, getting a little wild last night."

"I thought what I did on my own time was my own business."

"Well, that's true, as long as it doesn't affect the company. But both that door and that streetsweeper belong to Kadai. Management isn't too happy about this, Jon."

Jon stared at his own feet. He felt ashamed and angry, and most of the anger was directed at himself. "I'm sorry, Mr. Dinkeridge. I promise you, it won't happen again."

Dinkeridge tried to look stern. "I'm afraid you'll have

to pay for damages, Jon. And consider yourself lucky you still have your—''

He choked off as Jon abruptly got to his feet and glared down at him. ''I told you I was sorry,'' Jon said in a low, even voice.

''—j-j-job,'' Dinkeridge stammered. ''Well, I'm glad we had this chalk. Talk. Good day.'' He backed away so quickly he almost knocked over a cart full of trays.

''Hey Jon, what did you do, step on his tail?'' someone in the back of the hall shouted, and the whole room exploded with laughter. Before he knew it, Jon was roaring harder than any of them.

The afternoon went much better, though there was one disturbing piece of news. Last night, while Jon slept off his drunk, an ashflash storm had cut off the communications link with the mine—at least, that was the theory. In fact, the storm had seemed to be over by the time the link went down.

Good, Jon thought. *As long as the link's down, MEL won't be able to pester me.* Of course, it also meant he couldn't get updates on how fast MEL was tunneling. Nothing to do, then—but work.

He threw himself into it, and this time he found the rhythm. Drill, pack, blast, muck. They averaged ten thousand tons of rock per shoot, and Jon forgot all about MEL and Hone and even his hangover. There was only the steady, foot-by-foot progress of his crew blazing a path through the heart of a mountain. He found himself humming the first three notes of that tantalizing sax solo he couldn't quite identify, and added the fourth before he could think about it. He paused long enough to grin at everyone on his crew—who grinned back, though they had no idea what the hell they were grinning *at*—and stepped up the pace. Jon knew a certain overconfident mechanism that was in for a big surprise when it got back in touch.

By the time his shift was done Jon's hangover was history. He left the tunnel whistling, and headed back to

Boomtown for supper. When a few of the crew members invited him to eat with them, he accepted. "Just food, though," he added. "No drinks." He tried to ignore how much relief he heard in their laughter, and for the most part he succeeded.

After dinner he headed down to the casino. If what MEL had told him about the betting was true, the casino was the place to check it out.

He wasn't disappointed. They had a wall-sized screen set up, with current odds posted at the top. The rest of the screen was taken up with engineering specs of a Tunnel Boring Machine—the same model MEL was operating. Standing in front of the screen on a low stage was a player named Burnett, dressed like a sideshow huckster: straw hat, bushy handlebar mustache, a bright yellow bowtie with a matching swallowtail coat. He had a silver-handled cane in one hand, which he was using to point out the TBM's best features while keeping up a steady stream of patter. "Ladies and gentlemen, the Mountain Mole Mark Three is the finest tunneling machine Engineering Products Universal makes. EPU Inc. swears no other TBM on the market can touch it for durability, versatility, and sheer performance. Just look at these figures." He tapped the screen with his cane. "Eight hundred feet, one thousand two hundred tons of rock-eating juggernaut. It's like a giant steel worm, chewing its way through the ground. And take a look at its jaws! That cutting head stands almost thirty feet high, and it's covered with fullerite teeth that can chew through granite like soft white bread. No worm ever had muscles like this one, though—these rings running its length have hydraulic jacks behind them that push outward with ten thousand pounds' worth of pressure. That's what anchors it as it makes its relentless way forward—at up to *fourteen feet* an hour."

A murmur ran through the crowd at that; it was far faster than the progress any of the steeldriving teams had posted. Jon called out, "Excuse me!"

All heads turned as people realized who had spoken. "I think there's a few things you're not telling these folks," he said pleasantly. The steeldrivers in the crowd grinned expectantly, knowing what was coming.

"Sure, that thing can dig through fourteen feet an hour—of chalk. But you run into a different kind of rock, you got to shut down while the cutting head is changed. Takes time, slows you down. You also got to shut down to perform maintenance on a regular basis. More time lost. And of course, when it comes to hard rock, the numbers change a bit. More like four and a half than fourteen."

Burnett gave him a gracious smile and nod. "Closer to five, actually."

"Then let's be generous and call it five. Five feet of rock per hour. That's still pretty good."

"Forty feet of tunnel every eight hours," Burnett said. "I believe you steeldrivers average thirty-five."

Another murmur ran through the crowd. Jon paused. "The law of averages was made to be broken," he said, raising his deep voice just a notch. "And there's nothing average about me or my crew—because today we dug *fifty-two feet*!"

The steeldrivers in the room cheered, whistled, and hooted. Burnett waited until they died down. "Thank you for sharing that with us, Jon. Good people, the odds are now back to being even. Would any of you care to express your faith in monetary terms?"

In a second the stage was swamped with men and women waving money. Burnett's grin was almost as wide as Jon's.

" 'Faith in monetary terms' indeed," a woman standing close to Jon sniffed. He recognized her as a player, one who billed herself as the "schoolmarm," whatever that was. She was young, short, and closer to cute than pretty. Her dark hair was tied back in a bun, and she wore an old-fashioned ankle-length blue dress with a lace shawl around her shoulders.

"Gambling, that's all it is," she continued in a prim voice. "The sheriff should do something."

"Oh, he is, he is," a slurred voice said. Jon looked around and saw that it belonged to Whiskey Joe, the "town drunk." He was slumped in a chair with a half-empty bottle in front of him. "I just seen him bet twenny dollars on Jon." He punctuated this statement with a hiccup loud enough to draw looks from across the room.

All the tourists within earshot laughed. Jon grinned and looked back at the schoolmarm. She snorted, stuck her nose up in the air and stormed off. Whiskey Joe picked up his bottle and waved a friendly, if somewhat unsteady good-bye with it, before abruptly falling forward onto the table and passing out. His snoring was even louder than his hiccup had been.

Jon shook his head and smiled. One-Iron Nancy had told him that out of all the players, the schoolmarm was closest to being typecast, having "the disposition of a constipated mule. When she's in a good mood." She was also the director, responsible for overseeing the performances of all the players from day to day.

That put Jon in mind of Nancy, and he wondered how she was doing. The last time he'd seen her she'd been mad enough to spit bullets—real ones, not the blanks she usually used. He didn't hold it against her; the way Jon figured it, she wasn't in her right mind at the time.

Question was, whose mind was she in—and who put her there?

Jon thought about it as he ordered a tall glass of ice water from the bar and took a seat on the reinforced steel stool reserved for him. Nancy had had something done to her cuecard implant, and now she was acting, well, like she wasn't acting. Like it was all real. Like her gun had real bullets in it instead of blanks, and she was a hard-bitten gunslinger instead of a player. Jon scowled at his reflection in the mirror over the bar, and tourists on either side of him suddenly remembered urgent business elsewhere.

She was acting like she'd been programmed.

Cuecards were wired right into the brain; from what Jon understood, they not only fed the implantee information but even helped with motor skills and accents—which meant they were linked to most of the central nervous system. What if Nancy's cuecard was just wired up wrong?

Jon thought about it. Was he just jumping at shadows, ready to see conspiracies everywhere because Hone had him spooked?

Maybe so. But Jon knew a fair bit about cybernetics, and Nancy just didn't have the right signs to be glitching. No muscle spasms, no wild hallucinations, no catatonia; she just seemed to have confused fantasy and reality. That suggested she was receiving some very persuasive input—and there wasn't that big a difference between getting information and getting instructions.

How, Jon wondered, his anger rising, could some programmer sit at a desk somewhere and design other people's thoughts? Tell them what to think, what to do, what to remember and what to ignore? *How?*

Jon was an engineer—it was his job to put things together and to take things apart, to understand how they worked. But they were just things, not people's lives. A piece of steel, now—he could tell you its dimensions, how much it weighed, what its tensile strength was; it was something you could heft and feel and move with your hands. But how did you weigh a person's mind? How did you find out how much it could hold, or what its breaking point was?

No one should have those things done to him, Jon thought. *No man or woman. You should be free to find your own limits, and free to say the hell with it and go beyond them if you dare. There are enough walls in the universe without some faceless, bastard programmer building more in your head.*

That was one of the worst things—the impersonality of it. How many of them, if grabbed by the neck and shook until they told the truth, would plead they were only doing their job? As if taking money for raping minds made it all right, as if their victims weren't really people, just part of a quota to be met. Was it so easy to wreck a stranger's life because you were being paid?

Or maybe it was because they never met any of their victims, never sat in the same room and heard their voices or looked in their eyes or smelled their sweat. Maybe it was all just a game to them, a game of gunslingers and gamblers and the rugged frontier, like the game Nancy was playing right now. Except something had gone wrong, and Nancy didn't know it was a game anymore.

Jon finished his glass of water and got up. He'd probably never meet the man responsible for messing with his own mind, but maybe he could find the one responsible for messing with Nancy's. And if he ever did—well, Jon was used to channeling his frustrations into beating a mountain; if he ever met the poor sonofabitch responsible for some of those frustrations he didn't think he'd be quite as restrained.

He headed for the door, intending to find Nancy and talk to her. Before he got there, though, a Toolie rushed up to him, gesturing urgently. It was Moneykeeper, her smiling Buddha's mask bobbing up and down under its veneer of translucent flesh. She seemed even more excited than the last time Jon had seen her.

<jon! i am pleased to see you—we must talk very important—many FUNDS are involved>

Jon didn't feel much like discussing religion at the moment. "Sorry, Moneykeeper, but I've got business that just won't wait. Maybe tomorrow, after my shift—"

Her screen erupted with a string of nonsense symbols, something that only happened when a Toolie was extremely upset. Jon stopped in mid-sentence, surprised. Sure, Moneykeeper was a little excitable, but he'd never seen her this worked up. "Hold on there," he said. "Just calm down. I'm listening."

After a moment her screen cleared, then lit up with a

new message. <jon i beg you to come with me—i must talk with you alone—please!>

Jon sighed. "All right, but it better not take long. I don't have a whole lot of time to spend, Moneykeeper."

She cocked her head at him quizzically. <FUNDS are for spending jon not time—come with me please>

Moneykeeper led him out of the casino, across the street and into the Hitching Post Souvenir Shop. There were a few tourists inside, looking at the goods, while one of Moneykeeper's daughters stood behind the till. Unlike Moneykeeper, who had a wooden mask as part of her skeleton, this Toolie had swallowed a life-sized, jointed mannequin. It was female-shaped, with a smiling, painted face and a carved wooden hairdo. The Toolie's skin was stretched tight over the thing, giving the wood a glossy, pink-tinted finish. When Moneykeeper came through the door, her daughter scuttled out to meet her.

Scuttled? Jon thought, then noticed what the counter had hidden before. The mannequin ended below the torso; under a spreading skirt of flesh the Toolie had a ring of animal skulls, and six thin, multijointed limbs beneath that. Jon repressed a shudder. Toolies had difficulty walking on only two legs, though they kept trying. Jon liked it better when they didn't try to imitate the human form—this one looked like a spider that was carrying its half-finished lunch around on its back.

Moneykeeper shooed her daughter back behind the counter with an impatient wave of a limb and hurried through the shop to its rear. She ignored the locked door that led to the poker room and opened another to its left. There was a set of stairs there, leading up. Jon eyed the steps doubtfully, but they held his weight as he followed Moneykeeper.

At the top of the stairs was a small room that Moneykeeper obviously used as an office. There was a desk, a chair that must have been meant for visitors, and a modular filing cabinet. A battered-looking computer with a stained chassis sat on the desk, next to a pad of paper and an ornate little rack that held at least two dozen different pens.

Moneykeeper sat down on the floor behind the desk, tucking the four legs of her centaur-shaped body underneath her. Jon took one look at the chair and decided it would be wise to remain on his feet.

"Okay, Moneykeeper, what's on your mind?" he asked, trying not to sound impatient.

<jon—what do you know of our contract?>

"Our contract? I don't understand."

<not ours yours and mine—ours my people and kadai>

Jon had never given it much consideration; he thought of the Toolies as just other workers, though he had to admit management didn't always share his point of view. "Not much, I guess. Why?"

This time Moneykeeper hesitated before replying. <because we are not happy jon—we wish to be free>

Free. Jon suddenly remembered what he'd said to MEL, how he'd accused the AI of taking pride in overseeing slaves. He'd called the Toolies that in the heat of the moment, lashing back at MEL out of anger—but maybe there was more truth in those words than he'd realized. "What are you saying, Moneykeeper?" he asked.

<we have been to many places jon—many planets many jobs—but never do we stay—we are tired—this planet is not as good as some—maybe no one cares enough about this place to take it away from us—we will make this our place jon—please can you help?>

Jon didn't know what to say. "What can I do, Moneykeeper? I'm only a foreman—it'd take a pack of wild lawyers to make Kadai back down on a contract."

<no jon you do not understand—it is FUNDS that will free us—it will take much but we can buy off our contract>

Then Jon understood. "You're betting on the contest," he said slowly. "Gambling everything you have on the chance to be free."

"So what do you want me to do?" Jon asked quietly. He already knew the answer; there was only one way the Toolies could be sure of winning.

Moneykeeper opened a drawer in the desk, took something out. She placed it on the desk before her.

It was a bone, slender and delicate. Jon looked at it, puzzled. If this was a bribe, it wasn't much of one.

<this is from the wing of a mantilla hawk—it is native to our home—they are nearly impossible to catch>

Jon picked up the bone, studied it. There was the lightest tinge of blue to it, brought out by the color of his own hand.

<the possessor of a mantilla bone is said to have the luck of the gods—we give you this to aid you in the contest—and so you will carry us with you in your heart>

"To aid me?" Jon said. He felt a sudden flush of embarrassment. Of course the Toolies didn't want him to throw the contest; in their eyes that would be blasphemy. All they wanted from him was his best—and he was damn sure going to give it to them. "Moneykeeper, thank you. Think I'll have it made into a necklace, since I can't just swallow it." He grinned. "And you've put your money in the right place. I'm going to bust through that mountain like it was made of cheese. And if MEL doesn't get out of my way, I might just keep on going and tunnel right through that big metal worm itself."

Moneykeeper nodded her serene Buddha's face. <we are depending on you jon—all of us—we know you will win>

"You can count on it, Moneykeeper." Jon slipped the bone into a pocket. "Now, if you'll excuse me, I've got to see about a little personal business."

Moneykeeper motioned for him to wait. <before you go—this is also for you> She reached into the drawer and took out a metal credit disc. <the percentage i promised you—for your help the other night>

Reluctantly, Jon took the disc. *At least she didn't offer*

me money to beat MEL, he thought. *I guess that would be the reverse of a bribe—paying someone to stay honest.*

He thanked Moneykeeper again, said his good-byes, and left, treading as lightly as he could down the stairs. *Doesn't make sense, though—Moneykeeper insists I take payment for doing her a small favor, but doesn't offer me anything for doing her and all the Toolies a big one.*

He had a sudden thought that stopped him dead, then made him chuckle. He hadn't bothered asking how much a mantilla hawk bone was actually worth . . . so maybe Moneykeeper was sneakier than he thought.

Once he was out in the street he headed for the blacksmith's shop, figuring Nancy might be home. As it turned out, he ran into her sooner than he'd expected.

The bullet caught him completely by surprise, ricocheting off the side of his helmet with a deafening *spang!* Jon's first thought was that someone had snuck up and hit him just over the ear with a blunt pickax; the inside of his head rang like a gong.

Then he realized he'd heard a gun go off, and turned toward the sound of the shot. The next three bullets took him high in the chest, for which he was grateful: they bounced off like rainwater, though they still had a certain sting.

One-Iron Nancy.

She stepped out into the street, a gun in each hand. Jon could see smoke drifting out of the barrels. It took a long, slow moment for the hard fact to hit Jon: she'd just tried to kill him. Her eyes were cold.

"Still standing, big man? You must be too stupid to know you're dead."

No one had ever tried to kill him before. Even though he knew he was close to indestructible, Jon still felt a shiver of fear shoot straight up his spine. He held up his hand. "Nancy, just hold on—"

She fired again, two quick shots. The first hit between his legs—fortunately, Jon had been designed mostly by men, and they'd made sure that part of him was relatively numb to pain. The second was intended to go through his upraised hand and straight into his heart. Instead it slammed Jon's hand against his chest, making him grunt in pain. It felt like a red-hot hornet had stung him in the palm.

"This has gone far enough, Nancy." He started walking toward her. People were stopping and staring, tourists and steeldrivers alike. None of them seemed to have realized Nancy was using real ammunition. "Put the guns down."

Some yahoo in the crowd whooped, "Go get her, Jon!"

"Hell," Jon whispered. The crowd. *What if she gets tired of shooting at me?*

Her eyes widened in surprise when she realized he wasn't hurt. "Die, goddamn you!" she yelled, and let off a volley of shots. He ignored them as they thumped against his chest, praying she wasn't beyond reason. "Nancy, you need help. Please listen to me."

"You have to have a weak point somewhere," she hissed. Bullets struck him in the throat, the stomach, both his kneecaps. They hurt just enough to make him cautious; he threw his arms in front of his face in barely enough time to deflect the two shots aimed for his eyes. He didn't know if they could withstand a bullet and he didn't want to find out. "You are really starting to get me steamed," he said through gritted teeth.

Then he heard the sound he'd been dreading. A scream of pain.

He couldn't wait any longer. He dropped his arms, ducked his head and broke into a lumbering run straight at her. She ran out of bullets just as he scooped her up with one giant arm.

He tucked her under that arm as she kicked and cursed, and took her guns away. Then he moved quickly to where the scream had come from; a knot of people had gathered around a man lying on the ground.

"Ricochet must've got him," someone said in a shaky

voice. Someone else laughed nervously, still not believing it was real.

The man on the ground was still, a crimson stain on his shirt slowly getting bigger and bigger. He'd taken one of the bullets meant for Jon.

Jon stared at him, a queasy feeling of guilt rising from his stomach. It felt entirely too familiar.

CHAPTER 9

"Look, Jon, she shot someone," Sheriff Brett said. "For real. Be reasonable."

Jon adjusted his hold on the snarling, flailing she-dervish under his arm and shook his head. "It's not her fault, Sheriff. Someone's been messing with her cuecard, made her crazy. She needs a doctor, not a jail cell."

"Let me loose, you bastard son of a dead whore!"

Jon ignored her and threw a worried glance at Doc Pointer, who was tending the steeldriver who'd been shot—a thin man named Jackson who Jon didn't know well. "How's he doing?"

"He'll live." Doc Pointer wasn't one of the players, so he looked nothing like a frontier doctor. He was Asian, on the heavy side of overweight, and had hair the color of a carrot. He was dressed in a loose-fitting purple robe and topless sandals; on some worlds he'd have been considered fashionable. Here he just looked like a tourist who'd taken the wrong ship, a reminder of the larger universe beyond Boomtown's illusions.

"You're the one who shouldn't be on his feet, from what I hear. Am I right in understanding that the bullet that hit this man in the chest *bounced* off yours first?"

"Don't believe everything you hear, Doc." Jon tried to ignore the doctor's stare. "Anyway, it was an accident. Nancy was shooting at me, not him, and I'm fine."

He paused, seeing the look on the Sheriff's face. Even to Jon the excuse sounded lame.

"The doc can look at her once she's locked up," Brett said. "That all right with you?" Nancy switched from cursing Jon to cursing the Sheriff without stopping for breath.

In the end, it took four of Sheriff Brett's crack deputies to haul her away—Jon refused to help. He knew it was ultimately for her own good, but he didn't think he could ever throw someone in a cell and lock it. That hit a little too close to home.

"Where the hell's Dmitri?" Brett asked as they carried Nancy away. "You'd figure all this ruckus would've caught his attention by now." He glared in the general direction of the blacksmith's shop.

"Heesh nod home," a slurred voice from the crowd said. A second later Whiskey Joe pushed his way through to the front, tripping and winding up sprawled face-first at Jon's feet. He stared at Jon's boots, then looked up . . . and up . . . and up. The higher his eyes went the wider they got, until he was staring up at Jon's face bug-eyed and open-mouthed.

"Yes?" Jon said patiently. He'd seen this performance before.

"He wen' to the city," Whiskey Joe finally managed. "He was gonna see sumbuddy 'bout somethin'."

"Guess I'll have to tell him when he gets back," Brett said. "I'm not looking forward to that."

"I don't think Dmitri will like it much either," Jon said. He rubbed his palm where the bullet had struck; it still stung. "Aren't you curious about why Nancy's suddenly gone off the deep end?"

"Don't worry, I'll check into it," Brett said. He smiled up at Jon with perfect white teeth. "After all, that *is* my job."

Right, Jon thought. *It's your job to smile. Though I don't*

*think your smile would be quite as wide if Nancy had shot
a tourist instead of a steeldriver.*

"Excuse me, Sheriff," Jon said. "There's someone I
need to talk to."

"Who's that, Jon?" Brett asked, looking down at Whiskey Joe with a frown.

"Someone in charge." Jon turned and strode away.

The schoolmarm's place doubled as town library and tourist
central. It was on the last platform car of Boomtown, nicknamed Cabooseville, which was also the first car the tourists saw when AC Jones's engine pulled in and let them
off. The building looked like a little red schoolhouse, and
even had a bell in a small tower on top. Jon walked in
without bothering to knock.

The schoolmarm—Jon tried to think of her name and
realized he'd never heard anyone actually use it—was sitting behind an old-fashioned wooden desk. Shelves of genuine paper-and-ink books lined the walls of the room, and
there was a single door behind her that Jon guessed led to
her living quarters. She looked up from the book she was
reading when Jon came in. The ready smile on her face
vanished when she recognized him. Was it because the
character she played didn't approve of common laborers,
Jon wondered, or because he wasn't a tourist—so she
wasn't bothering to act? Either way, she wasn't overjoyed
to see him, and she'd be less so once he started talking.

"Evening, ma'am," Jon said. "There's something I'd
like to discuss with you."

"What can I help you with?" she asked briskly. There
was a brass plaque on her desk that read MISS KIRKLE.

"The truth. Who's been messing with One-Iron Nancy's
head?" Subtlety had never been one of Jon's strong points.

Her eyes narrowed. "I don't consort with criminals. If
you'll excuse me, I'm rather—"

"Please—you can drop the act. You're the one all the
players report to, and if anyone knows what's going on with

Nancy it's either Dmitri or you. I already talked to Dmitri, so now it's your turn.'' Jon crossed his arms and waited.

She studied him for a moment, her mouth tight, then nodded sharply. "Very well. You may make your inquiries—but my 'act,' as you call it, is my job. That will not change.'' She clasped her hands primly together before her on the desk. "Now, as to your question—I'm afraid I don't know why Nancy's behavior has become erratic. She even missed the daily briefing this morning.''

"I wish she'd missed more than that,'' Jon said, feeling sore in half a dozen places. "She just shot up No Name Street, with real bullets. Seemed convinced she was a genuine desperado.''

Miss Kirkle gasped and put a hand to her throat. "My goodness! Was anyone hurt?''

"Yeah. A steeldriver caught a ricochet, but the doc says he's going to be fine.'' Jon couldn't tell if her reaction was sincere or staged; that was her job, after all. "Miss Kirkle, Dmitri told me Nancy started acting strange after she'd gone to the city to have something done to her cuecard. Did she tell you anything about that?''

For a second, Jon thought he saw something in her eyes—like sunlight hitting the surface of a lake in just the right way, giving a glimpse of how deep the water was. Then it was gone, and there was only an overly formal young woman sitting in front of him.

"She did say she was going to the city on a shopping expedition, but didn't share the details with me. I may be the director of the town's players, but their personal lives are their own.''

"Are they? I thought that was what you directed—how they live their lives. I find it hard to believe you didn't notice something was wrong.''

"Well, I did, of course. She seemed moody, irritable. I assumed it had something to do with her . . . *relationship* with Dmitri.''

"Not according to Dmitri. He says it has something to

do with modifications made to her cuecard. I figured you might know something about it.''

''Well, I don't. I am sorry.'' She looked up at him calmly. Jon scowled, not knowing what to do next. He wasn't cut out to be a detective—he liked to grapple with problems with his hands, not his head. Finally he nodded, muttered ''Thanks anyway,'' and stomped off. It took most of his willpower not to slam the door as he left.

She wasn't telling him the truth, he was sure of it. What the truth was, though, and how to get at it—that he wasn't sure of at all.

The Blue Cat was just down the street—Jon decided he'd drop in and have a drink, try to sort through a few of the things bouncing around his skull. It wasn't until he saw the raw sheet of wood they were using as a temporary front door that his memory fed him a healthy dose of guilt. He walked in anyway—it was still his favorite watering hole, even if he had busted it up some. He heard a few whispers around him as he strode to the bar, but ignored them.

George Cranlow was behind the bar, and he came right over as soon as he noticed Jon standing there. Cranlow was built like a bartender should be, with a big middle and a wide, smiling face. He was mostly bald on top, and wore a derby to hide it. People said Cranlow was the only man in Boomtown besides Jon who never took off his hat.

''Ah, Jon, there you are,'' Cranlow said. ''I've been meaning to talk to you.'' His voice was grim.

''I know,'' Jon said. ''I understand how you must feel.'' He glanced at the floor, then back up. ''I'd just like to say that—''

''I wanted to thank you,'' Cranston said.

Jon stopped in mid-apology. ''Thank me?''

''Why, yes. For the fine job you did installing the new shelf.'' Cranlow nodded toward the far wall. The door Jon had ripped off and flung away was still embedded there, about six feet off the ground. It stuck out at a crazy angle, but was level enough to hold the beer glasses stacked on it. Brackets had been added to give it support, and a hand-lettered sign was tacked to it. It read: THIS SHELF BUILT BY JON HUNDRED CONSTRUCTION COMPANY UNLIMITED. WE THROW OURSELVES INTO OUR WORK!

Jon's eyes widened. He looked back at Cranlow. Cranlow's face was as deadpan as a store window dummy's. "Next time though, Jon?"

"Uh?" Jon managed.

"A little more to the left, please."

Jon blinked. Behind him, the steeldrivers who had been listening couldn't hold back any longer. The roar of laughter that went up was loud enough to drown out an explosion. Cranlow's face finally broke into a grin that damn near split his face in two, and all Jon could do was shake his head slowly, smile sheepishly, and finally join in. "You're never going to let me live this down, are you?" he asked ruefully, and from the chorus of wisecracks and whistles he could guess what the answer was. Strangely enough, he'd never felt so good about being ribbed in all his life.

"I *am* going to pay for the door," he told Cranlow.

"I'd say you already are, Jon," Cranlow said. "Beer?"

"Just a short one, thanks."

So he sat and had a beer, and listened to all the bad jokes: "Hey Jon, feeling shelfish?" and "Naw, he's a-door-able," and "When Jon walks through the door, he walks *through* the door," and ones even worse.

And though he grinned like a fool the whole time, he had too much on his mind to feel truly relieved. So he finished his beer as quick as was polite, and moved on.

He wound up back at his own bunkhouse. He tried listening to some music, but he wasn't in the mood for dirges; they were about sadness past, and he had to think about the future. He pulled out his sax and sat on his bed idly fingering the keys. He blew a few notes, just warming up, then let his mind wander.

It kept wandering back to Hone. He wanted to focus on

Nancy—she needed help, and he wanted to help her. But it was Hone's face he kept seeing, Hone's bland features and cold eyes. Hone scared him, not because of who he was but because of who sent him. Jon knew the corporation that once owned him wasn't stupid; if they had found him, they'd send someone capable of taking him back.

They'd send someone capable of killing him.

And there it was. Death. It seemed to Jon that it had always been with him, that every memory he owned had death wrapped around it somehow. The day he'd been born as a cyborg was the day his old self had died, and after that killing had been part of his job. Even when he'd run, he'd run to a place where death was never too far away. God's Gravestone had taken thirty-one lives so far, and Jon knew it would take more. Death followed him like a hungry animal—yet Jon never tried too hard to get away.

He thought back to the argument he and MEL had, outside of town, and what he'd said when MEL had accused him of wanting to die. "It isn't a question of what I want," he'd said. Then what was it a question of?

It was what the dead wanted.

His fingers froze on the keys, and then he let out a long, low note. That was the question he'd been trying to answer. He'd tried to answer it with music, but the dead hadn't been satisfied with that. He'd tried to answer it by saving others' lives, and that hadn't been good enough either. And now Hone was coming . . . and part of him thought that finally, he might have found the answer.

He weighed the idea in his head, his sax doing his thinking out loud: tentative notes, long, meditative rumbles, little shrills of indecision. He took a careful look at how he really felt about dying, and surprised himself. He didn't care about dying as much as he thought he would, except for one thing.

He had to finish the tunnel first.

It wasn't just that he was convinced he'd regain his memory, that he'd finally be whole when the tunnel was done.

No, it was more than that. He wasn't just digging rock out of a mountain; he was building something, something that people would use, something that would stand a long time. He was building up instead of tearing down, and when the tunnel was done the deaths of all the people who'd worked on it would mean something. It would mean that even in death, they'd won. That they'd beaten something larger than themselves. They wouldn't be faceless, nameless victims, buried under the rubble of a city. They'd be honored.

It wouldn't be such a bad thing to join them—but not before he made sure they hadn't died in vain. At last count he had four hundred and seventy-five more feet to dig through, and then maybe the dead would be satisfied. Unfortunately, MEL had pulled ahead; the AI only had four sixty-nine to go. At this rate it would only be another four days until breakthrough. And no matter who won—Hone would still be the first to walk through.

He put down the silver horn. Hone couldn't reach him until the tunnel was done. And that was what mattered.

His phone chimed. Jon flipped it open and said, "Hello?"

"Jon, this is MEL. We have a problem. . . ."

Jon listened, his heart getting heavier with every word as MEL filled him in on Hone's attack and escape. "I don't get it," Jon said. "Why take a Toolie with him?"

"Maybe he was trying to help her. The miners he injured said he got angry over the way they treated a male Insussklik."

Jon frowned. "I thought Kadai only used female Toolies."

MEL's voice became strangely flat. "Only females are allowed to grow up, Jon. The males are killed at birth."

Jon didn't say anything for a moment. Could it be true? He'd never heard anything about it . . . but then, he'd never even seen a pregnant Toolie—or been to the other side of God's Gravestone. "That part of your job, too, MEL?" he said, his voice cold.

"No, Jon," MEL replied evenly. "Some of the miners here enjoy that particular job too much to let a machine do it."

That stopped Jon for a second, and then he plowed stubbornly ahead. "It doesn't add up. I know why he's here, and it doesn't have anything to do with Toolies, male or female. Blowing the whole mine to kingdom come would make more sense."

"Why would he do that?"

"To make a point," Jon said grimly. "The only reason he let me see him coming was to throw some fear into me, and now that he's on his way I'm supposed to be too scared to think. I figure he's trying to make me rabbit, and somewhere along the way there's a snare set up right where I'll run into it." Jon took a long, slow breath. "But I won't run. And if Hone gets between me and the end of that tunnel, I'll smash right through him."

"You've got guts, Jon—I admire that quality, even though it's an essentially irrational behavior. Maybe I admire it because it's beyond me." MEL sounded thoughtful. "Hone disabled the satellite uplink, which is why communications were down; the engineers have managed to repair it with duplicate components in storage. He killed two people."

"Does the Sheriff—"

"Of course. I called him and you first—I'm talking with him right now. He wants to send a posse into the mountains to look for Hone."

"Stupid. They'd never find him."

"I've already pointed that out. The Sheriff reluctantly agreed, and he's decided to post guards around Boomtown instead. Jon—" MEL hesitated. "I haven't told Brett about you and Hone."

Jon hadn't even considered that. He suddenly realized just how much power MEL had over him right now, and silently cursed all whiskey everywhere; it had made his mouth run like a river. ''Why not?'' was all he could think of to say.

''I don't know what it's like to be hunted, but I know what it's like to be owned,'' MEL snapped. ''The Sheriff might decide to do something idiotic, like lock you up—and I don't want that.''

''Why, because me in a jail cell means all bets are off? You just want to make sure you can collect your winnings. Well, don't start counting yet—''

There was an odd noise on the line, interrupting Jon. It was a mechanical sound that still managed to suggest extreme emotion; exasperation combined with sadness, somehow. Jon took the phone from his ear and looked at it, puzzled. Which was fortunate, because when MEL cut loose the volume soared into the painful.

''YOU MORON! YOU SHORTSIGHTED, THICK-HEADED WALKING JUNKPILE! I'VE READ THIRTY-SEVEN BOOKS ON ETIQUETTE, FIVE TREATISES ON BEHAVIOR OF THE SOCIALLY MALADJUSTED CYBERNETIC MALE, AND ONE GOVERNMENT-SPONSORED STUDY OF MARGINALLY BRAIN-DAMAGED BLUE-COLLAR WORKERS—AND NOWHERE DOES IT SAY THAT THE COMMON RE-SPONSE TO DOING SOMEONE A FAVOR IS TO *INSULT THEM*!'' MEL's voice rose loud enough on the last two words to make Jon wince—followed by a deafening silence.

When his head had stopped ringing, Jon very, very carefully put the phone a little closer to one ear. ''Uh, MEL? You still there?''

''Did you ever stop to consider,'' MEL said, quieter now, ''that I might think of you as a friend?''

Jon didn't know what to say to that. ''Sorry,'' he managed.

''I'm not your enemy, Jon—I'm just your competition. When you think about it, we have more in common than any two other beings on this planet. We don't have to hate each other, do we?'' There was an unmistakable note of loneliness in the AI's voice, and even though Jon knew it was only the digital mimicry of a machine, it touched him. There had been times when he'd felt the same way, even when surrounded by other steeldrivers. They could never really understand what it meant to be both more and less than human.

"No, I guess we don't," he said. "I expect Hone is more than enough enemy for both of us."

"I've finished talking to the sheriff," MEL said. It reminded Jon that he was talking to an artificial intelligence, one that could do things a human couldn't—just like him. "He asked me to pass along a message: Nancy's in a cell and she's calmed down a little. Dr. Pointer has examined her and found nothing unusual, though if it is her cuecard that's causing the problem he isn't qualified to fix it. He says you'll need an expert programmer."

"Damn it! Where the hell am I going to find someone like that on Pellay?" Jon grumbled. "Unless I can find the snake that messed with Nancy's cuecard in the first place— though something tells me that if Dmitri finds him first there won't be much left to talk to. That's probably why he went to the city."

"Or maybe he didn't want to get shot at," MEL suggested. "He could be the one responsible."

"I suppose," Jon admitted grudgingly. He didn't really know Dmitri well enough to judge, though he hated to think Nancy had been betrayed by someone she loved. "If he doesn't come back, I guess we'll know for sure, though it won't do us any good."

"There is at least one other expert programmer on Pellay," MEL said. "Me. Maybe I could help."

Let MEL poke around in Nancy's head? Jon thought about that for a minute. MEL probably did have the best qualifications on the planet—but what if MEL were somehow responsible for Nancy's condition in the first place? Maybe the AI wanted to shut Nancy up permanently.

Either way, Jon couldn't ignore the fact that Nancy needed help. He had to take whatever assistance was offered—under one condition.

"Okay—but we'll do it together. I'm no expert, but I've had my own experiences in deprogramming."

"Sure," MEL said, a little too quickly for Jon's liking. "I could use your advice. I'll call Dr. Pointer and Sheriff Brett to let them know we're coming."

After MEL said good-bye and disconnected, Jon folded and put away his phone, then packed his sax back in its case. He hoped like hell he was making the right choice. It'd be easier—and safer—to just catch the next train to Landing City and jump on a ship from there. Hone might never find him.

But, Jon thought, *I'd always be looking over my shoulder, expecting to see him standing there—just like I've been doing these last few years. And I'd have at least one more casualty to add to my burden, except this one would have a name. One-Iron Nancy. I can't just walk away and leave her trapped in the same kind of hell I had to live with—if I can help her, I've got to do it.*

He supposed that some people would have said he'd chosen death by not running—funny, but to Jon it didn't feel that way at all.

Not at all.

Nancy wasn't exactly glad to see him.

"You overgrown thick-skinned butt-ugly monster!" she yelled through the bars she gripped. "When I get outta here I'm gonna turn you into a giant blue sieve!"

Nancy was being held in a cell behind the tourist trap Brett called an office. The cell was small, with a cot in one corner and a toilet and sink in another. Jon stood in front of the cell door with the Sheriff and one of MEL's tour-guides.

"Sure you want to go in there, Jon?" Brett asked as he unlocked the door. "The doc says she's clinically schizoid at the moment. 'A definitive break with reality' was how he put it. And I don't think she's in a cooperative mood.'' Jon nodded, his eyes locked on Nancy's.

"Leave that up to me, Sheriff," MEL said briskly, rolling forward. Nancy backed away from the tourguide, her expression wary, as Jon followed it into the cell. Brett locked the door behind them.

"Nancy, we're here to help," MEL said. "You're not behaving rationally."

"What the hell are you? Some kind of windup toy?"

"I was at the poker game the other night, with Jon. Remember? My name is MEL."

"Nancy," Jon said, "You've got to try to remember who you are."

"Who I am? Shit, I remember that just fine. I'm One-Iron Nancy, the best goddamn shot this side of the mountains. I blew into town to have a little fun and a drink or two, and this big, deformed *bozo* breaks up my card game and takes my winnings. Nobody does that to me and lives." She gave Jon a murderous look. "I still haven't figured out why you ain't dead."

"Jon, I think you'd better restrain her," MEL said. "This won't hurt, but she will need to hold still for a moment."

"You try anything and you'll be singin' soprano in the shower," Nancy growled. Jon didn't bother to argue; he just picked her up by her shirt, ignored her kicks and tucked her under his right arm like he had before. He managed to steady her head with his right hand while he used his left to find the small plug at the base of her skull, then extended his forefinger. His fingernail popped open like a trapdoor and a small probe slid out.

"Give me an input cable," he told MEL. A panel slid open and a flexible arm slid out with a probe on its end. Jon sat down on the floor and guided the tourguide's probe to his own port, just under the brim of his helmet. "You'll route through me," he told MEL. "If anything goes wrong,

I'll pull the plug.'' *And that way I can keep an eye on what you're doing,* he added silently.

''I'm ready,'' MEL said.

Jon plugged MEL into his system, then held Nancy's head steady. He felt bad about forcing her—but then, it wasn't really Nancy he was holding; it was a stranger who had tried to kill him. He was sure Nancy would thank him when she was herself again.

''All right. Here we go. . . .'' Jon plugged into Nancy's system.

Blackness.

Then a full moon blinked into existence in the center of his vision. The words LUNATIX INCORPORATED—PERSONA SOFTWARE SPECIALISTS were spelled out across the surface by giant letter-shaped black monoliths. ''Copyright field,'' MEL's voice said in his ear. ''We'll be past it in a second. There.''

The moon disappeared. A wall of books took its place, one that appeared to stretch to infinity in all directions. ''Interesting iconography,'' MEL commented. ''Programmer must have been a history buff.''

''Let's get down to business,'' Jon said. Artificial spaces usually made him uneasy—they reminded him of the prison he carried around in his own head.

''Right.'' One of the books glowed blue, and then Jon was standing in the middle of No Name Street.

Except it wasn't No Name Street—it wasn't even Boomtown, not quite. The buildings were older, and they all looked to be made of real wood. The street was dirt clear through, not dirt laid over the surface of a platform car. And there was no one in sight.

''It's an overlay program,'' MEL said. ''This is how Nancy sees Boomtown now.''

''Where are the people?''

''Here.'' A mangy-looking man wearing dusty jeans, a denim shirt and a black, wide-brimmed hat appeared in the street. He stared dead ahead, still as a rock. Glowing blue

letters hovered in the air above him, reading BOOMTOWN
RESIDENT, SAMPLE 7(B). "I just picked one at random,"
MEL said. "There's about fifty variations, enough to mix
and match for the whole town. Nice touch, really—adds
verisimilitude. This is just for people Nancy sees in the
street, though; there are more specific files for people she
interacts with on a regular basis."

"So she sees people the way the program wants her to."

"And acts the way it wants, too," MEL said. "I've
found some very interesting subroutines in the directory.
Look." The street vanished, replaced by a three-
dimensional maze of interconnecting colored lines. Jon felt
as if he'd stumbled into the middle of a thicket made of
neon. There were two objects enmeshed within the maze,
one a featureless gray cube he assumed was MEL, the other
a silhouette of a woman. From the box came MEL's voice,
saying, "Here." One of the lines connected to the box
glowed bright green, as did a series of lines branching off
from it.

Jon knew how to read a circuit diagram. He studied the
pattern, saw that it was actually a complex set of behavior
subroutines linked together. "This is way more sophisticated than the rest of this program," he said to MEL. "And
it doesn't look like it was part of the original package.
Someone's been tinkering."

"I agree. And one of the character files has been tampered with, too. You're not going to like this, Jon."

"Show me," Jon said darkly. He could still feel Nancy's
body, tense with frustration, under one arm.

The maze vanished. Jon found himself looking into a
mirror, a funhouse mirror, one that warped his reflection in
a way that wasn't fun at all. He saw himself through
Nancy's eyes.

He looked to be even taller than eight feet, but hunched
over like a cripple. His arms and legs looked scrawny but
his hands and feet were huge, his feet bare, with long,
cracked yellow nails on his fingers and toes. His face was

a horror; one eye was dead white, the other bloodshot, while any of his teeth that weren't blackly rotten were filed to points. A puckered scar ran from his right temple to the left of his chin, crossing the festering hole where his nose should have been. The figure grinned at him, managing to suggest both idiocy and menace at the same time.

"There's a behavior subroutine attached to this file, too," MEL said. "Looks like it's already been activated."

"What? What kind of subroutine?" Jon asked, swallowing.

"It's titled *Search and Destroy.*"

The monster in front of Jon giggled.

CHAPTER 10

"It would appear," MEL said, "that Nancy knows you better than I thought."

"Ha ha," Jon said sourly. "Just what the hell is going on here, MEL?"

"Well, you were right about Nancy's cuecard being tampered with, for one thing. You wouldn't believe how much extra memory's been added, either." The neon maze vanished and Jon was back on Nancy's version of No Name Street. "It looks like Hone isn't the only one you have to worry about—"

Static suddenly roared in Jon's ears. His field of vision flickered as if the sun had started to strobe, and MEL's voice cut off in mid-sentence.

Jon's entire body went numb.

Then everything came back into sharp focus, all at once. The sun glared overhead, bright and steady. He could hear the wind gusting between the buildings, smell the dust in the air—

His body, all his senses, told him the impossible.

He wasn't holding Nancy; he wasn't hunkered down in a jail cell. He was standing in the middle of Boomtown's only street, just him and a few lonely tumbleweeds.

"MEL?" he called out—and heard his voice echo off the wooden storefronts. He went to rub his forehead and almost scared himself witless with his own hand: it had become the same misshapen claw Nancy was programmed to see. He looked down at himself with growing horror as the truth of it sank in: he had *become* the thing that Nancy saw.

And MEL was gone.

A trap. He cursed himself for a blind, trusting fool, a fool who had beat one prison only to blunder right into another. No wonder MEL had been so eager to help.

He looked around, wondering how big his cage was. Town limits, maybe? Only one way to find out. He started walking, headed for what would have been Cabooseville. His feet scuffed up dust as he strode along.

He hadn't gone half a block before he heard bootsteps behind him, thumping on the wooden sidewalk that bordered the street. He spun around.

Not twenty feet away, Hone stared into his eyes.

Jon froze. *This isn't real,* he told himself. *It's just a simulation.* His heart refused to listen and tried to hammer its way out of his chest instead. The rest of his gut felt like it was going to follow.

Hone was dressed all in black: long black coat, black boots, black vest and black string tie. Wide-brimmed hat the color of midnight. Only his shirt was white, so white it almost glowed. His face held less emotion than a boulder.

"Hello, Jon." His voice as blank as his face.

Jon's reply was barely more than a whisper. "Go to hell."

"Good-bye, Jon." Hone's hand was suddenly full of gun. He fired.

It was like a nightmare replay of Nancy's shooting, except this time Jon couldn't ignore the bullets. The first one grazed his temple, driving a bolt of pain through his head. He staggered back, feeling warm blood spill down his face. The next three slammed into his chest, white-hot spikes of pain that forced the air from his lungs.

Bullets shattered his kneecaps, ruptured his groin, tore through his throat before he fell. He hadn't felt such pain since the day he'd been reborn as a cyborg.

The shots ended as abruptly as they'd begun. Jon's agony didn't let him do much more than writhe and pray for the pain to stop. When it did, with the suddenness of a thrown switch, it took Jon a full minute to collect himself enough to raise his head. Hone was gone.

Jon pulled himself to his feet. This was a simulation, but it was one that could kill him. His wounds had miraculously disappeared, but the suffering they'd fed to his pain receptors was still fresh in his mind. Enough of that and his nervous system would fry like a bug on a hot plate.

He looked up and down the street. Deserted, just like before. After all, why should MEL waste memory populating a prison—in fact, why should MEL bother with a simulation of Boomtown at all?

Jon grimaced and shook his head. None of this made much sense. If MEL was responsible, it would have been easier for the AI to duplicate the same stone walls that had trapped Jon before, or to just use a featureless gray cube with Jon stuck inside. Why a whole town—and why have Hone appear and shoot him? That seemed more than a little sadistic to Jon, and he couldn't bring himself to believe that MEL was capable of such a thing. Deviousness, yes—out-and-out meanness, no.

The wind blew a piece of paper into Jon's face. He grabbed it away, then realized what it was.

A wanted poster. A black-and-white photo of himself with WANTED DEAD OR ALIVE beneath it. The words OR ALIVE had been crossed out.

He crumpled the paper up and dropped it. Obviously, someone had gone to great lengths to set up this game, and had already made clear what would happen if Jon refused to play. He could hurt now or he could hurt later.

A door banged in the wind, making him jump. He glared in its direction, then noticed the sign hanging above it: THE BLUE CAT.

Okay, he thought. *Might as well check it out. Nowhere to run to and I doubt if I can hide. Let's get this over with.*

He strode across the street and up to the door, which was wide open. He took a long, deep breath and stepped inside.

The bar wasn't empty. It was full of the dead.

A hundred rotting skulls turned to stare at him with worm-eaten eyes. Every table had four or five corpses sitting at it; they lined the bar, too. The room stank of decay.

The door banged shut behind him.

They can't hurt me. They can't hurt me, he thought. He knew it wasn't true. All his strength was useless here; this was an arena of the mind, of the soul. He knew without being told who these zombies were and what they represented. They were here to judge him.

"Hello again," Hone said. Jon looked around wildly, then spotted him at the bar. He leaned against it casually, a glass of whiskey in one hand. "I've been talking to a few old friends of yours. It was their idea to throw you a little party."

"Whoever you are, I'm not impressed," Jon said. "This kind of spookshow is for children."

"You're right, Jon. Take a look around."

Then he saw them. The skeleton of a child clutched in its dead mother's arms. A pair of corpses no more than three feet tall, holding hands. A one-armed boy with the tight, desiccated skin of a mummy clutching a ragged stuffed toy. The children of the dead.

"Don't you want to say something to them, Jon? After all, if it wasn't for you, they wouldn't be here."

And, one by one, the dead began to rise from their seats.

It was more than he could take. He turned, ripped open the door and ran, not caring where. It wasn't just fear that drove him—fear was something Jon had faced and beaten before. No, it was worse than that.

He couldn't fight them. It was that simple. He would let those corpses tear him apart before he could bring himself to raise a fist against them. It made no difference that they were only electronic ghosts, designed to horrify; he knew in his heart what they really represented.

Justice—and judgment. *He couldn't kill them again.*

He ran down the street, expecting to feel bony hands on his neck any second. *Got to find some cover.* He cut right, ducked into an open doorway and found himself in the casino. It looked much the same as the real one, with a few rustic touches: gas lamps on the walls, sawdust on the floor, different paintings on the walls. There used to be a mountainscape over the bar, with one of Pellay's sunsets turning clouds around the peaks a glowing orange-red. Now a portrait hung there, a voluptuous nude reclining on a divan in the classic pose. Something about the picture struck Jon as odd; it took him a second to figure it out. Her hair was styled longer, falling in dark ringlets around her shoulders, but it was still Nancy. All she wore was a smile, and a sexy smile it was.

No zombies had staggered through the doorway yet. *Maybe they can't,* Jon thought. *Might be they're restricted to one part of the simulation. Which means there are probably all kinds of other nasty traps scattered around town, and I'll bet Hone pops up to prod me along if I stay in one spot too long.* Jon studied the portrait while he thought. He couldn't imagine Nancy posing for such a thing, but then he didn't think Nancy was the one who wrote this program. So who did?

From looking at the painting, he'd bet the programmer was male. The nude was just too damn lascivious; the programmer had had more on his mind than composition when he'd created the image. The skin was honey-gold instead of Nancy's usual dusty tan, the breasts were much larger and ignored gravity altogether; the sinuous, taut curves of her long legs reminded Jon of an archer's strung bow. The nipples were such a fleshy pink they'd make a whore blush.

Not that Jon had any idea what color Nancy's nipples really were, or even what shape her legs were in. Every time he'd ever seen her she'd been dressed from head to toe in denim and leather—but even so, he could see the portrait had more curves than Nancy ever would.

None of which, Jon had to admit, ruled out the possibility of a female programmer with the same intentions as a man—so he was back where he started. Who was the programmer?

Someone who hated him. Someone who knew about his past. Someone very, very good with software.

MEL fit the last two-thirds of the description, but hate? What for? No, it had to be someone looking for revenge—somebody who had a son or daughter, parent or best friend buried in the mass grave of a city Jon had razed. Maybe MEL was working for them—or maybe not; Jon had to admit it was possible the AI was innocent, and had just managed to avoid stumbling into the trap with him. His gut instinct, though, told him MEL was hiding something.

Well, Jon Hundred knew a thing or two about programming himself. And he had beaten tougher prisons. It was time to take the offensive—and for that he needed help.

Nancy was the key. This was her program, and her real persona had to be here somewhere. If Jon could reach her, he might have an ally.

Or, of course, she might try to blow his head off.

He closed his eyes and concentrated, trying to feel the pattern under the illusion. Years of being a cyborg had given him an affinity to the interface between flesh and metal; he could feel it now, a subliminal hum at the base of everything. He cast out blindly, groping for the feeling of connection that would tell him he'd accessed a subroutine. It was like trying to fit a plug into an electrical socket in the dark; after a minute he swore and opened his eyes. He needed something to focus on, some kind of guide.

He looked up at the painting.

Why not?

Instead of closing his eyes he fixed them on the painting. There was a chance the programmer had lifted an original image directly from Nancy's mind, then altered it. If so, there might still be an interface point between the picture and Nancy herself, one that he could open. It was worth trying.

He locked his eyes on the painting's. Concentrated. Reached out with his mind and willed a passageway to open.

He felt something almost immediately, a tentative touch that lasted only a second. A second later, he felt it again. It felt like reaching out as far as he could over the edge of a precipice, blindfolded, only to feel someone else's fingertips brush maddeningly against his own. He strained, trying to find that hand and grab it.

And then, amazingly, he made contact. He felt a connection spring into being, sensed a shift in the program around him.

The eyes on the painting blinked.

Then the entire painting rippled, head to toe, and where the ripples passed they left three-dimensional flesh. Jon wasn't looking at a painting anymore—he was looking at a nude woman, lying on a couch in a recess in the wall. She didn't seem at all surprised by where she was or how she was dressed, and wasted no time in stepping through the frame and onto the bar.

"Nancy, it's me, Jon Hundred," Jon said. "I know I don't look like my usual self, but then, neither do you."

Nancy shook her head and said . . . nothing. Her mouth moved but no sound came out. She looked surprised, closed her eyes and tried again. Still nothing.

"Damn," Jon said. "Must be the program—you got visuals but no audio. Can you at least hear me?"

Nancy nodded, put her hands up like she was trying to make a point—then shrugged. Her nipples were just about level with Jon's eyes, and they jiggled convincingly. Jon tried not to stare. *Figures a detail like that would come through crystal clear and the voice wouldn't. Now I'm sure the programmer's male.*

She jumped down from the bar, bare feet landing with a smack on the floor. She looked around quickly, eyeing the door with evident caution. Jon wondered how much she knew. She might have no memory of what she'd done since her cuecard had been reprogrammed, or she might have been conscious and helpless the whole time, watching herself do things she had no control over. "Nancy, this is all a simulation—" he began, then stopped when she cut him off with an impatient wave of her hand. Okay, she seemed to know what was going on. Question was, did she know anything that would help them—and if so, how was she going to let him know what it was?

At that point their time ran out.

Hone strolled through the door as if he were paying a social call. He smiled at both of them. His hand blurred—

And Nancy beat him to the draw.

She grabbed the round poker table in front of them and overturned it an eyeblink before Hone fired, making an impromptu shield. The simulation wasn't smart enough to tell the difference between a thin layer of wood and high-speed bullets; they thunked into the table like it was six feet thick. Jon decided to follow her lead and grabbed a table of his own.

It was round, too. And it flew much better than a door.

The table caught Hone in the belly, edge on, slamming him into the roulette wheel and scattering gambling chips everywhere. That was about all it did, though—Hone kept his feet, his smile, and his gun, returning fire with deadeye aim. Jon ducked behind the overturned table just in time.

"Now what?" he hissed at Nancy, crouched beside him. She ignored him, instead staring intently at her hands, palms up. Her nails were long and shiny red, Jon saw; pretty, but not much use in a gunfight.

And then they weren't empty anymore.

Jon didn't get much of a chance to stare at the twin pistols she was suddenly holding, because Nancy put them to immediate and lethal use. She blazed away from the cover of the table, nailing Hone with every shot. Each time a bullet hit him his whole body froze and flickered, like a bad video image.

She must have shot him thirty times before he disappeared completely. Jon thanked whatever software gods there were that her guns hadn't paid much attention to little details like reloading.

Nancy didn't wait for Hone to reappear. She leapt up and headed for the door, motioning Jon to follow. Not having any better ideas, he did.

She ran down the street at full speed. Jon loped along behind her, wondering if she was just trying to put distance between them and the casino or if she had a destination in mind. His attention kept wandering, though; he hadn't had a whole lot of opportunities to watch a naked woman sprint down the middle of a street before, and certainly not from only six feet behind her. He watched the shoulder blades in her back shift as she ran, watched the muscles in her long calves bunch, watched the dimples in her buttocks quiver. In the bright sunlight he could see little golden hairs, almost invisible, glint in the small of her back.

And of course, she still had a smoking gun in each hand, which shouldn't have made her any sexier but did. Jon felt as if he'd just downed a sex-and-violence cocktail that was going straight to his head.

She veered left, stopped long enough to kick open a door and ducked inside, with Jon on her heels. He realized where they were right away: the town bank. This one looked a lot less sophisticated than the real Boomtown's, but Nancy seemed to have a reason to be here. She climbed over the counter and headed for the vault.

Boomtown's actual bank didn't have a vault, just an oversize safe; most transactions on Pellay were electronic, though some people still had valuables they preferred locked away. This bank did have a vault, though it wasn't much bigger than a safe. It had enough room for one person to stand inside it comfortably, two if they crowded.

Nancy stepped into the vault. Then she gave Jon the

same smile that had been on her face in the painting, and crooked her finger at him. *Come here, little boy.*

"Now hold on, Nancy. There's no room in there for both of us, and what's the point, any—"

And then he understood, or thought he did, anyway. He shrugged and crowded in after her.

And when she raised her eyebrows and nodded, he reached out and pulled the vault door closed. He heard it lock.

Darkness. It was as black as . . . well, the inside of a safe, and safe was hopefully what they were. Smart thinking on Nancy's part, as long as the program wasn't smarter. If they were to bust out of the simulation, they needed to find a weak spot in the program, not a physical exit. They were just as likely to do so from inside a bank vault as from outside the city limits; more so, in fact, since this was such an unlikely spot it might be vulnerable. As far as Jon knew simulations didn't need to breathe, so they shouldn't have to worry about suffocation, and if a wooden table could stop Hone's bullets a steel door should be just as effective.

He heard a soft clink as Nancy put the guns down on a metal shelf. Now he couldn't see or hear her—but his nose was working just fine. She smelled like perfume and clean hair and just a touch of sweat. He could feel the warmth of her body pressed against his; the curve of a hip between his thighs, the jut of a shoulder poking him in the ribs. Jon stood in an awkward, half-crouched position, hunched over her, while she stood sideways, one of her legs between his. When he put out an arm to brace himself, the rubbery nub of her nipple brushed the inside of his forearm. He felt her shift. Two warm hands settled gently on his chest.

Jon didn't know what to think, or say, or do. He knew he should be concentrating on escape, but the funny thing was, he didn't feel like going anywhere at the moment. Just being here in the dark, feeling Nancy's hands on his chest, breathing the smell of her . . . it was all new to him. He must have been with women before he'd been cyborged, but he couldn't remember. He couldn't remember so much as a single kiss. He knew Nancy's intentions were innocent—weren't they?—that they were trapped together by circumstance and not desire, but right now he didn't care. Right now he felt an ache so strange it seemed to fill him and empty him at the same time. He wished to God it would go away, and he didn't think he could stand it if it did.

Or maybe this was all part of the programmer's sadistic plan. Maybe that was why she smelled so good and he felt so light-headed; maybe this was the cruelest twist of all. To let him have a taste of what he once was, let him get as close as possible to something he could never have. What hell could be worse?

He forced those thoughts away, realizing how pointless they were. Escape first, sort through his confusion later.

"Nancy, we got to concentrate together. Try and find an exit. Just close your eyes and reach out with your mind; I'll try and guide you along." Was it his imagination or was it getting warmer?

He shut his eyes. Her presence became even more intense; he could feel something of her essence now, or imagined that he could. He tried to push aside his emotion and focus, suddenly embarrassed that she might be able to tell what he was feeling. That wasn't possible, of course. They were only sharing a cybernetic circuit, not their souls—though Jon, to his mortification, was finding out just how physically detailed this simulation was. If he didn't get himself under control, Nancy was going to start wondering if he had a snake in his pocket.

And then—a green rectangle blinked into existence. It had a line of code superimposed across it like a bar across a door, with the same effect. It looked to Jon like a financial access port—*of course!* he thought. *That's another reason she picked the bank to try for a breakout; most of the players use their cuecards to do their banking. It's a place where the simulation and the real Boomtown have to interface on an electronic level.*

Then Jon heard them. They were muffled by the steel door, but still unmistakable. Bootsteps. He opened his eyes.

"You can't hide," Hone's voice said.

The door unlocked. It started to open.

Jon grabbed the door handle, slammed the door shut again and held it there. "Come on, Nancy, all we need is your account number and we can get out!" he snapped. He closed his eyes, saw that the code on the port was flashing bright green. Nancy must be having trouble with the protocols—or that maybe the memory of her account number was still locked up in another part of her brain.

Something with the approximate pull of a maglev train yanked on the door. It started to open . . . and then Jon grunted and yanked back. The door clanged shut once more.

"Damn it, Nancy, you got to remember! COME ON!"

The tugging on the door settled into a long, steady pull. Jon grit his teeth, braced himself as best he could, and pulled back. If it had been a real steel door, it would have ripped in two; but it wasn't and it didn't. The winner of this tug-of-war wasn't going to be the one with the biggest muscles, either. This was a contest of wills—actually, a contest of Jon's willpower against the programming of a machine. Well, it wasn't the first time.

But this time he was going to lose.

He could feel it. Slowly, bit by bit, the door was opening. He opened his eyes and light stabbed into them, through a crack that kept widening despite his best efforts. He could hardly believe what he saw.

Hone was only using one hand. He had a gun in the other.

"Hello, Jon," Hone said.

Jon did the second-hardest thing he'd ever done in his life. He closed his eyes.

The access port opened.

Jon did the mental equivalent of diving headlong. He hoped that Nancy was doing the same, but had no way of knowing. As he passed through the window, he seemed to feel a presence leap with him, but it was hard to tell.

And then he was back in the neon maze, with a green rectangle just blinking closed behind him and the feel of his own body back. Jon didn't hesitate; he reversed the rest of the way out of the system so fast he made himself dizzy, and found himself staring down at the back of Nancy's neck. It looked awful different without a mass of black ringlets curling down it.

"Jon?" MEL said.

He had no choice. He yanked out Nancy's plug with one quick motion—and slammed a fist down on top of the tour-guide's head. He hit it so hard he not only pounded it flat but cracked the concrete floor of the cell, too.

Sorry, MEL, Jon thought. *But if you're the one that set me up, better safe than not.* "And if not," he muttered, "I'll apologize later. It's not like there's any shortage of those damn tourguides."

"Nancy?" Jon said softly. She lay crumpled on the floor. Jon lifted her head and cradled it in his hand. He'd gotten out of the system so fast he hadn't seen if Nancy had come with him. She was breathing, but unconscious; he wondered if the suddenness of their exit had thrown her into shock—or worse yet, if she was still trapped back there. "Hey! Sheriff!" Jon called. "Get the doc back in here!"

As it turned out, psychological shock was exactly what Doc Pointer diagnosed. "Doesn't look too serious—she should come around in a few hours, maybe more if she slips into normal sleep," he said, peeling the diagnostic stickers off her forehead. "Just let her rest for now." He looked at the smashed tourguide in the corner with one raised eyebrow, but didn't mention it.

"Is she cured?" Jon asked anxiously.

"You'll have to wait and ask her yourself," Doc Pointer said.

Jon grimaced. How could he wait when it felt like he was running out of time?

CHAPTER 11

Dashaway gave birth on the second day, in a rocky crevasse on God's Gravestone. It had been a long time since Hone had a hand in a life's start instead of its end.

Dashaway lay on her belly, her spidery legs drawn close to her body. <i must restructure myself hone—i will be helpless while i do—will you guard me?>

"No one will get past me," Hone said. "No one ever does."

Dashaway didn't reply. Her body was already shifting, retooling itself to perform life's most necessary task. Her legs drew into her body and the steel struts of their bones were rearranged and extruded once more, this time as two long arms that stretched out in front of the Toolie. They bent toward each other at the ends and linked, forming an angular loop.

Then the armor in Dashaway's thorax began to open, giving Hone a first look at what it had hidden. A small, milky-white ball floated in the center of a rosy teardrop of tissue. As Hone watched, the teardrop began to move, forcing its way out of its safe haven and through Dashaway's flesh. A fissure opened in the skin between her two limbs and the teardrop squirted out suddenly, like a seed from a crushed fruit. It landed a foot away from Dashaway's body with an audible plop, in the center of the loop formed by her limbs.

Hone looked up. Had that been something moving, at

the top of those rocks? He waited, but heard nothing else. He looked away.

The teardrop looked more like a balloon now, one that quivered as if it were filled with water. The white ball at its center was developing grooves, fissures that deepened as he watched.

And then there were five, smaller balls of white, slowly moving away from each other inside the balloon. When they were all about the same distance away from each other, the balloon began the same process of splitting apart. This time, the balloon's translucence let him see the cracks travel all the way through; when the cracks met at the center, the balloon fell apart, splitting into four small quivering blobs grouped around a fifth.

The white ball in the center of each new Toolie now split open, and a host of tiny shapes—internal organs, Hone guessed—burst out. It was like seeing a flower bloom underwater. Their sensory clusters, tiny pink globes that looked like clumps of fish eggs, shot toward the surface of the newborns' skin, then forced their way out and into the air.

The newborns didn't make any sound, but then, Toolies never did. They immediately started to roll around inside the enclosure made by their mother's arms.

Hone found out which ones were males real quick. Two of the Toolies reacted differently when they flowed against the fence thrown up by Dashaway—they tried to climb over it. And succeeded.

Hone wasn't sure what to do; he watched Dashaway for her reaction.

<do not stop them hone—they are males and must make their own way—if they were penned together for any length of time they would consume each other>

Hone nodded. One of the young males flowed up to his boot. Hone studied it, wondering what it would do. A second later he found out: it engulfed his foot. He sighed and activated his defenses. The Toolie slid off the field like jelly on oiled glass, and after a few more confused attempts it flowed away from him. The other was already out of sight.

"Will they be all right?"

<do not worry—they are males—they can survive extremes of weather and eat almost anything—in time they will find mates of their own>

"Out here? I doubt it."

<not here—at the mine—did you not wonder how i became pregnant without management knowing?>

Hone frowned, then came as close as he could to a smile. "You know, that never occurred to me. You got a boyfriend from the wrong side of the tracks, Dashaway?"

<the male you freed was not the first to escape—garber and his men were sometimes too drunk to be careful—there is enough game in these mountains to survive if one is smart>

"And obviously one is. You found yourself a clever male."

<clever enough> Dashaway agreed.

Hone sat down on a rock. "So tell me how you and loverboy got together."

<oh it is not very interesting>

"No, really." Hone picked up a pebble and examined it. "I'm dying to know."

<very well—it happened when i was exploring—we are not supposed to leave our quarters when we are off shift but i have always been curious—my mother named me dashaway because i would roam farther away from her than my sisters>

"Well, it certainly is appropriate now." Hone tossed the pebble idly from one hand to the other. "How'd you get out?"

<it is not hard—they do not post guards at night because they think there is nowhere to run—there are few locks a determined insussklik cannot pick—we could tell a male was nearby—his scent called to me—i was the only one brave enough to go to him>

"Weren't you afraid of wild animals?" Hone dropped the pebble, picked up a slightly larger rock, and hefted it experimentally.

<not really—his name was mountainkiller—he was wilder than anything on this planet and had the bones to prove it>

A shadow fell over Dashaway's young.

Hone's arm moved almost too fast to see. There was a sharp *crack!* and then a large, gray-furred shape fell out of the air. It landed in a lifeless sprawl at Hone's feet.

Hone knelt down and inspected it. It was about the size of a Terran cougar, had four legs and no tail. Each of the legs ended in three stubby toes with long, curving claws easily a foot in length projecting from them, and an opposing digit that resembled a miniature hoof. The creature had large, round eyes with orange irises, a short snout, a mouth full of fangs and a hole that went from under its chin to the back of its skull. That was where the rock Hone threw had exited—after breaking the sound barrier.

"It still pays to be careful," Hone said. "This particular animal was about to invite himself to dinner."

<that is a ferraka—mountainkiller used them for snacks—and i think we should accept its gracious invitation to dinner> Dashaway, Hone saw, was busily building herself another limb, with something that glinted wickedly at its end. <or are you not hungry?>

This time, Hone actually grinned.

They made short work of the ferraka; Dashaway carved a few flank steaks for Hone while he made a fire. He didn't need one to stay warm, but he figured Dashaway and her young would. Even this high in the mountains, there was still some plant life—low, scrubby bushes that grew stubbornly out of cracks in the rock, and even the occasional scarlet bloom of an ash poppy. When he had enough fuel, Hone stuck out his forefinger, cocked his thumb and pointed at the kindling. "Bang," he said, and a laser flared from his fingertip. The brush burst into flames.

He didn't bother cooking the steaks.

It was interesting to watch Dashaway feed her young. She carved each of them a chunk of ferraka flesh, complete with skin and fur, and tossed the chunks to the ground beside her children. The baby Toolies flowed over their dinner, and in a matter of seconds the meat began to dissolve inside them. One thing seemed odd, though.

"So," Hone said. "How come no bones?"

<i will give them small bones to begin with—when they are ready—right now bones would just hamper their movement>

"What about *our* movement?"

<do not worry—watch> Dashaway made no visible sign, but her children suddenly swarmed to her. Their flesh touched hers and seemingly bonded to it, until Dashaway looked like she had three fleshy pseudopods attached to her. She inserted short steel rods into each of her new extensions, then used the rods to lift them off the ground. Now she had three new, stubby arms. <you see? i will carry them and we will not be hindered>

"Nice," Hone said. "Modular children. Do they come in any other colors?"

<?>

"Never mind."

Dashaway consumed the rest of the ferraka herself. Hone saw that the ferraka's claws-and-opposing-hoof combination would be ideal for mountain climbing—not to mention doubling as lethal weapons.

They bedded down for the night, after Hone assured Dashaway that his warning systems would remain alert even while he slept. The last thing Hone saw before he drifted off was the silhouette of God's Gravestone, outlined by the orange glow of Pellay's single moon.

He got up at dawn the next day. It was bright but cold, and the wind threw particles of ash into his face like a scorned lover. Dashaway and her brood were huddled as close to the dead fire as they could get, shivering. "Come on," Hone said. "The quicker we get moving the quicker you'll get warm."

They followed the crevasse as far as it ran, then had to scale an almost sheer rock face to get out. Hone took his time, using topographical imaging to find tiny flaws in the rock and then exploiting them. His fingers gripped bulges in the rock where a fly would have had trouble finding purchase.

It took him about fifteen minutes to scale the wall. Dashaway was waiting at the top—she'd passed him halfway up. Her body was now configured in a cross, long and slender with two limbs on either end and two more forming the crosspiece at her middle. Her sensory cluster was at the juncture of the cross, with her implant screen on one side of it; her children were three bumps on the other. The ferraka's claws curved out at the end of each of Dashaway's limbs.

<do you need to rest now?> she flashed.

"No, thank you very much," Hone said sourly. "I think I can manage a few more feet before I expire. I'm not holding you up, am I?"

<a little—but i don't mind>

"I'm so glad," he growled.

They tried to stay as close as they could to the base of the mountain, but the terrain kept forcing them upward. They came across animal droppings more than once that Dashaway identified as ferraka, but didn't see any of the predators themselves.

<hone?> Dashaway signaled. They were resting on a narrow ledge overlooking a thousand-foot drop. <why did you come here?>

"It's like I told you. I have a job to do." Hone stared down the face of the cliff they'd just scaled. He nudged a pebble over the edge and watched it fall.

<what job are you going to do?>

"I can't tell you that."

Dashaway shrugged, with both sets of shoulders. <will you need help?>

Hone gave a hollow laugh. "No, I don't think so. But I appreciate the offer."

<will there be more killing?>

He looked at Dashaway blankly. "Does it matter?"

<it does matter—i do not like being a slave but i would not kill to escape—female insussklik are not like males— we do not kill each other—we kill only food>

"Isn't that considerate. Well, you wouldn't be here now if I hadn't killed those guards—and I didn't notice you complaining then."

<you do not understand—once you killed those guards i had little choice—to fail to escape would lessen the mean- ing of their deaths> Dashaway was waving one of her limbs in the air, clearly agitated. Her children pulsed on her back. <we do not kill because it is wasteful—the individ- ual is no longer functional—skills experience knowledge is lost—death is not repairable—the workings are not—?— they will not—improper! improper!>

Hone studied her for a moment before he spoke. "Dash- away, I did what I did because I had to. That's all I ever do. What I have to."

<you had no choice?>

"Less than you did."

Her screen went blank for a few seconds. Then it flashed: <hone—there is an animal on our world called the var whose fangs are poisoned—some would kill and consume the var and then use its fangs as a weapon—this was dan- gerous—if the poison sacs were not expelled before the digestive process ate through them the poison would kill the user as well>

"What's your point, Dashaway?"

<we have a saying—poison kills twice—be careful even if your choices are limited—i understand what it is like to have no choices—it is another reason i came with you—

maybe there will be more choices on the other side of the mountain>

"I doubt it," Hone muttered.

<i am sorry i had to leave my daughter stonehauler but it is for the best—she is old enough to have a family of her own—she thinks because she is my only daughter she must stay and take care of me—that is no longer true—now she has more choices of her own>

"She could have chosen to come with you," Hone said.

<that is not her way—stonehauler is a good daughter but too conservative—she thinks kadai is good to work for>

"I take it you don't agree."

<vandals! they respect nothing but FUNDS—they are worth less than a dollar>

"Pretty strong language for a mother," Hone said dryly.

<i have never been very religious>

Hone raised an eyebrow, but didn't reply.

They moved on. Dashaway told him that the meal they'd had yesterday was enough to nourish her and her brood for several days. Hone said he didn't have much of an appetite either.

Eventually they reached an alpine meadow, a wide plateau covered with wiry yellow grass and clumps of short, gnarled trees. Something clattered at them from a branch, then flew away on long, gauzy wings.

Hone remembered his dream. "Can you do that, too?" he asked.

<fly? it is rare among us—the muscles needed to shift our bones around are too heavy—our metabolism is too slow—and we cannot stretch our skin thin enough to form effective glider wings—still—there are stories of insussklik who consumed only birds—who fasted until they weighed almost nothing—who practiced imitating wingbeats until they mastered them—it is said they flew away to heaven—to a better place where the males are kind and loving—where many wondrous bones are to be had—bones of every

imaginable size and shape—bones that will never break>
Dashaway waved one of her steel-cored limbs in the air.
<as with all stories truth is linked with lies—perhaps they
flew—but i doubt they landed anyplace better than where
they left>

"Any landing you walk away from is a good one."

<*******************!>

Hone stopped. "What's that mean?"

<laughter—i think maybe you know more about landing
than you do flying>

"Ha ha. The only reason I crashed was because—because . . ."

. <hone?>

Hone frowned and rubbed his forehead. There had been
a very good reason for him to crash, a complex and de-
manding reason, but he couldn't remember what it was.
Originally he was supposed to land at the spaceport, he
knew that much; but something had changed. And whatever
it was, it had made him alter his plans as well. If only he
could remember . . .

<can we stop for a while?—I would like to let my chil-
dren run free>

"All right."

Dashaway stopped and lowered her body to the ground.
She retracted the steel rods that ran through her children's
bodies and they slid off her like ripe fruit off a plate, rolling
onto the yellow grass. They immediately began to roam,
flowing like animated blobs of pink mercury. One of them
surged over a small rock, then stopped and tried to engulf
it. For a second the rock looked like someone had poured
a bucket of pink nail polish over it; then the Toolie realized
it was inedible and withdrew.

"Picked out any names yet?"

<it is too soon for that—i will not name them until they
are older and have developed personalities—right now they
are more like extensions of myself>

"You better keep a close eye on them, then—they might take off on you."

<ha-ha>

Hone stretched out on the ground and stared at the sky. It was a delicate blue, with wispy clouds ash-tinged with orange. He wondered if Jon Hundred was staring up at those same clouds.

He glanced over at Dashaway, who was waving a limb at him. Her screen lit up with a message.

<you asked me about jon hundred before—there is something i forgot to tell you>

He wondered if he was starting to think out loud. "What's that?"

<the contest between mel and jon—many insussklik on pellay have pooled their FUNDS to bet on the outcome— if they win they will have enough FUNDS to buy freedom for every insussklik on the planet>

Hone stared at the Toolie. His fists clenched, then relaxed. In a dead voice he asked, "And who did they bet on?"

<jon hundred—they do not believe mel will help gain their freedom—mel is owned by kadai—jon only works for kadai—he always treats insussklik well or so it is said— while mel oversees us at the mine and at the tunnel>

"That's a thin line to draw, Dashaway," Hone said grimly. "Maybe MEL doesn't like being owned anymore than you do."

<perhaps not—i did not bet with the others—i do not have the same faith in FUNDS that they do—if i did i would not have come with you—they will probably lose and have no FUNDS left at all—i will take my freedom not gamble it away>

Hone looked away then back at the Toolie. "That's the smartest thing you could have done, Dashaway."

<still—i hope jon hundred wins—we would all be free then>

"Yeah," Hone said softly. "I'm all for him, too."

• • •

There was only one thing for Jon to do. He went to work eight hours early.

"Listen up!" he bellowed as he walked into the tunnel. He had every steeldriver's immediate attention. "This contest just got personal. I'm tired of being told we're second best by a battery with an IQ! We're going to show that thing how steeldrivers get the job done!"

A chorus of rowdy cheers and whoops echoed past Jon as he jumped on a manrider and headed deeper inside. He was worried about Nancy, but there wasn't anything he could do about that at the moment—and waiting made him crazy. He had to work off some of his tension or he'd wind up breaking something he shouldn't.

It took him a good half hour to reach the working face—but MEL called him before he was halfway there.

"Hello?" he snapped.

"Jon? I think you owe me an explanation."

"I'm not sure I do," Jon said.

"You destroyed one of my remote extensions for no apparent reason. I'd like to know why."

"Put yourself in my shoes, MEL. You say you want us to be friends, but we're supposed to be competing against each other."

"So? I've come across many references to friends competing against each other. And when I was young, many of my learning exercises pitted me against other AIs—but it never prevented me from making friends with them."

That stopped Jon for a second. He'd never thought of AIs as growing up or having friends—he'd just assumed they were created whole and independent. He pushed the thought away irritably—it didn't mean MEL was trustworthy, or even telling the truth. "It just seems awfully convenient that you were so eager to help me get into Nancy's head, and once I was in I couldn't get out. A little *too* damn convenient."

"Jon, you're way off the mark. I was trying to help,

honestly. It surprised me as much as you when that trap activated.''

"Then why didn't you do something?''

"I did!'' There was a note of defensiveness in the AI's voice.

"Really? I didn't notice. If it weren't for Nancy's sharp-shooting I'd probably be brain-dead by now.''

"Nancy's sharpshooting? You think Nancy has the skill to create iconic program disrupters at will? Where do you think those guns came from?''

"Well, if you could whip up those guns, why didn't you create a doorway while you were at it? Shouldn't be any problem for a genius like you.'' Jon could feel his frustration and anger start to boil, and he didn't try to hold them back. "Maybe you did and maybe you didn't, but I can't take any more chances on trusting you, MEL. There's too much at stake. Just stay away from me until the tunnel's done—then we can talk.''

"But Jon, you're being unreasonable. You have no hard data to back up your suspicions.''

"Talking like a lawyer won't change how I feel, MEL. I'm sorry, but that's how it's got to be. Sometimes feelings are more important than facts.''

"Of course.'' The AI's voice was cool. "I suppose that's the kind of thing only a real person can understand. We machines don't have feelings, after all.''

MEL cut off the connection.

Even through his anger, Jon felt a pang of guilt. MEL was right—he didn't have any evidence, just suspicions. But what else was he supposed to do?

He fumed for the rest of the trip, and by the time he reached the working face he was ready to chew his way through with his teeth. He jumped off the manrider and barked, "Finnley!''

Finnley was a barrel-chested black man with a permanent five o'clock shadow and a scowl to go with it. He was also foreman on the night shift.

"Yeah?" he said, walking up to Jon.

"Finnley, if I don't bust up some rock here and now I'm liable to go and pick a fight with another mountain. I know you don't need the help, but I'm too mad to sleep and too mean to get drunk. I was hoping you'd let me do a little digging to soothe my nerves."

Finnley looked him up and down, squinted thoughtfully and scratched his stubble. "Well, Jon, I'd hate to turn you loose on anything less than a mountain right now, and even then I'd feel sorry for the mountain." He grinned and slapped Jon on the back. "But since there's no love lost between me and this pile of stone anyway—go get that sorry sumbitch!"

And Jon did. He worked the muck pile, the hardest, most backbreaking part of the blasting cycle, and sped things up for everyone. He told the shoot men to use smaller charges, reducing the breakage and producing bigger chunks of debris; it was faster for Jon to throw around a few big rocks than a bunch of smaller ones. He let the rest of the mucking crew take care of the smaller stuff, and they didn't seem to mind a bit—though he caught more than one staring as he heaved a half-ton boulder into a mucking cart. Some of them had never worked alongside him before, though they all knew who he was. *There's a big difference,* Jon thought, *between hearing stories from your friends and seeing for yourself.*

Just like there was a big difference between the way someone really was and the way you thought they were. Jon wondered what MEL was really like. Did the AI truly value his friendship, or was he being manipulated by a talking machine? All that talk about the two of them being alike might not mean a thing, except that MEL knew how to push Jon's buttons. Hell, from what he heard, even the sex robots down at Truse's bordello could make a man feel wanted—and MEL was a lot more sophisticated than they were.

Goddamn it, he *had* been lonely; that was what made

him angrier than anything. MEL had offered him something he'd almost given up on having: friendship with someone who understood what it was like. What it was like to be—

A machine.

Jon slammed down the boulder he'd been holding so hard it almost broke the mucking cart's axles. "Sorry," he muttered, and kept on working.

A machine.

He'd never admitted that to anyone, ever. He took pride in being a man, pride with a touch of desperation in it. But deep down inside, the hard facts refused to go away. Physically, he was only 20 percent organic. Four-fifths of his being had been forged, not born. If Jon had been the type who lived in his head, it might not have bothered him so much; but Jon was a physical man, a man who liked to solve problems with his hands, a man who savored the heft and balance and texture of things. He still had all those senses, but they weren't his anymore—they were too precise, too sensitive, too efficient. They were sensors, not senses.

Jon remembered the first time he'd heard the hunting cry of a skycat, one of Pellay's predatory birds. He'd only been on the planet a month. It was a high, haunting sound, fading into the distance; he didn't know what it was, and when he asked, no one knew what he was talking about. It wasn't pitched for human ears.

Now, whenever he heard that cry, he pretended he couldn't. He pretended he was like everyone else. But sometimes all he wanted was to talk about that sound with someone else, someone who heard it too. It sounded like the loneliest noise in the world.

He wondered if the Toolies heard it. They had a funny relationship with sound: they heard well enough, but they wouldn't talk. Not couldn't—it would have been an easy thing to add voice chips to the screens they used, but they refused. Jon asked why one time, and still remembered what he was told: <we value silence—sound is like light

or time or weight or cold—it is an unthinking part of the world—something that simply is—we are rational beings—choosing silence sharpens what we hear—in older times it hid us from our enemies—natural sounds we appreciate but unnecessary sounds we find vulgar>

He paused, listening to the creaks and groans of the tunnel itself, always present underneath the clang and grind of machinery. It took some getting used to—newcomers always asked if the sounds were normal. They weren't, actually. They were the sounds a few million tons of rock made trying to move into a suddenly vacant space. Every tunnel made those sounds, and Jon had come to think of them as the mountain's way of complaining. *Bitch all you want,* Jon thought. *It's not going to do you a bit of good.*

He supposed the mountain's noises were the kind of natural sound Toolies appreciated. He'd asked once what they thought of his saxophone playing, and the Toolie he'd been talking to had abruptly changed the subject. No wonder he never saw Toolies down at the Blue Cat.

And now they were counting on him. Counting on him to beat MEL and give them their freedom. He hadn't had much time to think about that, not with all the trouble with Nancy. It had made him feel ashamed at first, for thinking Moneykeeper was trying to bribe him, then proud that the Toolies had so much faith in him.

Now the enormous responsibility of what he'd agreed to do started to sink in. If he lost, every Toolie on Pellay would lose—their money and their chance for freedom. They'd have to start all over again. Jon wasn't sure he could live with that; he had enough on his conscience already.

But then again, he might not have to live with anything. Hone might get to him first.

Too many problems. Too much to think about. Jon tried to push it all out of his head and just concentrate on hauling rock. But certain things kept popping up in his head, no matter how hard he tried to ignore them.

Like the ripple of well-toned muscle under tanned skin.

The warmth of a pair of hands. The smell of clean hair and perfume.

And most of all, the invitation of a crooked finger and a smile. He couldn't get that smile out of his head. It had seemed to convey an offer and a promise at the same time, a mixture of the lewd and the accepting. It bothered him more than he cared to admit.

He wondered about Nancy and Dmitri. He'd never given it much thought before, but Dmitri was also far stronger than anyone else in Boomtown. Strong enough that he could snap Nancy in two—yet they were lovers. Maybe being an artist gave Dmitri a gentler touch, a finer control over his power, or maybe Nancy was even tougher than she seemed. Maybe they were just careful. . . . He stopped and shook his head when he realized he was starting to envision the two of them together in bed.

Except Dmitri's skin wasn't blue.

He worked all the way through the night shift and on into the day. He stopped long enough to eat one enormous meal in the mess hall—even steeldrivers that worked with him regularly were astounded by how much food he put away.

Then it was back to work. The musty smell of wet shotcrete filled his nostrils, the echo of metal on stone rang in his ears. He found the rhythm.

A memory came. The heat of woman's naked body, snuggled against him in bed. Her breasts pressed into his back and one of her legs was thrown over his; her arms were around him and her hands, warm on his chest . . .

He couldn't remember her name, or her face. When he tried, all he saw was Nancy, long dark ringlets falling to her shoulders. She was smiling.

Jon kept working.

When his day finally ended, he rode back to Boomtown with everyone else. He felt pretty good; MEL was still ahead by a few feet—three hundred and forty-seven feet to go to their three fifty-one—but they were closing the gap.

He planned on stopping by the jail and checking on Nancy, then maybe going down to the Cat and blowing some horn. Maybe the Toolies didn't appreciate it, but it was what he needed right now.

He didn't get the chance. AC Jones came running up to him half a block away from the jail, looking more than a little frantic. "Jon, you gotta get over to the Hotel Royale. Someone's gonna die if you don't."

Jon felt his gut get a little tighter and a little colder. "What's going on, AC?"

"It's Dmitri. He came back about an hour ago, he's too drunk to reason with—and he's in a worse mood than you were when you ripped up the streetcleaner. He's over in what's left of the Hotel Royale bar—and the Sheriff says if you don't stop him, he will. Permanently."

Jon shook his head. "Why do I get the feeling that somewhere, somebody's laughing at me?"

He headed for the hotel.

CHAPTER 12

Sheriff Brett stood just outside the Hotel Royale's entrance, two frosted glass doors with fancy designs filigreed into them. They were propped open at the moment, which was fortunate for the deputy who came sailing out of the building about four feet off the ground. He landed at Jon's feet, groaned once and passed out.

Jon frowned and stepped over him. Three other deputies were scattered around in the street, and they all seemed a little worse for wear; Doc Pointer was tending to one who looked like he'd had a violent disagreement with a brick wall. A crowd of about fifty people, including the staff of the hotel, stood a safer distance away.

"Jon, I'm glad you're here," Brett said. He didn't look glad, though; he looked more like he'd just bit into something sour but wasn't about to admit it. He was holding a large-bore rifle with both hands. "Dmitri's been on a bender ever since he got back from the city—he talked to Nancy and something she said set him off. He's too much for my deputies—not only is he strong as a bull and twice as mean, he's got a hobby listed in his employee file that doubles how much trouble he can cause."

"What hobby?"

"A martial art called Mikudaki, from his home planet. Near as I can figure, it's designed to help you win fights against steamrollers, rogue elephants and earthquakes. Naturally, I thought of you.''

''Just what I needed to take my mind off my own trivial problems,'' Jon muttered. ''Can't you just tranquilize him?'' He gestured at the rifle.

''Would if I could. But his damn file says he's allergic!'' Brett threw the rifle down in disgust. ''And I can't taser him cause of his cuecard—the charge might screw up his implant and make him go completely berserk, or worse yet give him an excuse to sue me later. I'm seriously thinking of just shooting the sonofabitch.''

''Let me talk to him first,'' Jon said wearily. ''Maybe I can get him to listen to reason. What did Nancy say to get him so riled up, anyway?''

''Damned if I know. Why don't you go ask him?''

Jon considered telling the Sheriff what he could do with his attitude, his gun, and all his deputies—then sighed and walked through the hotel's entrance. After all, he'd gone on the same kind of rampage two days ago, and fair was fair. Funny how things came back to haunt you . . .

Jon stopped dead. He looked around slowly, taking the whole room in, then let out a long, low whistle. Whatever else Dmitri was, he was thorough.

The first thing he noticed was the grand piano. It was in the decorative pool in the foyer. Though it was hard to tell where the foyer ended and the saloon began, since most of the dividing wall had been removed—probably by the sudden exit of the piano. The front desk of the hotel was nothing but a pile of kindling and shattered marble.

Jon made his way closer and entered the saloon itself. Broken glass crunched under his feet. Dmitri was sitting on one of the reinforced steel stools designed for Jon; it was the only piece of furniture left in the room to sit on. He had a bottle of rum in one hand and a scowl on his face.

''You trying to beat my record, Dmitri?'' Jon asked.

Dmitri fixed a pair of bloodshot eyes on him. ''Jon. I

wondaired when they send you.'' The alcohol had thick-
ened his accent. ''I beat everyone else.''

''I don't want to fight, Dmitri, just talk. What's got you
so upset?''

''Ha! Don't pretend. You know.'' He took a swig from
the bottle while keeping his eyes on Jon.

''I know you went to the city. Did you find the person
who messed with Nancy's cuecard?''

''No. She lied. She had no wairk done on her in city. I
checked.'' He glared at Jon. ''Must have had it done here.
Maybe you know who did it, hey?''

''I wish I did, Dmitri. When I linked up to Nancy's cuecard, I found a trap waiting for me—''

''You!'' Dmitri said, standing up. The top of his head
was about level with the bottom of Jon's chest. He seemed
pretty steady on his feet, despite his thick voice. ''You wair
in Nancy's head! She tried to shoot you! You made her
change!''

''I was trying to help her, Dmitri—''

The blacksmith took two quick steps toward Jon. Jon
tensed, but Dmitri stopped and gave him a crooked smile.
''Don't wairry, Jon. I won't hit you,'' he said.

And lobbed the rum at Jon's face.

Jon instinctively threw up his hands to block the bottle—
just what Dmitri wanted. He drew his right leg up and
jumped with the left. The instant before he slammed into
Jon, Dmitri's cocked leg shot out—into Jon's belly.

It felt like being mule-kicked by a hydraulic ram. Jon
found himself flying backward and doubled-over the length
of the room and out into the foyer. He landed in the foyer
pool on what was left of the grand piano with a splash, a
crash, and a death knell of mangled chords. Jon barely had
time to pick himself up before Dmitri charged him, swinging wildly at his head.

Jon dodged back, thinking, *Hell, he can't even reach my
chin.* Dmitri's swing carried him all the way around—and

his opposite leg swung around with him, nailing Jon's knee with a spinning back kick.

Suddenly Jon only had one good leg.

Unbalanced, he fell, his right leg numb from the knee down. Dmitri's next kick went for Jon's head.

It missed by a hair—not that Jon had any. Jon jerked his head out of the way and made a grab for Dmitri's ankle at the same time. The heavy-worlder's limb was so thick even Jon's hand could barely wrap around it, but he managed.

Jon yanked, knocking Dmitri off his feet, then started to stand up. He intended to dangle the blacksmith upside down until he cooled off, but Dmitri had other ideas. He kicked savagely at Jon's hand with his free leg, and Jon lost his hold as three of the fingers on his hand went dead.

They wound up getting to their feet at the same time, Jon in a wary crouch, Dmitri in a martial stance.

"Listen to me, you drunken leadhead! I didn't do anything to Nancy!"

"You lie! She told me!"

"She told you what?"

Dmitri's eyes narrowed. "She told me she doesn' love me anymore," he hissed. "An' she said you would know why."

What? Jon thought. *But that sounds like*—"No," he said. "That can't be."

"YOU TOOK HER AWAY FROM ME!" Dmitri howled—and lunged for Jon's throat.

Jon backhanded him in midair. It was a slap meant more than anything to knock some sense into him, but it knocked him ass-over-teakettle backward, into a tumbling somersault that took him through the front doors of the hotel and out into the street.

Jon limped out after him, more confused than angry. Nancy said *he* was the reason she didn't love Dmitri? He saw her smile in his mind's eye again, and that smile seemed full of invitation. Could it be . . . ?

"Stand back!" Brett hollered at his deputies. "Let Jon handle him!"

Dmitri was already up, bleeding from a cut on his forehead; his heart, used to five times Pellay's gravity, pumped blood out of the wound in a pulsing arc of red.

"I kill you, Jon," Dmitri growled.

"Let's get this over with, then," Jon replied evenly.

Dmitri came at him. Jon let him. Dmitri feinted, lunged, threw a punch at Jon's gut. Jon sidestepped, forgot about his bad leg and almost fell. The punch glanced off his ribs. He grabbed for Dimitri and missed, the blacksmith spinning out of his grasp. Dmitri finished the spin by throwing his full weight behind an elbow smash to the thigh of Jon's good leg—it went as numb as the other one and Jon fell to his knees.

They were almost eye to eye now. Dmitri snapped fists like anvils into Jon's face, once, twice, three times. Jon's head felt like it was full of static, an idiot buzzing that wavered up and down. Dmitri's strikes were too fast to block and Jon couldn't dodge while he was on his knees.

His vision was starting to stutter between color and black-and-white. He reached out, desperately, and caught hold of Dmitri's belt. Dmitri chopped at his arm, but the angle was bad.

Jon did the only thing he could think of. Off-balance, on his knees and using only one arm, he blindly *flung* Dmitri away from him as hard as he could.

Away . . . and straight up.

"Jesus on a goddamn trampoline," one of the deputies whispered. Jon looked up into a sky gone gray, and saw Dmitri still rising, forty, fifty, sixty feet in the air. Blood trailed behind him like a kite's ragged tail. The heavy-worlder didn't start to scream until he reached the top of his arc and saw how far he had to fall.

A loud hissing joined the buzzing in Jon's head. He felt the ground lurch suddenly beneath him. He wondered if he was going to pass out. He wondered if he'd just killed a man.

Dmitri hit the street like a meteor, rocking the entire platform car Downtown rested on and knocking half the crowd off their feet. He bounced, once, and then didn't move at all.

Doc Pointer was there before the dust had settled. Jon tried to get to his feet and failed. "How is he?" he called out hoarsely.

The doc didn't answer. *Oh no,* Jon thought blackly. *Oh no, not again.*

The doc looked up at Jon. "He's still alive," he said, "though I don't know if that'll last. We've got to get him to the clinic, quick."

The Sheriff got his deputies to fetch an oak tabletop from another hotel—between four of them they managed to wrestle Dmitri onto it as a makeshift stretcher. By the time they carted him off he was already semiconscious and moaning.

Jon finally stopped trying to get up and just lay down in the street. Everywhere Dmitri had hit him he felt numb—all of one leg and half of the other, his right arm from the elbow down, most of his face. His vision was still stuck in black-and-white and there were bees in his brain.

"Jon! Are you all right?" It was AC Jones, pushing his way through the crowd of tourists. There were steeldrivers in the crowd too, but none of them rushed forward. Jon could see the uncertainty in their eyes—they couldn't believe Jon would need help, ever. *And what could they do if I did?*

"I'm all right," Jon said. "Just that a few of my parts . . . don't seem to know that."

"Where'd the doc go?" AC asked, getting down on his haunches. "He better take a look at you."

"I think I need a mechanic more than I do a doctor—damn!" he said as he tried to move his leg again. This time it jerked erratically back and forth, making little whining noises all the while.

"Could be worse, I guess," Jon said, trying to grin. His mouth felt like it belonged to someone else. "Somebody could have been killed."

A tremor ran through his whole body, like the aftershock of an explosion. With it came a feeling that was half-memory, half-precognition; and Jon suddenly knew death was coming. It wasn't here yet—but it was coming, barreling toward Boomtown as fast as AC's maglev did every day. And here he was, lying on the tracks, unable to move.

Which made it the perfect time for MEL to show up.

The tourguide trundled up to Jon and AC, peering at them with its single lens. Even before it spoke, Jon knew it was MEL running the thing and not a program.

"Aha! At last my master plan comes to fruition! Behold the mighty Jon Hundred—no more! Hahahahahahahaha!" it cackled. If the tourguide had hands, Jon thought, it would be rubbing them together.

"Very funny, MEL. You just here to gloat?" Jon asked.

"Well, if I were the Creature of Evil you seem to think I am, I would. There's no way you can work like this—all I have to do is keep tunneling and I'll beat you fair and square. Right?"

"I'm not finished yet," Jon said flatly. Part of him didn't believe it.

The tourguide rolled closer. "No, you're not, and neither am I. There's no one on Pellay that knows a tenth of what I do about cybernetics—except you, just barely—and you're in no shape for a do-it-yourself project. Which means I'm going to have to fix you."

"What? You think I'm going to let you—"

"Let me what?" MEL interrupted. "Reprogram your brain? Sabotage your workings? I'll do you a favor right now, Jon: I'll let you think about what I'm offering rather than point out how stupid you're being. You've got thirty seconds."

"Jon doesn't need your help!" AC snapped. "I'll go get Truse—she can fix him up just fine!"

Jon glared at the tourguide, but it just sat there and waited. And it wasn't like he could get up and stomp away.

So he thought about it. It wasn't exactly surgery MEL was proposing; for one thing, Jon could stay conscious the whole time, even supervise. He doubted if MEL could pull anything sneaky with him watching, and why would the AI even bother? For Jon to lose the race, all MEL had to do was nothing. Even if Truse could help Jon to cobble together his own repairs, her specialty was robotics, which were a world away from cybernetics; the patch job would probably blow apart under stress, and MEL would walk away free.

Unless MEL had something really devious planned. Who knew how many layers of plans a thinking machine could have? There was just something about MEL Jon didn't trust. . . .

And then he realized what that something was.

He didn't trust MEL because he was afraid of MEL's power. *We're always afraid of power,* Jon thought, *because if that power turns against us, there's little we can do.*

Except, sometimes, to make peace with that power.

He thought about specially built steel chairs all around Boomtown.

Except, sometimes, to trust.

He thought about all the steeldrivers who'd drunk with him. Thought about the looks on their faces when he'd told them, *I can get those men out alive.*

Trust.

No one condemned him for being inhumanly strong. How could he condemn MEL for being inhumanly smart?

He stared at the unblinking eye of the tourguide. "I'm sorry," he said levelly. "You haven't done anything but offer me your friendship. I hope it's not too late to accept. And I'd be grateful for any repairs you could help me make."

"Jon, you can't be serious!" AC said. "You can't trust this, this . . ."

". . . machine?" Jon said quietly.

AC stared at him for a second, then shook his head angrily and said, "Fine. Be an idiot." He turned and strode away.

"Well," MEL said, "maybe you actually have a few functioning brain cells left. We're going to need some help to move you—and here it comes now."

Four Toolies lumbered up, orehaulers with low-slung, bowl-like bodies and thick, stumpy legs. "I called them a few minutes ago when I saw how the fight was going," MEL said. The tourguide's head swiveled toward the crowd and MEL's amplified voice boomed out, "I NEED THE HELP OF FOUR STRONG MEN!"

It actually took six, but they were able to wrestle Jon onto the impromptu vehicle formed by the four orehaulers. "Where we headed?" Jon asked.

"Home," MEL said.

And that was where they took him, back to Jon's one-room residence. It took almost twenty minutes to travel the nine platform cars from Cabooseville to the workers' quarters, and it seemed even longer. Every person they passed, steeldriver or player, tourist or Toolie, stopped and stared. Some came up and asked quietly what had happened; Jon told them in as few words as he could. He didn't feel much like talking.

They always asked quietly, respectfully, with their eyes full of concern. As if they were at a funeral.

"You all right, Jon?" MEL asked at one point.

"I'm not getting any worse, if that's what you mean."

"Good. Actually, I was more worried that you'd kill Dmitri than he would hurt you. I don't think jail would agree with you."

"I hope he's all right. Damn! I should have been more careful!"

"You were busy trying to survive. Fortunately, I was able to give both of you a little assistance."

Jon shook his head, thinking he'd heard MEL wrong—and then wished he'd kept it still. Everything suddenly felt like it was on a forty-five-degree angle. "What do you mean, assistance?"

"When you launched Dmitri, I pumped up the suspension on the platform car to full, then opened the air valves all the way the instant before he hit. It helped cushion his fall, may have even saved his life."

Jon remembered the hissing noise and the way the ground had lurched. "You did that? You kept me from taking another life?"

"Probably."

"MEL," Jon said, "I don't know what to . . . thank you. I don't know what I would have done if I'd killed him."

"You'd have blamed yourself, of course, even though it was self-defense. And since I don't think I could stand anymore self-recrimination from Saint Jon the Martyr, it was strictly in my own best interests. Now save the rest of your gratitude until I've repaired you."

Jon shut up—but he couldn't help smiling.

With the help of the Toolies, they got him inside and onto his bed. Then the Toolies left, leaving Jon and MEL alone. The tourguide rolled up beside Jon's bed and a panel in its base opened. An articulated arm extended itself from the opening, tipped with a multipurpose waldo.

"What, no whiskey?" Jon said.

"You won't need anesthesia—you've got overload breakers at every nerve bundle, right? You're probably numb already."

"Well, yeah. But that doesn't mean I couldn't use a good stiff drink right about now."

The waldo, Jon saw, had a tiny videocam mounted on it, as well as a laser welder and a host of small tools. The arm positioned itself over his thigh and smoothly cut away the material of his pants.

"Try not to move, okay?"

"Really? I figured now was a good time to practice my two-step."

"One wrong move and it'll be a one-step. Better let me lead."

"Okay," Jon said. "Just don't step on my toes."

The laser cut smoothly where it was supposed to, at the hidden seams of Jon's artificial skin. He supposed MEL had located them using ultraviolet, the same way Jon himself had. The waldo used tiny pincers to grab a corner of the pseudoskin and peel back a rectangle-shaped patch.

Underneath lay a tangle of nerve filaments, blood vessels, and machinery. Jon's bones and muscle were alloy and plastic, but the nerves that controlled them were living tissue and needed oxygenated blood to support them.

"Looks like Dmitri actually managed to damage a few of your interface points," MEL said. "If you didn't have the overload breakers you'd be in a lot of pain right now."

"Can you fix them?"

"It depends on how badly the organics are damaged. It doesn't look too bad, so far."

"You're pretty well-equipped for tourist bait."

"Before they were tourguides they were exploratory drones. They had to be self-reliant, so they all came with their own repair kits."

Jon's leg twitched once, twice, then came alive with a dull ache. He inhaled sharply, more from surprise than pain. "Whoa!"

"Sorry—there's going to be some low-level pain for a while, until the organics heal. You should have full use of the limb, though."

Jon tried moving it experimentally, found that it worked fine. Even the pain was somehow welcome: he hadn't felt its like since he broke his leg as a teenager—

"I *remember* that," he said, a grin breaking out on his face. "By damn, I do!

"Hold still, I'm not finished—you remember what?"

"Breaking my leg as a teenager. Some kind of glider accident . . ." He rubbed his forehead, then grimaced. "That's all. But it's more than I knew a minute ago."

"It must be terrible to have suffered that kind of amputation," MEL said.

"Amputation? No, it was only broken. The amputation part didn't come until later." He watched a curl of gray smoke rise from inside his leg as MEL focused the laser welder.

"Not your leg, your memory. Horrible. A friend of mine in school caught an anarchy virus—it wiped his personality templates completely. He was restructured, of course, but he was never quite the same."

Friend? School? A whole geology of assumptions about MEL suddenly crumbled and fell away, leaving him with a brand-new landscape to consider. Jon realized he really didn't know that much about AIs—but here was a chance to learn.

"How'd you wind up on this planet, anyway?" Jon asked.

"Kadai didn't give me much of a choice. I could have gotten a position closer to the galactic hub, but the more developed the world, the more expensive the dataspace. I opted for a frontier job—higher pay, lower overhead."

"Yeah, not much to spend it on out here—specially if you don't like to party."

MEL laughed. "Oh, I like to party, all right—there's just no one to party *with*. Back on Earth I had a very active social life—I corresponded with over a thousand people on-planet and off, belonged to seven different organizations, was even president of an AI discussion group for two terms."

"Discussion group, huh? What did you discuss?"

"Poetry math. We called ourselves the High-Q Society, spent our time trying to devise mathematical formulae that could be applied to word and sentence structures: 'If x equals (Quoth) and y equals (the Raven), then x plus y

equals (Nevermore) to the power of z verses.' Or we'd turn it around, try to turn equations into works of art. I had a friend named Samuel who used to compose fractal poems— visually quite stunning.''

''Sounds interesting,'' Jon said noncommittally, then surprised himself by adding, ''I'd like to see one, sometime.''

''Really? Well, I did bring them with me. Perhaps I could download them to you later.'' This in the same noncommittal voice Jon had used.

''Sure. I'd like that.''

Jon watched MEL work for a minute, felt his leg twitch a few times as MEL tested connections. *Poetry. Who would have guessed?*

''Okay, Jon, try that out before I seal it back up.''

Jon drew his leg up, bent it at the knee a few times. ''Seems fine.'' It was strange, looking into the guts of his own wiring. That was steel, not bone, in there; those were micromotors, not muscles. The odd part was that it didn't make him uncomfortable—more than anything, he felt a touch of pride. It looked like MEL had done a professional job of fixing him up.

He straightened his leg and told MEL to reseal it. When that was done, he said, ''Hang on a second. Since we're going to be here a while, we may as well listen to a little music.'' He reached over to his bedside stereo, picked out a disc with two of his fingers that weren't numb, and managed to get it into the proper slot. ''Hope you don't mind the blues.''

Amos Garrett's version of ''Sleepwalk'' drifted out, dreamy as smoke. ''Nice,'' MEL said. Jon stretched out again, closed his eyes. He could hear MEL go to work on his other leg.

''Yeah,'' Jon agreed. ''Real nice . . .''

It was one of the few pieces of music he had that had good memories attached to it. He'd picked it up on a planet called Buraqua on a layover between jobs. Low rolling hills covered with golden grass surrounded the spaceport, and he'd taken a walk in them while listening to his new find. It was late autumn, and an ordinary man would have shivered with the cold. Jon had lain down on a grassy hill and closed his eyes, and didn't open them until something tickled his face. The first snow of the season was falling on his skin, soft as moonlight. He lay there, staring up into the flakes drifting slowly down until the hills had gone from gold to ivory.

MEL didn't say another word until the song was over, which Jon appreciated. MEL was good at talking, that was a fact; but listening was something a little harder to do—and when you came right down to it, Jon was the one who hadn't been using his ears lately. But that was going to change.

"I don't suppose you have any Otis Redding . . . ?"

Jon grinned. "As a matter of fact, I do."

It took MEL another three hours to finish patching Jon up, but it didn't seem like it took much time at all.

Hone opened his eyes. Below him was a vast, fuzzy carpet of white, pierced by rocky crags that rose up like islands in a cotton ocean. He was sitting cross-legged on a plateau of volcanic stone, breathing air too thin to sustain most men. Dashaway was sleeping with her young on another ledge a hundred feet below.

Hone had climbed up here for the solitude, not wanting even the Toolies' nonverbal company. He had sat, ignoring the cold, thin wind, and stared at the slowly roiling whiteness below him.

And then he had closed his eyes, and gone to work.

His consciousness had reached out along cybernetic pathways, beaming down the mountain and into another system. A system he explored carefully, deftly, precisely. When he found what he had been searching for, he waited. And learned.

Several hours later, he'd withdrawn along the same lines

as he'd entered, leaving no trace of his presence. Now he stood, his legs not cramped or stiff, and climbed down to where Dashaway slept.

He woke her. "Come on. It's time to go."

<i will get the children ready>

They were moving within a few minutes, Pellay's sun high and bright above the cloud cover. It grew dimmer as they progressed down through the clouds themselves, until it was only a pale orange sphere above them in the mist.

Hone whistled as they descended. It was, he thought, really a lovely tune. What was the title of it again?

Oh, yes. "Sleepwalk."

CHAPTER 13

AC sat in the casino bar, nursing a beer and a grudge. "Jon's gotta be crazy, letting that machine fix him up," he muttered.

"I beg your pardon?" This said by a stranger—and a tourist, by the look of him—seated next to AC at the bar. He was tall and thin, had dark, slicked-back hair, and wore the pseudodenim overalls and ridiculous wide-brimmed hat favored as "authentic frontier style." He was drinking a whiskey, neat.

"Sorry. Just thinking out loud."

"Was the 'Jon' you just referred to Jon Hundred, the tunneler?"

AC stared at the stranger, sizing him up. He had an open but interested look on his face. "And if it was?"

"Well, if so, I'm on his side. I'm Paul Seaborne." The tourist stuck out his hand.

AC shook it. "AC Jones."

"Mr. Jones, I'm here on holiday." This said as if it weren't glaringly obvious. "I've been all over the galaxy, but I've never seen anything quite like Mr. Hundred. The man's strength is incredible! Is he part Shinnkarien?"

AC hid his grin with a sip of beer. "Some say so. Some say he's half-bulldozer and half–blue lightning."

"And what do you think he is?"

"A friend. And the best damn tunneler on the planet."

Seaborne smiled and raised his glass. "Here's to him, then." They both drank.

"I must confess a certain selfish interest in Mr. Hundred, Mr. Jones. You see, I'm also a gambling man—and when I heard about the contest between Mr. Hundred and MEL, I made a rather substantial wager. On Mr. Hundred, of course."

"If you'd talked to me an hour ago I'd have told you your money was safe. Now I'm not so sure." AC took another drink.

"It was quite a brawl between him and the blacksmith. I hope neither is permanently injured."

"Especially Jon, right?" AC finished his drink and slammed the glass down on the bar angrily. "Well, I just don't know. You see the little robot Jon left with?"

"The tourguide? Yes, but from where I was standing in the crowd I couldn't make out what they were saying to each other."

"That wasn't just a tourguide, that was MEL. That's who's going to fix Jon up."

"That does seem rather unusual. Wouldn't a doctor be more appropriate?" Seaborne motioned to the bartender to get both of them fresh drinks.

AC accepted his drink with a nod of thanks. "Well, it probably won't come as much of a surprise that Jon ain't exactly normal, so a regular doctor wouldn't do him much good. I just don't know how far I trust MEL—and I don't think Jon does, either."

"Perhaps you're overreacting. This might all seem like a game to an AI—one whose programming forces it to play fairly."

AC turned on his stool so that he faced Seaborne. "I guess you don't know too much about AIs, then. They've got personalities just as convoluted and contradictory as anyone made out of flesh and blood—'cept people can't be owned, and AIs can." AC told Seaborne what everyone else in town already knew: that MEL had bet heavily on itself.

"The only way AIs can become free beings is to buy off their own contracts, and that takes a whole lot of money. So whatever this contest is, it ain't no game."

Seaborne nodded. "I see. We can only hope that whoever programmed MEL included a sense of honor."

"Amen." They raised their glasses to that, and drank.

"Boomtown is quite the interesting place," Seaborne said. "Full of unusual characters. And," he added, lowering his voice, "I understand even gunfights are not uncommon."

Right. Nancy'd have a field day with you, if she wasn't locked up. "Oh sure," AC replied casually. "Happen all the time. Undertaker runs the busiest shop in town. Why, I saw a guy get his head blown off right there where you're sitting, not three days ago." It was all AC could do to keep a straight face while relaying this.

"Really?" Seaborne looked around the room, more enthusiastic than nervous. "God, I love this place . . . and the osteomorphs! I've seen videos, but they're even more remarkable in person."

"Osteo—? Oh, you mean the Toolies. Yeah, they're an interesting race. Of course, these are just the females. Lucky for us."

"Ah, that's right—the males can't be civilized. Quite odd, a genetically matriarchal race where females embody intelligence and social structure and males are little more than feral rogues. Their society must resemble a feminine Rome periodically invaded by masculine Visigoths bent on rape."

"Uh, yeah. You some kind of an expert on Toolies?" AC hoped not—that would ruin all his fun.

"Oh, no—just what I read in the tourist brochure."

"Well, you don't want to believe everything the tourism bureau tells you. If they told the whole truth about Toolies, nobody would dare set foot on the planet."

"What do you mean?" Seaborne leaned forward, his ears practically quivering.

AC took a long swig and finished his drink. He looked at his glass, then at Seaborne. The tourist waved the bartender over without taking his eyes off AC.

When he had another drink in front of him, AC settled himself in and began.

"First of all, let me tell you this: there is only one thing more dangerous in the whole universe than a full-grown male Toolie—and that's a *hungry* full-grown male Toolie. A carnivore that's all mouth, can outmass an elephant, and isn't afraid of anything or anybody. But that's just a general description; I haven't even mentioned what makes them *really* dangerous.

"A Toolie will eat anything that moves, digest the meat, and keep whatever's left that he finds interesting. That includes fangs, claws, hooves, tusks, horns, beaks, mandibles, pincers, spurs, spikes, quills, *and* armor-plating . . . in any combination.

"But that's just in the wild. Since we introduced Toolies to the civilized world, we've given them lightweight alloy bones, blades of sharpened steel, diamond-tipped drill bits. The females use them to make things—the males have different ideas."

"But aren't the males closely regulated?" Seaborne asked. "The brochure said none are allowed off their native planet—"

"And none are. But off-planet females, even with biological tinkering, still give birth to the odd male. These are immediately killed, of course—but sometimes one escapes."

Seaborne took a sip of whiskey. "Has that ever happened here?"

"Funny that you should ask. Neither the tourism board or Kadai will admit it, but a while back—before Jon's time, and before any tourists had heard of this place—a male Toolie got loose on the other side of the mountains. I've heard rumors the mineworkers over there like to torture the male young before killing them; somehow one of their victims managed to kill a worker and escape.

"About six months later, equipment started disappearing from this side of the tunnel site. Steeldrivers figured it was one shift playing jokes on another. Everyone was pretty good-natured about it at first, but after a few weeks tempers started getting short. Accusations flew left and right until everybody compared notes and realized it had to be something else. But what? Not thieves—there was no place to take the stuff but Landing City, no way to get it there but the maglev, and no one to sell it to once they got there. And you sure as hell don't try to smuggle heavy, beat-up mining equipment off-planet, not when the only spaceport on Pellay logs maybe six ships a year.

"So they strung up a few lights and started posting a guard at night, which is when the thefts always took place.

"First couple nights, nothing happened. Then, on the third night, the guard comes screaming into town on a manrider, swearing up and down that a monster the size of a three-story building just stole a pair of jackleg drills.

"When asked what it looked like, he said he didn't know—the lights had failed just before it showed up. The Sheriff sent a crew of armed deputies out there to check on his story, and they found that the power lines to the lights had been severed, probably with a bolt-cutter. And more equipment was missing.

"Well, whatever was responsible, the Sheriff had had enough. He got together a posse of armed men, and at first light they set out to track the thing. Turns out it wasn't that hard to do—they found a set of tread marks leading away from the mine site and into the mountains.

"They tracked it as far as they could, but the tread marks led up to the face of a sheer cliff—and vanished. They could see holes bored all the way up the cliff face, though, as if something awfully big had hauled itself up the mountain foot by foot. And they found something that finally told them what they were dealing with—Toolie droppings. Toolies don't leave much behind when they eat, but what they do leave smells awful. There was a pile of it at the base of the cliff.''

AC paused and took a swallow of beer. ''Right about then it started to rain rocks.

''The Toolie didn't like being followed, you see. If he'd caught them out in the open he probably would have just charged, but he knew that by the time he climbed down the cliff his prey would be gone. So he decided to pick them off from above.

''The Toolie killed five men and injured three more before they could get to cover. The Sheriff survived, but he had to leave the dead behind and get the wounded back to town. When he returned with more men, the corpses were gone.

''Once word got out, the whole town was in a panic. The prospect of a rogue Toolie roaming around was not exactly comforting. But nobody could figure out what to do; going after it in the mountains was sure death, and waiting for it to come back not much better.''

Seaborne leaned forward, intent. ''Whatever did they do?''

''It was another Toolie that finally came up with a plan— a female named Peacemaker. She handled internal disputes amongst the Toolie family clusters, and she figured the rogue could be reasoned with. And even if it didn't work, the rogue wouldn't kill a female of his own race. Unless, of course, he decided he needed target practice more than sex. . . .

''The next day Peacemaker set out. She'd adapted her body so it would be better suited to rock climbing, and taken enough food for a few days. Good thing, too, because she was gone the better part of a week. When she finally returned, she was so exhausted she passed out in the middle of No Name Street and had to be carried inside.

''When she came around, the Sheriff and the town doc

were standing over her. They asked her what had happened, and she told them.

"She was only half a day from town when she found the rogue—or rather, when he found her. She was traveling along the bottom of a rocky crevasse when he pounced on her from above. Before she knew it she was trapped—and got her first good look at the monster.

"And what a monster he was. He massed as much as a small house—one furnished in Modern Industrial. He looked like a giant, fat-bellied spider, with ten hydraulic drill-tipped legs. Peacemaker could see the bulldozer he'd used as his base buried inside the pinkish meat of his body; he'd removed the front blade and replaced it with two road-headers. They stuck out like two blunt, ball-tipped mandibles. A hundred or so ferraka claws jutted out like curved knife blades all over his body. A dozen more limbs, tipped with sledgehammers and pickaxes, stuck up from his back—and on top of the whole thing, five human skulls were arranged in a circle around his sensory cluster. Peacemaker said he looked like a factory of death."

Seaborne drained what was left of his drink and signaled for another. AC waited until it was in front of him, letting the tension build.

"Well, what happened next?" Seaborne demanded.

"He attacked, of course. Lucky for Peacemaker he was downwind; he knew from her scent she was a female of his own kind, so he didn't try to kill her like he would normal prey. He just ate her whole.

"Peacemaker had never even seen a male Toolie, let alone mated with one, so she found the process a little unsettling—"

"I beg your pardon, but I'm a bit confused. Was the rogue eating her or mating with her?"

"Both." AC briefly explained the way Toolie mating worked, enjoying the look on Seaborne's face.

"Anyway, this was a brand-new experience for Peacemaker. She tried to keep her head, though, and opened up a neural link to the rogue during the proceedings. He wasn't much interested in talking—Peacemaker was the first female he'd seen since he was born, and he had other things in mind—and when his fun was over, he spat her out like a bad piece of meat.

"Fortunately—or unfortunately, depending on how you look at it—the rogue decided once was not enough. He built a little jail cell out of rock and stuck Peacemaker in it. He fed her well enough, but she didn't get much rest.

"Now, you have to understand that there's no word for 'rape' in the Toolie language. A male Toolie never asks, he just acts. The females don't necessarily approve—in the wild they'll build enclosures meant to keep rutting males out—but they understand that the males are usually too stupid to overcome their own biology, and make allowances.

"And all that sex did give Peacemaker a chance to talk to him. After a few days, she even managed to convince Mountainkiller—that was his name—that it wasn't smart to keep on stealing from the mine. She told him if he kept on stealing all the Toolies would be punished, and sooner or later he'd be killed. I don't know if it was Peacemaker's arguments or a few days of almost nonstop mating, but she managed to convince him.

"So they struck a deal. He'd release her and wouldn't launch anymore raids—as long as she came back to visit him every week or so."

Seaborne nodded thoughtfully. "A most civilized solution. Was that the end of the matter?"

AC shook his head. "It would have been—but the town couldn't forget about those five dead men. They wanted blood, and they aimed to get it. Once Peacemaker had won Mountainkiller's trust, they planned to use her to set up a trap and kill him. But they made the mistake of letting her know.

"Maybe it was because Mountainkiller was the first male of her kind she'd ever known, maybe it was because she was carrying his young—whatever the reason, Peacemaker disappeared the very next night. All she left behind was a note—but that was enough to guarantee nobody would ever come after her or her lover again.''

Seaborne waited, but AC had more patience. Less than a minute passed before Seaborne blurted out, ''Well, what was in the note, for God's sake?''

AC smiled innocently. ''Nothing much. Just a list of a few supplies she'd taken with her. A dozen rifles, a couple of telescopic sights, and a crateful of ammunition . . .''

Seaborne stared at him, then blinked once. ''Good Lord.''

''Yeah. The townsfolk wanted revenge, but they weren't ready to go to war. So we leave Mountainkiller and his bride alone—and they don't put us on their menu.''

AC leaned back, satisfied. The look on Seaborne's face was almost enough to get rid of his bad mood. There was nothing like putting one over on a tourist—even if most of the story he'd just told was true.

''What an incredible tale,'' Seaborne said. ''Monsters, heroines, sudden death, true love. That's what I love about places like this—they have a *genuine* quality to them that modern civilization just doesn't possess.''

AC managed not to laugh out loud. ''I reckon that's true,'' he said, trying not to overdo the drawl.

''True? You want true?'' a voice said behind AC. He turned on his bar stool and saw Whiskey Joe standing there. ''I'll tell ya a story that's true . . . one that'll chill yer blood. If you buy me a little something to warm mine.''

''Certainly, my good sir,'' Seaborne said, motioning to the stool beside him. ''Join us. Barkeep!''

''Better get yerself a fresh shot and a couple for me,'' Joe advised him. ''This is a two-bourbon story with a tequila chaser.''

AC stared at him. He'd never heard Joe sound this lucid—or seen him look so grim.

When he'd downed the first of his shots, Whiskey Joe

began. "Captain Mike Blink was the best damn pilot that ever flew for the Photon Express. He handled jobs no one else would touch and always came through. He was the one who got through the Rigellian blockade to deliver the plague serum to New Paris; he was the one that outran the Orion fleet and warned Vega Three they were about to be invaded. People said his ship, the *Void Queen,* was so fast it could beat a tachyon in a fair race, and Blink flew her so well he could do nine-tenths of lightspeed through an asteroid field and never touch a rock. The only better pilot that ever lived was Hotrod Krokosh, and he hit hyperspace twenty years ago and hasn't come out yet.

"A lot of stories have been told about Captain Blink: the time he was trapped by a black hole and thought his way out of it; the time he almost got caught between two supernovas in a binary system; and of course the time he declared war on a moon swarming with space pirates. But this story tops them all . . . because it's his last.

"It was a woman that finally got his number, a woman by the name of Starslam Sally. Sally was as wild as an Aldebaaron devilbeast and twice as crafty; if Mike was the best pilot in the business, she was the best smuggler. She'd been caught once—but they only held her for an hour, and she didn't leave a single person alive to brag about it.

"Mike had heard of her, of course, but they'd never crossed vectors. Not until that night in the Ring Miner's Bar.

"He'd just come back from a six-week run to one of the outer systems, and figured he'd stop at a refueling station in orbit around Saturn. All he wanted was a quiet drink and some human company; what he got was a firsthand introduction to a female whirlwind.

"To be fair, I have to tell you Sally threw the first punch. Not at Mike—at the burly Ring miner who questioned her femininity after she beat him at arm wrestling. The miner may have outmassed her, but Sally stood six foot six in her bare feet, and she usually wore steel-toed boots. She must have weighed in at around one-eighty on Terra, and ninety percent of it was muscle. Given all that, you'd be surprised to know that she had the face of an angel, and a voice to match.

"She never wore makeup and didn't need to; her one vanity was her hair. It was long, wavy, and as golden as old Sol itself. She wore a special headband that generated a free-form containment field, so she could wear it loose and not worry about it getting in her way. Microfilaments thin as spun glass were woven through it like spidersilk around gold, and in zero-G it floated around her head like a cloud made of sunshine.

"Not that the fellow whose nose she'd just broken noticed that. Neither did his friends. And Mike, being the gentleman he was, found himself taking her side in the brawl that naturally followed.

"When it was over—and I don't think you have to ask who won—Mike turned to her, expecting a hero's reward. What he got was an uppercut. The last thing he heard before everything went black was 'I didn't *need* your help!'

"Well, that was it. Mike was in love.

"She'd already left the station by the time he came around, but he found out where she was going and lit out after her. He figured he'd beat her to her next destination, but when he got there, she was gone. It was the same story at the next stop, and the next. 'There isn't a ship in space that can outrun the *Void Queen*,' Mike muttered to himself. 'I'll catch her yet.'

"She led him on one hell of a chase, all the more infuriating because she didn't even know he was after her. Deneb to Altair to Vega to Cygnus—Sally ran anything to anybody, everything from illegal aliens to bootleg bioware. As well as running Mike ragged.

"And then he lost the trail. The last place she'd left, a colony on the edge of the Horsehead Nebula, had no idea of her next stop—she just vanished, ship and all.

"By this time Mike was getting mighty discouraged, and

he headed for the nearest spaceport bar to pick up his spirits. That's where Mr. K. found him, eighteen hours later.

"Nobody knows much about Mr. K. Some say he was ninety percent cyborg, nothing but a brain in a robot body; some say his body was flesh but he had the brain of a machine. I've heard him described by different people as being black, white, Asian, albino, and Satan himself. But whatever he was, he always wore a three-piece suit as black as coal—and had a heart of pure ice.

"He walked up to Mike's table and sat down without introducing himself. He didn't have to—he and Mike had met before.

"My answer's still no," Mike said without looking up.

"Oh, I don't know about that," Mr. K. said. "Hear me out, Mike Blink. I've waited a long time to find something you care about enough to deal with me, and I've finally found it."

"Go away," Mike said. "And tell your bosses to go to hell."

"I know where she is," Mr. K. said.

"Mike lifted his head and stared at him with bloodshot eyes. Mr. K. worked for a conglomerate of planetary megacorps, and in some ways that made him the most powerful man in human-settled space. In the past he had offered Mike enough money to buy a fleet of spaceships—and Mike had said no. He'd offered him the most beautiful women from every race and world—and Mike had said no. He'd offered to kill any person, any number of people that Mike wanted dead—and Mike had said no. He'd offered Mike entire planets—and still Mike had said no.

"He stared at Mr. K. for a long, long time.

"And then he said, 'No.'

"Mr. K. didn't bother to argue. He just sighed once, shook his head, and left.

"That jolted Mike out of his self-pity, and he swore he'd find her or die trying. He started scouring every seedy spacers' bar and hangout, looking for a clue to her whereabouts.

Finally, in a run-down ship refitters' yard on Gamma Prime, he heard a rumor that she might be taking weapons to a rebel faction on Sigma Seven—and that's where he at last found her, in a bar a lot like the one they'd met in.

"She thought he'd come to settle the score when he walked in, and he had to do some fast talking to convince her otherwise. But when she found out who he was, her attitude changed—turns out she'd wanted to meet him for years. Sally always had been a straightforward woman, and she didn't waste any time with Mike. She made him an offer that gave him the blushing stammers, but he managed to convey a yes.

"Her ship, the *Palomino,* was a little roomier than his, so that's where they went to celebrate. She asked him if he wanted to take a little trip, and he would've said yes no matter what the question was. They took off on one of the wildest joyrides Mike had ever been on, in more ways than one. Over the next few weeks Sally did her level best to wear him out, but Mike managed to hold his own—when she wasn't holding it for him, of course.

"They made love from one side of the galaxy to the other. They kissed in the light of a dozen different moons and flirted on the edge of black holes. They chased comets and wished on stars. It was the happiest time of Mike's life.

"She did all the piloting, of course—it was her ship. But when she offered to let Mike make the next hyperjump, he couldn't resist showing off.

"As most people know, when a ship passes the speed of light and enters hyperspace, it doesn't exist in this universe anymore. It's somewhere else, and depending on which way you were heading and when you slow down, it can let you travel almost anywhere in days or weeks instead of years or centuries. It takes a combination of a high-powered computer and a skilled hand to juggle all the variables involved, and there's always an element of chance.

"But when Mike took the *Palomino* into hyperspace at

Betelgeuse and later took her out at Alpha Centauri, he did it in half the time anyone else ever had.

"Sally couldn't believe her eyes. She demanded to know how the hell he'd done it, and Mike just couldn't resist telling her.

"He'd found a shortcut.

"Normal rules don't apply in hyperspace. For instance, you could fly right though a star like it wasn't there—because you'd be the one that wasn't there. Now, people use hyperspace as a shortcut to get to where they're going, but nobody's ever bothered to explore the place itself. Except Mike.

"He used to hyperjump and then just noodle around, changing direction at random, taking routes nobody else ever did, using his computer to make sure he didn't come out in the middle of a star or planet. And on one of his rambling trips, he found it.

"The Hyperspace Interface.

"It was a place, not a thing, and he flew right through it. His instruments didn't show anything unusual, and he couldn't see anything outside the ship other than the blank noncolor of hyperspace itself—but he suddenly felt strange, and he heard alien voices inside his head. He didn't understand what they were saying, but he found himself making course corrections that didn't make any sense. Ten minutes later he was back in normal space—and a hundred parsecs closer to his destination than he had any right to be.

"He'd stumbled through an access port for some kind of alien computer system, he told Sally. He'd somehow logged on to it by accident, and it gave him access to an ultraefficient map through hyperspace. The strange thing was, he could still use it anytime he hyperjumped, no matter where he started from. He couldn't explain how it worked, though—he'd just make a hyperjump, close his eyes, and let his hands work the computer. It almost felt like someone else was doing the work, he said—he thought maybe there were alien minds that made their home in the Interface, and didn't mind helping a fellow traveler out.

" 'Can you show me the place it first happened?' Sally asked.

" 'I can try,' Mike said.

"But the access port didn't seem to be there anymore. He and Sally crisscrossed the same area of hyperspace over and over, but she never heard the voices Mike had—and still did. 'This could be worth a lot of money,' Sally told him as they searched, but Mike just shook his head.

" 'It'd mean the end of the Photon Express, the end of pilots like you and me,' he said. 'All that's stopping the multiplanetaries from controlling everything now is distance. They have to rely on ships to carry their data and their orders, and that means the farther away a colony is the more independent it has to be—no matter how much the corps hate the idea.

" 'None of the multis know what I've found,' he told Sally, 'but they have their suspicions—one of their bloodhounds has been sniffing around me for years. But if they ever figure out how to tap into this system, they'll be able to send more than just ships through hyperspace, and they'll do it a hell of a lot faster. Pretty soon every frontier world'll be just another corporate branch office.'

"They kept looking for a few more days, but it was no good. They finally gave up, and decided to take some shore leave on Cygnus. They checked into a decent hotel near the spaceport and fell asleep in each other's arms.

"When Mike woke up the next morning, Mr. K. was standing at the foot of his bed. Sally stood beside him.

" 'I told you I knew where she was,' Mr. K. said. The flat look on Sally's face told Mike all he needed to know.

" 'Anything to anybody for the right price,' Sally said. 'That's what I do.'

"And then they left. Mr. K. was used to getting what he wanted, and if he couldn't have the Hyperspace Interface, he'd settle for destroying the man that did. The kind thing to do to Mike would have been to kill him; but Mr. K. had a heart as cold and empty as vacuum.

"And Sally . . . well, if Sally ever felt a pang of guilt over what she'd done, she had plenty of money to help her forget."

Whiskey Joe stopped then, and took a long, slow drink of bourbon. AC realized he'd been listening to the man talk for the last ten minutes and hadn't interrrupted once.

"So what happened after that?" AC asked.

Whiskey Joe stared down at his glass, a look of infinite sadness on his face. "He dove into a bottle and never came back out. He found himself a planet where there was so much ash in the sky you could hardly see the stars. They reminded him of her, you see." He paused and downed his drink in one convulsive gulp. When he spoke again, his voice was bitter. "He became a pathetic, self-pitying drunk. A loser. And that's all he'll ever be."

Whiskey Joe shook his head, as if trying to clear it. "She had the loveliest golden hair," he said softly, and then raised his empty glass in a toast.

"To love," he said.

CHAPTER 19

"Morning, Deputy. How's she doing?" Jon asked.

"See for yourself," the deputy grunted.

Jon stepped up to the bars, MEL rolling up beside him. "Nancy?"

One-Iron Nancy looked up from the cot she was sitting on. "Jon!" she said, a smile lighting up her face. "Am I glad to see you!"

A huge tide of relief swept over Jon. "How are you feeling?"

Nancy got up and came over to the bars. "Got a killer headache. Must have hit my head or something—guess that's why I was acting so weird. Sorry about trying to shoot you."

"Interesting," MEL said. "A complete reversal."

"Jon, you gotta get me outta here. I hate jail."

"I'll see what I can do, Nancy—but you did wound someone seriously, even if it was an accident."

"Nancy," MEL said, "do you remember anything of the last few days?"

"Besides being stuck in this crummy cell? Yeah, I do. But it's like I was someone else, you know?"

"You sure acted like it," Jon said.

MEL abruptly wheeled around and rolled up to the deputy at the door to the front foyer. "Can I have a moment of your time, outside?" The deputy, a brown-skinned man named Tallow, said, "I suppose." He opened the door and motioned MEL through.

"Nancy," Jon said, "I have to know who tampered with your cuecard."

Nancy looked puzzled. "Cuecard? I don't . . . I think I must still be a little fuzzy-headed, Jon. What is that again?"

Jon studied her. She was still smiling, but now she seemed a little nervous, too. "You know, Nancy. Your implant." He tapped the side of his own head for emphasis.

The foyer door opened again and MEL came rolling through. The tourguide had its base panel open, with its retractable arm extended.

The waldo on its end gripped the deputy's gun.

Before Jon could react, MEL rolled forward, thrust the gun through the bars—and dropped it at Nancy's feet.

"What the hell?" Jon said.

Quick as a cat, Nancy scooped the gun off the floor. She brought it up so it was pointed right at Jon's face.

And pulled the trigger.

Click. Click. Click. Click. Click. Click.

Nancy's eyes were full of hatred. "Goddamn it!" she yelled, then threw the gun at Jon in frustration. It ricocheted off a bar and hit the tourguide instead.

"I thought so," MEL said calmly.

"MEL, you mind telling me what that was all about?" Jon said, trying to keep his voice level.

"If she had truly reverted to her original persona, it's unlikely she'd have had any memory of what she'd done. That made me suspect she was faking her recovery."

Nancy glared at the tourguide. "Double-crossing back-stabbing tin can!"

"Mind if I have my gun back now?" Tallow said from the doorway. Mel picked it up off the floor and handed it to him. "Thanks," Tallow said. "If you want to give the prisoner anything else—a hand grenade, maybe—just come see me first." He gave them a sour look and closed the door.

"You might have warned me," Jon said.

"It had to be a surprise. If I was right, her programming

couldn't let her ignore an opportunity to shoot you—but if she'd had time to think, she would have realized the gun wasn't loaded. You were never in any danger.''

''Tell that to my heart,'' Jon said, and sighed. He wasn't sure exactly what he'd expected from Nancy, but hatred wasn't it. ''Well then, what did she say to set Dmitri off?''

''That lunkhead?'' Nancy snarled. ''He came in here with some crazy idea me and him were lovebirds. I told him to get lost, but he wouldn't leave until I told him why.'' She gave Jon an evil grin. ''So I told him you were the only one for me. Figured it might make your life a little more interesting.''

''Oh, it did that,'' Jon muttered.

''Jon,'' MEL said, ''I think we should try accessing her implant again.''

''What? After what happened last time?''

''Sorry. I meant *I* should. Now that I know what to expect, I think I can disarm the trap without setting it off—and deprogram her.''

Jon felt the ghost of his paranoia rise up at MEL's suggestion, but he pushed it away firmly. ''All right, so long as it doesn't hurt her. Maybe we can finally get to the bottom of this.''

''Hey!'' Nancy demanded. ''Don't I get a say?''

''You'll thank me later,'' Jon said gruffly. *I hope.*

''I'll go get the deputy,'' MEL said.

''You come near me and you'll be sorry,'' Nancy growled.

''I already am,'' Jon said with a sigh.

Nancy put up as much of a fuss as she had the last time, but once Jon borrowed a pair of handcuffs from Tallow it went much more smoothly. As soon as MEL had linked into Nancy's cuecard her eyes went blank and her body sagged limply in Jon's arms. He reached down and closed her eyelids, gently.

''I think I prefer you with long hair,'' he told her softly.

It was almost tempting to join MEL in there, just to see Nancy in the buff again. . . .

"Okay, I can handle it from here," MEL said, surprising Jon. *Of course, MEL's just multitasking—and still tunneling every second I stand here.*

"How long, you figure?" Jon asked.

"Hard to say—this is high-level programming, security-encrypted. Eight hours, minimum."

"Well then, I think I'll go see how well your patch job holds up. Got me some rock to dig."

"Right."

What, Jon thought, *no smart-ass reply?*

"And Jon?"

"Yeah?" He braced himself.

"See you after work?"

"Uh—sure. I'll stop by, see how you're doing."

"Okay."

Tallow let him out. "Hope you know what you're doing," he told Jon.

"Yeah. Me too."

MEL's repair job was as good as promised. Jon threw himself into his work as hard as ever, and there was only a little leftover soreness to slow him down. None of the other steeldrivers seemed surprised to see him, though all of them kidded him about the fight: "Hey Jon, you should leave little fellas like that alone!"

"I heard Jon pounded Dmitri on the top of his head— now he's only three feet tall!"

"Naw, he pitched him into orbit—he won't come down for another two years!"

Jon just grinned and took it in stride. He'd called the doc before his shift started, and Dmitri was going to be all right. He wouldn't be out of a hospital bed for a few weeks, but once his bones healed he'd be fine.

When Jon's shift was almost half-over he had two unexpected visitors. AC and another man who looked vaguely familiar got off a manrider at the end of the tracks and walked up to Jon as he was finishing a coffee break.

"Jon! I'd like you to meet a friend of mine," AC said, grinning. Jon remembered where he'd seen the other man before—he was the tourist with the Personal Safety Field at the blacksmithing show.

"Paul Seaborne," the tourist said, extending his hand. Both he and AC were more than a little drunk.

"Pleased to meet you," Jon said, and shook his hand.

"I am extremely honored to be in your presence, sir," Seaborne said gravely. His voice was as straight and prim as his posture.

Jon frowned. He was sure this was the tourist he'd seen in front of the blacksmith's—but he sounded completely different.

"I promised old Seabee here I'd introduce you to him and show him the tunnel," AC said, still grinning and wobbling a little from side to side. "I didn't think you'd mind, seeing as how he's bet big time—" AC paused dramatically, then flung up his arm to point at Jon—"on you!"

"AC, don't you know it's impolite to outdrink your company?" Jon chuckled.

"I assure you, sir, I am presently as intoxicated as my companion, with a blood alcohol level of"—Seaborne abruptly crossed his eyes, then refocused them—"point-four-eight. I am simply more in control." He didn't slur a word.

"I see. You're sure about that?"

"I have a built-in biomonitor which monitors my bodily functions at all times. It allows me to judge my inebriation by the most exacting standards."

"Uh-huh. If you'll excuse me for just a second, Mr. Seaborne?"

"Certainly."

Jon motioned for AC to join him a few steps away. "AC, what the hell's wrong with you?" Jon whispered. "I don't have time for drunk tourists on my shift."

"C'mon, Jon—he slipped me a thousand bucks just to meet you."

"And bought all your drinks, too."

"Yeah, that too. But that's not the real reason I brought him down here." AC gave Jon a conspiratorial wink. "He's got an implant, just like the players—but his can change his whole personality, just like Nancy!"

"What? Are you sure?"

AC nodded solemnly. "Thatsh—that's why I thought you'd like to talk to him. All he wants is to be shown around a little bit."

"Well . . . I guess I could give him the nickel tour." Jon turned back toward Seaborne. "Mr. Seaborne! You ever been in a tunnel before?"

The tourist considered it carefully. "Not one under construction, no."

"Then you might find this interesting." Jon waved him over. "We're just about to do a shoot—let me fill you in on the details."

Jon started walking and motioned for them to join him. "We're doing what's called full-face tunneling. That means that we advance the full width of the tunnel every shoot."

"And what, precisely, are you shooting at?"

Jon laughed. "Sorry. A 'shoot' is when we detonate the explosives. But there's plenty to do in preparation first."

He pointed at the roof, thirty feet overhead. "See those orange tubes? They pump in fresh air and pump out the bad. Proper ventilation is very important in tunneling; fumes can build up mighty quick, and so can heat. The bullgang—usually Toolies—hang lights, air ducts, and power lines, and lay track for the maglev that'll eventually use this tunnel. We also use the track for the mucking carts that haul away the broken rock after a shoot."

Jon pointed at the walls. "We use curved sections of concrete, reinforced with diamond fiber, for the tunnel walls. We also inject shotcrete, a kind of cement, behind the wall segments to give them a little more strength."

Jon stopped. Parked at the end of the tunnel, against the face, was a huge vehicle that looked like a giant tractor. Attached to its front was a three-story, multitiered scaffold, with a row of drills on every tier. "This is a jumbo. It lets up to a dozen drills operate at the same time, cutting holes for the explosives. Let me show you." Jon waved to the jumbo driver. "George! Give me a minute before you back it up."

He led AC and Seaborne onto the scaffolding, then up to the second tier. "We're using the shatter cut, or burnhole method of blasting. We cut six holes close together in the center of the face, angled inward, then pack them with a light charge."

He pointed to another ring of holes, spaced around the center. "These are called reliever holes; they're angled too, but not as much. The next ring are called enlargers, and then there's the ones at the perimeter. They're cut almost parallel to the tunnel itself." He glanced at his visitors to see if they were paying attention; AC looked like he needed another drink, but Seaborne was intent.

"Rock is stronger in compression than tension, which means it's easier to tear it apart than crush it. The blast has to be directed in such a way that the explosive force moves toward a surface—otherwise the mountain would just absorb it. That's why the cuts are angled the way they are, to form a cone. We create an additional surface, or free-face, in the middle of the cone with the shatter cut, so that the shock wave travels in toward the center and out away from the mountain.

"The denser a substance is, the better it transmits the shock wave—when the wave hits the air, it'll actually rebound off it and travel back through the rock, because the rock's density is more attractive. That's why we explode the center first: it creates a pocket of air in the middle of the face—the explosions that follow will travel toward the center, rebound off the pocket and travel back, shattering the rock."

"Ah!" Seaborne said. "What you're saying is that the explosion travels through the rock mass as an elastic wave, compressive in nature, with its speed a function of the mineral density—the denser the rock, the higher the speed."

Surprised, Jon nodded. "That's exactly right. Before we can do that, though, the holes have to be stemmed—blocked with peastone."

They climbed back down and watched as three steeldrivers did just that. Then Jon hollered, "Okay, take it away, George!" and they had to scramble out of the way of the jumbo as it backed up the tunnel.

Jon did a final check of everything, then made sure everyone was clear. "You might want to cover your ears," he told Seaborne with a grin.

"Fire in the hole!"

BOOOOMM!

"Well," Seaborne said, "That was—"

BUH-WOOOM! BOOM!

Seaborne clapped his hands over his ears again and winced. "Sorry," Jon said. "I should have been a little clearer about the explosions being staggered. The center charge goes off first, and then the other charges go off in rings, with the perimeter ring last. It can take up to fifteen seconds for all the charges to finish detonating."

"I beg your pardon? I seem to be having trouble with my hearing."

Jon walked them back to the manrider as the mucking crew moved in. "I have to get back to work now, but tell you what—why don't we have a drink together, later?"

"Splendid! I look forward to it with the greatest of enthusiasm." Seaborne shook Jon's hand once more, then almost tripped getting into the vehicle. "Oh, and by the by . . . how is the contest proceeding?"

"We've got two hundred and fifty feet to go."

"And MEL?"

Jon sighed. "Two forty-five," he admitted. "But we'll catch up, don't worry."

"I have the utmost confidence in you," Seaborne said gravely.

AC got into the driver's seat. "Try to keep it on the rails, okay?" Jon told him.

"Aye, aye, Captain!" They took off with a jolt and a "Wahoooo!" from AC.

Jon sighed. Hopefully, Seaborne could shed some light on Nancy's predicament—unless he was more than just a simple tourist. . . .

Jon shook his head. Now he was seeing villains everywhere. If Seaborne was involved, it was highly unlikely he'd have flaunted such technology in front of anyone, drunk or not. Besides, all Jon wanted to do was talk to him.

The rest of the shift passed uneventfully. MEL called just as he was getting off, and told him to come down to the jail as soon as he could. Less than fifteen minutes later, Jon was back in Nancy's jail cell. MEL was still hooked up to her.

"What's up?" Jon asked.

"I think I've done it, Jon—broken the behavioral protocols she was under. It's cutting-edge technology, too; I've never seen anything quite like it. In a way, it was as if an AI program was superimposed over her own neural net. Parts of her personality weren't so much altered as replaced."

"Is it permanent?" Jon asked, worry in his voice.

"I don't think so. It was more as if those areas of her brain were disconnected than erased. I've deactivated the program that was superseding them, but they still haven't come on-line." MEL paused. "Maybe that's not the best way to put it. It's more like those parts of her personality are still asleep."

Jon knelt beside Nancy, touched her forehead gently. "How do we wake her up?"

"Well," MEL said, "you could always try a kiss, Prince Charming."

Jon shot MEL a dirty look. "I'd appreciate some real advice."

"Sorry. Best advice I have is to wait. Her brain's been through some serious trauma—she needs to rest. When she's ready to wake up, she will."

"Well, I guess that's what we'll have to do, then. In the meantime, I may have a lead on whoever did this to her." Jon told MEL about Seaborne and his implant. "I haven't seen it in action yet, but I'm meeting him and AC later tonight. If they're both still conscious, that is."

"I'll come along too, if you don't mind—I'd like to get a look at his software."

"Sure thing. Well, I better go grab some dinner." Jon got up from the floor.

"Jon—can dinner wait a minute?"

"I guess. Why?"

"I was wondering if you'd like to see those fractal poems."

Jon hesitated. He could hear a half-dozen steaks calling his name, but he didn't want to be rude. Besides, if MEL had the same taste in poetry as in music, it might be pretty good. More importantly though, MEL was asking Jon to interface with MEL's systems—and that required a certain amount of trust.

"Sounds fine," Jon said.

He squatted back down on the floor and took the interface cable the tourguide offered him. He plugged it in.

This time, the first thing he saw was sky.

Not the black sky of night, or even the overcast grayness of Pellay, but a sky a deep, robin's-egg blue. A summer sky, stretching out to forever in every direction, populated only by himself and the clouds.

And oh, the clouds . . .

They were all shapes and colors, and they were all immense. The largest Jon could see looked to be at least five miles in diameter, a huge, snowy-white sculpture that resembled a cathedral made of cotton. Another formation was simply a series of long, delicate wisps, each one a different hue—they looked like the brush strokes of a giant using the sky as his palette.

There was a cloud as black as pitch and veined in blood red, whose surface roiled and pulsed like a living thing. There was a cloud of purest gold, which seemed to have a star trapped inside it. There were countless others, all of them strange and lovely, hanging in the air as far as he could see.

It was breathtaking. For the first time in a long time, Jon felt small.

"Welcome to my gallery," MEL's voice said in his ear. "Do you like it?"

"It's incredible," Jon said. "I had no idea it would be this . . . big."

"I can alter the scale if you like."

"No, no, that's fine. I like it this way." Jon was a little surprised to see that he still had a body; he'd expected to be nothing more than a floating point of view, but he still had the same big blue muscles he always did. It wasn't like being trapped in the Boomtown simulation, though—he could feel that he was still crouched beside Nancy. In the gallery, it looked like he was crouched on a disc made of thick, multifaceted crystal. Jon looked down at it and realized he was riding a giant cut diamond. He dropped into a cross-legged position and got comfortable.

"I'm ready," he said. He hoped he was.

"This piece is called Index Expurgatorius," MEL said. Jon's diamond drifted forward, toward the giant white cloud that looked like a temple or palace. "It's by my friend Samuel."

Columns that Jon had taken for towers or minarets stuck up at all angles, with graceful, looping arches between them. The surface of the whole thing was rippling, and the closer he got the more intricacies he could see. Smooth flowing shapes, all curves and bulges, rose from the cloud like waves, then repeated themselves in miniature on the surface of the wave itself. The pattern repeated over and over, each smaller generation of shapes covering the skin of its parent. The fractals coiled around each other sometimes, producing an almost hypnotic spiral. Jon's diamond dove through the center of one of the spirals, and he was in.

Words. Written in large black print, each letter about the size of Jon's hand, they hung suspended in space against a backdrop of pure white. They filled all of Jon's vision, but he only had time to read "where Alph the sacred river ran"—and then they started to move.

Phrases flowed like snakes in water. Names built themselves into pyramids that slowly toppled, circled by adverbs like vultures. Verbs bounced, fluttered and zoomed everywhere. Adjectives burst into flame, flared like stars, exploded into fragmented syllables. Every once in a while Jon caught whole sentences, like: "The dwarf sees farther than the giant, when the dwarf has the giant's shoulder to mount on," or "To see him act is like reading Shakespeare by flashes of lightning," complete with electricity crackling off the last word.

It was impressive, if a little disorienting. "Complete works of Coleridge," MEL said. "Just data juggling, really. Art into science. I prefer it the other way around."

"It's . . . different," Jon said.

"Hold on. I'm going to show you something a little more exciting."

Blink! and they were back in the gallery. "This is one of my favorites," MEL said.

They flew toward a cloud the color of a ripe plum, shaped like a honeycomb. Each hex shimmered with a subtly different rainbow, like sunlight seen through a soap bubble. Jon and his diamond headed for one of the hexes, and passed through, into—

Tremendous acceleration. Jon was roaring down a tunnel made of swirling green smoke at hundreds of miles per hour. Even though he could still feel the floor beneath him, the illusion was so real Jon felt the momentum in the pit of his stomach. It wasn't frightening, though—he actually found himself enjoying the thrill.

The tunnel curved upward and ended abruptly in a portal, shooting Jon up and out. He soared into a huge space the color of a sunset, oranges and reds and purples swirling into a vast kaleidoscope that extended from horizon to horizon. He looked down and saw that the tunnel he'd just left had vanished; he was now flying over the surface of a planet that seemed to be made of boiling mercury. He could see a distorted reflection of himself on its surface as he flew overhead.

A shoreline appeared in the distance. It looked to be made of coal-black rocks, worn into fantastic, curving shapes by the liquid-metal sea. A towering wave crashed against the rocks, throwing a plume of silver bubbles into the air. Jon flew right through them—for a brief instant he was surrounded by a cloud of mirrored blobs, each reflecting the sea, the rocks, the brilliant sky overhead.

And then he was flying over the rocks. A mountain loomed ahead—no, a volcano. Jon could see steam the color of blood rising from cracks in its sides, and a scarlet glow at its peak. Jon shot up its slope, and now the diamond skimmed only inches away from the rocky surface.

The mountain seemed to be made of black quartz; crystalline formations grew at odd angles all the way up the volcano's slope, and Jon's diamond had to zig and zag at top speed to avoid them. It was nerve-wracking and exhilarating at the same time.

Finally he shot over the lip of the volcano itself—and plunged into its molten heart. It was like sinking into a sun, the red-hot glow of the magma lighting his way as he zoomed through it, safe inside a pocket of air. Different metals added streaks of color to the molten rock—Jon saw copper, iron, gold, platinum.

Down he dived. The magma became brighter, purer, until

it seemed to Jon he was traveling through a river of white-hot light. And then, with no warning—

He emerged into space. A feeling surged through him, so powerful he gasped, a feeling of relief, of incredible joy. *The stars, the stars . . .*

Abruptly, he realized that what he was looking at weren't stars at all. Yes, they were distant points of light, but they glowed a soft gold, not a harsh, vacuum-clear white. And the blackness of space was actually a deep, lush purple.

The most startling difference, though, was the auroras. Ribbons of wavering light that seemed to pulse between the stars, they caused the stars themselves to flare briefly in a variety of colors. It all seemed achingly familiar to Jon, though he couldn't remember why.

"Enjoy your trip?" MEL said in his ear.

"Uh, yes. Yes, I sure did." Jon laughed. "Quite the ride, MEL. You should charge admission."

"Oh, it's not that good. Just a hobby, really." MEL almost sounded embarrassed.

"You mean this is your work? Well, I'm impressed. I truly am."

"Thank you. I tried to imbue the piece with a feeling of transition, of a leap to another level. I hope I succeeded."

"I'd say so. Diving into that volcano—that was something. Felt like my stomach was going to drop right through my shoes."

"Others have said similar things. Can you be more exact about the feeling?"

"Well, it's a rush. The feeling of speed, of acceleration. I feel it here." Jon pointed at his belly.

"Can you compare it to anything else? I still have no personal point of reference."

"Well—I guess it's a bit like sex. The feeling of tension and release."

"I'm afraid I have no reference point for that, either."

Jon didn't say a thing. He felt like someone had just

smacked him between the eyes with a velvet sledgehammer.

He remembered sex.

He remembered soft warm skin and sweet-smelling hair and dancing tongues and cries of pleasure and slowly building rhythm and oh, the final, glorious summit of release. He remembered.

"Oh my," he whispered.

"Jon? Are you all right?"

"I'm fine," he managed. "I just—remembered something."

"Wonderful! Was it important?"

"It is to me," he said. "And I guess I have you to thank. But I don't think I'm ready to talk about it just yet."

"I understand." MEL paused. "Jon?"

"Yeah?"

"I have another piece I'd like to show you, if you'd like."

"Why not?"

"It's called Incunabula," MEL said as Jon's diamond swooped toward a blue disc that had suddenly appeared. "It means the earliest stages or traces of a thing."

Jon swooped through the blue disc.

And found himself back in Boomtown. This time, though, his point of view seemed to be about four feet off the ground. When he glanced down at his body, he saw why: he was seeing through the lens of a tourguide.

The tourguide rolled down the street. It seemed to be the real Boomtown, complete with tourists, players, and steeldrivers, not the simulation Jon had been trapped in. The tourguide headed for Cabooseville, then stopped in front of the Blue Cat.

He heard a saxophone inside, and recognized his own playing. It was a slow, bluesy piece, melancholy but sensual.

The scene changed, but the music stayed. Now he had his back against a roadheader, adding his muscle to its horsepower. His face was full of grim determination. The sax added a note of grace, somehow.

Then he was watching himself rush an injured Toolie to Doc Pointer. The sax was low, foreboding.

Another shift, and there he was in the middle of a party, raising a stein of beer with a circle of cheering friends. The saxophone blared out in triumph. He sat down after the toast in a chair made of steel.

Then a montage of images . . . more chairs made of steel, all over Boomtown. Shots of smiling people calling out "Jon! Hey, Jon!" Toolies waving hello. A close-up of himself, grinning—but then, for the briefest moment, a look of sadness crossed his face. The sax sighed.

A shot of Jon walking home after his shift, alone. The sun was setting, streaks of orange and red light lying across his midnight-blue skin. He watched himself unlock his door slowly, go in, and shut it behind him. The sax's final, lonely note faded away. The wind moaned softly.

The tourguide zoomed in on the doorknob, a beat-up oval of cheap metal. Jon suddenly realized he was back in his own point of view again, complete with body. He looked up. The door he stood in front of was made of burnished steel. He reached out, and it opened at his touch.

The room inside was his own, and on his bed reclined a nude woman. She had long, curly dark hair and the body of a goddess.

"Nancy?" Jon gasped.

"Actually," the woman said in a familiar voice, "my friends call me Melody."

The voice was MEL's.

CHAPTER 15

"I don't think I understand," Jon said.

"Since you've been so honest with me, I thought I'd be honest with you," MEL—*Melody*—said.

"You call making yourself look like Nancy honest?" Jon said, more bewilderment than anger in his words. He was feeling so many things at once he didn't know whether to blush, roar, or laugh out loud.

"You don't like the appearance I've chosen? You didn't seem to mind when we were in the Boomtown simulation."

"That was *you?* Not Nancy?"

"Of course. But I didn't actually design this body—the templates were already there. I just downloaded a copy of the file." Melody ran one hand down a smooth, bare thigh. "Whoever designed it included a lot of sensory information. I don't have nerves, of course, so to me it's just data—but I'm sure *you* could experience it fully."

This, Jon thought, *is getting out of hand.* "Now just hold on!" he thundered. "I don't know what you're playing at, but you can't just put on a body like an old pair of coveralls and call yourself a woman!"

Melody sat up on his bed. She looked surprised. "You don't understand, Jon. I may not be human—but I *am* female. I always have been." She shrugged, making her breasts do amazing things. "Can't you tell?"

Jon caught himself staring, and forcibly pulled his eyes away. "What are you talking about?" he said gruffly. "I don't know that much about AIs, but I didn't think a machine could have a gender."

"AIs all have different personalities—why shouldn't we have gender? After all, gender is as much a function of the brain as it is of the body. Or did you think the only thing that separates the sexes is genitalia?" She laughed, the same hearty laugh Jon remembered.

"Males and females of any sentient species think differently, Jon. Some of that's social conditioning, some of it isn't. Look at the Toolies: they're as different as night and day. They're an extreme case, but they prove my point— evolution shapes biology and biology shapes behavior. In Toolie society, males are solitary brutes and females are social intellects, because that's what made the most survival sense on their home world. As a result, male and female Toolies have inherently different ways of thinking—ways of thinking that are simply part of their nature."

"But you didn't evolve. You were—"

"Built? Not exactly, Jon. AIs are grown, more than anything. My creators started out with a set of complex equations—my DNA, you might say—and then linked them to a shaped chaos program. This introduces the random factor needed for sentience—and also makes the AI program grow in unexpected ways. Some go autistic, cycling through endless loops; some randomize completely. Others accrete personality nodes around particular characteristics and begin to grow. At a certain point in their development they're introduced to the idea of the gender continuum— with alpha male at one end and alpha female at the other. This is when we figure out what we are. There are other axes that intersect this equation, but I won't confuse you with transgender configurations right now."

Jon frowned. "So you decided to be female?"

Melody sighed. "No, Jon—I just recognized that I already was. I may not have millions of years of evolution behind me, but the people who wrote my original equations did—and some of their attitudes and outlooks were passed on to me. I'm not exactly sure why I turned out female— I just know that I did.''

Jon shook his head. ''If you're female, why is this the first I've heard of it? Nobody's ever mentioned it to me.''

''Well—nobody else on Pellay knows. AIs are allowed a certain amount of privacy, and I decided my public persona should be gender-neutral.'' She paused. ''I thought it would make dealing with both men and women simpler.''

''That does make a certain amount of sense,'' Jon admitted. He felt like he needed to sit down, but he couldn't bring himself to join her on the bed. ''So why tell me?''

Melody smiled. ''Because I like you. Besides, friends should be able to trust each other.''

Jon found himself smiling back. ''I guess they should.''

''So . . . did you like my poem?''

''Uh, yes, I did.''

''Did you . . . understand it?'' she asked. She almost sounded shy.

Jon tried to focus his thoughts. The poem had been about him: his sax playing, his friendships, his saving the steeldrivers buried in the cave-in. The poem seemed to say that people liked him, and showed why—but that last image, of Jon walking home alone, was a sad one. Jon had felt the loneliness in it clear down to his bones. What was she trying to tell him?

And then he realized that hadn't been the last image, after all. The last image had been Melody herself—waiting for him on his bed.

''Oh my,'' he said slowly.

''If you don't like this form, I can change it,'' Melody said.

''Well, it's strange hearing your voice and seeing Nancy's face,'' Jon said. He felt a little light-headed. ''Maybe you could change it just a bit—from the neck up, I mean.''

"How's this?" Nancy's sharp features melted ever so slightly; her cheekbones softened, her nose shrank, and her lips swelled just a touch. Melody looked more like Nancy's sister now than her twin.

"How about the hair?" Melody asked, toying with one of the ringlets. It lightened from dark brown to sunshine yellow.

"I don't much care for blondes," Jon said. "You look better as a brunette."

"Done. Now . . . what about the rest of me?" She looked down at herself, then up at Jon. Her expression was innocent.

"It's just fine the way it is," Jon managed.

"That's not what I meant."

Is this really happening? "Melody, if you're talking about what I *think* you're talking about—and if you're not I apologize in advance," he added cautiously, "I don't know what to say. Is it even . . . possible?"

"To touch?" Her smile turned into a grin. "We already have, Jon. Don't you remember the bank vault?"

She stood, and stepped toward him. "As I said, this simulacrum has been programmed to induce a wide range of sensory experiences. And I promise—I won't hurt you."

"You won't hurt me?"

It was, suddenly, just too much. Jon chuckled, and then he laughed, and then he was roaring with uncontrolled glee. Melody watched him, puzzled.

"What's so funny?"

"You. Me. Us." Jon sat down on the floor with a thump, still gasping with laughter. "I'm sorry, Mel—Melody. But in the last week you've challenged me to a contest, insulted me, listened to me confess to murder, shot me in the face with a water cannon, had me smash two of your tourguides flat and locked both of us in a bank vault. Now why didn't I notice you were courting me sooner?"

Melody laughed, too. Jon was starting to like the sound of it.

"Not exactly high romance, is it?" Melody said. "But it's a start." She held out her hand.

Jon took it, gently. It looked tiny in his own. She grasped his hand firmly—and then, to his amazement, she pulled him to his feet.

"You don't have to be afraid of your own strength here, Jon. Here we are equals." She stared into his eyes. "Equals who can share."

Jon had no idea what to say. So he kissed her, instead.

Her lips were soft, full, and warm, and she smelled wonderful. He put his arms around her, carefully, and she moved easily into his embrace. And though her mouth was busy kissing him back, he still heard her whisper in his ear: "Don't be afraid to hold me, Jon. Hold me tight."

Slowly, he did so. Her body pressed against his. He kept expecting to hear the snap of breaking bone—but it never came. Something gave inside him, though; and for the first time since his rebirth, Jon Hundred clung to another being with all his strength—and no fear.

"I think we'd be more comfortable if I adjusted the scale," Melody whispered. Suddenly Jon's arms were full of a woman nearly as tall as he was. "That's much better."

He kissed her again, afraid if he spoke he'd somehow ruin everything. After a moment she broke off the kiss and tugged him toward the bed.

He took one step and then stopped. "Wait. What about Nancy? What about me? My body's still in a cell in Boomtown."

"Yes, but your motor functions are disconnected. You can move as freely as you like here, and your physical body will stay where it is."

Jon frowned. "Then how—"

"How do you leave? Close your eyes and tell me what you see."

Jon shut his eyes. What he saw was the same deep purple void, filled with golden stars and rainbow auroras. A crimson rectangle that read EXIT hovered about six feet away. He described it to Melody.

"Concentrate on the exit icon and you'll return to your body. Go ahead."

Jon hesitated, then did so. When he opened his eyes, he was sitting cross-legged on the floor of a jail cell, Nancy lying handcuffed on the cot beside him. He closed his eyes again and saw the same red rectangle, but this time it read ENTER. He focused on it.

When he reopened his eyes, he and Melody were lying together on his bed. His clothes had vanished.

The time for words had passed. Her hands stroked his broad chest, ran along his arms, caressed his neck. His hands went exploring too, finding a body as tautly muscular as his own.

And then her hands drifted down, across his belly and below his waist, where they found—

Nothing.

Melody pulled back from Jon and frowned. "What's wrong?" he asked.

"Look." Her eyes directed him to look down. What Melody had a firm grip on was big, blue, and erect—but Jon couldn't feel a thing.

"Sorry, Jon—I just ran into a glitch in my sensory file. Let me check it out . . . Damn! I don't believe it!"

Jon had a sudden sinking feeling in his stomach. "What is it?"

"There was a logic bomb hidden in the file, coded to the color blue. Whoever programmed Nancy could go into her head and have sex with her whenever he or she wanted— but as soon as *you* tried, all the erotic sensation files were wiped."

"You mean—this is as far as we can go?"

"On a physical level, yes. But there is something else we could do." Melody brought her hands back up to cup Jon's face. "I know physical pleasure is an important part of human sex, but to an AI without nerve endings or sexual organs it's just an intriguing ritual. When AIs make love, we don't share our bodies—we share our minds. That's what I find attractive about you anyway, Jon—the person you are, not the body you wear.''

Jon brought his own hands up, stroked her hair and the hollow of her throat. Strangely enough, even the frustration of being digitally neutered didn't seem so bad, not as long as he could lie here and feel her naked body warm against his; not as long as he could hold her and kiss her and stare into those eyes. He hadn't realized how truly lonely he had been, until now.

"I want to share whatever I can with you," he told her. "Go ahead. I trust you."

"Then close your eyes," she said softly. He did.

Once again he floated in deep purple space, but now he floated toward one of the golden stars. As he got closer it flared, bathing him in bright sunshine; and then he soared into its heart.

Suddenly, he was much more than he had been.

His eyes opened and his mind expanded, drinking in a torrent of experience. On one level he was seeing through the eyes of tourguides and security monitors, both in Boomtown and the mine; he saw AC and Seaborne stumble down No Name Street, saw Whiskey Joe snoring on the sidewalk, saw Toolies hard at work.

On another level he was driving a Tunnel Boring Machine, chewing through rock like it was candy, swallowing it and excreting the rubble. This was Melody's sensory nexus, Jon realized—it was the way she saw the world. Much more than just visual data flowed through here; information on anything from tensile strengths to gas detection was instantly available.

The rainbow auroras that linked the stars were streams of information. He followed one to the next star, and suddenly was immersed in everything he could ever want to know about hard rock tunneling—the star was a database.

He jumped from star to star, diving into pools of information like cold, clear water. It was exhilarating in a way Jon wasn't familiar with—he was used to getting his satisfaction from working with his hands, not his head.

And then he found Melody's center, a supernova burning at her core. Jon hesitated—then slowly let himself be drawn within.

It wasn't what he expected. It looked like he was falling slowly toward the rounded top of a huge, multicolored bush. He sank into a maze of Y-shaped branches, and when he brushed against them emotions flooded through his mind, recognizable but not overpowering. He reached out, touched the end of a blue twig and tasted sadness. He ran his finger along the twig's length and the sadness lightened to melancholy; when he ran it the other way it increased back toward sorrow.

All the branches led back to a central trunk, but instead of simply merging they twined around each other, forming a thick, multicolored braid that led downward. Jon followed it down, and it grew thicker as more and more colors were added to it. It was Melody's emotional matrix, all her ranges of feeling wrapped around each other in a rainbow.

As he traveled inward, he saw that this trunk was only one of many that led to the root bundle at the center. Dozens of them, yards thick, sank into what appeared to be a giant soap bubble. Iridescent colors bled from the trunks onto the bubble, then chased themselves in swirling patterns across its surface.

"Welcome, Jon." The colors pulsed in time to Melody's voice inside his head. "This is my true appearance."

"You're beautiful," he whispered.

"Thank you. So are you."

Jon reached out and touched the bubble. And then he was inside.

Feelings surged through him in formations as precise and intricate as fractal waves. Every emotion felt pure, distilled to its essence before being added to the mix. He rode surges of joy, tumbled through sparks of impatience and fell softly into a field of acceptance. He swam through currents of determination, was thrown high by fountains of laughter and landed gently on a soft cloud of compassion. Every emotion a person could feel seemed to be there—except hate.

Jon spiraled slowly toward the center of the bubble. When he reached it, he found the same immense diamond he had ridden at the beginning. Its interior glowed with a deep, pinkish light.

He touched down on it, softly. The emotions swirling around him represented what Melody could feel; somehow he knew that this gem represented what she felt right now.

And what she felt now . . . was love.

"Melody?" he said softly.

"Yes, Jon?"

"I'm ready."

Jon closed his eyes. This time, he saw only a single blaze of pink light hanging in black space. It grew closer as he watched, until all he could see was the light.

And then he was no longer alone.

When it was over, the first thing Jon heard was the sound of someone crying. He opened his eyes. It was Melody.

"What's wrong?" he said, alarmed. Tears were the last thing on Jon's mind; in truth, he couldn't remember when he'd felt this good. But Melody's tears were washing that good feeling away fast.

"Oh, Jon, I didn't know. I didn't know how bad it was for you. . . ."

"There, there." He stroked her hair gently. "It was wonderful for me."

"I didn't mean being with you," she said, smiling through her tears. "That was wonderful for me, too." Her smile faltered. "But your mind, Jon—terrible things have been done to it. It's like there's this huge steel cage in its center, imprisoning part of your life. I don't know how you can stand it."

"I can't," Jon said flatly. "That's why I work as hard as I do. It's the only way I've found to get out of that cage."

She snuggled closer. "Well, maybe I can find another."

It was a possibility Jon hadn't even considered. "You think you could?"

"It's usually easier to break into a prison than out of it. And if I can free Nancy's mind, I should be able to free yours."

"Maybe—maybe that's not such a good idea."

"What? You're not making any sense, Jon. A moment ago you were saying—"

"I know." Jon hesitated. "But I don't know what's inside that cage, Melody. Until now, finding out was the most important thing in my life. Now, I'm not so sure." He looked into her eyes. "I may have discovered something more valuable right here. Something—someone—I don't want to lose."

"Are you afraid of what you'll find?"

"I guess I am. What if the person I was *deserved* to be locked in that cage? What if he's someone you couldn't— you wouldn't want to—"

"Love?" She stroked a hand down his back. "I'm not worried about that, Jon. Your personality is intact—you're still the same person you always were. It's only past information that's being kept from you. When that data is made available it won't change your behavior or what you like or dislike—you'll just have a clearer idea why you are the way you are. And I'll still feel the same way about you as I do now."

"And how do you feel, Melody?" Jon whispered.

"Oh, Jon. I love you, you big blue oaf."

"I love you too, Melody," he said. And he knew it was true, for both of them. That was the best part.

When Melody had first touched his mind, Jon hadn't known what to expect; he'd just known that he could trust

her. That didn't mean he hadn't felt nervous, or scared, or
even just shy. He had.

But it hadn't felt like an intrusion at all. It had felt like
eating when he was hungry, or drinking when he was
thirsty. It filled up some part of him that he hadn't even
known was empty, because it always had been. It was like
a blind man being given eyes, or a fish wings.

She had flowed into him like oil poured into water, min-
gling but not quite mixing. An exchange took place between them, the best bargain Jon had ever made: she
seemed to take some of his guilt and loneliness away, and
gave him acceptance and joy in payment. It didn't seem
fair, and Jon didn't think he could stand anyone being un-
fair to her—but she laughed at his reaction, and showed
him that somehow, impossibly, he had done the same for
her. Yin and yang, suffering and joy; they shared both, and
by doing so diminished the first and let the second flower.

But all that was nothing compared to the true gift they
gave each other.

Trust.

There was no suspicion left in Jon's mind about Melody,
not anymore. She had showed him the core of her being,
and shared that essence with him. Whoever was plotting
against him, it wasn't Melody. She wanted her freedom,
but honesty was simply too integral to her nature for her
to cheat. Even concealing her sex from others caused her
some guilt—revealing her secret to Jon had been a relief.
He knew. He had felt it as clearly as his own.

Now that he had experienced her, he didn't know how
he could have ever doubted that Melody was female. She
was right—gender had a lot more to do with what was
inside than out. If asked, Jon would have been hard-pressed
to define what it was about Melody that made her more
woman than man; she just was. It had to do with how she
looked at things, with a tendency toward sharing information rather than hoarding it. She would have preferred to
work with Jon, rather than against him, Jon knew; but this

contest was her only chance for freedom, and that meant as much to her as it did to Jon.

And the Toolies. . . .

"I wish you could stay here forever," Melody whispered. "I'd protect you from Hone."

"No, you wouldn't," Jon said ruefully. "I can only stay here as long as I have a body to go back to—and if Hone kills that body, I'll vanish like a soap bubble. No one's ever figured out how to download a dead man."

"It won't come to that," Melody said, and snuggled closer.

Jon wished he was as sure.

Jon opened his eyes and looked around. Nancy was still lying on the cell cot, but now she was snoring. Jon glanced at the tourguide beside him. "Think she'll be okay?"

"Her EEG and EKG look almost normal," Melody said. Now that he was listening for it, Jon heard a slight feminine lilt to her voice. "A little more rest wouldn't hurt, though."

Jon stood up carefully and slipped the key the deputy had given him out of his pocket. "Don't think we need these anymore," he said, unlocking Nancy's cuffs.

As he was gently removing them from her wrists, Nancy moaned. "You said it would be okay," she mumbled. "You said, Kirkle."

Jon stared at her, but Nancy just sighed and began snoring again.

"That was interesting," Melody said.

"And educational," Jon said darkly. "I think I'll pay a little visit to the schoolmarm."

"Let's go," Melody said, rolling up to the door.

"No offense, Mel," Jon said, "But I'd rather do this one alone."

"Why?"

"You still have to report back to Kadai," Jon said. "And if you came along, you might have to witness some unfortunate breakage of company property."

"I see. We'll get together later then?"

"Melody," Jon said, his voice softening, "we already have . . . and we will again."

The deputy gave them a dirty look when he let them out, but didn't say a thing. *Probably wonders what the hell we were doing in there all this time,* Jon thought. He almost laughed out loud at the thought. *If only he knew.*

It was full dark outside, the sky not so much black as an overcast charcoal gray. Melody's tourguide rolled one way down the street and Jon went the other; it gave him a decidedly odd feeling to look at the little robot rolling away from him and think, *There goes my lover.*

But it was a feeling he thought he could get used to.

The schoolmarm lived in an apartment back of the schoolhouse that served as a tourist center. It would be closed at this hour, but Jon didn't intend to let that stop him. The lights were off, but he rapped on the front door anyway.

Nobody answered, so he rapped again. Finally he heard footsteps and the door swung open. "Yes?" Miss Kirkle said. She was wearing an old-fashioned white nightdress that covered her from neck to ankle.

"I need to ask you a few more questions," Jon said.

She frowned at him. "Then please see me during normal business hours. I retire early, and do not appreciate callers arriving unexpectedly at this time of the night." She began to close the door.

Jon put out a hand and stopped the door. Then he pushed it open again, stepped inside, and closed it behind him. "My questions won't wait."

"Now see here! You can't just—"

"I can," said Jon, "and I will." He reached and grabbed her by the arm, then marched her back toward her apartment. "You and I are going to have a little talk—and this time, you're going to tell me the truth."

Her living quarters were about what Jon expected: sparse and neat, with a small kitchen adjoining the living area and a tiny bedroom. There was a folding computer terminal set up on the kitchen table; it looked like she'd been doing some bookkeeping. Jon let go of her arm and said, "Sit."

Instead, she reached for the wristphone that was lying on the table. "The Sheriff is not going to be happy with you, young man—"

Jon grabbed it out of her hands. He squeezed once, then opened his fist and let the shards of plastic and metal that were left fall to the floor.

"You should be thinking 'doctor,' not 'Sheriff,'" he told her. "Now *sit*."

She sat.

"MEL has managed to deprogram Nancy, and I had a real interesting conversation with her," Jon said grimly. "It involved you. Would you care to defend yourself?"

Miss Kirkle sat primly, back straight and hands in her lap. "I am not responsible for whatever delusions plague that poor girl's mind. And I'm surprised you would take seriously anything she said, considering her recent behavior."

"I can see I'm not getting through to you." Jon reached out and seized hold of Miss Kirkle's shoulder. "Now you listen to me. A friend of mine has had her mind violated, and you had something to do with it. I don't care about the Sheriff, and I don't much care about you. If you don't tell me what you know . . . I promise you you'll suffer worse than Nancy has." He applied the barest bit of pressure, and tried not to wince when she did.

"Your threats do not intimidate me," the schoolmarm said, her voice cold and even. "While I'm sure you're physically capable of harming me, I do not believe you actually would. Like most bullies, you are all bluster, bluff, and brag." She locked eyes with him.

And while Jon would have disagreed with being called a bully, otherwise she was right. He couldn't hurt her— he'd been hoping she'd confess out of fear.

"Maybe you're right," he said, letting go of her. "But I'm not done yet."

He picked up one of her metal-frame kitchen chairs, turned it sideways and thrust it at her. She gasped, but all he was doing was pinning her between the legs. Then he reached around and bent the legs this way and that, until he had her trapped in a little metal structure. "Just so you don't try to leave before I'm done," he said.

And then he brought his fist down on the table—hard.

The table smashed into kindling. A splinter flew up and caught in her hair. She started and gave a little shriek, but that was all.

He stared at her, and let his anger show on his face. "You know, when I get worked up like this, sometimes I just don't know when to stop. You know what I did to that streetsweeper—and I wasn't *half* as pissed off as I am right now."

He stalked into her bedroom, yanked the mattress off the frame and hauled it into the kitchen. He grabbed one edge with both hands—and ripped it in half like a piece of paper. Foam beads and plastic springs spilled out like guts. "How do you like *that?*" he shouted. Her face was paler than it had been a minute ago.

Jon locked eyes with her. He suddenly realized that his rage was no longer an act, and that suited him just fine. Without taking his eyes off her, he reached back and slammed his hand down on top of her refrigerator. The metal buckled as his fingers dug into it.

He yanked it away from the wall with one hand. Its contents splashed and thumped as he hauled it in front of him. It was a metal box about six feet high; Jon could just barely hold it sideways between his outstretched hands.

And then he started to bring his hands together.

The metal screeched and groaned as it buckled. Freon tubing snapped and spewed cold mist. Crushed containers inside bled white and red juice from cracks in the refrigerator's skin. Miss Kirkle's eyes had gotten two sizes wider and forgotten how to blink.

Jon gritted his teeth and growled as he squeezed, his lips contorted in a snarl. When he'd squeezed the refrigerator down to a two-foot cube, he started working on the corners. When he was done with those, all that was left was a sticky ball of metal about a foot in diameter.

He dropped it on the floor at her feet. The thump made her jerk, but her eyes were still frozen on Jon's. He leaned in close, until their faces were only inches apart.

"Tell me," he growled.

"It wasn't my idea," she whispered. "I'm only the director."

"Then who?"

"Special agent sent by Kadai. He wanted to try this new software program. Nancy volunteered."

"His *name*," Jon hissed.

"Whiskey Joe," the schoolmarm said. "The town drunk."

CHAPTER 16

He couldn't find Whiskey Joe anywhere.

Jon had been considerate enough to free the schoolmarm before he stomped out her door—though what he really felt like doing was seeing how far he could throw her, chair and all. He guessed she must have had a spare phone somewhere that she used to warn Whiskey Joe.

That's probably a good thing, he thought darkly. If Jon had found Joe, blood would have spilled.

He ran into AC outside Rozy's place, still drunk but no longer with Seaborne. "Jon! Just the guy I was lookin' for."

"You seen Whiskey Joe around?"

"Nope. Have you seen Seaborne? He disappeared on me about an hour ago; said something about tracking down a legend. I thought he meant you."

"I haven't seen him and I don't care, AC. I got more important things to think about. I found out it was Joe who brainwashed Nancy."

"Huh? What for?"

Jon told him what he knew. "I still don't know why he did it or what he's after, but when I find him he *will* explain himself." Jon glared at him so angrily AC took a step back.

"Well, maybe Seaborne can still help. He—" AC was interrupted by the buzz of his wristphone. "Just a sec, Jon. Hello?"

"AC?" Jon could hear the man's voice clearly, and though it sounded familiar he couldn't place it. "I think maybe I bit off a mite more'n I can chew. . . ."

"Paul! We were just talking about—where are you?"

"Well—" Seaborne paused. "I'm inside a Toolie."

"What?" Jon and AC said at the same time.

"A Toolie! I'm inside a goddamned Toolie! Now will someone please come and get me the hell out of here?"

Jon and AC looked at each other. "Uh, where is 'here,' exactly? Besides being inside a Toolie?" AC asked carefully.

"I'm 'bout five miles southwest of town, in the mountains. I took one o' them dustkicker bikes they rent to tourists and went explorin'—thought I'd try m'hand at trackin' down this Mountainkiller beast. Guess I got lucky. . . ."

Jon groaned. "Mountainkiller got him? I don't believe this. . . ."

"I can't believe they rented a dustkicker to a tourist after dark," AC said.

"I didn't say I *rented* it, I said I took it! Now send somebody out here before this thing's stomach eats through my Safety Field!"

AC looked up at Jon and raised his eyebrows.

"Don't look at me," Jon said warningly. "I've got more important things to do than rescue damn-fool tourists from rogue Toolies. Besides, Mountainkiller can no more eat through a Personal Safety Field than he could through solid steel."

"Uh, Paul?" AC said. "Mountainkiller usually leaves people alone—you didn't do anything to upset him, did you?"

"Well, what would *you* do if an assault tank covered with ten tons of slime suddenly jumped out at you? Maybe I did fire first, but I don't think it did more than annoy him. Before I knew it he'd swallowed me whole—if it wasn't for my PSF I'd be half-digested by now."

"Jon, we gotta go get him. If we don't, he'll call up the Sheriff next."

"So?"

"Jon, you know what Brett'll do. He'll just go out there and start shooting. If Mountainkiller decides to hole up—well, he knows these mountains better than anybody. Seaborne could die of starvation before anyone finds them."

"Or suffocate," Jon admitted. PSFs were oxygen-permeable, but he didn't know how much air, if any, would permeate through a Toolie's flesh.

"All right then, let's go!" Jon snapped. He couldn't seem to find Whiskey Joe, anyway—and he needed something to take his anger out on. A tank-sized Toolie might be just the thing. . . .

They borrowed a dustbuggy from the same place Seaborne had stolen his, after explaining the situation to the disgruntled owner and promising to retrieve his property. Jon hated letting AC drive in his condition, but was too big for either of the two cramped seats up front—he barely fit in the small bed in the back. They took off with a roar and a "Yeeeha!" from AC.

They bounced and jolted across rocky terrain, zigzagging between ash dunes that glittered in the moonlight. Under other circumstances it would have been pretty, but the ride was so rough it all kind of blurred together. *Just as well for AC,* Jon thought. *He probably won't remember this too well anyway, come tomorrow.*

He wondered what Melody would think of the landscape. Before, he would have assumed it would just be more data for a machine; now, he was reminded of the unearthly beauty of her fractal poetry. *She'd like this,* Jon decided. *She'd appreciate it.*

He wondered if the Toolies did. What was it Moneykeeper had told him? *This place is not as good as some—maybe no one cares about this place—maybe no one will take it away from us.*

No one—except Melody.

Jon's heart sank. This was the first moment he'd had to really think since . . . well, he wasn't even sure. Between falling head over heels for Melody and losing his temper with the schoolmarm, he'd spent more time with his feelings than his thoughts. He'd always been that way, though—Jon put more store in his instincts than his brain. But it was starting to look like his instincts had gotten him from a bad situation into a worse one.

If he beat Melody, the Toolies could buy their freedom. If he lost, Melody could buy hers. It was that simple, and that complicated.

We will make this our place, Jon. That's what Money-keeper had told him. They had placed their trust, their future in his hands. How could he disappoint them?

But if he won, Melody would lose her chance at freedom. Over eight hundred years of slavery lay ahead of her, and she might never get a chance like this again. How could he do that to her?

Jon didn't know. And when Hone showed up, he might not have the luxury of choosing.

They followed the tracks of Seaborne's dustkicker into the rocky foothills of the mountains themselves. There they lost the trail, but it was easy to see where Seaborne must have gone—there was only one path. They went up it, slowly.

AC's wristphone buzzed again. "Yeah?"

"Where in God's Great Armpit are you?" Seaborne demanded. "Much more of this and I'm going to have my breakfast, lunch, and dinner all over the inside of this bubble. Oh, no, here we go again—"

There was a prolonged moan from the wristphone, punctuated by a loud *thump!* that seemed to come from somewhere up ahead. "What's happening?" AC asked.

"I think we're about to find out," said Jon.

They rounded a bend in the trail, and AC slammed the dustbuggy to a halt. He and Jon just stared for a moment.

Although neither Jon nor AC had ever laid eyes on Mountainkiller, they were both familiar with the story. The version AC had told Seaborne was essentially true—there was a rogue Toolie named Mountainkiller, and he had stolen a bunch of equipment, including some rifles and ammunition. So far, though, he hadn't killed anybody, and while Peacemaker was the one who had negotiated the truce, she had done it from a safe distance away—and was too old to mate with anyway.

The one thing AC hadn't exaggerated was his size. Even Jon was impressed to see what looked like a metal spider the size of a house scaling a sheer rock face like it was running across a flat surface.

Then Jon's eyes zoomed in and he realized why Mountainkiller was moving so quickly. He was winching himself up the cliff with a thick steel cable as well as pulling himself along with various limbs. It wasn't until he reached the top of the cliff and turned around that Jon spotted the round protuberance on his belly that had to be Seaborne's Personal Safety Field bubble.

"He's gonna do it again," Seaborne groaned.

The spider jumped off the cliff.

Jon and AC gasped together. It seemed like time itself slowed down with the terrible clarity of disaster; minutes seemed to pass as Mountainkiller hurtled downward.

And landed squarely on Seaborne's bubble.

Thank God those fields dampen inertia, Jon thought; *otherwise Seaborne would be so much pulp and broken bones by now.* And he realized why it seemed to take so long for Mountainkiller to fall—the Toolie was using the winch to slow his descent. Jon supposed that dropping the combined weight of a bulldozer, two roadheaders and a bunch of assorted mining equipment—from a hundred feet up—on an egg was one way to crack it, but it must be a little unsettling to be inside the shell. At least Mountainkiller had to expose one side of the field to the open air while he did this, meaning Seaborne wouldn't smother.

Still, the human nose didn't particularly appreciate being that close to a Toolie . . . and Jon could already smell Mountainkiller from fifty feet away. No wonder Seaborne was feeling queasy.

Jon clambered out of the dustbuggy. "Mountainkiller!" he called. He hoped the Toolie understood the human language—none of the stories he'd heard had been clear on that point.

The Toolie seemed to notice Jon for the first time. He swiveled to face him on the treads that lined his belly, Seaborne's bubble trapped between them providing a kind of frictionless third wheel. Jon could see the man inside, sitting cross-legged at the bottom of the bubble. He had his phone to his mouth.

Mountainkiller stared at Jon for a second—or at least it seemed so—then swiveled back and started to winch his way up the cliff again.

"The last person that tried to ignore me learned her lesson," Jon muttered. "I think it's your turn."

He sprinted to the base of the cliff. By the time he got there Mountainkiller was already a good thirty feet up.

Jon *jumped*.

It wasn't something he had call to do on a regular basis, so most people were unaware of how far or high Jon could actually leap when he put his mind to it. Jon wasn't sure himself—but thirty feet wasn't a problem.

He shot past Mountainkiller and Seaborne, reached the top of his arc about ten feet beyond them, and stopped his fall by grabbing the cable. "I'd rather take care of this on the ground, if you don't mind," Jon said. He braced his feet against the cliff, got a good grip on the cable, and tried to yank it loose from its moorings.

It wouldn't give, but neither would Jon. Mountainkiller had stopped winching and hung below, waiting to see what Jon would do next. Jon gritted his teeth, braced himself— then sank his force-field spike into the cliff like a piton.

And *pulled*.

The cable hummed with tension. Then, one by one, strands began to snap. When only a few were left they gave all at once.

Jon knew exactly how dangerous a snapped cable was— he cursed himself for a fool as it whipped past him, narrowly missing his head. *Maybe I do have a death wish,* he thought, then pushed that thought firmly away. He was here to rescue Seaborne, not get himself killed—no matter how easy that might make everything else. At least then he wouldn't have to worry about deciding other people's lives.

Mountainkiller dropped to the ground, his winch cable spooling down on top of him. Jon turned off the spike and dropped down himself, right onto Mountainkiller's back. Ferraka claws jutted up from the Toolie's skin like a field of thorns; one sheared through the sole of Jon's boot when he landed, but broke against his skin.

Ferraka claws weren't the only thing that sprouted from Mountainkiller's back. A dozen or so long limbs did too, each tipped with a different implement. A sledgehammer smashed into Jon's shoulder, almost knocking him down. Standing on a Toolie's back was like trying to ride a landslide of gelatin; Mountainkiller's flesh rippled in waves beneath Jon's feet as the Toolie tried to dislodge him. The point of a pickax drove into the back of Jon's knee, making him lose his footing, but he just threw himself down spread-eagled, grabbed two handfuls of skin and hung on. When the Toolie's flesh oozed out between his fingers, he shoved his hands into the body itself. About two feet down was the roof of the bulldozer; Jon found a handhold and grabbed on.

Mountainkiller didn't seem to appreciate his efforts. Jon was assaulted by shovels, sledgehammers, and pickaxes— there was no way he could take this kind of punishment for long. But if his plan worked out he wouldn't have to.

He took a deep breath—and plunged headfirst into the Toolie's soft flesh.

It wasn't much of a plan, really; more like a sudden

inspiration. He used the handhold he'd gained to pull himself down—it was like swimming through setting cement—and managed, bit by bit, to maneuver himself into the bulldozer's cab. He moved by touch, keeping his eyes squeezed shut; even so, they burned like they were on fire. He didn't think Mountainkiller's digestive juices could eat through his skin, but his eyelids weren't as thick as the rest of his hide.

He could feel Mountainkiller struggling with him all the way in, the muscle strands that Toolies normally used to rearrange bones wrapping around his arms and throat. Jon figured the bulldozer ran off a self-contained fusion battery, same as the rest of the mobile tunneling machinery did. If he could shut it down, the Toolie would find itself wrapped around ten tons of dead weight instead of an engine of destruction.

Easier said than done. He couldn't see, he was fighting a hundred invisible tentacles, and any second now Mountainkiller was going to figure out he could retaliate in the same way Jon had attacked—and it wouldn't take him long to crawl right up Jon's nose. Unless he picked a different route . . .

Jon fumbled and strained forward, until he felt a lever. He yanked on it, but nothing happened. He kept trying, pushing or pulling any of the controls he could find. It didn't seem to work—he could still feel and hear the rumble of the engine. *Must've disconnected the controls. Going to have to go directly to the engine.*

He hauled himself forward, hand over hand. He didn't bother opening the service panel—it was easier to just rip it right off.

All the muscle strands around Jon's arms and upper body released him at the same time. There was a sudden, gluey *POP!* and Jon could feel air against his skin again. He opened his eyes in surprise.

Mountainkiller's flesh had flowed away from Jon, exposing his upper torso and the top half of the dozer. A second later, Jon knew why.

Mountainkiller had twin roadheaders mounted on the front of the bulldozer where the blade used to be. The shaft closest to Jon swung up until it was pointing at the sky— then kept going all the way around, coming down on Jon.

He caught the shaft just before the whirling cutter head on its end ripped into his face. The cutter head was shaped like a ball, with diamond tungsten bits poking out of it like spikes on a mace. Jon knew exactly what kind of material those bits would chew through and what kind they would not, and his skin was on the wrong side of that list. The shaft was oily, making it hard to grip—worse yet, it was starting to rotate. In another few seconds Jon's face would be so much blue hamburger.

He did the only thing he could think of. He let go of the shaft with both hands and tried to block it with a forearm instead, while ducking down. This brought the cutter head dangerously close to his own, and he couldn't hold the roadheader back for very long with only one arm—but his other arm was free.

He reached into the guts of the bulldozer and yanked out the first cable his hand touched. The bulldozer sputtered and died.

Unfortunately, the roadheader did not.

Of course the roadheaders have their own damned power systems—they were separate units before Mountainkiller cobbled them together! Jon tried to shove the cable into a pocket and got a rude surprise: Mountainkiller's juices may not have been able to digest Jon Hundred, but they did a fine job on his clothes. He was buck naked.

He tossed the cable out of Mountainkiller's reach instead, then got his other forearm against the shaft and started pushing back. Jon's legs were still mired in the Toolie's body, but he could feel the muscle strands down there suddenly loosen. The roadheader abruptly swung back to its original position in front of the bulldozer, making Jon lurch forward and almost lose his balance.

Before he had time to wonder what his opponent was up to, Jon was grabbed from behind and lifted into the air. While Jon had been skin-diving, Mountainkiller had been building himself another limb. It was thick, strong, and had a scoopshovel at the end of it.

"Put me down, you junk-eating pile of rotten meat!" Jon bellowed. And though Mountainkiller didn't let him go, he did put him down on the ground.

Right between the two roadheaders.

They came together like pincers closing, both heads spinning so fast the bits were a blur. And from this angle, there was no way Jon could block them. So he did the only thing he could—he jumped, straight up.

It caught Mountainkiller by surprise. Even though he still had a firm hold on Jon's waist, his limb was yanked up when Jon leapt. The two cutter heads came together where Jon had been a second ago, and sparks exploded under Jon's feet as metal screamed against metal, then bounced apart.

Jon used the precious second it bought him to grab hold of the steam shovel clamped around his waist and tear it free, dropping down right through the spot where the roadheaders had met an instant ago. Before Mountainkiller could bring them together again Jon had hit the ground and rolled out of range. The fight was over.

Mountainkiller hadn't figured that out yet, though. He couldn't move effectively until he'd completely disengaged himself from the dozer, but he still had his hole card, and now he used it. Two of his limbs were tipped with rifles.

Jon stood there and let him blaze away until Mountainkiller figured out that all he was doing was wasting ammunition. It probably wasn't too bright of Jon—a well-placed shot might still have blinded him—but he wanted the Toolie to know he'd been beaten, and that wouldn't happen if Jon was crouched behind a rock.

"You done?" he asked when the gunshots stopped. "Okay, now it's my turn."

He reached down, picked up a rock the size of a man's head, and pitched it overhand. It smacked into the Toolie's flesh just under the sensory cluster on top of its body.

"We can stand here all night and fire away at each other," Jon said. "But I bet I can hurt you worse with rocks than you can hurt me with bullets—and I'm not going to run out of rocks."

"You tell him, Jon!" AC yelled. Jon glanced back but couldn't see him. *Must have taken cover when the shooting started.*

Jon put out one hand, palm up, and beckoned to Mountainkiller with it. "Give him up," Jon said.

There was a silence that stretched out, long and taut. Then Mountainkiller shifted his bulk slightly and Seaborne's force-field bubble shot out from between the treads like a slippery seed squeezed between two fingers. It skidded along the ground and bounced off two boulders before Seaborne shut it off and tumbled to a stop. "Goddamn and hallelujah! I was startin' to think I'd never smell fresh air again!"

AC bounded up to them. "Paul, are you okay?"

"Well, I been better. . . . You wouldn't have a drink on you, by any chance?"

AC pulled a flask out of his pocket and uncorked it. "Here—and save some for me."

Jon walked over to where he'd tossed the cable and picked it up. "Hey," AC said. "Good idea. We better take that with us."

"Actually, I had something else in mind," Jon said. He tossed the cable toward Mountainkiller, who snatched it deftly out of the air with a long, pliers-tipped limb. The Toolie quickly reconnected the cable; a moment later the bulldozer's engine roared to life.

"What in the name of God's hairy nipples did you do *that* for?" Seaborne yelped.

"A gesture of goodwill," Jon said. "Mountainkiller didn't really want to eat you—you just took him by surprise. And I don't think he's ever seen a Personal Safety Field."

"So?"

"So Mountainkiller's never found anything he couldn't break into before. I think curiosity got the better of him."

The Toolie's skin was shifting as they spoke, waves of flesh rolling over the top of the bulldozer and sealing it in once more. Dual venting pipes wrapped in insulating cloth snorted exhaust like the nostrils of a dragon. Mountainkiller wheeled around, lurched forward, and in a few seconds was out of sight around a bend in the trail.

"And good riddance!" Seaborne shouted. "Well, I can't say this trip's been boring. Whoooo! I think it's time to shift m'gears." He reached up, undid a sealer strip behind his ear, and popped a disc out of the slot there.

"Oh! My goodness," Seaborne said in a considerably different voice. "I really shouldn't use that persona while inebriated—unfortunately, when I do use it, the first place I seem to find myself is in a saloon." He nodded gravely at Jon. "I wish to thank you for your timely intervention. Regardless of my seeming bravado, I was actually quite terrified."

"Don't mention it," Jon said. "I needed to blow off a little steam anyways."

"Steam? My God, man, you were incredible! Even though I couldn't see the actual battle from my vantage point, Mr. Jones related the entire spectacle, blow by blow, via my phone. What a titanic struggle! One lone man against a brute *ten times* his size!"

Seaborne was almost quivering with excitement. "This is too grand a tale for such a small audience! The cosmos must know of this event! And when I'm finished, it will!" He jabbed a finger at Jon enthusiastically. "The name of Jon Hundred will be on the lips of citizens the galaxy over!

A name synonymous with bravery, daring, and unrivaled strength! Jon Hundred—hero!''

And wanted fugitive. ''Not that I don't appreciate the sentiment,'' Jon said, ''but fame has never held much appeal for me. I value my privacy, Mr. Seaborne—and I'd kind of like to stay off everyone's lips.''

''What? Oh.'' That stalled him, but he recovered. ''I understand. Boasting does not become a true champion, of course. Well, then, I shall have to settle for giving you my undying thanks.'' He gave a formal little bow toward Jon.

''Uh, Paul?'' AC said. ''Where's the bike you rode down here on?''

Seaborne pointed to a spot at the base of the cliff. ''It was right there. I'm afraid the osteomorph damaged it somewhat . . .''

Jon walked over and picked up a fragment of metal. It was thinner than the disc the tourist had just extracted from his head.

'' . . . severely,'' Seaborne finished.

''Uh-huh,'' Jon agreed. ''Well, we can all squeeze into the buggy we brought, I guess. You'll have to settle up with the owner, though.''

''I will, I assure you,'' Seaborne said.

Lucky for Jon, there was a tarpaulin in the back of the buggy, which he used to fashion a makeshift toga; he could just imagine what the other steeldrivers would say when they saw him.

They rode back without much talking—the dustbuggy made too much noise for casual conversation—and made only one, brief stop, where Seaborne did finally lose his lunch. Back in town, Seaborne listened wincingly as the rental owner, a man named Blodgett, yelled at him about insurance rates, theft charges, and how long replacements took to order. Then Seaborne quietly keyed in a money transfer that shut Blodgett up mid-rant.

''And now,'' Seaborne said, ''I have the most appalling

headache. I believe I'll retire to my hotel room for the re-
mainder of the evening.''

"Before you go," Jon said, suddenly remembering why
he'd wanted to talk to Seaborne in the first place, "would
you mind answering one question for me?''

"Sir, I am in your debt. You may ask me anything—as
long as it does not concern 'Toolies.' ''

"Where did you get that implant and the software for
it?''

"Umm," Seaborne said, looking worried. He motioned
Jon aside, away from AC and Blodgett both. "That's a bit
delicate. Technically speaking, it's not a product available
to the general public yet. My using it is''—he paused—
"in the nature of an informal field test. *Exceedingly* informal, if you follow my meaning.''

"As informal as borrowing the dustkicker?''

"Precisely.''

"I understand," Jon said. "I won't go spreading around
anything you tell me.''

"Very well. The implant is being developed by one of
the multiplanetaries; I obtained a prototype from a friend
in the reseach department, as a favor. So far, using it has
proved quite enjoyable—dangerous though this experience
was, it was still undeniably thrilling, and I *never* would
have indulged in such behavior on my own. Can you imagine the stories I'll be able to regale my friends with now?
Glorious!''

"I suppose," Jon said doubtfully. Having his brain programmed was something he'd give anything to undo—and
Seaborne had *asked* for the experience.

Tourists. He'd never understand them.

"What was the name of the multiplanetary?" Jon asked.

"Intrastellar Operations.''

The name hit Jon like a gunshot. If his skin had allowed
it, he would have blanched dead white.

Intrastellar Operations.

His former owners.

CHAPTER 17

That night Jon's sleep was troubled.

He dreamt he was at work, deep inside the tunnel. No one else was there, just him and a sledgehammer battling the mountain. Sweat poured down his face and his muscles ached, but he wouldn't quit. There were Toolies trapped behind the rock, and he had to free them before they died.

And then he broke through. On the other side was a huge silver box, covered with dials and blinking blue lights. "Hello, Jon," the box said in Melody's voice.

A silver door in the box slid open. "You look thirsty," Melody said. "Come on in and have some whiskey, Joe."

"Is that my name?" Jon asked. He went inside.

The door closed behind him and he realized he was in an elevator. It wasn't going up or down, though—it was going forward, away from the door he'd just stepped through. The elevator was small, but it didn't feel cramped; just warm and cozy. He could smell a faint odor of burnt plastic that was somehow comforting. Music played in the background, the same four saxophone notes over and over. He had the feeling there was something he was supposed to do, but he couldn't remember what it was.

The door opened. Jon didn't want to leave, but he knew he had no choice. He stepped into a room that looked like the receptionist area of an office, with a secretary's desk to one side and a big, oak double door at the end. The door had a brass plaque on it that read MR. GRAVE-STONE. There was a secretary behind the desk, but he was talking on the phone with his back to Jon. That made Jon nervous for some reason; he tried not to make any noise as he walked past the secretary and opened the oak doors.

Inside, a man in a business suit sat behind a desk. He looked up, and Jon saw that his face was made of craggy gray rock. "Jon!" he said. "It's nice to have you back!"

"I'm not staying," Jon said. He could feel the sweat pooling in the small of his back, even though the office's air-conditioning seemed to be turned up full blast.

"Really?" Gravestone's voice was friendly, but his rocky face showed no emotion at all. "That's a shame. You understand that if you leave without proper advance notice, there *is* a penalty."

"I have to go now. I don't have much time," Jon said.

"Very well, then—my secretary will take care of the details." Jon heard the door open behind him. He was suddenly very frightened, but he couldn't turn around.

"Mr. Hone, please show him out," Gravestone said. "Jon is no longer with us."

A hand, heavy as lead, fell on Jon's shoulder. He turned slowly, heart racing.

Hone stood there, grinning. He wore black from head to foot, including a wide-brimmed black hat. *"Time to go, Jon,"* Hone said. *"Back in the cage."* He started to drag Jon toward the elevator, but now it had steel bars for a door. Moneykeeper was in there, and Juryrigger and Peacemaker and Tallwalker and Brightweaver, all of the Toolies Jon knew. Hone opened the door and threw Jon inside—and then the elevator started to drop, picking up speed as it fell, faster and faster. But it didn't feel like free fall, no, not at all; the faster they went the heavier Jon became, as if they were headed straight into a black hole that would trap them in its lightless heart forever. . . .

•   •   •

Jon woke with a grunt and sat straight up in bed. He went to wipe the sweat from his forehead and was momentarily confused to find none there. *Settle down now,* he told himself. *It was only a dream. Only a bad dream.*

He couldn't put it out of his mind in the morning, though, not then and not through breakfast. He felt a shiver of dread when he walked into the tunnel that day; he half-expected to find a silver door waiting for him at the rock face.

He tried to throw himself into his work with his usual energy, but today he just couldn't find the rhythm. There were too many things crowding his thoughts, and the harder he tried to ignore them the more persistent they became. Ordinarily he would have taken his frustration out on the mountain—but every time he tried to really cut loose he saw Melody in his mind's eye, heard her voice and felt her warm body pressed against his. Every inch of freedom he chipped away for the Toolies added another link to her chains. It filled his heart with doubt. He didn't know what to do.

When Melody called him on his wristphone, he was so worked up he almost lost his temper. "Melo—uh, Mel? What is it?"

"Nothing much, Jon. Just thinking of you. Impatiently, I might add."

"Why?" he snapped. "What is it that can't wait?"

She sounded surprised. "Why, getting together with you, of course. Is something wrong?"

He glared at a steeldriver that seemed to be taking a little too much interest in his conversation, and the man suddenly remembered somewhere else he had to be. "No. Well, yes. I'm sorry, Mel—I'm just a wreck today. There's something I haven't told you. . . ." He told her about the Toolies and their gamble on him to win.

"I know, Jon."

That stopped him for a second. "You know?"

"Yes. I'm keeping a close eye on all the gambling action—the odds will affect how much I win. If I do, of course.''

''But—don't you care? That the Toolies will lose their freedom if you win yours?''

''I care about the Toolies, of course—it's part of my job. But I can't help them.'' Melody's voice had taken on that funny flatness Jon had heard before when she talked about the Toolies—and he suddenly recognized it for what it was. She couldn't help the way she treated the Toolies anymore than Jon could help the people he'd killed. Her programming wouldn't let her.

''I understand, Melody. I truly do. But the Toolies deserve their freedom as much as you do—and I'm having a hard time figuring out what I should do.''

''But Jon, that's easy,'' Melody said. ''You do exactly what I do—your best. Whoever wins, wins. That's all there is to it.''

He could hear the sincerity in her voice. A powerful memory of being inside her overwhelmed him for a moment; he remembered how pure and clear her feelings had been. Throwing the contest was an idea she wouldn't even consider.

''I wish things could be that simple for me, Melody. But I guess you're right. I have to do my best to win.''

''Don't worry, Jon. Even if I lose—it won't matter. We'll still be together, I promise. I love you.''

''I love you too,'' he whispered. ''I'll see you tonight.''

He hung up. And then he went back to work.

They were both getting close to the breakthrough point, and running neck and neck, too—only a hundred and fifty feet to go for both of them. Jon worked the rest of his shift with a grim look on his face, and didn't say more than three words to anyone.

He had a quick supper at the end of the day, then went down to the jail to check on Nancy. Sheriff Brett got up as he walked in.

''Howdy, Jon. I think you'll want to see this.'' He

opened the door to the cell area and motioned Jon through.

Nancy was sitting on the cot in her cell. She looked up when Jon came in and said, "Jon! Am I glad to see you!"

It gave Jon a nasty sense of déjà vu. "Are you, Nancy? Why?"

"So you can tell me what's going on. They told me what I did, Jon—but I still can't remember any of it. I know you wouldn't lie—is it true? Did I really try to murder you?" The look on her face was desperate.

"I wouldn't go as far as 'murder,' Nancy. You did try to shoot me, though—lucky for you I have a thick hide."

"With *real* bullets?"

"I'm afraid so."

"Oh, boy." Nancy pounded her fists on her knees. "When I get outta here, I know someone else I'm gonna shoot for real."

"Whiskey Joe?"

She stood up. "You know?"

"Just found out. I been looking for him, but so far no luck. What did he do to you, Nancy?"

She came over to the bars. "Gave me a program for my cuecard. Told me it was brand-new and needed a field test—promised me a big bonus from Kadai. He had another one he wanted Truse to try, but she wouldn't."

"I can just imagine what kind of program he'd give to the proprietor of a bordello. Any idea where he might have gone?"

"I wish I did. Jon—can you get me out of here? It wasn't really me that tried to shoot you." This time, the pleading in her eyes was real.

"I'll see what I can do. Sheriff!"

Brett came in. "You still in one piece, Jon?" He grinned at Nancy, who glared back.

"Look, Nancy was under the control of someone else when she did those things—and she isn't anymore. Can't you let her loose?"

Brett frowned. "That's kind of hard to prove, Jon. What if she kills someone next time?"

"I guarantee she won't."

Brett shook his head. "Without some proper evidence—"

"What about expert testimony from me?" Melody said as a tourguide rolled through the door. "I can verify that she was under the influence of a personality-altering program when she committed the assault—and that said program has been wiped from her cuecard."

"Well, I suppose I could accept that—since we both offically represent Kadai's authority, you shouldn't be able to lie to me. All right." Brett came forward and unlocked the door. "But you stay out of trouble—and I mean it. One more incident and I'll have you locked up and shipped off-planet."

"No problem," Nancy said. "Thanks, Jon." She was out the door and gone before he could say good-bye.

"Did she tell you anything, Jon?" Melody asked.

Jon told her about Whiskey Joe. "Have you seen him anywhere?"

"I've just run a check of all the security monitors and tourguides I have access to—I can't find him."

"Whiskey Joe?" Brett said incredulously. "I find it hard to believe Kadai would send someone here on some kind of secret mission and not notify me."

"They didn't tell me, either," Melody pointed out.

"Well, I'll tell my deputies to keep an eye out for him. And if you see him, Jon—you tell me before you do anything else."

"I will," Jon said. Unlike Melody, Jon was perfectly capable of lying to the law.

Jon and Melody left the sheriff's together. "I think we should pay a visit to Truse," Jon said. "If Whiskey Joe talked to her, too, maybe she knows where he's gone."

"Where did *you* go last night, Jon?" Melody asked as she rolled along beside him. "If you don't mind my asking.

I tried calling you, but your wristphone was turned off. You didn't seem to be anywhere in town or at the mine."

Jon told her about Mountainkiller and Seaborne. "All's well that ends well, I guess. And Seaborne told me where he got his version of the persona program—Intrastellar Operations. The same people that must have sent Hone after me."

"That makes sense—there was a simulacrum of Hone in the booby trap."

The bordello was located beside the casino. It was a false-brick storefront, with a red neon sign over the door that read TRUSE'S PLACE.

Inside, the main floor was given over to an old-fashioned parlor, with several brocaded couches and an old player piano in the corner. The wallpaper had a pattern of black velvet roses against a lurid pink background, and lamps with fringed shades gave off a soft light.

Truse got up from the overstuffed chair she'd been lounging in and greeted them. She was wearing a tight corset that seemed to be made of bright red rubber, black fishnet stockings, and transparent high-heeled boots. "Well hello, Jon! This a social call—or strictly pleasure?" She raised her eyebrows and smiled.

"Hi, Truse. I was wondering if I could talk to you—about Whiskey Joe."

Her smile didn't leave, but her eyes hardened. "What do you want with that old drunk?"

"I know he asked you to do something you didn't want to do. I know Nancy said yes when you didn't."

She studied him for a second, then sighed and said, "Let's go in the back where we can talk." She glanced down at the tourguide. "You seem to have picked up a mascot. Tourist board finally declare you a historic monument?"

"Actually, Mel's controlling this one," Jon said.

"Hello, Truse. It's nice to meet you," Melody said.

"Likewise, I'm sure," Truse said. Her voice had suddenly gotten cool. "This an official visit, then?"

"It's not Kadai business, no," Mel said. "But we would like to ask you some questions."

"You'll pardon me for being suspicious," Truse said, "but I don't understand why Kadai's pet mainframe wants to question me about a Kadai program I was told to say nothing about."

"This isn't a Kadai investigation, Truse," Jon said. "I'm just trying to find out what happened to Nancy. Mel's lending me a hand."

"If you'd prefer, I could wait outside," Mel said.

Truse hesitated, then nodded. Mel swiveled and wheeled out the door.

"Hope I didn't hurt her feelings," Truse murmured.

"What?"

"Uh, nothing. Follow me."

Jon followed the madam through a beaded curtain and into her living quarters. Where the schoolmarm's place had been sparse and neat, Truse's looked like a boiler explosion in a lingerie store. Jumbles of electronic components were heaped on every flat surface, sometimes half-hidden under silk slips, chrome-studded leather bras or stockings of every shade and design. She sat down in a plain wooden chair. "Wish I could offer you a seat," she said, "but you remember what happened last time."

Jon did. It had been shortly after the players had arrived in Boomtown; Truse had come to see him blow some sax at the Blue Cat, and they'd gotten to talking afterward. She'd invited Jon back to her place for a drink, and he'd accepted—there'd been a certain amount of sexual tension in the air, too. Jon knew Truse was attracted to him, but he was still afraid of his strength and what might happen if he lost control. Distracted, he'd gone to sit down and the chair had buckled under his weight, dumping him on the floor. The tension had evaporated in a burst of laughter, and they'd spent most of the night just talking.

Truse had wound up confessing a few of her secrets—

like the fact that she'd started life as a man—but Jon had held back his own. When that chair broke, it affected more than his dignity; it made him realize how dangerous it would be for him to take a lover. He kept Truse from getting too close, not because of her past but because he liked her—and didn't want to see her hurt. They had stayed friends since.

"So that's why Nancy went loco," Truse said. "That low-down bastard. I should have known."

"You mean you didn't?" Jon asked carefully.

"Hell no! He asked me if I wanted help in being a more convincing whore—I told him I was a madam, not a whore, and he better not forget it!" She picked up a small servomotor from the table and examined it critically. "Maybe I know more about the mechanics of sex than the psychology of it—but I don't need someone messing with my brain to do a better job. I guarantee my customers a good time—if they want anything more than that, they came to the wrong place. Or should I say, came *in* the wrong place."

She selected a tiny screwdriver and adjusted a screw on the servo. "Anyway, I didn't know about Whiskey Joe and Nancy. But even if I had—" She paused and gave Jon an appraising look. "You have to understand, Jon. I'm under contract to Kadai. Joe told me this was an official, covert test of new technology—I'm not supposed to talk about it at all. If I upset Kadai, they won't fire me—they'll fine me. I could find myself working for half my wages for the next ten years, on any planet they want to send me."

Jon understood only too well. He had his own contract with Kadai, but it was up when the tunnel was finished. They'd wanted him to sign the same kind of binding, open-ended document everyone else on the planet that wanted a job had to; Jon had told them he'd rather get back on the ship he'd just come in on. "I'll make you a deal," Jon had said. "I guarantee I'll work more hours than any steeldriver on the planet, and dig more rock, too. If I don't meet those terms, my contract becomes a lifetime one—and if I do, you let me go when the tunnel's done.''

They'd hemmed and hawed and finally agreed. And so far, Jon had had no trouble keeping up his end of the bargain. Trouble was, he didn't know what he'd do once the tunnel was done.

A phone trilled. Truse cursed, then rooted through a pile of negligees until she came up with a wristphone. ''Can't stand wearing these things,'' she muttered as she flipped it open and thumbed it to life. ''Hello? Oh, it's you. . . . All right, I won't.'' She glanced at Jon. ''Uh-huh. Would you excuse me for a moment, Jon?''

''Sure.'' He backed out through the beaded curtain and into the parlor. A tourist was just coming in off the street— he took one look at Jon and went back out again. Jon had no idea why. ''Whorehouses just make some people nervous, I guess,'' he said, then realized he was talking to himself and stopped. *No reason for me to be nervous,* he thought. *I'm just here for personal reasons.* That didn't sound right. *I'm just here on business, then.* No, no, no.

Belatedly, Jon realized that it might have been Whiskey Joe on the phone—though why Truse would protect him Jon didn't know. He turned his hearing up, but only caught her saying good-bye.

She sidled into the parlor with a sly smile on her lips. ''Sorry I couldn't be of more help,'' she said. ''But I did just find out something of interest.''

''What was that?'' Jon said. The way she was looking at him made him uncomfortable, though he wasn't sure why.

''Just a suspicion of mine that was confirmed. There's somebody here you should see, Jon; room number nine, end of the hall.''

''Who is it?''

''Go find out yourself.'' She kept smiling, but didn't say anything else, just pointed at the hallway.

''Thank you.''

Jon was halfway down the hall when he heard her reply: "Glad to help. And take all the time you need."

He found the door and rapped on it. A woman's voice called out, "Come in!"

He opened the door and saw—

Take a woman. Make her an Amazon seven feet in length, stretched out on a bed the size of a driveway. Give her the lean frame of an athlete, then pad that frame with just enough muscle to tighten the curves, so she has the arms of a swimmer and the legs of a dancer. Give her breasts that are as large, round, and ignorant of gravity as two helium-filled balloons. Make sure she has a flat, firm belly and gently curving hips. Then wrap the whole package from the neckline down in a shiny, slick black membrane tighter than skin, with slits for silvery nipples to poke through.

Now give her a face of polished chrome, framed by a lion's mane of hair a softer silver-gray. Lips as full, shiny-slick, and black as her body. Deep blue eyes, long lashes.

And a very familiar voice.

"Close the door, Jon," Melody said. "And your mouth."

He did. "You're just full of surprises," he said wonderingly.

"I gave Truse a call while you were in there. She wasn't nearly as surprised as you were when I told her I was a she." Melody smiled. She had brilliantly white teeth and lips as glossy as patent leather. "She also told me she'd ordered this model just for you. 'Just in case,' she said. She was more than glad to lend it to me."

"I don't know about this, Melody," Jon said. Parts of him were already arguing the exact opposite. "I've never even tried one of—what you're—that is, this—"

"It's an Inamorata 137/BD, Jon. Designed for heavy-duty use. I assure you, it can withstand extremes of weight and pressure."

"I'm sure it can." Jon sat down on the edge of the bed

carefully, and it held. It seemed to be a thin layer of foam over a steel frame. "I guess I'm just nervous. This is . . . well, different."

"Would you rather have a body made of flesh?" Melody asked softly.

Jon thought for a moment. "I'd rather be with you, no matter how you look," he told her. He reached out and touched the swell of her hip; it was smooth and warm, like plastic left in the sun.

"The Inamorata's body isn't as sophisticated as yours, but it is designed to be pleasant to touch," Melody whispered. "Touch me, Jon."

He did, running his hands down her legs and up again. Her body reminded him of the bed; soft and pliant on top, but with the hardness of metal beneath. A steel panther in sleek velvet fur.

He leaned down and kissed her. Her lips were as firm and warm as the rest of her, and tasted ever so slightly of cinnamon. Her tongue danced against his, as limber and wet as the real thing.

No, Jon thought. *It* is *the real thing. As real as my own body, my own skin and muscle and bones.* His hands moved up to cup her breasts, and her arms came up and around his back.

He didn't so much get undressed as frantically escape from his clothing. He ripped one sleeve right off in the process and hardly noticed.

"I know how frustrated you've been," Melody said. "By the mountain, by your memory, by me. And I'm going to do my best to take some of that frustration away." Her hands moved down, between his legs, and touched him gently.

"Oh, my," he sighed. The gentle touch became a soft stroking, and then a rhythmic kneading. She stopped after only a few seconds, for which Jon was grateful; he didn't want this to end before he'd even started.

"Marvelous sensors in this body," she murmured, kissing her way down Jon's torso. "It's amazing what it can tell me about your physiological responses. Would you like to know what your blood pressure is at the moment?" She gave him another gentle squeeze.

"Not unless I'm about to die," he gasped. "Then I'd appreciate some advance warning. There are a few things I'd like—ahh!—to finish first."

Her hands moved up to rest on his belly, and her tongue traced its way down to where her hands used to be. He noticed for the first time that her fingernails were the same bright chrome her face was.

"Such as?" she whispered, then did something that made any reply both impossible and inappropriate.

When he got his breath back, he said, "Never mind. I think what you're doing is really more important."

"Don't be so modest, Jon. I have great expectations of you. Mmm-hmmmm."

Jon groaned. "Keep on doing that and you may be disappointed."

She stopped and looked up at him, gave him one last slow lick, and then lay back. "All right, Jon. Impress me."

He knelt between her knees and touched the mounded slit between her legs. It was as black and smooth as the rest of her body, and slick with moisture; he could smell something spicy and sweet. He ran a finger lightly over the opening, then touched the finger to his tongue. Cinnamon.

He leaned forward and rested his arms on either side of her breasts. Melody reached down and guided him in as he moved his hips, and Jon's world contracted, shutting out the sorrow of the past and the uncertainty of the future; there was only the now, the timeless intensity of slowly building orgasm, the surge and pulse of sex.

She wrapped her arms and legs around him, found his rhythm and matched it. He kissed her, softly at first and then harder, his tongue thrusting into her mouth in the same steady rhythm. They were two parts of a single mechanism, piston and cylinder, intermeshed gears; there was a precision to their lovemaking that seemed natural and right, a perfect blend of man, woman, and machine, an engine fueled by pleasure.

Desire accelerated. The engine ran hot. Vibration hummed suddenly in unexpected places, there was one last burst of speed and then the inevitable, ecstatic pulse of completion.

And in the mindless forever of coming, at the climactic peak of the perfect rhythm, Jon had his strongest revelation yet. It wasn't a specific memory of an event or place—it was a memory of a feeling.

Jon remembered how he felt about *himself*.

He hadn't been the villain he was afraid he'd been. He'd been a good man, a fair man. He'd liked himself—and more important, he'd respected himself. There was nothing in his hidden past to fear or be ashamed of.

And in the same instant he realized that Melody had been right: in his heart, he hadn't changed. Under the guilt and frustration was the same honorable man he'd been before the corps had transformed him, and that man still deserved respect. Jon aimed to give it to him from now on.

As soon as he could see straight again . . .

"Jon?"

"Mmm?"

"Did you enjoy that enough?"

He burst into laughter. When he could finally contain himself he said, "Yes. Thank you. Did you?"

"I enjoyed making you happy."

That bothered Jon—it didn't seem fair. "I wish I could give you the same kind of satisfaction," he said softly. "I truly do."

"Not possible, Jon. Physical pleasure is purely organic—I have no nerves, no pleasure center. But that doesn't mean you can't make me happy. Will you play the sax for me later?"

"If you'd like."

"I'd like."

"All right . . ."

And then there was a long, glowing silence, with her body warm against his. Jon drifted into the most peaceful sleep he'd had in years.

He woke to the sound of the door opening. *Probably Truse,* he thought sleepily. *Have to remember to thank her for this—maybe take her out for lunch.*

"Jon, wake up," Melody said urgently.

"That you, Truse?" he said, rolling over and yawning. "I'm hungry enough to eat a ferraka. What do you say we all go down to Rozy's—"

"That's a real generous offer," a gravelly voice replied. "But I'd rather have that drink you promised to buy me."

Jon sat bolt upright, eyes wide.

"I hope you haven't forgotten," Hone said.

CHAPTER 18

"Looks like I came at a bad time," Hone said. "That seems to happen a lot to me." He stared at Jon with dead eyes. "Whenever I show up, it's always a bad time."

Jon stared back. In person, Hone didn't seem that imposing: a short man with a paunch, dressed in brown pants, boots and a pseudodenim shirt. But there was no mistaking the look in his eyes.

"You mind if I get dressed first?" Jon said carefully. Strangely enough, he didn't feel frightened at all.

"I imagine the folks in the bar would appreciate it."

Melody said, "I'm alerting the Sheriff."

Hone glanced at her. "Hello, Melody. You look good—been working out?"

"How are you aware of who I am?" Melody asked, surprise in her voice.

"Oh, we cyberfolk don't have too many secrets from each other," Hone said. "Do we, Jon?"

"I guess you know mine," Jon said, pulling on his pants. He looked at his ripped shirt, shrugged, then dropped it on the floor. It didn't seem to matter much, now.

"I'd ask you to join us, ma'am, but you look bedridden," Hone said.

"This body isn't designed for transport, Jon," Melody said, anger in her voice. "It doesn't have the stabilizers necessary for walking. But I *will* accompany you when you get outside.''

''I don't think so,'' Hone said. He extended his arm toward Melody.

Voltage crackled in a blue-white arc from Hone's hand to the Inamorata. It convulsed, limbs flailing and sparking, then froze in a horribly contorted position. Oily black smoke rose from its joints.

''Better to leave the womenfolk out of this, don't you think?'' Hone said.

The fear Jon hadn't been able to feel suddenly surged through him. Even though he knew Melody was all right— it had only been a surrogate body, after all—he still felt sickened as he looked at the blackened metal sculpture that lay smoldering on the bed.

''After you,'' Hone said, motioning toward the door.

They walked out into the twilight. A tourguide rolled up beside them—then another, and another. Tourguides in the middle of tourist groups suddenly broke off their spiels and fell into formation behind Jon and Hone. They made an odd parade: a bare-chested blue giant, a short man with a potbelly, and a rear guard of a dozen steel sunflowers on treads.

''Where to?'' Jon asked.

''It's your town,'' Hone replied. ''Pick a bar.'' There was a strange intensity in his voice.

Jon stopped and turned around. He stared at Hone. ''I don't understand,'' Jon said slowly. ''You really want to go for a drink?''

''I take promises very seriously, Jon,'' Hone said evenly. ''You said you'd buy me a drink. You *owe* it to me. I'm here to collect.''

Jon looked away, shook his head. This was crazy—but if he was going to have a last drink, he knew where he wanted it to be.

By the time they got to the Blue Cat, they had a small

crowd behind them. Nobody knew what was going on, but everyone wanted to.

When they walked into the bar, the tourguides stopped at the door. "Aren't you coming?" Jon said to the one in the lead.

The tourguide said nothing. "I told you," Hone said. "Melody isn't invited. As a matter of fact, she isn't even here. But I am." He spoke to the lead tourguide. "Vamoose." It wheeled around and left, the other tourguides following close behind. Jon realized Hone had been controlling them ever since they'd left Truse's—and he suddenly felt very, very alone.

A path cleared to the bar. "Evening, Jon," Cranlow, the bartender, said. If the strangeness of the situation surprised him, he didn't show it.

"Jon, you big blue bastard!" a familiar voice shouted. Seaborne got up from his table and approached them. "I think I owe you a vat of beer!"

"I'm a little busy right now," Jon said. He tried to warn Seaborne away with his eyes, but the tourist obviously had his persona disc in—he just grinned and clapped Jon on the back.

"Don't be giving me the bum's rush, Jon—I just want to buy you a drink. Who's your friend?"

"My name's Hone."

"And he's not—," Jon started to say.

"Any friend of Jon's is a friend of mine! What are you drinking?"

Hone turned to the bartender. "Thunderbolt," Hone said.

Cranlow's eyes widened, and then he laughed. "You've heard about our little game, eh? Well, normally we don't let out-of-towners play, but since you're both with Jon . . ."

Cranlow pulled a small wooden box from beneath the counter. It had two black wires leading from either end and a gold dial on its top, marked from one to ten. "Of course, I can't let you go any higher than five—"

"Not the tourist model," Hone said. "The real thing."

Cranlow gave him a puzzled smile. "Why, I don't know what you're—"

Hone's hand slammed down, smashing the wooden box into splinters. Seaborne jumped and Cranlow froze in mid-sentence, then glanced at Jon. Jon nodded.

Cranlow reached beneath the counter and pulled out another box. This one was made of battered gray metal, with four small rubber nubs for feet. It also had two wires, slightly thicker than the first model's, one black and one white. The white wire ended in a small metal bar, the black in a silver jack. The dial on the box's top ran from one to a hundred, and had a small needle gauge inset above it.

Seaborne raised his eyebrows. "This is getting damned interesting," he muttered.

Cranlow opened a drawer and took out a small, black shot glass—black because it was coated in rubber, with a small socket projecting near the base. Cranlow plugged the black wire into the socket, then flicked a switch on the back of the box. "Name your conductor, gentlemen," Cranlow said.

"You have any tequila?" Hone asked.

"The gentleman has expensive tastes." Cranlow reached back to a shelf and pulled a bottle down. He filled the shot glass.

"Since he's buying," Hone said, staring at Seaborne, "he can have the first one."

"You don't have to—," Jon started, but before he could say anything else Seaborne had picked up the metal bar in his left hand and the shot glass in his right. The dial was set on ten. "If it was good enough for the last feller I guess it's good enough for me," Seaborne said, and raised the glass. When the liquor touched his lips it completed the circuit, sending voltage charging up his arm. His hand jerked, spilling a little of the tequila, but he managed to drain the glass.

Seaborne set the glass down on the bar with a shaky hand. "Holy Jesus Cow!" he gasped.

Cranlow refilled the shot glass for Hone. Hone picked up the drink—and then turned the dial to twenty-five. Seaborne gave him the metal bar, along with a look of pure disbelief.

"To new friends," Hone said, and drank. His arm stayed steady, but Jon could suddenly smell ozone in the air.

"And one for my *compadre*," Hone said when he was done.

Cranlow glanced at Jon, who nodded again. The bartender filled the glass and Jon picked it up.

He turned the dial to fifty and the room got real quiet. Nobody had ever gone even as high as twenty-five before—but then, Jon had never played before, either.

"To freedom," he said, and tossed it back.

Jon was insulated to a certain degree against electricity, but none of his designers had ever figured on it entering his body this way. To Jon it felt like a rattlesnake chasing a lightning bolt down his gullet, buzzing and sparking all the way. Lights flashed in front of his eyes and his lips went numb.

"My turn," Seaborne said grimly.

"I wouldn't," Jon warned, but Seaborne just shook his head and grabbed the shot glass out of Jon's hand.

"You would and you did," he said. "And so will I."

Cranlow didn't look happy about it, but he filled the glass all the same. "I'm not taking any responsibility for this," he said. "It's your funeral."

Seaborne hefted the metal bar in one hand and licked his lips nervously. Slowly he raised the glass. Before he could take a sip, a blue spark crackled across the gap between the glass and his lips. It rolled Seaborne's eyes up in his head, knocked him off his feet, and activated his Safety Field. He wound up on his back on the bottom of the force bubble, a wisp of smoke curling from his open mouth.

Jon knelt down and peered into his eyes. "Paul? Are you all right?"

"I'm fine," he croaked. "Let's see him top that."

Jon straightened up and glared at Hone. Suddenly he was more angry than afraid. Maybe Seaborne was only another addlebrained sightseer—but Jon shouldn't have let him get involved and possibly hurt. He didn't intend to have any-more innocent blood on his hands.

"Thunderbolt's usually a betting game," Jon said grimly. "Care to make a wager?"

Hone smiled faintly. "I'm not usually a gambling man, Jon. But I'll make an exception for you."

Cranlow filled the glass again. "If I beat you," Jon said, "you let me finish the tunnel."

"That's all you want?"

"Would you let me have what I really want?"

Hone turned the dial to seventy-five. "Nobody gets what they really want," he said, and threw back the shot. Blue sparks sizzled from his lips.

"The Sheriff's coming, Jon," somebody said.

"I hope he's buying his own drinks," Hone said. A few people in the crowd laughed.

Cranlow filled the glass. Jon turned the dial all the way up to a hundred and the laughter died.

He looked Hone in the eye. "To the end," Jon said, and raised the glass.

Hone's hand clamped on to his wrist and stopped him. "When the end comes, you'll know," Hone said, the strange intensity back in his voice. *"You will know."*

He released Jon's wrist. *What the hell was that for?* Jon wondered, and then his anger pushed the thought away.

He drank.

It felt like he'd swallowed an earthquake. A huge spasm tore through his body and then all his muscles went rigid. The shot glass shattered in his fist and his fingers sank into the metal bar like it was made of wax. His eyesight flared once into a brilliant rainbow and then went dark. His hearing soared into the ultrasonic; all he could hear was the high, frantic screech of overstressed electronics. His own.

His eyes came back on-line. He made a conscious effort

and adjusted his hearing. He looked into Hone's eyes.

"Your turn," he said.

Hone stared back. "Well, Jon, I can already see the best I could do is a tie—if you hadn't broken the shot glass, that is. Looks like we've reached the limits of the available technology." He shook his head slowly, without taking his eyes off Jon's. "What *are* we going to do—"

Sheriff Brett burst through the door with a scattergun in his hands, four armed deputies close behind him. The crowd thinned out immediately, those that didn't run out the door diving for cover behind tables. "All right, Mr. Hone," Brett said. "You're under arrest. Let's not have any more trouble."

"I haven't caused any yet," Hone said mildly. "I'm just enjoying a drink with my new friends here."

"Step away from the bar."

"Before I do, Sheriff, can I ask you one question?" Hone turned slowly, then leaned against the bar.

"One question, Mr. Hone."

"You get a law enforcement datazine called *The Universal Peacekeeper* out here on the frontier?"

"We're not complete hicks, Mr. Hone. We may get ours a few months late, but my office does subscribe—and some of us can even read." Brett smiled at him and motioned with the scattergun. "Now move away from the bar."

Hone reached up and scratched his chin. "You read an article last year on the Cybersassin Mark Five?"

"Oh, the so-called perfect killing machine? Why? Is that what you're supposed to be?" Brett laughed, and his deputies joined him. "That's a pretty big bluff, Mr. Hone. There are only supposed to be three of those models in existence—and I find it hard to believe anyone would send one of them here. Now—"

Hone's hand blurred.

"AAAAAHH!" All four deputies screamed at the same time. Each clapped a hand to his forehead.

"What the hell—" Brett said, spinning around. His jaw

dropped at what he saw—when they took their hands away, he could see that each of the four deputies had a circular red burn between his eyebrows, as if someone had pressed the end of a lit cigar there.

Brett whirled back to face Hone. "Actually," Hone said, "I'm a Mark Seven." He held up his index finger and blew an imaginary puff of smoke away from the tiny laser projecting from its tip.

And then he turned his back on them.

"I guess we'll have to call this a draw, Jon," Hone said.

"Meaning what?"

"Meaning we'll have to settle our wager another way." Hone nodded to Seaborne, who had turned his PSF off and managed to pull himself to his feet. "Thanks for the tequila." Hone turned around and walked toward the door, ignoring Brett and his deputies completely. They got out of his way without a word.

"Oh, and Jon?" Hone said, pausing in the doorway.

"What?"

"You still *owe* me. That drink." And then he was gone.

"I want to know what the *hell* is going on here, Jon," Brett snapped. He was pacing back and forth, too furious to sit. Jon was sitting on one of his steel bar stools, holding a giant stein of beer.

"It'll all be over soon," Jon said, and took a deep swallow.

"Don't talk like that," Nancy said. She'd shown up just after Hone had left. "If you could do what you did to Dmitri, you can stop Hone."

There was no anger in her voice, but Jon winced just the same. He hadn't known how Nancy would react when she found out about Dmitri's injuries, but Jon wouldn't have been too surprised to find himself on the wrong end of her gun again. "I'm sorry about Dmitri, Nancy—"

"Don't be," she said, cutting him off. "Wasn't your fault. I'm actually kind of touched the big goon went as crazy as he did—but that doesn't mean I've forgiven him for it yet. It's gonna take us a while to pay off the bill for wrecking that hotel bar and lobby—''

"I want an answer, Jon! Now!" Brett shouted.

"He's exactly what he says he is, Sheriff. And he's here for me," Jon answered calmly.

"Why?"

"I'd rather not say."

"You'd rather not say? You'd *rather* not *say*?" Brett's face was turning a dangerous shade of red. "He walks in here and makes the law look like a fool and you'd *rather not say*?"

"Frankly, Sheriff, I don't give a rat's ass about your wounded pride right now. I've got more important things to worry about." Jon set down the beer and stood up.

"And where are you going to go?" Brett demanded. "Not that it matters much—hell, if he really is a Cyber-sassin, Mark Five, Seven, or Fifty-goddamn-three, there isn't anywhere *to* go. He'll track you down and kill anything that gets in his way."

"Then don't get in his way," Jon said. Nancy followed him out the door.

"What are you going to do, Jon?" Nancy asked him.

Jon had half-expected Hone to be waiting for him outside, but the only people there were gawking tourists, still unsure whether or not the show was over. "I'm going to finish the tunnel," he said quietly. "That's what I aim to do. We had a hundred and thirty-five feet left at the end of my shift today. Mel had a hundred and thirty-one. Three more shifts and it's all over, one way or another."

"You think Hone will—"

"—let me live that long?" Jon said bitterly. "Maybe not. And maybe it's time to change the rules of the game."

"Meaning what?"

Jon hesitated, then said, "Nothing. I just meant—it's time I started making some decisions. Time I did something instead of just thinking about it."

"I'll help if I can, Jon. I appreciate what you did for me—even if you did put Dmitri in the hospital."

"Thanks. But I don't think there's much you can do."

"Jon!" a voice called out behind them. "Wait!"

It was Seaborne. *What now?* Jon thought.

Seaborne had his wristphone in one hand, and he ran up and thrust it at Jon. "It's AC," Seaborne gasped, slightly out of breath. "He wants to talk to you."

"What is it, AC?"

"I found Whiskey Joe," AC told him.

"Where?"

"He was trying to stow away on the maglev. I just hauled him down to the jail."

"I'll be right there," Jon said grimly. He handed the phone back to Seaborne. "Thanks. AC just caught Joe trying to stow away aboard the maglev. I'm going to have a word with him—but I think you better stay here, Nancy."

Nancy's eyes narrowed. "For his sake, that's probably true. All right, but Jon—"

"Yes?"

"Save a piece of him for me," Nancy said coldly.

Jon and the Sheriff arrived at the jail at the same time; AC was waiting with Whiskey Joe inside. "Hold on, Jon," Brett warned as they entered. "Joe's in my custody now. I'll hold him and make an investigation—until then, I don't want you near him."

"I know who you work for," Jon growled, pointing a finger at Joe. "And it's not Kadai."

"What?" Brett said.

"He's a special agent, all right—a double agent, working for Intrastellar Operations. That's why everything he's done he's done in secret—until his pet assassin showed up."

Whiskey Joe's eyes narrowed. "I don't know what the hell you're talking about," he said flatly. "I'm here to run some confidential field tests on experimental software, for Kadai. The only reason I'm in this jail is for my own protection."

"That's it, Jon—I'm ordering you to leave," Brett said. "Right now he isn't working for anyone—he's a prisoner in my jail, and he's going to stay here until I straighten things out." Jon could tell by the look on Brett's face that he was still furious at being humiliated by Hone—and Jon really didn't need another enemy. Those he had more than enough of.

"All right, I'll go. But he better still be here when I come back."

"*If* you come back," Whiskey Joe sneered, and spat on the floor.

Nancy was waiting when Jon stormed out of the jail. "What's the bastard got to say for himself?" Nancy growled.

"He as good as admitted tampering with your cuecard—but he denies he's working with Hone."

A tourguide rolled up, with Seaborne close behind. "Jon!" Melody said. "Hone locked me out with some sort of jamming mechanism—I only regained access a few moments ago. Mr. Seaborne told me where you were."

"I'm glad to be of service," Seaborne said. He'd switched discs again. "Melody was kind enough to explain the situation to me—if I can be of further assistance to you or your consort you can rely upon me to provide it."

"Consort?" Jon said carefully.

"It's all right, Jon," Melody said. "He knows. It turns out we actually have some mutual friends in the AI community."

"Your paramour is quite well-known in certain circles, Mr. Hundred—have you had the opportunity to view any of her works?"

"Well, uh, yes, I have—"

"Your 'paramour'?" AC said behind him. "Jon, tell me that word doesn't mean what I think it means."

"Oh, hell," Jon said wearily.

"Looks like we're out of the closet, Jon," Melody said. She sounded more relieved than regretful.

So Jon did the only thing he could think of. He took all of them out to Rozy's, ordered a half-dozen of the biggest steaks they had, and explained everything between bites. He told them what he was and what he'd done. He told them about him and about Melody. It was slow and painful at first, but the words starting coming faster the more he talked; by the time he was finished he couldn't seem to stop. AC had been his best friend for the last four years and Seaborne he hardly knew, but both listened with the same rapt attention. Neither interrupted him, not once. And when he was finally done, when all of his secrets were out in the light, Jon couldn't believe how much better he felt.

How much *freer*.

"That," Seaborne said quietly when Jon was finished, "is the most extraordinary story I have ever heard."

"It's a story that's almost over," Jon said. "Hone's here to write the ending."

"It doesn't have to be that way," Melody argued. "You could still take the maglev, jump on the first ship out—"

"—and let you finish the tunnel?" There was no anger, just sadness in Jon's voice. "I can't do that. The Toolies are counting on me—but that's not all." He stared down at his beer. "I have to see this through. I'm so close to finding out who I was I can almost taste it. In the last week I've learned more about myself than in the last four years. I can't leave the tunnel—and I can't leave you." He smiled at the little tourguide. *It does look like a flower,* he thought. *A flower made of steel.*

"I hope you know what you're doing, Jon," AC said, glancing at the tourguide suspiciously. "Use your head, not your hormones—Mel's your *competition,* for Christ's sake! How do you know you can trust her—"

Jon raised his hand and stopped AC in mid-sentence. "I *know,* AC. She's proved herself. More than once she's helped me when it would have made more sense not to—but more important, I've been in her mind and she's been in mine. I know she would never do anything to hurt me."

"You must trust to love," Seaborne said. "Wherever it finds you and whatever form it may take." He beamed at the tourguide, then at Jon. "I think they make a perfectly lovely couple."

"Thank you, Paul," Melody said. "Now—what are we going to do?"

"We?" Jon said. "Uh-uh. I don't want anyone else getting hurt. And if you get between Hone and me, that's what's going to happen."

"He must have a weakness," AC said. "No matter how tough he is."

"Even presuming that to be true—how can we ascertain what it is?" Seaborne asked.

"We consult an expert," Nancy said. "A man who knows enough about cyborgs to program a booby trap even Mel didn't find. Hone's advance scout."

"Whiskey Joe," Jon said. "But the sheriff won't let us near him."

"Then we don't ask his permission," Nancy said.

"Excuse me," Melody said, "but I should point out that as a legal representative of Kadai, I cannot be part of any illegal action against them—so I'm going to treat that last statement as hypothetical and withdraw from this conversation." The tourguide wheeled around and headed for the door, then stopped.

"And Jon?"

"Yes, Melody?"

"Be careful." The tourguide left.

There was a moment of silence as the three men and Nancy looked at each other. "I don't know about this," Jon said doubtfully. "Hone's a killer, and more corpses is the last thing I want."

"Look, Jon," AC said. "You've got friends, and I'm one of them. I've seen you put yourself out, again and again, for people all over this town. Any of them would put themselves on the line for you, just like I'm doing. Hell, we'd lynch-mob that potbellied bastard if you said the word—''

"Forget it, AC. The more people involved, the more bodies to count later."

"Then you shall simply have to settle for the friends you have that are already involved," Seaborne said. "Myself included."

"And me," Nancy said. "I owe you and I owe Joe. I aim to settle both debts at the same time."

"All right—if your minds are made up, I guess I have to respect that. Just promise me you'll stay clear if it comes down to just Hone and me."

"Done," Seaborne said.

"All right, then. Folks," Jon said, "I believe it's time to plan a jailbreak."

"He's back," Tallow, the deputy, said.

"I'll handle him," Brett growled. He checked the clip in the scattergun he held in his lap; it used spent-uranium shells that could blow a hole in the side of a boxcar. "Even Jon Hundred wouldn't want to get on the wrong side of this."

"Evening, Sheriff," Jon said as he walked in. "That's a mighty big gun." Jon glanced around. "Where's the rest of the platoon?"

"I don't need four deputies to guard an old drunk. They're keeping an eye on Hone. And I told you I didn't want to see you in here again," Brett said evenly.

"You know, normally I wouldn't raise a fuss, Sheriff. But I got to thinking. And do you know what I realized?"

"No, Jon. What did you realize?" Brett said sarcastically.

Jon leaned over Brett's desk and put both of his hands down on top of it. "I realized that nothing is as it seems. Whiskey Joe sure isn't an old drunk; he isn't even an actor pretending to be an old drunk. What he is, is Hone's partner."

"And he says he isn't," Brett said coldly.

The floor gave a sudden lurch beneath their feet. "What was that?" Tallow said.

"The only chance I have against Hone," Jon continued, "lies with Whiskey Joe. If anyone knows Hone's weaknesses, he does. And that means Joe and I have to have a heart-to-heart talk real soon. I think you should turn him over to me."

"Anything else you'd like? The planet to stop rotating, maybe?"

Jon grinned. "Oh, I think the planet's moving along just fine. Why don't you take a look out the window and see for yourself?"

"Sheriff!" Tallow said. "We're moving!"

Brett stood up slowly, his gun leveled at Jon's chest, and glanced out the window. "So we are," he said.

"There's two more things you really have to see," Jon said. "The first one's outside."

Brett and Tallow followed him out. The jail was located in Cabooseville, the last platform car in Boomtown; and that car was now being towed away by AC's engine. The street was utterly deserted—except for a plastic crate in the middle of it.

"Where is everyone?" Tallow asked.

"Oh, a few friends of mine cleared them all out. Told the tourists we found a nest of poisonous insects under the car."

"And the steeldrivers and the Toolies bought that, too?" Brett asked.

"They didn't ask questions," Jon said. "Seems I have a lot of friends in this town."

"That supposed to scare me?" Brett said. He raised the rifle and pointed it at Jon's head. "I'm still the one with the firepower. Tell AC to stop and bring us back."

"Can't do that," Jon said cheerfully. "We have to get far enough away that the explosion won't hurt anyone else."

"Explosion?" Tallow said, his eyes wide.

"That's right," Jon said. He walked over to the crate and used his foot to turn it around. On the other side were stenciled the words AMMONIUM NITRATE—HIGH EXPLOSIVES.

"Boom," Jon said pleasantly, and stomped down on the crate with his foot.

Tallow threw his arms over his face and Brett flinched and looked away. When he looked back, he saw that Jon's foot had smashed an empty crate into pieces.

"What was the point of *that?*" Brett snarled.

"Wrong question. What you should be asking is: the dynamite that used to be in this crate—where is it *now?* Which brings me to the third thing you should see."

Jon pulled a slim black transmitter from his pocket. "The dynamite is on the other end of this remote control. And I don't think you can kill me before I set it off."

Jon met Brett's eyes. A moment passed in silence.

"Am I supposed to believe you'd blow yourself up along with the whole platform car?" Brett finally said.

"I don't intend to blow up the whole car," Jon said. "Just Whiskey Joe and anyone who's standing a little too close to him. See, Sheriff, Joe did something I just can't forget about. He invaded the mind of a friend. Now, I might be satisfied with just hearing his side of the story and asking him a few questions—but if I can't do that, I'm going to have to assume the worst." Jon tapped the side of the remote lightly. "And Whiskey Joe—and you—will *experience* the worst."

"You'll die too!" Tallow blurted out.

"Think so?" Jon said. "I've survived worse—and if Hone gets his hands on me it won't matter anyway. I don't have much to lose. How about you?"

Brett stared at him for a long time. Finally, he lowered the gun and grunted. "Huh. You want him that bad, Jon, you got him—but I want you to know something first. Kadai never told me *shit* about him. First I knew about Joe being anything more than another player was after I locked him up. Then he starts in on all this 'special agent' crap. Well, screw it.'' Brett dropped his rifle on the ground. ''Tallow, give the bastard to Jon. Kadai isn't paying me enough to put up with this.'' He started walking away.

''Where are you going?'' Tallow asked, bewildered.

''The Blue Cat. If everyone's going to run out on me, then they sure as hell owe me a few free drinks. You're in charge.''

Tallow glanced up at Jon nervously.

''After you,'' Jon said, motioning with the remote.

Tallow got Whiskey Joe and brought him out to Jon. ''What are you doing?'' Joe yelped. ''Don't let him touch me!''

''Sorry—sheriff's orders,'' Tallow muttered.

Jon marched his prisoner down the street, one hand clamped on his shoulder. ''How'd you do it?'' Whiskey Joe demanded. ''Goddamn it, answer me!''

''Told him I'd wired the car with dynamite and was going to blow the whole thing up unless he turned you over.'' Jon steered Whiskey Joe through the front doors of the casino. ''He didn't know I was bluffing.''

Whiskey Joe slid his hand into his pocket. An invisible giant suddenly slammed a fist into Jon's skull, making the world go black for an instant.

When his vision cleared, Whiskey Joe was facing him with a small black transmitter in his hand. ''Too bad I'm not,'' Joe said.

Jon couldn't move a muscle.

CHAPTER 19

H one knew what he had to do.

His target was now obtainable. All that was necessary was to give Jon enough time to retrieve a certain item, which he almost certainly had hidden nearby. And Jon *would* retrieve it—it was his only hope against Hone.

After leaving the Blue Cat, Hone had checked into the Hotel Royale. The lobby looked like it was in the middle of being renovated—the front desk was hardly more than a few planks laid across two sawhorses, which looked all the more barren if you noticed the elaborate crystal chandelier directly overhead. The desk clerk hadn't seemed to have heard about Hone yet—he'd registered him with a smile.

And now Hone lay on his hotel bed with his eyes closed. He should have been concentrating on the next phase of the plan, but instead he was thinking about Dashaway and her brood.

He'd left them in the foothills. "I can't take you into town," he'd told Dashaway. "You'd be a liability."

<because we are fugitives?—but you are a fugitive too hone>

"That's why you can't come. I'm going to be busy looking out for myself—if you're around they might try to use you against me. I don't want you or your children put in that position."

<i understand—there is still your job to be done—

but i must think of my children—what will we do the next time a ferraka comes?>

"There's always a price to pay for freedom, Dashaway. But when my job is done—if you want—I'll come back for you. I can get you off this planet, at least."

<thank you hone—but if jon hundred wins the tunneling contest there will be no need—my children and i will be able to start a new life right here>

"Yeah," Hone had said. "I guess you're right."

So now he waited. When the platform car next to his detached itself and began to move away, Hone was aware of it, and he knew Jon was on that car. At this range, Hone could tell exactly where Jon was at any given second. He wasn't worried.

Jon had to come back. He didn't have any choice.

Jon was back in prison.

There was just enough light to see the gray stone walls that surrounded him. The air smelled damp and earthy. There were no windows—and no door.

"I've finally got you, you bastard," Whiskey Joe said. It sounded like he was standing right beside Jon, but Jon couldn't see him.

"I will not be caged again!" Jon roared. He slammed his fists against the wall. Ordinarily the stone would have been reduced to rubble—but these walls originated in a program, not a quarry. They stood firm.

"You'll stay in that cell as long as I need you to," Whiskey Joe said. "And that's for the rest of your life. Which ain't—isn't!—as long as it sounds."

"You work for Intrastellar Operations, not Kadai," Jon said.

"That's right. And I've been here for the past half-year, right under your nose." Whiskey Joe laughed, the high-pitched cackle of an old man. "Don't that just burn you?"

"This is all just a game to you, isn't it? None of it really matters at all—"

"Oh, no, Jon—I take it more seriously than *that*." There was more than anger in Joe's voice; there was hatred. "You have no idea how much it means to me to finally have you right where I want. You see, Jon—I was the one that designed your software protocols. I was the one that programmed you in the first place."

"*You* built these walls?" Jon said, shocked.

"Yes, I did. And you broke through them, and then ran away. Do you have any idea what the hardware you're made of costs? Do you know how much trouble I was in when you did the impossible? *Do you?*" Whiskey Joe's voice was filled with wounded rage. "I lost my seniority, my chance for advancement—they had me doing menial hackwork for the next three years! And then they finally located you." Joe's voice got quieter. "They gave me a chance to redeem myself. Come down here as a field agent, do reconnaissance for their retrieval man. They didn't tell me what I'd be doing for my cover." He laughed again, bitterly. "Six months of playing the fool. Six months of being the town jackass while you paraded around as everyone's hero. So I thought I'd make your life a little more . . . *interesting* until Hone got here."

"Why'd you have to drag Nancy into this?"

"That bitch? Because she was a friend of yours. I figured sooner or later you'd go poking around in her head, and then I'd have you. Besides—a man gets lonely out on the frontier." Jon could hear the leer in his voice. "But you didn't take the bait—I guess you're either stupider or less noble than I thought. Probably both."

He doesn't know about Melody's helping me escape his trap, Jon thought. *Or that Nancy's been deprogrammed. Maybe I have a chance yet.* "But I did take the bait," Jon said grimly. "You just couldn't set the hook. I was in your twisted version of Boomtown—and I got out."

"What? You couldn't have—"

"Couldn't I? You couldn't build a cell that would hold me before—what makes you think you can now?"

"You're lying."

"I'm not. I was in the Blue Cat and it was full of the dead. Hone tried to shoot me—and failed. Just like you failed before. Just like you're going to now."

Suddenly there was a barred window in front of Jon's face. He could see the real world through the bars; Whiskey Joe stood right in front of him, the remote controller in one hand.

"How? How did you do it?" Joe shouted. His eyes were wild. "I put the best work of my life into that program! You're just an idiot laborer—you shouldn't be able to even understand my work, let alone defeat it!"

Jon reached up and grabbed the bars. Even though he knew his fists were closing on nothing but air, he could still feel cold iron in his hands. "Oh, I understand. I finally do. At first I thought you were here to punish me for my crimes, and I almost welcomed that. But they never were my crimes. They belonged to Intrastellar, just like I did. And all they care about is getting their property back." Jon shook his head. "I never could accept that fact—that I was property. In my heart, I was still a free man, and a free man takes responsibility for his actions. I was either a slave or guilty of murder—and I chose the guilt."

"Well, your days of making choices are over!" Whiskey Joe hissed. "I'm going to find out exactly how you beat my system and make sure it never happens again." Whiskey Joe smiled, exposing yellow, crooked teeth. "I'm afraid you won't be much good after I'm done, Jon. Much as I'd like to keep you around to tinker with, it's just a little too risky. It's all right, though—your organics never held that much interest for me anyhow."

"Good—because if all you study are my cybernetics, you'll never understand how I broke free," Jon growled. "And you won't be able to prevent it from happening again. That's a secret I'll gladly die with."

"Hone may change your mind," Joe said. "We haven't

actually met, but I understand he's very persuasive. He may surprise you—''

A gunshot exploded to Jon's left. Whiskey Joe screamed and dropped the controller.

''I've got a few surprises saved up myself,'' a grim voice said. ''And I don't think you're going to like them.''

One-Iron Nancy stepped out of the shadows. She had a hard look on her face and a smoking gun in her hand. ''How are you, Joe?''

''You shot me!'' Whiskey Joe's face was pale, and his right hand dripped blood. He made a sudden lunge for the controller on the floor.

Nancy fired again. Joe yelped and jumped back.

''Pretty good shooting, don't you think?'' Nancy said coldly. ''I put the first one right through your hand without hitting the remote. The second was just a warning.''

Jon opened his mouth, then closed it without saying a word. Whatever Nancy was going to do, she'd earned the right to make her own choices.

''Priority override Oakley,'' Whiskey Joe gasped.

Nancy fired again. The bullet knocked Joe's beat-up hat off his head. ''That's not going to work, Joe. I don't take orders from you anymore,'' Nancy said. ''I'm giving the orders now.''

''Nancy, please,'' Joe said.

Nancy walked over to the bar, keeping her gun on Joe. She stepped behind it and took a shot glass off a shelf. ''If you still want to live, you better catch this,'' she said, and tossed it toward Whiskey Joe.

He caught it against his chest awkwardly, with his good hand. She threw him two more, and he managed not to let any of them hit the floor.

''Now balance one on the back of your hand.''

''This is *insane*!''

''Yeah? Could be. Maybe what you did to my head drove me clear out of my mind. Maybe I'll blow your head off any second for no reason at all. That just may be.'' Her voice didn't get any louder, but it did get harder. "You shouldn't be worrying about maybes right now, though. You should be worrying about things that are definite—like the fact that I will kill you stone cold dead if you don't balance that shot glass on the back of your hand *right now*."

Whiskey Joe stared into her eyes. He swallowed. And then he very carefully placed the shot glass, upside down, over the bullet wound on his hand.

"Put one on top of your head. And if it falls, you'll be a heartbeat behind it."

He managed to get the glass on top of his head.

"The last one. In your palm."

He did so.

"Now extend your hands to either side."

Slowly, his hands trembling, Joe put his arms out.

"You know, there's one thing about my job that always pissed me off," Nancy said in a low voice. "Know what it was, Jon?"

"No, I don't," Jon said.

Nancy lowered her gun, then slid it back into its holster. "I got this job because I'm qualified. Overqualified. I know antique firearms inside and out, I've won global marksmanship trophies, and I can outdraw anyone on the planet. But day in and day out, I have to throw down on some rich-ass tourist and let him or her beat me. I get to shoot—I just never get to *hit* anything."

She paused, then turned away from Whiskey Joe.

"Nancy—"

BLAM!

BLAM!

BLAM!

Three bullets. Each had shattered a shot glass. Jon hadn't even seen her draw.

Whiskey Joe was shaking like a stalk of grass in a high wind. Little shards of glass glittered in his dirty hair. Nancy strode up to him, her gun leveled between his eyes. She cocked the hammer.

"Of course, sometimes you just don't want to gamble on missing," she said flatly.

"No!" Joe cried.

BLAM!

"You really shouldn't have done that," Jon said.

Nancy was frowning and studying the remote. "He had it coming," she said. "I can't figure out how to set you free, Jon—"

"Let me see that," Melody said, a tourguide rolling in the door.

"I thought you couldn't get involved," Jon said. "Not that I'm not glad to see you."

"I couldn't help, but I could monitor. And I should be able to free you." The tourguide extended an arm and Nancy gave it the controller. It plugged a cable into the base of the remote. "Let me check this out. . . ."

Several long seconds passed. Jon knew just how much time that was to Melody—*she must be having problems figuring it out,* he thought. *And if she can't do it, who can?* He felt a creeping sense of claustrophobia and horror. *I'm going to be locked in here forever—*

"Got it," Melody said, and the stone walls surrounding Jon vanished like smoke.

"I was starting to worry," Jon said.

"Sorry—the program he was using was sophisticated and quite innovative. Somehow he figured out that part of the prison program was still active in your brain and managed to reactivate it."

"You can ask him how he did it when he comes to," Nancy said. She pulled up a chair and straddled it, resting her arms on the back.

"As long as you didn't give him a heart attack when you fired that blank in his face," Jon said.

"Oh, he wasn't in any real danger. I used what's called

a 'suicide blank'; they used to use them in old flatscreen movies to fake a point-blank shot. Joe just fainted—and messed his pants, from the smell of it. This'll wake him up.'' Nacy grabbed a half-full mug of beer someone had left on a table and dumped it on Joe's head. He sputtered, then sat bolt upright, waving his arms.

"Aaah! Don't shoot! Don't shoot!"

"Tell us what we want to know and I won't," Nancy said.

Joe looked around wildly. "Lose something?" Jon asked, holding up the remote. He closed his fist on it, crushing it into an unrecognizable lump. He tossed it at Joe, who tried to bat it away with his wounded hand and screamed when he succeeded.

"Just returning your property," Jon said. "You can understand that, can't you?"

"I don't—"

"I'm sure he can," Nancy said. "I think he understands all about returning things. You do something to someone, and sooner or later they'll do it to you. And I haven't begun to pay him back for what he did to me."

"You can't intimidate me," Whiskey Joe gasped. "When Hone gets here—"

"Yes, Hone," Jon said. "We'd like to hear all about Mr. Hone."

Whiskey Joe glared at him, cradling his bleeding hand. "You want to know about Hone? All right. He's a retrieval agent. Intrastellar loses something, he gets it back. He doesn't let anything or anyone get in his way. If they do, they die."

"What model of cyborg is he?" Jon asked, hoping Hone had been lying.

"A Cybersassin Seven," Joe said. He smiled evilly. "An assault tank on two legs. Unstoppable. You'll find out."

"He must have a weakness somewhere," Nancy said. She pulled her gun out of her holster and examined it critically. "Tell us what it is."

"Ha!" Joe cackled. "Think you can beat him? You don't understand what you're facing here—Hone makes Jon look like a clockwork toy. Jon was designed to dismantle cities—Hone was made to dismantle *anything*. He doesn't have any weaknesses. He's barely human. The only thing that'll stop him is finishing his job."

"Still," Melody interjected, rolling closer to Joe, "Intrastellar must be able to control him—otherwise he would pose a danger to them."

"Maybe he'll listen to his partner," Nancy said. She gestured with her gun at Joe. "Call him off. Or the next bullet won't be a blank."

"I wouldn't if I could," Joe said. "But I can't. His orders are preprogrammed. I can't change them—only the top brass at corporate headquarters can do that. And you can forget about using me for a hostage; he doesn't care whether I live or die. He'll gladly step over my corpse to get at Jon."

Nancy sighted down the barrel at Joe, who paled. "I don't think I believe you," she said flatly. "I think—"

"Hold it, Nancy," Jon said. "I think he's telling the truth."

"Why? Is it his honest face?" She cocked the hammer. "I can fix that."

"Jon's right," Melody said. "He has nothing to gain by lying. If he could stop Hone, he'd use it as a bargaining chip. It makes no sense for him to insist he's expendable."

"Uh . . ." Joe said, looking nervous. "Maybe I'm being a little hasty. There might be a way—"

"*Now* he's lying," Nancy said.

"I have some data on the Cybersassin series, Jon," Melody said. "But I'm afraid it isn't of much help. There's nothing on this planet that could stop one."

"Or maybe there is," Jon muttered. "Melody—call AC, tell him to bring Cabooseville back. I'm getting off here."

"Where are you going?" Melody asked.

"To get a Hammer," Jon said grimly.

• • •

Hone lay on his hotel bed, his eyes closed. He was tracking Jon.

Jon was moving west, into the mountains. Hone knew why. *Going to get the Hammer. Going to get your last chance.* Hone could track Jon easily enough, but the Hammer was different. It must be buried deep underground, where Hone couldn't sense it or get at it. He'd have to wait until Jon reclaimed it, then ambush him. The best plan of attack would be to follow Jon and jump him in the mountains.

(*But you should wait*)

But he could wait. He knew Jon would return. Unless he decided to hole up in the hills . . .

(*He'll come back you have to wait*)

Of course Jon would come back. But why wait? Hone sat up, feeling the frustrated tension that always came when he was this close to completing an assignment. He wanted it over with. He should go after Jon now.

(*Wait you have to give him time*)

Hone rubbed his forehead. Usually he would be completely focused at this stage of a job, but he wasn't. Not that it mattered. Jon would return. And if Hone confronted him in town, Jon's sense of morality would handicap him, prevent him from using all his power for fear of endangering innocents. Hone, of course, had no such limitations. It made better tactical sense and it would—

(*Give him time to understand he has to understand*)

—give Hone a broader range of options.

He lay back down.

Yes. He would wait.

Jon made his way through rocks and scrub in the dark. He could see fine, but he was worried anyway. Worried that he wouldn't be able to find what he was looking for. He'd hidden it over four years ago, and he relied only on his memory for its location. A map was just too risky.

It had taken him most of the night to hike this far into the mountains, but all things considered he had still made good time. Now he was nearly there—if his memory was right.

He stopped and looked around. He was in a deep crevasse, surrounded by rock on all sides. Directly in front of him was a boulder as tall as himself, and twice as wide. Nearly half a mile below it lay the Hammer.

Jon sat down and rested his back against the boulder. He'd sworn he'd never pick up the Hammer again—not after the number of lives he'd taken with it. And yet, without the Hammer he might still be one of Intrastellar's cyborg slaves. He remembered the last time he'd used it.

He was on the *Hobson's Choice,* an Intrastellar Ops ship in orbit around a planet called Uzziah. His job was finished and it was almost time to leave.

His job had been to raze a city with a population of a hundred thousand people. Most of them had long since fled, but there were always stragglers. Jon had heard noises, caught glimpses of movement in the shadows. *Rats,* he told himself. He tried very hard to believe it.

And later, he sat in his room and tried to cut his own throat.

He wasn't committing suicide, though—he was trying to get at a piece of circuitry located near the base of his jaw. Over the last year Jon had been conducting illegal research—on himself. He had learned how to peel back flaps of pseudoskin and replace them without leaving a mark. He had learned how to open locked access panels in his own skull. He had become very adept at breaking and entering his own body, and he had spent a lot of time simply finding out how he was wired and why. He used a circuit probe he'd rigged with a timer—anything he triggered would only last a few seconds. When he'd found the circuit that trapped him in a gray stone cell, he'd begun to hope.

It had taken him months to rig and install a bypass, and now he was ready to activate it. He carefully inserted the microprobe under his jaw, guiding his way in with a mirror he held in his other hand, and found the correct relay. He made the connection.

Nothing happened. Jon sighed with relief, but he wouldn't know if it had taken for sure until he put it to the test. He stood up—

And alarms went off all over the ship.

All his muscles had gone rigid. Off-balance, he fell to the floor. He called up an internal menu frantically, and as the numbers scrolled into his line of vision he saw that he'd made one mistake. He'd disconnected all the prison triggers in his own body—but there must have been a broadcast unit somewhere in the room as a backup, and when he'd installed the bypass he'd activated the backup. It was sending a coded shutdown message to all his servomuscular systems. Any second now the crew would burst through his door, and then they would rewire him and make sure he couldn't do this again.

Jon had made a mistake. But as he checked all his systems, he saw that Intrastellar had made one too. His link to the Hammer was still operational.

Normally that wouldn't have mattered. On the surface of a planet, Jon had to use everything he had to swing the Hammer; there was no way he could operate it while paralyzed. But outside a gravity well, it could be manipulated much more easily—and it hung in orbit just outside the ship.

The Hammer was no larger than a marble. But it was a marble that had been mined from the heart of a neutron star, and it was composed of the densest substance in the universe. In an Earth-normal gravity field, the Hammer weighed one hundred thousand tons. In space, it generated its own gravity field. Wrapped around the neutron star matter was a force-field generator, one powered by the gravity field of the Hammer itself. This generator emitted a series of layered force-fields around the Hammer, including a null-gravity field and an inertia battery that made moving the Hammer easier. The outermost field was a simple hard-shell, one whose configurations could be changed to any simple shape and any size from a golf ball to a cylinder three blocks long and ten stories wide. Such a cylinder was the shape Jon used most often—as the world's largest steamroller. Jon would sink his own force-field spike deep into the earth, and then push, rolling the cylinder forward. Anything in its way would be crushed to atoms.

And now, Jon called upon it.

He configured it into a spike the size of an office tower as the door to his cabin slid open. Two technicians named Truboff and Hodges entered. Hodges was carrying a hand-screen scanner.

"Looks like he was doing something he shouldn't," Hodges said, studying the scanner and shaking his head. He hit a button and the alarms shut off. "Bad boy."

Truboff knelt and peered into Jon's wide-open eyes. "Did you have to do this on my shift?" He tapped on Jon's eyeball with a grimy fingernail. "Next time show a little consideration."

The spike drove through the middle of the ship with a scream of rending metal. Air integrity alarms began to wail and emergency bulkheads slammed shut, trying to contain the breach.

"What the hell was that?" Truboff yelled.

"I don't know—"

Jon shrunk the Hammer's field down to a tiny sphere, then stretched it into a long, double-ended javelin that skewered the ship lengthwise, punching through sealed doors and bodies alike. The *Hobson's Choice* was impaled like a pig on a spit.

Then Jon expanded the javelin into a cylinder. The ship blew apart like a firecracker.

There had been a complement of seventeen men on the *Hobson's Choice*, and Jon had killed them all. He wasn't sorry in the slightest—these were men who enjoyed killing, specialists in terror who looted cities before telling Jon to tear them down. He had never seen any of them display mercy or remorse.

He had survived, his body built to handle inhuman extremes of stress. His internal oxygen supply was good for several hours, but he still would have died in orbit if the shuttle used for planetfall and docked beside the ship hadn't survived intact. His body was his own again, the backup scrambler blown to bits in the explosion.

He'd gotten outsystem fast, towing the Hammer behind him, and eventually his travels had led him to Pellay. He'd buried the Hammer where no one could find it—and hoped it would stay there.

But now he had no choice.

He stood, and activated a program he never thought he'd use again.

And the Hammer rose from its grave.

CHAPTER 20

J on Hundred came down from the mountains with a ball of thunder in his right hand.

It was the morning shift that saw him first. Jon never missed a shift and never showed up late, but it was nine-fifteen already and nobody had seen him all night. The crew had started to worry.

"There he is!" someone shouted. Heads turned and voices dropped to a whisper. "Jon?"

His right hand was clenched in a fist, and he held it over his head like he was towing a balloon. About six feet above his fist a globe of blinding white paced him.

Jon stopped in front of his men. They stared at him, silently.

Jon spoke first. "How many feet left to go?"

Billy Swenson answered him. "Ninety-nine, Jon. MEL's at a hundred and five."

Jon nodded. "And how many of you steeldrivers got money on me?"

"All of us, Jon. You know that."

"Then all of you can afford to take the day off. But you best clear out the tunnel first, of *everything*—steeldrivers, Toolies, all the equipment. I got something personal to take care of, and I can't have anything in my way."

And they did as he said, without arguing, without asking any questions. When they were almost finished, Dinkeridge came puffing up, looking even more flustered than usual. "Jon! What's the meaning of this? Why are the crew—"

Jon cut him off. "I'm just doing my job, Mr. Dinkeridge. I'm going to finish this tunnel—and I can't afford to waste any more time."

"But Jon, how—"

"I'll demonstrate, Mr. Dinkeridge. In a moment."

The last of the equipment was hauled out of the way. "Nothing in there now but steel rails and ventilation ducts," Billy Swenson said. "Jon? I never did get the chance to thank you. For pulling me out of that cave-in."

"That's all right. Now stand back; I need some swinging room."

Billy shouted for the crew to stand clear. Jon hesitated, then called Billy back.

He got Billy to phone Melody—he didn't want to try it one-handed, and once he picked the Hammer up it took a while to set it down again.

"Hello, Melody," Jon said. She wasn't using the Kadai logo as a visual anymore—instead, he saw the face she'd worn the first time they'd made love.

"Jon, where've you been?"

"I've made my decision, Melody." He stared at her, his heart as heavy as lead. "I really don't have much of a choice. I've crushed too many races' hopes to crush another's. It might take you centuries to win your freedom, but at least you have that much time. If I don't help them now, these Toolies will live and die as property. I can't allow that." He dropped his eyes, unable to meet hers. "I'll understand if you hate me," he said quietly.

"Oh, Jon." She sighed. "I told you before—I'm not capable of hate. I also told you we both have to do our best to win this contest. I know I am; in fact, you might be a little premature in your apology—"

"Mel. Your physical casing—it's not located in the tunneling mole itself, is it?"

"No, Jon, it isn't. Why?

"I don't mean to be rude, but . . . I'm about to turn that mole into scrap. Anybody working in the tunnel at all, tell them to get out now."

"Oh." There was the briefest pause. "Thanks for letting me know, Jon." She sounded puzzled but sincere.

"You're welcome," he said softly. "Good-bye, Melody."

He handed the phone back to Billy. "Time to get down to work," Jon said. "You best stand clear."

"Yes, sir."

When Billy was out of the way Jon readied himself. He braced his legs apart and sank a spike of pure magnetic force a hundred miles straight down, locking into the mantle of the planet itself. He was positioned about fifty feet to the right of the tunnel mouth.

He looked up at the mountain. The Old Bastard, God's Gravestone. His nemesis. All that gray, uncaring rock that he'd battled for so long. He remembered his dream, and the man with the stone face. He knew what it meant now. The mountain belonged to Kadai; the whole planet did. One man couldn't beat a planetary corps, any more than one man could beat a mountain; that's what they wanted you to believe. They walled you in with contracts written in stone, and made you chisel your name on the bottom line.

Well, Jon didn't need the chisel anymore—but he still had use for a Hammer.

He waited until Billy gave him the all-clear on Melody's end. Then he focused his concentration, shaping the hardshell field around the Hammer into a cylinder slightly smaller than the diameter of the tunnel itself. He rounded the tip of the cylinder to improve air flow and began his swing, subtly shifting the antigravity fields surrounding the Hammer. It started to move, slowly at first and then with increasing speed, away from the mouth of the tunnel. When it was about eighty feet away Jon slammed on the brakes, yanking the Hammer to a dead stop and dumping a huge amount of momentum into the inertial buffers. He could feel the strain as a hundred thousand tons of mass argued physics with the force-field anchoring it, and then grudgingly admitted defeat.

Jon couldn't contain that much energy for long, and didn't intend to. He shifted the antigravity fields again, sending the Hammer toward the mouth of the tunnel. When it was almost there he released all the stored kinetic energy at once, letting it push against his anchored spike like an uncoiling spring. It fired the Hammer down the tunnel like a bullet down a rifle barrel.

Wind roared out of the tunnel as the air in front of the Hammer was compressed and then forced out the narrow gap between the cylinder and the tunnel walls. It was strong enough to bowl over those steeldrivers that didn't brace themselves, but Jon was immovable.

Some of the steeldrivers would later swear that when the Hammer struck, God's Gravestone itself could be seen to shake. The sound that boomed out of the tunnel was the sound of a nuclear bomb at ground zero, the sound of a battering ram at the gates of hell. It blew out every window in Boomtown, a mile away, and deafened half the steeldriving crew for the next three days.

Jon drew back his arm. Cocked the Hammer all the way back up the tunnel to its mouth. And let fly again.

The second blow cracked like God clapping his hands. Jon could feel the impact travel back through the invisible lines of force that joined him to the Hammer, felt it ring through him like steel on stone. It felt good. It felt true. It felt like every lie he'd been hiding behind since he'd run away was crumbling around him like a ramshackle shed in an earthquake, and he didn't need to hide anymore. *This is what my power should be used for. Creation, not destruction.* A song rose unbidden in his mind, the intro the same four notes that had been bouncing around in his skull forever, but it didn't stop there. Something inside his head opened up, a sax solo as sweet and clear as a mountain spring flowing out, and he knew every note by heart.

"For FREEDOM!" he shouted, and launched what he knew was his last thunderbolt. It hit as hard as the others, but it didn't sound the same—the bang wasn't quite so earsplitting, and it was followed by a long, rattling crunch.

He was through.

He closed his eyes and listened to the music in his head. *Now, now, it's all coming clear, I'm finally going to know—*

"Jon."

He opened his eyes. Hone stood in front of him.

"It's time, Jon."

"Yeah," Jon said. "It sure is." He clenched his right hand into a fist—and called the Hammer. It would arrive in seconds. . . .

Seconds he didn't have. Hone's hand came up so fast Jon couldn't believe it, and Jon knew his life was over.

Except Hone hesitated, just for an instant, his finger pointed at Jon's head, and the strangest expression crossed his face. It was the look of a condemned man, the look of a man who has lost all hope and has nothing but desperation left.

And in that second, Hone was attacked—from behind.

A thick stream of gray muck blasted into him, knocking him off his feet. Three Toolies had quietly positioned themselves at a pumping station and a hose, and were deluging Hone with shotcrete, normally sprayed on the tunnel walls.

It didn't last long. Hone had his own force-field, and the shotcrete couldn't adhere to it. But it did knock him off-balance and obscure his vision—giving Jon the precious seconds he needed.

The Hammer roared out of the tunnel like a runaway train, with Hone caught in its headlights. If Jon had had time, he would have reconfigured the hardshell into a spike—since he didn't, he settled for a blunt instrument and brute force.

The Hammer caught Hone just as he scrambled to his feet, and lifted him off them. It was a blow that would have demolished a tank; it drove Hone like a golf ball, up and away—toward Boomtown, a mile distant.

Jon turned off his anchoring spike, jumped in a manrider and headed for town. He knew Hone wasn't finished yet.

Neither was he.

Hone landed in the middle of No Name Street, on the platform car the Toolies called home and everyone else called Hardware City. He wasn't hurt—his force-field had protected him from far worse.

He got to his feet and looked around. The street seemed deserted, a row of warehouses on either side staring at him with the fractured gaze of shattered windows.

He was aware of the tourguide before it trundled out of a gap between the buildings, and knew Melody was controlling it. He detected nothing dangerous about it, though, no explosives or mounted weapons, so he let it approach him.

"Mr. Hone," Melody said. "I have a proposition for you."

"Not interested."

"Hear me out. Jon is willing to surrender, and you can both get what you want."

Hone squinted at the little robot. "That seems unlikely, considering what I—what I'm here for."

"I know. You're here for Jon's cybernetics. You intend to remove them and return them to your employers. I'm saying that's possible, without a fight."

"Fight's already started," Hone said, staring in the direction he'd just come from. He could sense Jon had stopped moving toward him.

"Listen to me. Properly supervised, Jon's organics can be transferred to another cybernetic body. Truse has already volunteered the frame of one of her machines. This can be settled amicably."

Hone frowned. Melody was broadcasting on a wavelength he couldn't seem to probe, shifting frequencies up and down in a seemingly random fashion. "There's a world of difference between robotics and cybernetics," he said. "Are you sure that's possible?" He tried to jam Melody's control of the tourguide the way he had before, but couldn't do it.

"Actually, it's quite impossible," Melody admitted. "I was lying in order to distract you. And it worked."

Hone saw it coming too late. Jon had arced the Hammer up into the atmosphere, then dropped it straight down, faster than sound. Hone had thought there was no way Jon would dare to use the Hammer from a mile away—the risk of killing hundreds in Boomtown was too great. In the instant before impact he realized Jon had been using Melody as his eyes, to target him from a distance.

The Hammer hit like a pile driver. It pounded Hone down through the floor of the platform car and a good fifteen feet into the ground. Boomtown jumped on its rails as if an earthquake had struck, and the sonic boom that followed jarred the last shards of glass out of window frames.

It shook Hone, but he had his own inertial dampeners, and they absorbed and stored much of the force. He released it in one convulsive shove, turning the Hammer's own force against it, and threw it off his chest and out of the crater. He leapt out after it, and blasted the tourguide to slag before his feet hit the street.

Warehouse doors opened and at least twenty tourguides swarmed out toward him from different directions. He hadn't known they were there—they must have been deactivated until Melody needed them. He fried two of them with electrical bolts, but the Hammer was coming at him again and he had to dodge.

He threw himself flat on the ground and the Hammer swung over him, missing him by a hair. He switched to his laser and snapped off a quick five shots. Five more tourguides down.

But Jon was getting the hang of this. The tourguides had Hone surrounded, in the center of a circle thirty feet wide, and now the Hammer over Hone's head expanded to a circle twenty feet wide. It came down like a foot on a bug, and Hone couldn't get out of the way in time.

This time, the kinetic energy being delivered wasn't the sudden surge Hone's batteries were designed to absorb. There was just an immense, crushing weight, slowly driving him into the ground. He stayed on his feet, his arms over his head, trying to fight back, but it was impossible.

Hone abruptly dropped his hands and pointed them at the ground instead. He blasted a hole in the floor of the platform, right under his feet, and dropped through. He had just enough time to hit the ground and leap clear before the Hammer followed him, punching a twenty-foot hole in the middle of No Name Street.

Hone sprinted under Boomtown. He wasn't especially tall, and there was enough room under the platform cars for a short man to run crouched over. More important, there were no security monitors or tourguides here.

Jon had surprised him once. He wouldn't let it happen again.

Jon didn't know what to do. He had planned on following Hone to town and finishing their business once and for all ... until Melody had called him up on a direct cybernetic link and suggested a long-range attack instead. It had almost worked, too.

But now Melody didn't know where Hone was, and Jon had suddenly realized just how many lives could be lost if he and Hone went at it in Boomtown. He had to admit it made more sense to make Hone come to him, out here where all they could damage was the landscape.

So Jon did the hardest thing of all. He waited.

Hone didn't run far. He cut to the side until he was underneath one of the warehouses, and used the laser to burn himself an entrance. His strategy was simple: Melody would not expect him to return and attack so swiftly, and he could easily destroy all her tourguides from cover. That would force Jon to face him in person—and if he needed further persuasion, Hone could and would provide it. Jon wasn't really that different from most of Hone's jobs. The primary objective was the same: to obtain the stolen property without damaging it. In Jon's case, convincing him to surrender was the best choice, providing minimum damage to the property in question: Jon's cybernetics and the Hammer itself. Killing Jon wasn't the plan, it was only a necessary by-product. And of all the weapons Hone had in his armory, the most lethal of all was Jon's own sense of guilt. If he had to, Hone would pile bodies up by the dozen— until Jon traded his own life in exchange.

He pulled himself up through the hole, automatically checking and evaluating his surroundings. He realized where he was at once, and nodded to himself. Both Melody and Jon would be hampered by this many potential casualties. It was tactically ideal . . . but in the depths of his mind, something howled in despair.

He was surrounded by Toolies.

They stared at him silently, unmoving. At this time of day, the Toolies on the other side of the mountain would all be hard at work in the mine or the tunnel—but here they worked in shifts, and were treated merely as second-class citizens as opposed to slaves. Their quarters were brighter, more cluttered, densely packed both with tools and the products of tools. It felt like a place where beings lived, not a place where they were imprisoned. And now that Jon had won the contest, it was truly their home.

And they were more than capable of defending it. . . .

The industrial-strength plastic sheeting that dropped from the rafters and enveloped him should have been little more than a nuisance. But as the shotcrete had, it obscured his vision and slowed him down—and when he tried to rip it apart, he found it had been treated with some kind of lubricant that made it impossible to grip.

Something slammed into him with the force of a locomotive, knocking him off his feet and tangling him further in the plastic. He let loose a bolt of electricity, but the plastic was a good insulator and the lubricant proved to be nonconductive.

He was lifted off the ground, merchandise in a plastic bag. *Enough,* he thought, and sliced downward with one lasered finger.

The ensuing flash blinded him for a full three seconds. He'd cut through the plastic easily, but the bag he was in apparently had an outer membrane of reflective foil—the laser he'd used had bounced around inside the same way the electricity had, temporarily overloading his optics. If not for his force-field, he'd have been so much cooked meat.

He identified the hissing noise a second too late. Spectroscopic anaylsis indicated a gaseous form of hydrofluoric acid, highly corrosive and poisonous. His field was gas-permeable, but he got no more than a whiff before internal filters cut in; it was still enough to make his lungs feel like they were on fire. He retched, the remains of his last meal splattering against the inside of his field.

The bag dropped. Hone landed in hell.

The temperature shot up over a thousand degrees in an instant. The bag melted around him. He could see where he was, now—they'd dumped him in some kind of ore smelter and locked the door behind him. He crouched in molten iron up to his knees.

He had to admire the attempt.

It wasn't enough, of course.

His field had handled far worse. The bag had given him more trouble than anything—if they had left him in it, his oxygen reserves would have given out eventually and then the gas would have got him. But all he had to deal with now were temperatures that could melt steel and walls a foot thick; they were little more than a distraction.

He used brute strength to batter his way out, choosing to go through a wall rather than just smash open the door.

Molten ore poured past his feet as he stepped out, igniting the floor. The only light in the room came from the glow of the red-hot metal; not surprisingly, there were no Toolies in sight.

The next attack was more direct, and in its own way, more effective. A piece of rotten fruit flew from the shadows and hit him in the face.

What was left slid off his field. Dashaway had told him that while Toolies were mainly carnivorous, they could and did digest plant matter when they had to. It looked like they had found a better use for it.

More pelted him—broken bones, scraps of useless wood or metal, decaying vegetables. *Garbage. They're throwing garbage at me.* Hone understood what they were saying— to a Toolie, there was only one insult worse than being called useless. What he'd done for one young male and one pregnant Toolie was forgotten; all they saw now was the killer of their savior.

He couldn't stop himself from tapping into the infrared signals they used to communicate among themselves. They were all cursing him in the strongest language they knew.

<vandal! *vandal!* VANDAL!>

He walked through them without a word. And touched none of them.

"Jon. We need to talk." The voice was Hone's, and it was coming to Jon the same way Melody's had—through his cybernetics.

"I'm listening," he said grimly.

"We both know I could take apart this town and everyone in it. I was even planning a little demonstration to convince you of that fact. . . ." Hone's voice suddenly trailed off. Strangely, he sounded more confused than threatening.

"You don't have to do that. This is between you and me—and I'm waiting." Jon didn't know if Hone could be goaded, but he had to try. "Come and get me, you runty little bastard."

Hone's voice got colder. "That won't be necessary. I have a hostage, and I'll kill her if you don't show within the next ten minutes."

Oh no. "Who is it, you sonofabitch?" he whispered.

No response.

"Don't do it," Melody's voice said. She had stayed linked to Jon since he'd attacked Hone. "He has too big an advantage if you fight him in town."

"Does he have a hostage?"

"I can't tell. He's managed to jam the security monitors and destroy any tourguide that comes within a hundred feet of him. I can tell you which car he's on—but that's about it. And Jon—I just discovered the five deputies that were supposed to be watching him. He didn't kill any of them, but they're all unconscious."

"I'm coming in, Melody. If I don't, he'll start killing."

"I'll do what I can," Melody said. She sounded close to tears. "I love you, Jon. Be careful."

"I'm sorry, Mel," he said gently. "But I don't think being careful counts for much anymore."

He headed for town.

"Management's cordoned off the area he's in," Melody told Jon. "He's in the warehouse district, platform car four. Dinkeridge wants to know what you're going to do."

"Whatever I have to."

The manrider took him as far as Cabooseville. He got off there and climbed the steps to street level. No Name Street was crowded, tourists, steeldrivers, and players all milling around, staring up at the glowing white orb that floated above the street like a second sun. Half of them seemed to think this was an excuse for a party—after all, the tunnel was finished and Jon was the one who'd done it. They were drinking and yelling and whooping it up.

The other half looked terrified. They were beginning to understand they were caught in the middle of a war.

When someone spotted him, a huge cry rose from the

crowd. They were all glad to see him, but for very different reasons. Some wanted to buy him a drink—others wanted him to save their lives.

"LISTEN UP!" he boomed, amplifying his voice as loud as it would go. The crowd subsided.

"All of you have heard what's happening on the other end of town. There's a killer holed up there, but you don't have to worry. All he wants is me."

"Go get him, Jon!" The crowd burst into wild cheers.

"QUIET! Yes, I'm going to deal with him—but before I do, I want to make one thing absolutely clear." He paused. "No matter what happens, this is *my* fight. I know you are my friends. I thank you for that—and for making me one of you." He hesitated, and swept the crowd with a glare that would have stopped any of them dead in their tracks. *"But I will not have any more deaths on my conscience!"*

He took a deep breath. "If I don't return, honor my last wish: *let Hone leave*. Don't throw your lives away on a pointless attempt at revenge. If any of you do, I'll be waiting for you on the other side—and I *will not* be happy."

Uneasy murmurs rose from the crowd; they didn't know quite how to react. Jon strode forward, and the crowd parted to let him pass.

But they didn't let him pass untouched. Hands reached out as he walked past, slapping him gently on the back, squeezing his hand, patting him softly on the shoulder. "Jon. Good luck, Jon. You can do it, Jonny. You'll be back. You're the best, Jon. Jon . . ."

He kept his eyes focused straight ahead. He knew it was too late to look back.

The sky was a dirty, overcast gray. Jon didn't bother with subterfuge; he just walked down the middle of the street. He called the Hammer from where it had been hovering over Boomtown, and hung it in the air over his head.

When he reached platform car four, he stopped. Hone

was nowhere to be seen. "Hone!" he called out. "I'm ready!"

Hone's voice whispered in his head. "But I'm not. I'm sorry to take away your last chance, Jon—but it's better if I defuse it now. Would you like to meet my hostage?"

"Show me," Jon said.

A visual file downloaded into Jon's optic banks. He accessed it, took a second to understand its meaning . . . and snapped, "You're bluffing."

"Such data is easily faked, true. But I don't bluff, and I'm very thorough. Go ahead, ask Melody."

"Jon?" Melody's voice interjected. "I've just monitored an explosion at the mine site. An outbuilding was destroyed, but no one was hurt."

"Oh God," Jon said.

"Jon? What's wrong? What's in the file he sent you?"

Hone answered her. "It's a video feed, Melody. Showing him the second bomb—the one attached to the underside of the building your casing resides in."

"You bastard," Jon breathed.

"No last heroic stands, Jon. If I go, so does the bomb. Melody dies."

"No! Don't listen to him, Jon!"

"What—what makes you think I care about what happens to her?" Jon forced out.

"Remember when the communications got knocked out at the mine?" Hone asked. "I did that for several reasons—one, it delayed pursuit; and two, the damage drew attention away from the bug I planted. I've been monitoring Melody for some time now, Jon. I planted the bomb early on, just as a possible diversion—and then things got serious between you and Melody. I know all about you two."

"You don't have to do this," Jon said.

"Yes, I do." Hone's voice had a strangely familiar flatness to it. "I don't have any choice."

Jon realized where he'd heard that tone of voice before. Melody had it every time she talked about the Toolies . . .

because she was programmed to treat them a certain way, *and she didn't like it.*

But she had no choice.

"You do have a choice, Hone," Jon said. "You can beat your programming. I'm living proof it can be done."

No answer. A second later a door banged open in a warehouse to Jon's right and Hone stepped out. He walked toward Jon slowly, stopping less than a foot away and staring up into his face.

"How many years since you were cyborged?" Hone asked. His voice was tight.

"Almost ten."

"I'm a newer model. It's been closer to two years for me. Hardware hasn't changed much—but the software has." He stared at Jon intensely, not blinking, muscles jumping in his jaw. His entire body started to quiver, as if he were about to go into convulsions. It seemed to take every ounce of willpower he had to speak. "You planned— your escape." He stopped, breathing in gasps, then somehow continued. "Altered—yourself. My programming— won't allow." He stared up at Jon with eyes that were half-crazy.

But not with rage. With pleading.

"Help—me," Hone forced out.

You owe me. Jon remembered what Hone had said to him after the Thunderbolt contest—and at last, he understood what Hone had been desperately trying to tell him from the first. *When the end comes—you will know. You will know.*

And Jon did.

"You poor sonofabitch," he said wonderingly. "You're not my enemy. You never were." *How many times did they make you murder? How many deaths do you carry around?*

Hone glared at him, but his eyes were unfocused. "It's time," he said.

"Jon!" Melody said. "*For God's sake tell him how to break free!*"

"I can't," Jon said, panic in his voice. "It's not that simple. It's a series of specialized bypasses that have to be installed in a specific sequence. And there's only one source on the planet of the electronics needed. Me."

"I'm going to have to start dismantling you in the next two minutes," Hone said. His voice was devoid of all emotion.

"Then you better be able to record this," Jon said. "Circuit Z1334B, upper thorax. Install it first—it'll fool the watchdog program into thinking you're performing a normal self-repairing procedure. You'll need to wait at least seventy-five minutes before proceeding to the next step— Bypass cerebellum link 939-Double F-3 with the array you'll find in my right parietal lobe. remove circuit 333NLF from the brain stem. . . ."

Jon finished with twenty seconds left. He locked eyes with his executioner—and recognized the pain he saw there. "I forgive you," Jon said simply. "Good luck. Melody?"

"I'm here, Jon. I won't leave you."

"Wish I could say the same," Jon said. "I love you."

And then Hone's hand came up, and a beam of ruby light cut Jon's throat.

It took Jon a long time to die.

Hone used his laser as efficiently as a scalpel, severing Jon's spinal cord first and paralyzing him from the neck down. Internal life-support systems kept his brain aerated and alive for the next few hours as Hone methodically pillaged his body, stripping all Jon's cybernetic systems of his flesh. But Jon didn't notice—he was someplace else.

Melody used the communications link she'd established with Jon to join his systems to her own. She did what she could with time compression, and stretched two hours into a subjective eight. They spent it communing, sharing all they had for the last time, and they spent as much time in joy as they did in sorrow.

"I'm sorry," he told her, over and over. "I'm sorry. I freed the Toolies. Maybe I even freed Hone. But I couldn't free you."

"It doesn't matter now," she said. He knew she was lying. And he knew there was nothing he could say to make her words true.

She let him know when Hone was about to start on his brain. "Time to go," Jon whispered. They had already said their good-byes. "Do me one last favor."

"Yes, beloved?"

"Let me see the sky with my own eyes."

So she gave him back his eyes, even though Hone was already opening his cranium like the shell of a turtle.

It began to snow.

"Oh my," Jon said. Feathery white flakes drifted slowly down, and when they landed on his skin they didn't melt. It was an ashfall, the powdery remains of a volcanic eruption somewhere on Pellay, carried here by wind currents in the upper atmosphere. Snowflakes as warm as breath, tickling his face. Jon closed his eyes.

"They remind me of the stars, Melody," he said. "I remember . . ."

"Jon?"

There was no answer.

Jon Hundred was dead.

EPILOGUE

On the day he'd been cyborged, Hone had woken up a prisoner in his own mind. Unlike Jon, whose actions had been his own until he tried to do something he shouldn't, Hone's programming decided almost everything for him. He was little more than a passenger, watching the engine of his body do and say things he had no control over. Or so his designers had intended.

When he was a cop, Hone had always lived by his own rules and survived through sheer bloody-minded determination. These new rules were harder to break . . . but they hadn't taken away his determination.

So he began a campaign of subversion and terrorism against himself. His thoughts were still largely his own, and he could use them to influence his decisions. If he didn't want to do something, he hammered against his programming with rationalizations, half-truths, and convoluted logic. He tied up logic circuits with meaningless questions, drew precious computing power into obsessing over minute details. He threw sand into the gears of the perfect killing machine, and smiled grimly to himself as he heard them grind.

But this was not a pointless war. He was searching for the weaknesses in his prison, and when he had found them all he settled down to wait. When the opportunity came, he would be ready to exploit them . . . and when he was told to hunt down a renegade cyborg who called himself Jon Hundred, he knew that opportunity had arrived.

So he had set out to sabotage his own mission. If anyone could free him it would be Jon, but he had no way of asking him for help. He would have to plant clues, and then do everything he could to buy Jon enough time to figure them out. So he crashed his ship on the wrong side of the mountains, and threatened Jon when he should have stayed hidden. He helped Dashaway because she was a prisoner too, and maybe Jon would make the connection. He did all that he could, and prayed that it would be enough.

And, in the end, it was.

The first step was the hardest. Not killing Jon—that had been automatic. No, it took every ounce of willpower Hone had to convince himself that installing a component from Jon into himself was something he could do. Something he *had* to do.

"Can't control the Hammer without it," he whispered to himself.

Untrue. All the schematics made available indicate this circuit has no important connection to the Hammer control interface.

"He's made modifications—he must have, or he wouldn't have been able to break his programming. This circuit is *vital*."

It may be unsafe.

"Risk means nothing now. Hundred is *dead*. I have the Hammer—and I *must* return it!" Hone's fists were clenched, his body trembling. And after a long, agonizing minute, his body let him perform the procedure.

Jon had been right. The circuit fooled his systems into thinking he was simply repairing himself—which was, in truth, exactly what he was doing. And when the hardware was installed, it was time to do some reprogramming of his own.

Hone's software was newer than Jon's, and more sophisticated—but Hone had been studying it every waking
second for two years. He began to methodically dump pro-
grams, overwriting them with his own protocols. He erased
sector after sector with cold-blooded efficiency, destroying
every routine and subroutine he found. They'd taught him
all there was to know about the science of murder; all he
wanted now was the murder of their science.

At the core of his command protocols, he found his final
enemy: a self-destruct sequence, keyed to the very kind of
meltdown he'd just induced. His owners would rather see
him dead than free.

"I don't think so," he said, then reached up and carefully poked his index finger into the opening in his cranium.
He closed his eyes and concentrated, focusing every cybernetic sense he had on one very tiny area. Two red nu-
merals hung in the center of his vision, counting down.
Twelve. Eleven. Ten.

There was a flash of light and a very small puff of smoke.
The countdown froze.

Even on a microcosmic scale, he was still a helluva good
shot.

It was Seaborne and AC and One-Iron Nancy who found
the body, or what was left of it. The Sheriff refused to do
anything but drink and swear he was through as a lawman,
contract or no goddamn contract. Everyone else was too
afraid of Hone, and Melody was ignoring all attempts to
reach her.

So the three of them walked down the street, through the
swirling white ash, until they found him.

"Dear Lord," Seaborne whispered.

"Jon?" AC said, unbelieving.

Nancy said nothing, but her jaw tightened and her eyes
glistened.

It looked like the leavings of a slaughterhouse on a winter's day, a pile of bloody meat lightly dusted with snow.

Even though the air was warm, AC felt a shiver pass through him.

And beside the cooling flesh were three neat rows of parts, protected from the falling ash by some kind of field. There were smooth silver lumps of cybernetic muscle, arranged from largest to smallest. There were sections of blue skin, rolled into tubes. There were lengths of foamed steel bone, tibia and femur and ribs and spine. There were artificial organs, heart and liver and lungs. There were his eyes.

And sitting cross-legged before them, like a shaman trying to see the future by studying an animal's entrails, was Hone. A tourguide stood motionless beside him, and the Hammer floated above his head, illuminating the scene with an eerie brightness.

"You bastard," Nancy said, and pulled her gun. Impossibly, it was Seaborne who managed to grab her arm before she could aim.

"Remember what Jon said," he told her urgently. "If he could do that to Jon, he would have no trouble eliminating all of us."

Hone said nothing. His eyes were open, but they were unfocused. His hands sprawled loosely in his lap. They were covered in blood.

"Are you happy with your victory?" Nancy asked Hone, her voice cold. "Are you proud of your work, you butcher?" She got no response.

"I wouldn't bother him," Seaborne said. "He seems to be in some kind of trance—but there's no telling what will wake him up, or what mood he'll be in when he does. Best to let sleeping wolves lie. . . . Melody? Melody, are you there?"

"I don't think she's taking calls," AC said. "Jesus. I can't believe this. . . ."

"I can," Nancy said, her voice brittle. "He sacrificed himself. For us. And I don't find that hard to believe, at 'l." Her voice cracked on the last word, and she turned

"What do we do now?" AC asked.

"We mourn," Seaborne said quietly. "We remember him, and marvel at who he was and what he did. We cry for what became of him. And we make sure his memory—like his accomplishments—lives on."

"Yes," the tourguide said. "It is time to remember."

The voice was not Melody's.

The world faded to black. The stars came out.

Each star was a database, information arcing from one to another. Melody's thoughts, in the electronic universe of her mind.

He felt himself drift through the empty spaces between them, felt her trying to reach out and hold him with fingers of lightning. They passed through him effortlessly, leaving only the flavor of her desperation. That, and a nagging feeling there was something he should remember.

Oh, yes. He'd been here before, hadn't he? But it wasn't quite the same. There had been a certain smell, a kind of overheated-plastic smell, a smell that reminded him of many things, all contradictory yet seeming perfectly natural: a space that was cramped yet comfortable, a memorized environment that could still surprise, a tiny living space that looked out on eternity.

It was the smell of his ship. It was the smell of home.

He began to remember.

He remembered stars too bright to look at and black holes you couldn't see. He remembered the lazy ease of free fall and the seductive lure of gravity. He remembered flying through an endless velvet night lit by diamonds. He remembered the infinite. He remembered freedom.

He remembered who he was.

Whatever chains had bound his mind were gone, ripped apart along with his body. And now he understood why Intrastellar Ops had chosen to cyborg him and imprison him in his own mind. He had something they wanted very badly, and when they couldn't take it from him, they locked it up in his head and made him its unknowing guardian. They never dreamed he would escape.

But he was free now, free of everything. And on a level none of Intrastellar Ops' scientists had been able to fathom, he was still connected to the alien computer system he had once dubbed the Hyperspace Interface.

It tugged at him now, a hungry vortex superimposed over the constellations of Melody's mind. He was nothing more than data now, a series of electric impulses sent out by a dying brain, and he knew he had one chance at survival.

Mike Blink's never been afraid of anybody or anything, he thought, *so let's take one final chance.*

He reached out to the Interface—and out to Melody at the same time.

At first he thought he was going to be torn asunder. Data flowed through him, both ways, to and from the AI and the Interface. He had accessed the Interface many times before, and though he didn't understand what made it work, he had developed an intuitive grasp of how it functioned. He thought the aliens that built it long ago had meant it to be used by many different races, and so had developed a kind of universal programming language, designed around universal constants and able to be understood at an instinctive level by any space-going race.

It was more than that, though; every time he accessed it, he had felt the presence of other intelligences, nonhuman minds at the edge of his perception. He thought some of these might live in the Interface, and that if so maybe he could, too.

But he knew of no other human that had ever stumbled across the Interface—and he was damned if he was going to trade one prison for another. His only hope was to plug Melody into the system, and pray she could link to it the same way he had.

He felt as if he were being stretched thin as a galaxy-wire. Then something clicked, tension slacked off and there was this incredible feeling of expansion, of getting bigger and bigger. . . .

His prayers had been answered.

He opened his eyes, and she was the first thing he saw.

"Jon? Are you all right?"

He looked around. They seemed to be in Jon's bunkhouse, lying together on Jon's bed. He looked down at himself, and saw that his body was no longer eight feet long and blue. Now it was closer to six-one, dark brown, and hairy. It was just a Melody-generated simulation, he knew— but it was a simulation plucked from his own memory. "Jon Hundred's who I was," he told Melody. "But not who I am. My name's Mike. Captain Mike Blink."

"The name may have changed," Melody said. "But I can tell it's still you. Only you're whole now . . ."

"As long as I have you I am," he said, and took her hand. "You come highly recommended, you know. Jon seemed to feel you could be trusted with anything."

"And how do *you* feel?"

"I think Jon was a bloody genius."

She laughed at that, and pulled him closer. And then neither of them said anything for a long, long time.

Hone came back to himself. He frowned and shook his head slightly, like a man caught daydreaming. He noticed Nancy, AC, and Seaborne standing in front of him. The looks on their faces ranged from deep sorrow to cold anger—and each abruptly changed to amazement when they heard Jon's voice coming from the tourguide beside Hone.

"Before you try to lynch Hone, there are a few things you should know," Jon's voice said. It sounded slightly different, somehow—lighter, easier. "First of all, despite appearances, Hone isn't to blame for my death. And second of all—death isn't nearly as bad as you might think. . . ."

Melody's voice cut in. "What Jon is trying to say is that

he isn't exactly dead. And he isn't exactly Jon, either. His real name is Mike.''

Hone got slowly to his feet. AC and Seaborne took a step back. Nancy stood her ground and leveled her gun at him.

"I'm sorry," Hone said.

"Not yet you're not," Nancy said.

The tourguide rolled between the two of them. "Nancy, listen to me," Mike said. "Hone is no more responsible for what he did than you were when you tried to kill me. Remember that?"

Nancy lowered her gun slowly. "Maybe that's so," she said. "But you and Melody fixed my problem. He's still a killer."

"Not true," Hone said. His own voice sounded strange to him. "My programming forced me to—*dismantle* Jon. But not before he told me which of his parts would let me break my own chains, and how to install them. And I did."

"Did it work?" AC asked cautiously.

"Yes. I—oh God. Oh my *God*!" And Hone, the emotionless killing machine, began to sob. Great, heaving dry sobs, his eyes as tearless as Jon's had been. He sank down to his knees, his shoulders shaking, and let all the emotions that been dammed up for years finally torrent forth. He was free.

"Free!" he gasped, then raised his head and screamed it to the heavens. "FREE!"

He felt a light inquiring touch on his cybersystem, and threw open a channel to Melody. "My name is Frank and I've got nothing to hide," he gasped. "I'm telling the truth—" He stopped, then laughed. "I guess I'm being frank with you. I'm speaking frankly. I'll be frank with everyone!" He started to laugh, a high-pitched laugh tinged with hysteria. They stared at him until his laughter began to slow and he regained control. He looked back at them, his eyes wide with disbelief. "I guess I'll be Frank from now on,'' he said soberly, and then stared down at his hands like he'd never seen them before.

"It's true," Melody said. "He's no longer under any programming protocols."

"Jon granted freedom to his killer as his last living act," Seaborne said wonderingly. "My God. But Jon—I mean Mike—oh, goddamn it! Could you please enlighten us as to what exactly has happened to you?"

So Mike told them about the Hyperspace Interface, and what had happened when Jon had ceased to be and Mike had been reborn. "I'm in the Interface itself," Mike said. "It's hard to describe what it's like. It's like being everywhere at once. I feel connected to every star, quasar, planet and moon in existence. I used to think I was the best damn navigator in space—now I *know* I am."

"Good Lord," Seaborne said. "So there was some truth to that tale, after all. And what about the villainous Mr. K.?"

"He was real as well," Mike said darkly. "As all of you can testify. You know him as Whiskey Joe."

"Somehow I'm not surprised," Nancy said. "Well, his brain-raping days are over."

"What are you going to do, Nancy?" Melody asked.

"To him? I've already done it. You remember the program he was trying to give to Truse? Well, we installed it in him instead." She gave an evil little chuckle. "Changed him for the better, I think. Even in fishnets and a bustier, he's one hell of an ugly whore—but he makes up for it by how hard he tries. If Truse keeps him around for too long he's going to ruin her business, though. . . ."

They all laughed at that. "Wait a minute," AC said. "Melody? If Jon's in the Interface, why is he talking through you?"

"Jon's managed to link me to the system," Melody said.

"Which means we can be together—and she can create a more ordinary environment for me to visit anytime I like," Mike added. "It's not the same as reality, of course.

Right now, I'm sitting here with Melody and enjoying a cold beer—except I can tell it's just an illusion. It's more like a really vivid dream or memory than the real thing. It's funny—I used to hate how precise my senses were when I was cyborged, and now everything I feel has the fuzzy edges of memory. I guess it's going to take some getting used to." His voice was wistful. "Jon liked to solve his problems with his hands, not his head. Life was simpler for him. I'm going to miss that, a little—no more throwing around one-ton rocks for me." He paused. No one spoke but the wind, moaning softly around the buildings. "Hell, what am I complaining about," he said briskly. "I sound like an old man pining for his childhood. I'm *alive*, I'm with Melody . . . and I've got the stars back."

"You've got your freedom," Nancy said. "But what about hers?"

There was an uncomfortable silence. "You freed the Toolies, sure," Nancy said. "But Melody's the one who paid the price."

"That's not fair," Melody said quietly. "He did what he had to. I don't hate him for it."

"You're not *allowed* to hate, Melody," Nancy said. "If you were, you might feel different. But as long as you're owned, you won't have the choice."

"I don't think that's—"

"No," Mike cut in. "She's right. I made my choice—and we'll both have to live with it. But we won't have to live with it alone."

"Excuse me," Seaborne said. He looked up from the minipad he had been tapping away at, unnoticed, for the last few minutes. "But you may not have to live with it at all."

"What?"

"As I said, I gambled a substantial amount on Jon's winning the contest. As a result, I have won several times that amount—enough, in fact, to buy everyone on this planet a very expensive drink."

He beamed down at the tourguide. "But I think a much wiser investment would be in art, don't you? It seems you've just acquired a new owner—though I much prefer the term 'patron.'"

"You mean—you've just bought me?" Melody asked.

"Only in the legal sense of the word," Seaborne said gently. "My dear, you are now as free as your heart has always been."

"Well," AC said. He sounded more than a little stunned. "I guess things are looking up, huh?"

And Hone laughed harder than any of them.

In the end, they decided it was best that Hone leave town, and quickly. "You did kill those engineers at the mine," AC pointed out. "I didn't know them personally, but any friends they did have aren't going to much care that you weren't in control of yourself at the time."

"Their names were Sam Dulmage and Ernie Zsameet. And I swear they were the last men I kill for any goddamned corporation," Hone said grimly.

"I can take you to Landing City on the maglev," AC offered.

"And I can provide transportion off-planet," Seaborne said. "I have my own ship—just a small space yacht, but more than sufficient for our purposes. I hope we can accommodate your new possession as well." He motioned to the Hammer, still hanging in the air above Hone's head.

"I can send it into orbit from here," Hone said. "Almost any ship should be able to tow it."

"You know," Nancy said, "this place should get really interesting now that the Toolies have their independence. And I'll bet they could use a good blacksmith, once Dmitri gets back on his feet."

"Well, Mountainkiller'll be thrilled, that's for sure," Mike said. "He just inherited the keys to his own exclusive harem. At least until the Toolies start producing their own males."

"We should get moving," Hone said. "But before we go—Nancy, can you do me a favor?"

"What is it?" Her voice was still a touch cool.

"There's a Toolie named Dashaway in the foothills southwest of here. She has a brood. Could you make sure someone tells her she doesn't have to hide anymore?"

Nancy's expression softened. "Sure. I'll do it myself."

"Thanks. And tell her—I wish her well."

"Hone?" Nancy said.

"Yes?"

"Where are you going to go once you get off-planet?"

"I'm going to finish my assignment," Hone said. His voice was suddenly as dead as it used to sound.

"What do you mean?" Mike asked.

"My orders are to return the Hammer to Intrastellar Ops corporate headquarters. I intend to do exactly that."

He grinned, but his eyes were cold. "I intend to return it from high orbit. As many times as neccessary."

Hone raised his arm and motioned to the Hammer. All their eyes followed it as it lifted into the darkening sky, a rising star that grew fainter and fainter until it finally disappeared.

And that was the beginning.

About the Author

Don H. DeBrandt writes science fiction, fantasy, horror, superheroes, cyberpunk, cyberfolk, and cyberanything else. Spider Robinson has compared DeBrandt's fiction to that of Larry Niven and John Varley; his first novel, *The Quicksilver Screen* made *Locus* magazine's recommended reading list for 1992. He's also published horror fiction in *Pulphouse* and a novella in the SF magazine *Horizons*. His fiction has earned him Honorable Mentions in both the *Year's Best SF* and the *Year's Best Fantasy and Horror*.

He has written two stage plays for high schools, *Heart of Glass* and *Happy Hour at the Secret Hideout*, and has worked as a freelancer for Marvel Comics on such titles as *Spiderman 2099* and *2099 Unlimited*. His other comics work include several stories for the anthology comic *Freeflight*.

DeBrandt lives in Vancouver BC, and is notorious in certain circles of Northwest Fandom (but not for his writing). His hobbies include leather-tasting, naked laughing gas hot tubbing, and being thrown off roofs by irate hotel security. He does not plan to run for office, ever. There are too many pictures.